JED THE DEAD

Alan Dean Foster

ACE BOOKS, NEW YORK

This book is an Ace original edition,
and has never been previously published.

JED THE DEAD

An Ace Book / published by arrangement with
the author

PRINTING HISTORY
Ace edition / January 1997

Cover art by Gary Ruddell.

For information address: The Berkley Publishing Group,
200 Madison Avenue, New York, New York 10016.

The Putnam Berkley World Wide Web site address is
http://www.berkley.com/berkley
Make sure to check our *PB Plug*, the
science fiction/fantasy newsletter, at
http://www.pbplug.com

ISBN: 0-441-00399-0

ACE®
Ace Books are published by The Berkley Publishing Group,
200 Madison Avenue, New York, NewYork 10016.
ACE and the "A" design are trademarks
belonging to Charter Communications, Inc.

PRINTED IN THE UNITED STATES OF AMERICA

10 9 8 7 6 5 4 3 2 1

DON'T MISS THESE THRILLING NOVELS
BY *NEW YORK TIMES* BESTSELLING AUTHOR

ALAN DEAN FOSTER

LIFE FORM

On the faraway planet Xica, nine scientists from Earth have established first contact with a humanoid civilization. Now all they have to do is live to tell about it . . .

GREENTHIEVES

The crime wave of the (next) century is on, as high-tech pharmaceuticals keep disappearing right through the world's most advanced security system . . .

CODGERSPACE

The galaxy is threatened when an industrial accident triggers a revolution . . . by the world's electronic appliances!

CAT*A*LYST

The fur flies in this *purrfectly* out-of-this-world adventure of a movie star's cat who acts like she rules the planet—and maybe she does.

QUOZL

The furry Quozl *knew* they'd love the third planet from the sun. But it never occurred to them that anyone *lived* there!

GLORY LANE

A punk rocker, an airhead, and a nerd are swept up into the wildest, weirdest war of all time!

Also by Alan Dean Foster

THE LAST STARFIGHTER

SLIPT

GLORY LANE

MAORI

QUOZIL

CYBER WAY

LIFE FORM

GREENTHIEVES

CODGERSPACE

SMART DRAGONS, FOOLISH ELVES
(coedited with Martin Harry Greenberg)

BETCHA CAN'T READ JUST ONE (ed.)

CAT*A*LYST

FOR MUDDBONE . . .
Brock Lacock
Whit Mercer
Billy Edmonds

Thanks for the friendship, the music, and
for bringing back the girl I married.

ONE

It's a toss-up as to whether the dullest stretch of interstate highway in the United States is the section of I-10 in Texas between Van Horn and El Paso or Van Horn and Midland-Odessa. Either one makes the badlands of the Dakotas look positively verdant.

Ross Hager had opted off the interstate long before, so that he wouldn't have to drive the mind-numbing monotony of either segment. Highway eight-two shot straight through Hobbs, New Mexico, and on to Artesia before crossing the Sacramento Mountains and dropping down into Alamogordo. He'd have to hook back up with I-10 eventually, but not until it entered the more scenic country to be found around Las Cruces.

Meanwhile he delighted in the green foothills which gave rise to the eastern slopes of the Sacramentos, lush with spring snowmelt. Old gray barns listing on their sides stood lazy sentry over orchards spotted with spring color. Cattle cropped new grass amid mesquite-posted fields. Food hadn't been a problem, not with each little town boasting its own kindred Dairy Queen. He'd been told that once he reached Arizona, Dairy Queens would become scarce, a notion difficult for any son of the Lone Star State to grasp. Texas health food such as fries and gravy and steak fingers would be hard to find.

Well, he'd get by somehow. Where food was concerned, Ross Ed Hager's concern wasn't quality so much as it was quantity. At six-foot-six and two hundred fifty pounds, he needed a fair amount of fuel. He was used to hunting down his own food. The only kind of gun his family wasn't familiar with was a salad shooter. Mention bok choy to Mama Hager and she likely would have reached for a map instead of a cookbook.

For someone who'd been raised in the country tradition of fried cholesterol, Ross Ed had turned out just fine. His mom and dad were still cruising on a lifelong diet of fried chicken, fried steak, fried crappie and catfish, fried corn bread, fried okra, fried potatoes, fried corn-on-the-cob, and fried cheesesticks. Just about the only food in the Hager family that wasn't regularly deep-fat-fried was dessert, whose signature dish was his mother's hog-lard coconut-cream cake.

Yessir, he told himself, you couldn't beat down-home Texas country cooking for good health. Everything else, his daddy insisted, was rabbit food. In consequence, Ross Ed had grown big enough to terrorize more than a few opponents both on the football field and on the basketball court, making honorable mention all-state in the former.

Too easygoing to play college ball, he'd gone straight to work in the oil fields, where his good nature, size, and strength had served him well and assured steady work in an industry noted for the capriciousness of its employment practices.

The heavily laden pickup that appeared in front of him was making slow work of the steady grade. Biding his time until they reached a straightaway, he depressed the accelerator and leaned left on the wheel. The massive V-8 block under the capacious hood of the '72 Fleetwood growled softly as he passed the pickup with a friendly wave. The driver's return wave was visible in the rearview mirror.

"Atta girl." He gave the steering wheel an affectionate pat. He'd bought the big white Caddy years ago from an old rancher on the lookout for a new one. A few bucks here, a little tuning there, and he had a car that not only ran splendidly but that almost fit him.

It was cooling off nicely outside and he lowered the window, letting his arm rest in the opening. The peaks ahead loomed loftier than any he'd ever seen, much higher than the buttes down in the Hill Country around Austin. A few teased ten thousand feet. On the other side of the range would be White Sands National Monument, another local highlight he'd been advised not to miss.

Except for the pickup he'd had the road pretty much to himself all the way from Artesia. Late spring preceded the summer tourist season and schools were still in session. It was a good time to be traveling.

One Saturday morning it had just up and hit him that he was about to turn thirty without ever having been outside Texas and Louisiana. He'd been sprawled in his easy chair in front of the TV. Some dumb artificial sports show was on between games. It had been shot in Southern California, which seemed to be populated entirely by people under the age of twenty-four. All had perfect bodies and sprayed-on complexions and hair that was never out of place. From what he could see there was no natural dirt in Southern California; only asphalt, sand, and landscaping.

It wasn't the people who caught his attention, however. Not even the pretty girls, of whom Texas had more than its fair share. It was the ocean. He'd worked oil rigs out in the Gulf, but this different. Dark green and slightly dangerous, far more wild and undisciplined, it touched something deep inside him.

Going to be thirty and I still ain't seen the Pacific Ocean, he'd thought to himself. Whereupon he'd called in to his current place of employment and given notice.

That had been . . . let's see now . . . four days ago. So far he'd had no reason to regret his decision. He'd bade farewell to a few close friends, listened politely to their suggestions and admonitions, checked out the Caddy, tossed his few belongings in the trunk, and set out from Abilene.

Now, for the first time in his life, he found himself in real mountains, climbing a road flanked on both sides by trees taller than the more familiar oak or mesquite. He considered the loaded boom box on the passenger seat, decided to leave it be and listen to the air for a while longer yet.

Though he'd never been farther west than Sweetwater, he wasn't worried about getting lost. Pick any highway heading west, keep going that direction, and sooner or later you'd hit the Pacific. The longer he could avoid the frantic, monotonous interstates, the more of the country he'd be able to see. Like these beautiful, uncrowded mountains, he told himself.

Twenty-nine and traveling, he thought. Just because you came from a poor family didn't mean you couldn't see the country. You just ate cheap, slept simple, and got a job when your money ran out.

He accelerated to pass another vehicle. The car was new, streamlined, and just a little too big to fit in his trunk. Ponderosa pines and the occasional fir hugged the paved shoulder. It wasn't Maine or Montana, but it was the closest he'd ever been to a northern forest.

Slowing, he passed through the quaint mountain community of Cloudcroft. Ten minutes past the last building he pulled off the highway into a well-marked picnic area. Ignoring the blackened, industrial-strength public steel grills and soot-stained barbecue pits which marked assorted pullouts like so many fossilized robots, he drove to the farthest parking space and killed the engine. Birdsong replaced the a cappela rush of moving air.

From the trunk he extracted a gurgling plastic ice chest and a cardboard bucket filled with deceased fowl (fried, of course). Except for a couple of battered, transient trailers whose semipermanent occupants regularly tried the tolerance of the Park Service, the picnic pullout was deserted.

He was considering the most isolated of the concrete picnic tables and its accompanying oil-drum trash cans when a brand-new minivan pulled up and parked not twenty yards from him. Via multiple doors it explosively disgorged two brightly dressed adults and three hyperkinetic children.

He could tell from their footwear as well as their demeanor that they were from the city. Not a normal city, either, like Fort Worth or Austin or Lubbock, but some overly urbanized coast city. Instead of work boots, the father wore imitation Tevas probably purchased from Kmart or Wal-Mart or some other discount mart. The kids boasted designer sneakers. Mother wore combat boots.

Then there was the slick tablecloth, carefully spread out to separate sustenance from Nature. Expensive plastic picnic utensils followed, laid out as neatly as scalpels in a surgery. Meanwhile the children raced after each other, threw whatever they could pick up and kicked what they couldn't, and squealed nonstop.

Ross quite liked rugrats, but in their place. These quiet mountains weren't it. With his size he could easily have intimidated the family into leaving, but it was a public picnic area and besides, that wasn't Ross Ed Hager's nature. Grimacing in resignation, he turned and started up a gentle slope that led deeper into the woods.

Before long the sounds of children contesting inconsequentialities faded, sponged up by stone and tree and distance. He kept moving, searching for just the right place to park himself, wanting to ensure that he was far enough away so that his prospective midday idyll would not be disturbed.

Finding himself facing a steep granite outcropping, he scrutinized the gradient before starting up. With his long legs the slope was not an obstacle for him, but it would be sufficient to discourage any inquisitive children who happened to come bounding in his direction.

An overhang near the top kept part of the mound in perpetual shade, allowing winter snow to linger. He considered climbing farther, but the slight chill didn't bother him and there was a natural seat formed by the junction of two slabs of stone where he could dine in comfort. Set into the flank of the modest cliff, it offered a pleasant prospect across the gently undulating treetops.

Might as well soak up some cool before heading down into the desert, he told himself as he laid down his burden.

Just past his chosen bower a narrow cleft in the rocks beckoned inward. It wasn't a very big cave, but he decided he'd better check it out. He'd never seen a bear outside a zoo and didn't want his first wild encounter to occur while he was seated on a bare hillside above a fifty-foot drop.

Bending, he peered cautiously into the opening and sniffed. No animal smell emanated from within. Would a bear still be hibernating this late in the spring, with most of the snow hereabouts already melted? He doubted it.

Satisfied that he was safe from marauding bruins and screeching kids (or screeching bruins and marauding kids), he settled back to enjoy his lunch. Cracking the cooler, he popped the cap on a Lone Star and excavated an unidentifiable section of chicken from the cardboard bucket. Having cooled to the consistency of a used tire, the drumstick was just right. Blissfully attuned to his surroundings and at peace with the world, he washed down huge bites of greasy fowl with long drafts of ice-cold suds.

A second beer soon followed the first, with a third for dessert. Sitting the empty bucket aside, he snugged down between the rocks and let the brooding sun warm his legs. Three beers wouldn't affect his driving, Ross Ed's capacity for Lone Star being proportionate to the rest of him.

Always something of a loner, he luxuriated in the solitude. It was a characteristic which had driven more than one lady friend to distraction . . . or to other men. Not that he was in any hurry to get married. In fact, Ross Ed had never been in much of a hurry to do anything, unless it was watch a Cowboys' game. There was no sign of the invading suburbanites and the only sound was the occasional querulous squawk of a scrub jay.

After an hour or so of enthusiastically doing nothing he thought it might be fun to have a last look at the little cave. The sun now illuminated part of the interior, but to see all the way in he'd need the flashlight from the car. The possibility of encountering a bear no longer concerned him, but rattlers did. Still, it was mighty cold for rattlesnakes, and early in the season. If there were any slumbering inside, they'd like as not be pretty torpid.

Taking out his car keys, he switched on the mini Maglite he kept on the steel loop and directed the tiny beam inward. It revealed a broken, stony floor and little else. Smooth-sided walls of gray granite, coyote droppings, and a few old, gnawed bones. No beer cans, a few abandoned cobwebs, and no sign of snakes, musical or otherwise. Turning to leave, his light glinted off something in the far depths of the recess.

He frowned. Could some fool have dumped bottles or cans all the way in the back? He'd fancied himself the first traveler to picnic on the isolated ledge and didn't like the idea of having been preceded by some indifferent, littering slob.

He could depart secure in the knowledge that few would make the same distressing discovery. But what if it was a bottle and some poor bear stepped on it? Or worse, a busted can with sharp aluminum edges? He hesitated, torn between the need to get back on the road and a desire to do the right thing.

What the hell, he muttered to himself.

Using the compact light to illuminate the way, he entered the cave on hands and knees. Occasionally he would pause to locate his target. The nearer he got, the less it looked like a can or bottle. The reflective portion appeared to be attached to a much larger, nonreflective mass.

Gallon jug, he thought, with a shiny cap. Or a busted picnic cooler with metal handles. Traveler's trash. Whatever it was he'd drag it out and dump it in one of the fifty-five-gallon oil drums that served the picnic area as trash containers. It would be his good deed for the day.

The cave narrowed and when he whacked his head against the shrinking ceiling he had a few choice words for Mother Nature's imperfect design, both of the tunnel and his own hulking, ungainly body. Feeling gently of the bruise and coming away with dry fingers, he shuffled on.

It looked like glass, but he still couldn't make out the nonreflective remainder. Though bright enough, the mini Maglite's beam was very narrow. He lowered it slightly and picked out what appeared to be a bundle of old clothes on the cave floor.

Sure enough, there was a cache to it. Isolated from prowling kids and forest rangers, the cave wouldn't be a bad place for some transient to spend the summer while scavenging the leavings of hundreds of picknickers. It certainly beat a shelter in Albuquerque or a flophouse in El Paso. The only drawback was that its occupant would have to shift to warmer climes during the winter months, perhaps leaving a few simple possessions behind in the process. Ross searched for the expected wine bottle.

Instead of glass, his light glimmered on a curved faceplate. This was attached to the bundle of clothing. And both were inhabited.

This time when he hit his head on the ceiling he drew blood.

Too startled to utter an oath, he sat down heavily on the peeling granite, gaping at the thing behind the transparent visor. It was clear and unmarred and the Maglite picked out ample detail within. Aware that he was breathing much too hard and fast, the way he sometimes did when he was working on top of a rig in bad weather, he forced himself to keep calm.

Easy now, he told himself. The most likely explanation was that he was the victim of an elaborate practical joke.

But by whom? Besides the family that had arrived after him he'd seen only the couple of old trailers. Their probable occupants didn't seem the type to concoct such an intricate gag. Or such an expensive one.

No giggles reached him from outside the cave and there was no sign of hidden cameras. He was precisely as alone as he imagined.

So if it wasn't a gag, then what the devil had he found, and how had it come to be here?

Advancing slowly, he leaned over his discovery and played the narrow flashlight beam across the strange shape, stopping at what he'd originally believed to be a glass jug or bottle. Behind the gently curving transparency a face stared back up at him. The eyes were shut tight. All three of them. The lids were shiny and slightly iridescent, like mother-of-pearl, and the sockets smaller than those of a human child of comparable size.

From the top of the faceplate to the bottom of the brown, crinkly fabric the figure was barely three feet in length. Triangular in shape instead of flattened like a human, it boasted three arms and three legs along with the triple oculars. The face featured a prominent bony ridge or keel down the center, with concave cheeks or depressions on either side. The middle eye occupied a depression on this ridge, and was positioned slightly higher than its two counterparts.

Below lay a narrow slit about an inch in length and below that, a slightly wider, longer slit framed by a pair of fleshy protuberances like silvery cockscombs. There was no evidence of external ears. The head itself was a rounded dome divided by the continuation of the facial ridge, which in turn was a continuation of the unseen spine.

The facial keel was matched by one that ran the length of the body. An arm emerged from the upper portion and a leg from the base, each duplicated by counterparts at the back portions of the skeletal triangle. Though they were hidden from view by stiffened pads that were an integral part of the suit, he could feel tripartite toes or hooves at the end of each leg. Similarly, each arm ended in a gloved, three-fingered (or at least three-digited) hand.

The suit itself was nonreflective and ribbed with embedded wires and cords. These terminated in a lumpy metallic backpack of some kind that appeared to flow seamlessly into the material of the suit itself. Similar lumps and bumps embellished the front of the suit and the three arms. The rear half of the faceplate or helmet was opaque.

Upon concluding this preliminary inspection, his reaction was one of pity rather than disgust. He knew men who'd been caught in oil fires or rig collapses who looked a whole lot worse.

As to what it was, unless it was an exceptionally clever fake placed here for who knew what incomprehensible purpose, Ross Ed figured that it had to be an alien. Though not an especially imaginative individual, he'd seen enough television and movies to know that much. It wasn't a very impressive-looking alien, either. Certainly not intimidating. Ugly, yeah, but pretty sensibly put together if you thought about it. That tripod-leg setup ought to provide a lot of stability, and the three-eye arrangement good visibility. He wasn't sure how the arms worked together.

Both the suit and the creature within looked to be in an excellent state of preservation. Enough dust and dirt had accumulated on and around the body to suggest that it had been lying *in situ* for some time. There was absolutely no sign of life, not when he had felt of the arms and legs nor when he began to brush away the accumulated grime. Exactly how long it had been resting there, in the back of the little cave, he couldn't begin to estimate.

A cluster of mushrooms grew from the blown-in soil that had nearly buried the left arm. As he shook and brushed it clean he saw that their filaments hadn't penetrated the space suit. Or Earth suit, he corrected himself. Though thin, the material did not stretch or tear under his sometimes clumsy ministrations.

When he'd finished he sat back and stared afresh at his find. "Howdy." His voice echoed slightly in the confines of the cave. He didn't feel especially foolish, and there were no snickering onlookers to mock him. "How're you feelin'?"

There was no response, no reaction whatsoever. The otherworldly figure lay as he'd left it, still and unmoving. A raven complained somewhere outside. A bumblebee whizzed past the cave entrance, uninterested in the extraordinary confrontations taking place within. Otherwise it was dead silent in the dead cave with the dead alien.

Where had it come from? he wondered. Was there a ship tucked away back in the trees or buried beneath the seemingly undisturbed rocks? He'd spotted no signs during his short climb. While the cave itself was difficult to reach, the surrounding mountaintops frequently played host to hikers and horseback riders. Even a small ship or the fragments of a damaged one would surely have been seen by now.

But if there was no ship, how had the alien come to be here? Had it been abandoned in a moment of haste or confusion like the proverbial E.T.? Ross could only theorize.

One thing that did not surprise him was his continuing calm. After all, he'd seen plenty of *Star Trek* and *X-Files* and *Twilight Zone* reruns. The reality of the alien was not shocking so much as it was poignant. Poor little critter, he found himself thinking.

Lost or marooned here to die all alone and abandoned in this cold, dark place.

He certainly couldn't just leave it. While the alien hardly qualified as litter, it begged to be removed. And while Ross Ed wasn't the owner of a particularly vivid imagination, unlike many of his friends, at least he had one. The alien corpse embodied certain . . . possibilities.

Surely scientists would want to examine it, he mused. As its discoverer, he would be famous. That didn't interest him, however, as much as the financial potential. Roughnecking was a tough life dominated by uncertain prospects and a short future. He could use a couple of easy bucks.

As he reached for it he considered again the possibility that it might be nothing more than a clever fake, like those phony Bigfoot footprints they kept finding up in Washington and Oregon. An elaborate hoax placed in the cave for some gullible country boy like himself to flash on national TV.

Bending low and using the flashlight, he found he could see porelike pits in the drawn skin of the triangular face. If it was a fake, it was a mighty good one. He wondered at the color of the eyes concealed by the opalescent lids.

With the remaining two fingers of his left hand he gently stroked the vitreous, transparent material of the faceplate, wishing he could feel of the skin beneath. The material felt more like metal than glass. It was surprisingly warm to the touch and slightly roughened.

As rough as the surface of the planet he found himself gazing down upon.

TWO

Stately white clouds swirled above patchy blue oceans, more numerous and smaller than those of Earth. The continent in the center of his vision seemed almost familiar. Isolated from the other landmasses, it straddled the equator in tropical splendor. A chain of large, high islands trailed in majestic procession from the eastern shore like a disembodied tail. Ross Ed's knowledge of geography was rudimentary, but he knew he wasn't looking at Africa, or South America. Australia, perhaps, flipped upside down and nudged northeastward. No, he decided. This landmass was too rounded, too green across the middle.

His perspective tipped and three moons swung into view. Two were jagged and irregular in outline while only the third formed a gleaming disk like Luna. Outward his perception rushed, past a triple-ringed gas giant whose bright pastels put the bands of Saturn to shame.

Other worlds rushed by in bewildering succession, to be replaced by visions of gigantic nebulae and clusters of multihued comets. In one system a dozen separate asteroid belts separated an equal number of planets, while in another the gravitational wrestling of twin worlds generated enormous tides on each other's surface. There were astronomical objects for which he had no name: titanic, tenuous red suns and minuscule black spots around which inconceivable energies raged, parallel bands of incandescent gas ejected by an artificially shaped supernova, lines of force which strained mathematical probabilities, and most spectacularly of all, a triple-sun system that somehow managed to sustain half a dozen worlds in comparative stability, a grand cosmic juggling act in which gravity performed tricks unsuspected by the finest theorists. Two of the six planets supported carbon-based life-forms so bizarre and specialized that they could not have survived anywhere else, despite the most stringent and careful preparations.

Outward again, racing at physics-defying velocity through the galaxy in search of additional wonders to unveil to his startled eyes. Whirling, twisting, and plunging down into another system, uncataloged and unrecognizable. Everything spinning, a universe gone mad, sucking him into a whirlpool of forces beyond his understanding or control.

The throbbing in both legs made him blink. He was back in the cave, still kneeling before the alien body, his left hand having slid off the faceplate to lie limply at its side. A check of his watch revealed that he'd been kneeling thus for nearly an hour. The pain in his thighs came from badly cramped muscles.

Wincing, he sat back and stretched both legs out straight, wriggling them to restore the flow of blood. The resultant tingling was momentarily unbearable. He kneaded the muscles with both hands and the fiery prickling gradually faded.

The dead alien hadn't moved.

Ross Ed was now completely convinced it was not a hoax. No one could have faked what had just happened to him. He'd heard of virtual reality, but knew you had to don special equipment to experience it. He didn't think it could be projected into someone's head through simple hand contact. What he'd just experienced was unreal reality, initiated when he'd made contact with the suit's faceplate.

As soon as he felt that his legs would cooperate again, he crawled forward. It was time for decisions. The light from the mini Mag was fading and he had no desire to be caught out in the dark.

In case the experience he'd just undergone was repeated, he assumed a comfortable sitting position next to the alien. Tentatively, he reached out and touched the faceplate for the second time. Because of what had happened to him, the proximity of that alien face to his tracing fingers made him a little nervous.

This time there was no distortion of reality, no breathtaking tour of unseen worlds and distant plenums. He caressed the faceplate with his fingers, feeling the alien material. After a little of this he allowed his hands to trail off the transparency and down onto the suit. He could neither see nor feel a seam, buckle, zipper, or any other type of connection. The material of the faceplate seemed to flow into and become the dark brown fabric of the suit.

Nothing reacted to his touch or played with his head. He might as well have been inspecting a common cadaver in the Abilene morgue. There was no way he could know that any astronomer on the planet would gladly have traded a year of his life for Ross Ed's past hour.

Tilting his head back, he tried to see through the tons of rock above his head. No new visions enhanced his view of the universe. If mere touch could generate such revelations, what would happen when he tried to move the body? Something equally apocalyptic but more personal? Something perilous instead of enlightening?

Might the body be protected against movement, and was he about to disturb a grave? Would aliens booby-trap a burial site?

He tried to see it anew; as a small, unimpressive, inhuman corpse jammed in the back of a nondescript cave high in a range of little-visited mountains. Using the Maglite, he examined the body from all sides. There was nothing to show that wires, leads, or connection points attached it to the ground, or to anything else. It appeared wholly self-contained.

Wasn't anything else to do but to do it, he decided laconically. He'd worked most of his adult life in a dangerous profession and knew that sometimes you just had to throw the valve and see what resulted.

Gripping the mini Mag in his teeth, he slowly slipped his right arm beneath the corpse. Nothing arose to contest the gesture and he felt only cool dirt beneath the dry suit. His left hand went beneath the three legs. He lifted, and the body came up easily in his arms.

The alien felt light but might have been more of a burden to someone smaller than Ross Ed. It weighed no more than fifty, sixty pounds, he estimated. Certainly nothing he couldn't handle with ease.

Crouching low, he turned and started back toward the entrance. Once through the cleft he was able to straighten. Cradling the alien against his chest, he slipped the Maglite and keys back in his pocket.

The three legs and three arms lay slack, but the head remained upright. Whether this posture was a consequence of alien anatomy or some internal support mechanism he didn't know and couldn't tell. Rigor mortis, maybe, he told himself. Did the alien even have a skeleton? Feeling of the dangling legs, it was hard to tell.

Returning to the picnic site, he found no sign of the boisterous family which had impelled him to climb the granite outcropping. That suited him fine. He had no desire to encounter them or anyone else, lest he might be asked to explain his peculiar burden. A light was visible in one of the distant transient trailers, but no one emerged from within.

The big Caddy remained as he'd left it, sunlight glinting off the chrome. The same light allowed him to view the alien face with greater clarity. The dun-colored, slightly mottled flesh did not appear mummified or desiccated. Ross Ed suspected that in life his prize was just naturally gaunt.

The same went for the rest of the body, though there was a noticeable thickening where shoulders and hips ought to be located. Pressing one ear to the faceplate, he heard nothing.

Unlocking the car, he put the ice chest and the half-empty chicken bucket back in the trunk. He was about to add the alien when a mildly mischievous thought caused the corners of his mouth to twitch upward.

Slamming the trunk shut, he walked around to place the corpse in the spacious passenger seat, taking care to seat it in an upright position. No telling how long the poor fella (despite the lack of any proof he had decided to think of it as male) had been stuck in that damn cave. Time he saw something of the country. It would be nice to have a driving companion the rest of the way to California.

While the head remained perfectly upright, the limbs lolled loosely. Splaying out the three legs kept the body securely positioned.

Leaving his find, he relocked the car and returned to the cave. An extensive search revealed nothing else; no signs of a ship, no tools, no bits of suit fabric, no other caves, nothing. But on occasion, when stepping over a log or kicking aside a pile of pinecones and needles, or gazing up through the branches, he would see strange skittering creatures or great suns or hazy worlds rotating ponderously on their endless path through the cosmos. They would pop up unannounced and then fade from view, like the dots that appear when a bright light is abruptly flashed in one's eyes.

Flashbacks, he told himself. The longer he walked the less frequent they became.

Convinced there was nothing else to be found, or at least nothing else that he could find, he returned to the parking area. The alien was as he'd left him, seated motionless in the passenger's seat. Ross flipped the key in the ignition, pulled off the dirt, backed onto the pavement, and headed down the highway toward Alamogordo.

No one glanced in his direction as he made his way down the winding road and out of the mountains. To see his passenger another car would have to come within a foot or two of the Caddy. Even if someone did, at most they might think there was a funny-looking mannequin propped up in the passenger seat.

Ignoring the usual tourist-oriented billboards and blandishments, he drove straight through Alamogordo, not stopping until he reached the town's western outskirts. There he pulled into a Quickstop. A glance at the fuel gauge had revealed that the Cadillac was almost as thirsty as he was.

Popping the massive hood, he checked water, oil, and battery while the gas pump *click-click*ed away dollars as efficiently as any slot machine. Throughout, his passenger offered neither comment nor advice but instead sat patiently, awaiting a return to the road. Iridescent eyelids flashed briefly as Ross Ed worked his way back to the pump.

He winced at the amount on the meter, a by-now-reflexive response. The total was always greater than he expected. The price of comfort, he reminded himself resignedly.

Drawing his battered wallet from a front pocket, he entered the store and found himself in line behind a slim teenager who had adopted the protective sandy coloration of the nearby desert and a stout rancher slicked with grease. Patiently the man counted out dollar bills to pay for the two tanks of gas consumed by his enormous, extra-cab pickup.

While he waited to pay, Ross Ed let his gaze wander around the rest of the store. Sticky Slurpee machine, magazine racks, room-length glass-doored refrigerator crammed full of cold drinks, box displays of candy, cookies, road medicine and cheap souvenirs, forlorn baby cactus, and in the distance, a scarred restroom door whose cryptic handprint hieroglyphics all but cried out, "Abandon hygiene all ye who enter here."

His eyes came to rest on the single book rack, eighty percent of which was devoted to the tattered works of Louis L'Amour. The remainder was a mixed bag of large and small paperbacks. Several in particular not only caught his attention, but succeeded in drawing him out of the line.

All dealt with the same subject matter. The titles meant nothing to him. *The Roswell Incident. Cover-up at Roswell. UFO Compendium 1945–1995.* Nor did the cheap reproductions of photos and drawings purporting to show flying saucers particularly intrigue him.

The book he did pick up showed an alien, the same sort of alien everyone seemed to be seeing these days. There was the narrow, egg-shaped head featuring gigantic eyes much too large for the skull, the minuscule nose, and the tiny, pinched arc of a mouth. All in all it looked about as much like the being he'd removed from the cave as his aunt Pamela.

Flipping through the book supplied nothing of interest. Replacing it on the rack, he sampled another, with the same result. Each volume seemed to have its own agenda to push, each author claiming to be the one in sole possession of "the real facts." The thread that unified them was something called "the Roswell Incident," which claimed that the air force and the government had conspired to cover up the crash of a UFO near the town of Roswell, New Mexico, back in 1947.

He hadn't gone through Roswell, having passed well to the south of it, but the presence of so many books on the rack together with that of a certified alien in his car compelled him to read on. Not only was he a fast reader, but living and working on an oil rig out in the Gulf of Mexico afforded one the opportunity as well as the desire to indulge in every available type of literature.

Each book included long-winded discussions of such matters as weather balloons, government warehouses, witnesses of dubious probity, and secret laboratories. To the assorted authors a government cover-up seemed a foregone conclusion, though Ross Ed thought their arguments, as presented, pretty specious. Real *National Enquirer*–type material.

Except . . . right now he was traveling through southern New Mexico with an alien in his car.

Could the proponents of the Roswell theory maybe be half-right? All sorts of scenarios were possible.

Regardless of the truth, the supposed incident appeared to have spawned an entire local industry founded on the premise that *something* odd had happened in New Mexico back in the late forties. He considered purchasing one or more of the books, reflected on his present penurious circumstances, and decided that he'd acquired the gist of the story through his browsing. For all the bored young man behind the cash register cared, Ross Ed could have spent the rest of the afternoon reading everything in the store. It would take a far braver soul to shout "Hey, bud, this ain't no library!" at someone the size of the visiting Texan.

The line of people waiting to pay had evaporated and he shelled out cash for the gas, thanking the attendant as he departed. His thoughts were churning. There was no longer any question in his mind that he had not only *an* alien, but the famous Roswell alien. So what if it didn't resemble any of the drawings? Farmers and ranchers made notoriously poor witnesses and were inclined to tell interviewers anything they wanted to hear.

Suppose his alien's spaceship had actually looked like a weather balloon? Talk about your potential for confusion. In that event it meant that both the air force and the eyewitnesses were telling the truth. Contradictory truths.

"How 'bout it?" he asked his motionless companion. "Mighty long walk from Roswell up into those mountains." As expected, the child-sized corpse did not reply.

He'd have to proceed carefully, he realized. His book browsing had revealed the existence of a coterie of enthusiasts who would probably stop at nothing to exploit his discovery.

"What should I do?" he deliberated aloud. "Should I turn you over to the saucer folk, or to the government? Should I set up a tent and charge folks to look at you? Or should I just dump you at an auction house in Dallas and have 'em sell you to the highest bidder?" As before, the corpse did not respond.

I've been on the road too long, he thought. Bad enough when you start talking to yourself. But talking to dead aliens? He shook his head slightly and grinned. Still, you never knew when a dead alien might reply.

"Guess we'll keep thinking on it," he murmured softly. "I'm headed for California. Want to see the Pacific. If that's okay with you, well, you don't have to say anything." He paused briefly before adding, "That's what I thought."

As he motored westward he found he could no longer think of his passenger as simply "the alien." There'd been an uncle on his father's side who'd never said much. Just walked around wearing a little smile all the time that suggested he knew more than everybody else. The rest of the family thought he was weird, but Ross had always gotten along well him. Uncle Jedediah had been a good fella.

Though a fine and solid old name, Jedediah was a bit unwieldy for everyday use. Plain old Jed, now, that was easy on the palate. He glanced over at the alien.

"You ever seen the ocean, Jed?" He allowed a moment for the expected no-response. "Didn't think you had. Me, I've seen a lot of the Gulf, but people say the Pacific's a lot different. We'll decide what to do with you once we get out there. If that sounds good, you just sit tight and relax and leave everything else to me." Jed complied with admirable restraint.

As the miles between Alamogordo and White Sands slid past, Ross Ed kept up a steady patter with his companion, describing the passing scenery with jovial gusto. Unlike some passengers he'd had in the Caddy, Jed never griped or tried to act the backseat driver. He was a fine fellow traveler: clean, neat, uncomplaining, and an excellent listener. Nor did he need to go to the bathroom every five minutes like some of Ross Ed's ex-girlfriends. Only in the area of reciprocal conversation did he fall noticeably short.

Ejection seats, Ross found himself wondering. Were they or some similar device standard equipment on alien spacecraft? Maybe that's how Jed had arrived on Earth. It would explain the absence of a crash site in the vicinity of the cave.

A station wagon full of gray-haired retirees came up behind him and hummed past. One of the passengers studied the Caddy's occupants and did a double take worthy of Harpo as she caught sight of Jed, but the wagon didn't slow. It accelerated until it disappeared.

Ross Ed chuckled to his new friend. "Got 'em that time, Jed." If the rest of the trip was going to be this much fun, he might even be able to survive the absence of Dairy Queens.

He let both hands rest easy on the wheel. "Bet they don't have Lone Star on your planet. Do they even have beer? For that matter, do you drink? What's supposed to go through that funny-looking mouth of yours, anyway?" He grinned as he swerved smoothly around an unidentifiable lump of roadkill. "Seein' as how I found you in New Mexico, that makes you practically a Texan." He gestured at the fields of gold that lined both sides of the highway.

"California poppies. Calling us west. Too bad you won't be able to see any bluebonnets. This country's too dry for them." Resting his arm on the doorsill, he broke into song. The wind rushing past was warm, but not hot enough to justify running the gas-hungry air-conditioning. Certainly his passenger wasn't sweating.

He ran through some Guy Forsythe and Muddbone tunes before his attention was distracted by the flashing lights in the rearview. They shattered his mood as effectively as a fishbowl dropped from the top of a rig.

"Damn!" Reflexively, he glanced down at the speedometer. He was only doing sixty, a relatively safe speed in a fifty-five zone. Insofar as he knew, everything on the Caddy was in working order, and he wasn't trailing any loose bits. So what was up with the cop? Maybe his girlfriend was riding the rag.

He slowed gradually to make sure it was him the patrolman was after, then eased off onto the gravel shoulder. Sure enough, the big Kawasaki pulled in behind him, its lights alternating merrily. At least the officer hadn't used his siren, which meant he wasn't *too* exercised. Maybe he just wanted to deliver a warning, though for the life of him Ross Ed didn't have a clue as to what he might have been doing wrong.

Had the cop had a bad day? Had his favorite team lost badly last night? Was his digestion bothering him? Had the coffee been hot enough this morning? On such small incidents did large fines frequently hang.

Ross leaned out the window, careful to keep both hands on the wheel and in plain sight. "Something wrong, Officer?"

The patrolman was in his late forties, tending to puffiness, with too-pale skin blotched pink by the unyielding sun. The dark black shades he wore masked his eyes.

"You were wandering over the line back there a few times, son. Had anything to drink?"

"Couple of beers a few hours ago. That's all. I ain't drunk."

"Didn't say you were. License and registration. Slowly, please."

Ross Ed complied, passing the wrinkled forms to the officer's waiting fingers.

"Be just a minute." The man returned to his bike. In the sideview mirror Ross Ed could see him working his two-way, heard the crackle of static and distorted voices.

Was his registration up to date? He always tried to pay early. He couldn't remember the last time he'd renewed. Funny how your insides could tighten up at such moments, even when you were certain you'd done nothing wrong.

The patrolman returned, his expression neutral. Ross Ed waited to hear the dreaded words, "Would you please step out of your car, sir?" Instead, the cop passed back the Caddy's papers.

"Everything in order, Officer?"

"Seems to be. Try to stay on your side of the road, will you? We only get accidents out here when somebody does something stupid, like taking it too easy. Where you headed?"

"California. Never seen the Pacific, and I thought I'd get out of Texas for a while."

"Don't hear that from many Texans." The officer smiled and removed his shades.

Ross Ed relaxed and allowed himself to smile back. "I admit it ain't common." Now that it was clear he wasn't going to be fined, he was willing to be generous with casual pleasantries.

"Never seen the ocean myself." The cop nodded toward the western horizon. "Never been to California, either. Hell, I still have to make it to Arizona. I hear Tucson's pretty. I guess you'll be going through there."

"Don't know. I'm kind of taking it easy and enjoying the ride."

"Yeah, I can see that. Most people come up I-10, not through the mountains. It's nice up there this time of year."

"Sure is." Ross Ed waited patiently.

The patrolman was reluctant to leave. "You sure you haven't had more than a few beers?" Ross nodded reassuringly. "Okay. Just no more wheel-walking the center line." He grinned. "If you'd said one beer I would've known you were lying and might've had to haul you in."

"I'll be careful, Officer. I was trying to think and sing at the same time."

The cop pushed back his cap. "I'm sure not going to spoil the day for a man who's feeling good enough to sing. Don't have too many days like that myself. You take care now, son." As he started to turn and leave he caught sight of something that made him pause.

"Now what the blue blazes you got there?" He bent to squint past the Caddy's driver.

Ross Ed thought fast. How much imagination did the patrolman possess? His mom and dad had brought him up not to lie to the police, but in the oil fields and honky-tonks he'd been introduced to conflicting opinions on the matter. His thoughts milled about and collided furiously with one another, like a major accident he'd barely escaped one time on the outskirts of Houston.

The longer he hesitated, the edgier and more alert the cop grew. He had to say something, anything.

"It's a dead alien," he heard himself blurting out.

"Is that a fact? Funny, it doesn't look Mexican to me." The patrolman roared. After a moment Ross Ed joined in, though he was wincing inside. He had plenty of Hispanic friends back home and the crude joke didn't set well, though he knew this wasn't the time or place to make an issue of it.

"'A dead alien.'" The cop made a face. "I know, I know; you mean like one of those bug-eyed critters from *Star Trek* or *Star Wars* or one of those other *Star* movies. An E.T."

"That's right." Having shown his hand, Ross Ed figured he might as well play it. "His name's Jed."

"'Jed,' oh yeah, right." This time the patrolman laughed so hard he had to wipe tears from one eye. "Okay, Ross Ed Hager, what're you doing with a dead alien?"

Ross considered briefly, then shrugged. "I reckon I'm taking him to California with me."

"Right, right, I can see that." The cop checked his watch. "California'd be the proper place for one, that's for sure. Where'd you meet up with him?"

"Found him in a cave." Ross purposely neglected to identify the location lest it stir latent proprietary impulses within this jolly enforcer of the law. "Figured he might want to see the ocean, too."

"Of course. Who wouldn't?" The patrolman manufactured a mock frown. "You sure you haven't escaped from somewhere, Ross Ed?"

"As a matter of fact, Officer, I have. You know Abilene? I've escaped from there."

The cop grunted understandingly. "I've seen pictures. Mesquite and hills. Don't care much for it myself. Give me the desert any day. At least it knows what kind of country it wants to be." He leaned in slightly. "Can I touch it?"

"Why not?" Ross swallowed. Denial risked piquing the officer's suspicions. "He's dead."

He lowered the passenger-side window as the patrolman walked around to the other side of the car. Without a word the man reached in to feel first of the faceplate, then the suit. Ross tensed. As it turned out, needlessly.

The officer withdrew his hand. "Not a very good job. My sister could do better with papier-mâché. Some kids make it up for you, or did you buy it in a store? No, wait, you said you found it in a cave." He chuckled. "Probably stored there till the next Halloween. I can see a bunch of kids doing something like that. Scaring the shit out of their friends and then concealing the evidence. What're you going to do with it?"

"Haven't decided. Got to get to California first."

"That's right, you do. Well, you won't get there sitting around here." He stepped back and Ross Ed gratefully raised the passenger-side window.

"You take it easy now," the cop called out from behind the car. "You've still got a lot of road ahead of you. And when you get to California, whistle at a couple of those beach babes for me, will you?"

"I'll do that." Ross stuck an arm out of the open window and waved.

As the big Caddy started up and pulled back out onto the blacktop, the patrolman walked back to his bike, shaking his head. The weirdos you meet on the road, he mused. The guy was clean and polite. So he'd had a few beers? In his time the cop had downed a few himself, with no cataclysmic consequences. It wasn't like the driver had been throwing down vodka shots.

He climbed back on his bike with the intention of turning around and making a check of the east side. As he keyed the ignition and rolled the accelerator, the Kawasaki took off like a cat with a terrier locked on its tail.

Ross Ed estimated the patrolman was doing no less than a hundred and fifty and accelerating rapidly when he went rocketing past. It was hard to tell because he hadn't seen the bike coming up on him. It vanished over a low rise like dissipating heatstroke.

A mile down the road he slowed only long enough to make sure the cop was all right. His uniform in tatters, he was bending over the exhausted motorcycle, which lay on its side in the soft sand behind the shoulder. Smoke rose from the front and rear wheels, which sheer speed had reduced to globules of metal and rubber slag. As he surveyed the scene in his rearview Ross found himself wondering how fast the bike had been going when the wheels had finally melted and the cop's uniform had shredded. He glanced to his right.

Jed the dead sat stolidly in the passenger's seat, head facing forward, blankly eyeing the road ahead. Apparently, making contact with the alien, or the alien's suit, resulted in repercussions as unpredictable as they were astonishing. Ross Ed had received an hour-long tour of the known cosmos. The unsuspecting patrolman had been granted the ability to accelerate to speeds with which the physical structure of his vehicle was ultimately unable to cope.

Leaning over, Ross cautiously stroked an alien arm. Nothing happened. There was no reprise of the astronomical tour he had received in the cave. Perhaps the extraordinary happenstances were one-shots, delivered only upon making initial contact.

Another look in the rearview showed no sign of the dazed patrolman. Ross Ed doubted the man would draw any connection between the "fake" dead alien and the fact that his bike had inexplicably gone berserk. How he was going to explain to his colleagues that his motorcycle had been traveling three or four hundred miles an hour before it died was something Ross didn't have to worry about. No one would believe him anyway. Probably they'd think he'd set fire to his own vehicle. In that context the mention of a dead alien traveling cross-country in a white Cadillac in the company of a Texas roughneck would not be likely to endear him to his superiors.

He'd have to be careful, Ross reflected, not to let passersby make casual contact with his companion.

"You may be dead," he informed his passenger, "but danged if you ain't full of surprises. What other tricks can you do?"

Predictably, Jed was his usual nonresponsive self.

THREE

Thanks to the mutual appetites of car and man, Ross Ed was just about bust by the time he pulled into Las Cruces. Knowing he'd have a better chance of finding a good temporary job in the much larger metropolis of El Paso, he swung south and made the half-hour detour to that center of southwestern culture, smuggling, Tex-Mex cooking, discount boot outlets, and other widely assorted local enterprises that would remain forever inscrutable to anyone born or raised east of the Mississippi or north of the Ozarks.

The city clung like a piece of weathered river driftwood to the rambling north shore of the Rio Grande, where it slammed into Chihuahua state before turning southeast toward the Gulf of Mexico. The river was the only reason for the town's presence, since a bachelor coyote would have had a hard time making a living off the surrounding countryside. Compared with the dry desolation from which the city had been raised, distant Phoenix was the proverbial Garden of Eden.

Passing through downtown, he entered a highway hell of endless motels, truck stops, convenience stores, gas stations, and the ubiquitous discount stores. The presence of the latter caused him to examine his own footwear. His boots were scuffed and worn, but still serviceable and, more importantly, broken in. Leather still concealed the embedded steel toes, and the sharkskin uppers had not yet worn through. Stingray would've been better, but he'd yet to see a pair of boots fashioned entirely of that particular exotic material. Too tough to work, he'd been told.

You could saw wood with the leather. In his profession reliable boots were a necessity rather than a fashion statement. Try to get by on an oil rig with sneakers or sandals and it wouldn't be long before you acquired an interesting nickname. The Toeless Wonder, for example.

He calculated it would take at least a couple of weeks to replenish his finances. Meanwhile the Caddy would get a rest. He knew there was no oilfield work to be had this far west of Monahans, but over the years he had perfected a second skill for the times when roughneck work was scarce.

There were two professions which enabled any man or woman to get a temporary job anywhere in the world; that of nurse, or bartender. Ross Ed never had much cared for hospital ambience.

An exit sign shouted AIRPORT and he eased down the off-ramp. Driving north, he began to check out the line of hotels and motels. He knew he'd be able to get a job because he'd done so repeatedly in the past. Someone his size who didn't drink while on duty, was careful with the money and good with the customers, was always a welcome addition to the staff of busy bars. In Ross Ed a manager acquired not only an experienced mixologist but a backup bouncer, all for the price of one. It enabled him to be somewhat selective.

Spotting a conveniently located Howard Johnson's, he pulled in. Slightly more expensive than many chains, they had better security and the occasional extra-long king-size bed. While still not expansive enough for him, these at least allowed him to sleep with his knees situated somewhere below his chin.

Arranging a weekly rate with the duty manager, he pulled the Caddy around back. The interior hallway was air-conditioned, just like a bigger hotel, and his second-floor room looked out on a collection of drought-resistant trees and contented sparrows. The bed was almost big enough. The shower was impossible, but then they always were.

No one observed him as he transferred his suitcase and alien from car to room. Most travelers were still on the road and the parking lot wasn't likely to get busy for another several hours.

He sat his patient companion upright in one of the two chairs, taking care to keep him away from the window and the blast of the air-conditioner. Relatively invisible from outside, Jed still had a good view of the trees and birds. Pity he couldn't see them, Ross Ed thought.

"There you go. Time for me to get cleaned up."

It took him five minutes to unpack, following which he climbed into the shower tub and sat down. That allowed the spray to hit him on the head instead of in the navel. It was the only way he could do his hair in a motel bathroom without imitating a Mongolian contortionist.

Washed and reinvigorated, he shaved and carefully combed his thick black hair. Under Jed's unwatchful eye he drew forth from the suitcase fresh underwear, clean black jeans, and a neatly pressed, long-sleeve western shirt.

"Be back soon," he told the alien, and made sure the door locked firmly behind him.

He found the nearest car wash and treated the road-weary Cadillac to a bath of its own. A few judicious questions while it was being dried directed him to the better airport hotels, where within the hour he had a secured a job tending bar at the Sheraton. He much preferred working hotel bars to local clubs. They were clean, the tips were better, and the neighborhood drunks did not patronize them.

His job application consisted of demonstrating for the bartender how to make a frozen daiquiri and a screwdriver. That, a few questions, and he found himself hired.

The first few nights were a little rough as he struggled to learn where everything was. After that it went smoothly. Usually he worked alone, occasionally in tandem with a second bartender. Tips came from a steady procession of traveling businessmen, regulars, and soldiers from Fort Bliss. The three-minute commute from the motel was easy on both him and the Caddy. On-the-job entertainment was provided by boisterous patrons and the overhead TVs, which were perpetually tuned to different sports channels.

He settled in for a brief but remunerative stay.

"*Dios,*" murmured Corrina Martinez. What was that? Absently she shoved the two-dollar tip that was always waiting for her on the sink counter of Room 225 into an apron pocket. She'd already stripped the bed preparatory to remaking it when she thought it might be nice to change the pillows as well. According to the records, the room was occupied by a single gentleman. It was unusual for someone like that to tip the maids daily and she wanted to reciprocate.

The spare pillows were located on the top shelf inside the single closet. Sliding one of the mirrored doors aside, she'd started to reach for the pillows when she'd been startled by sight of the thing. It hadn't frightened her enough to make her scream, but she had drawn in her breath sharply.

When it didn't move, she crossed herself reflexively before turning on the light in the dressing alcove so she could examine it more closely. It was a doll of some kind, exceedingly grotesque in appearance but not notably of the devil. Having worked as a seamstress, the material of the little suit puzzled her, but she did not linger over it.

There were all manner of strange toys in the stores these days, as her children were fond of pointing out whenever they could drag her to a mall. It was a game. She could never afford any of them, and the kids knew she couldn't, but they would play at picking out their favorites and she would play at feigning interest. Then they would go for sopapillas and ice cream.

Was this a present for the gentleman's children? It was big, but she'd seen walking, talking dolls that were bigger. Probably it was a tie-in to some popular movie or TV show. It lay propped up against the back of the closet, the light shining off its three little button eyes. It didn't react when, feeling silly, she waved at it. Of course it wouldn't. If it "did" anything at all there would be a button or pull string somewhere in the back to activate it.

It was certainly well made. Her kids, especially the eldest two, would think it was "cool." She could see them making faces and funny voices behind it, flapping the multiple arms and legs to frighten the younger children. Recalling her own initial reaction to the sight of it made her smile.

She stretched to reach the pillows on the upper shelf, and found herself hesitating. What was that rusty brown fabric? Not leather, or satin. More like a very smooth foil, or crumpled, heavily starched silk. Who would starch silk? Her professional interest was piqued.

Bending, she used two fingers to pinch up a bit of the material covering the left arm.

The place where she found herself was dominated by a sky of silver that reminded her more than anything else of the mercury in a thermometer. How a sky could be silver she didn't know, any more than she knew how a sun could be bright red instead of a soft, warm yellow.

So unstable was the ground beneath her feet that they sank into it for a couple of inches before stopping. She took a tentative step forward and found the sensation to be not unlike walking on Jell-O. All around her long, coiled, ropy creatures composed of similar material wiggled their rounded ends at the sunlight. A flock of bright green ropes speckled with pink undulated through the sky. Their flanks gleamed metallic and sparkled like the paint job on some of the neighborhood low-riders.

Off to her right something like a bright blue faceless pig trotted along on stumpy legs through the forest of drunken coils. It was trailed by three little ones. Half a dozen filaments terminating in turquoise-colored nodules protruded from each forehead, bobbing up and down with every step. The pseudo-pigs seemed to skip along the slick, gooey surface without getting bogged down.

Lowering her gaze, Corrina was surprised to see that in place of her maid's uniform she was clad in some thin, bronze-hued material which covered her from head to foot while leaving significant gaps in unexpected places. Twenty years ago she wouldn't have thought twice about flaunting so much skin. Now there was simply too much of it, but somehow in this place the design seemed natural and normal.

Instead of a vacuum cleaner she found herself holding a long black tube in both hands. This was connected to a pack on her back by means of several flexible black conduits. A semitransparent black globe bulged the center of the tube. Holding it up to her face, she found she could make out dozens of tiny obelisks floating inside, like string beans in a consommé. Each was inscribed with detailed writing.

Her right index finger rested on a plastic spur that jutted down from the underside of the tube. Was it a gun, she found herself wondering, or a window washer?

Something hiccuped violently off to her right and she turned sharply in its direction. Bear-sized and extravagantly tusked, it looked like nothing she'd ever seen in a zoo or on one of the television nature shows her *tío* Gabriel favored. Sprouting behind the tusks was a snaggle of fangs that glistened razor-sharp in the argent twilight.

Each of the creature's five legs was the height of a man. They splayed out at the base into broad, flat pads that resembled a pair of swim fins fused together front to back. These enabled the

monster, despite its size, to tread
gealed ground.

A single sinister eye set in a facial
her, the slitted pupil narrowing threaten
mat of brown hair ran the length of the bu
inspection she saw that it wasn't hair but a of
eellike creatures that were parasitic on the cre

The toothy mouth parted and the hiccup und was repeated, challengingly this time. Lowering its foreparts, it started toward her, lurching from side to side and gathering speed with each pentuple stride. Massive tusks bobbed and pink slobber trailed from between the fangs.

Instinctively, she swung the black tube around. On its expansive footpads the monster seemed to glide over the quivering ground. Running was out of the question. She'd get one shot, she knew, and one shot only. Her finger contracted on the plastic spur.

Something went *splash* in her ears as the tube kicked like a restive ocelot. The front of the beast splattered all over the undulating ropy coil-creatures, which shrank back in horror from the gelatinous ruin. The force of its charge sent the rest of the massive body careening onward and she threw herself to one side . . .

. . . Pulling her hand away from the motionless figure propped up against the back of the closet.

Breathing hard, one hand on her chest, Corrina Martinez reached out to touch the figure a second time, jerking her fingers back as if from a hot plate. Nothing happened. The dream, or hallucination, or whatever it had been was not repeated. She was alone in the motel room. Sparrows chattered incessantly outside the window.

She'd had strange dreams before, of course. Didn't everyone? But this had been so vivid, so real, that she could still smell in her nostrils the peculiar fruity odor of that preposterous, unstable world and the distinctive muskiness of the monstrosity which had come charging down upon her.

What had happened? She gazed at the uncomely seated figure out of wide, staring eyes. It was some sort of demon. Something would have to be done about it.

But how could she be sure that her hallucination was connected to it? She'd touched it again and nothing had happened.

..g her eyes from the motionless figure, she began ..ıg away from the closet.

When the hand grabbed her, she very nearly did scream.

Despite his intimidating size, the stranger's gentle smile and easy manner quickly reassured her. "Sorry, ma'am. Didn't mean to startle you. Is something wrong?"

Panting and still unsure of what she'd just experienced, she struggled to regain control of her emotions.

"I'm sorry, sir. This is my room. I mean, I am doing the cleaning." She indicated the upper shelf. "I was going to change pillows for you."

"Thanks. That'd be nice." He showed her the large brown sack he was holding before putting it down on the floor. "Had some shopping to do. You sure everything's okay?"

She saw that he was looking past her, into the closet. "I didn't mean to touch it. It was an accident. I just wanted to get new pillows for you."

"No problem." He started to put a hand on her shoulder, changed his mind. The well-meaning gesture had a tendency to intimidate instead of reassure people. "Something happened, didn't it, when you touched the figure?" At the look on her face he smiled again. "Go ahead, tell me: I won't laugh."

The maid spoke slowly. "I thought it looked interesting. I was going to get you some new pillows, and I touched it."

"Yes, you've already said that. Calm down, ma'am. Everything's okay. Now, you saw something. Pictures in your mind that were new to you?"

Her eyes widened again. "Yes. I seemed to be someplace else. *Dios,* I seemed to be *somebody* else." She gestured into the closet. "What is that thing?"

He thought fast, the speed of his response helped by the fact that he'd given some thought to the matter already. "It's a new kind of electronic toy." He fought to recall what he'd recently seen on television. "You've heard of virtual reality?"

She shook her head. "No sir, I haven't."

"You put these special goggles on and they send you into another, imaginary world." He indicated the corpse in the closet. "This is like that, only they put it in a doll's body instead of a helmet and goggles. To make it seem more alien. All you have to do to see the pictures is touch it." Stepping past her, he reached in and ran a hand over Jed's faceplate. "There, I've turned it off.

Shouldn't have left it on. Go ahead," he urged her. "You can touch it now and nothing will happen." I hope, he added silently.

Slowly, uncertainly, she reached for the diminutive body. Ross Ed tried not to hold his breath. Her fingers contacted the middle arm . . . and drew back. The relief on her face was palpable.

"I see. It is very new, this toy?"

"Very new. Not really on the open market yet. Impressive, isn't it? It's intended for adults, not kids."

"I can see that. Can . . . can I try it again?"

"Uh, I'm afraid not. It uses a special rechargeable battery and I left the charger in my car. Maybe some other time. Now, you go on with your work." He motioned for her to leave.

"But, sir, I haven't finished your room yet."

"I just came back to drop off these groceries and pick up a few things. I'll be out in ten minutes and then you can have the place to yourself." He picked up the vacuum and shooed her outside, shutting the door on her bemused expression.

Would the story he'd hastily concocted satisfy her? He wondered what she'd seen. A vast astronomical panorama . . . or something else? Something new and different? His gaze wandered to the closet and its sole uncomplaining occupant.

"Well, Jed, I guess we're lucky she wasn't the house detective. What the blazes are we going to do with you? Can't have you sitting around frightening the hired help." The unmoving alien corpus offered no response.

Ross Ed had thought his companion safe. Obviously that was no longer the case. Next time the maid might come back with fellow workers, or maybe the manager. Among them might be someone who wouldn't accept facile explanations so readily.

He could change motels, but he was moved in, comfortable, and had established a friendly relationship with the management. He liked the location and his room, and the motel was convenient to everything. He couldn't afford the Sheraton.

He put the matter to his companion, who as usual had no suggestions. Since there were no objections from the alien quarter, he decided to stay. The maid seemed to have accepted his explanation. Unless she brought it up again, he'd proceed on that assumption.

Meanwhile something would have to be done about Jed. It wouldn't do to have a procession of curious maids fumbling around the alien. The trunk of the Caddy was a safe place, but it could get seriously hot in there and he'd found the body in a cold cave. He didn't know how well the corpse could tolerate extremes of temperature. And there was always the possibility of car thieves.

The only way he could be sure of the alien's safety was to have him someplace where he could keep an eye on him. He tried to remember his father's hunting lessons. What was it the old man had said about "hiding in plain sight"?

FOUR

Walter Siminowski hailed from Cleveland and sold medical instruments city to city, hospital to hospital. He didn't much like El Paso, finding the pace of urban life slow and the ambience as dry as the weather. But the Southwest was his territory and he could sell only so many devices in Las Vegas and Reno. He would have preferred California, which was a sales territory unto itself, but that bastard Novak still ranked him. Someday, he told himself, dreaming of beaches and starlets.

Siminowski was good at his job and made a nice living, but like so many in similar circumstances he hated the constant traveling. Fortunately for him and his colleagues, the electronic marketplace still had a long way to go before it found a way to replace the traveling salesman. Hospital managers weren't ready to buy the latest in bulk instrument sterilizers through a catalog, no matter how glossy. They wanted hands-on demonstrations of electronic efficacy.

He was pretty much done here, unless there were any messages waiting for him up in the room. That meant time enough for a two-drink afternoon instead of one. First thing in the morning he'd push off for Albuquerque.

With a grunt he put the sports section from *USA Today* aside, wondering if the Cavaliers would ever be healthy for the play-offs. His attention wandered absently around the room, passing over the nattering televisions suspended from the ceiling, the many small, round, and largely unoccupied tables, until it came to rest on the bar. Specifically, on the odd object on the back counter.

It sat propped up between a tall bottle of golden yellow Frangelico liqueur and a lighted Budweiser bas-relief of Clydesdales and beer. Siminowski stared at it for a long time, occasionally pausing to sip at his drink. When he'd inhaled the last of the liquid residue, he picked up the glass and ambled over to the counter. There were plenty of empty stools and he chose one directly across from the entity.

A couple of fellow travelers were seated several stools to his right. Their uniforms (conservative suit and tie, too much hairspray, white shirts laundered to the point where it was the starch and not cotton fiber that held them together, shoes that would stink of airports) marked them as migrating businessmen like himself. Farther down, a pair of army types were chatting up the young woman seated between them.

It was just after five. Soon now people would be coming in from work, ready to relax with a drink or two before dinner. The bar would get noisy, the restaurant next door would get busy, and he wanted to get to bed soon enough to rest up for the early flight next morning.

But his curiosity had a tight grip on his imagination and refused to let go.

He sat and nursed his empty glass and stared. Three legs hung over the edge of the shelf on which the object had been propped. Even within the integrated boots, the feet looked funny. Of the three arms, the right one was looped around the slim Frangeligo bottle, the left rested atop the Budweiser sign, and the one in the middle relaxed in what passed for a lap. Stiff and erect, the head and its reflective eye surfaces seemed to stare right past him.

"Excuse me?"

Responding, the bartender, who looked big enough to play pro football, ambled over. "What'll you have, sir?" Siminowski instantly recognized the lazy Texas drawl.

Mesmerized by the figure seated on the back counter, the salesman took a moment to think. "Jack on the rocks."

"Right away, sir." Like a magician working the three-cup trick, the bartender made Siminowski's empty glass disappear.

He returned a moment later with a fresh squat glass full of ice cubes stained brown, which he sat before the salesman on a clean, compact napkin.

Siminowsky extracted a five from his wallet and flipped it onto the counter. "Keep it."

The bartender nodded appreciatively. "Thanks." The bill vanished with the same facility as the previous glass.

"Just a minute." Siminowski gestured and the big man paused expectantly. He wore a western shirt and black jeans. The buckle at his belt looked like it had been run over by a backhoe, not once but several times.

"Something else, sir?"

The salesman raised a finger and pointed. "What *is* that, anyway?"

"What?" The bartender turned his head and grinned. "Oh, you mean Jed."

"'Jed.' Yeah, I guess I do."

Ross Ed chuckled gently. "A lot of people ask that question, sir"

"Walter," the salesman corrected him. "Walter Siminowski, Cleveland." He extended a hand, which the bartender enveloped in his own.

"Just call me Ross," the big man replied.

"Okay, Ross. Tell me about that thing. Where'd it come from? How long has it been here? Who does it belong to?"

As Ross Ed was formulating a reply a couple of younger business types claimed the stools on Siminowski's left. Their ties were undone and the top buttons of their shirts open. There was no sign of their jackets. Probably left them in their car, Siminowski decided. Their accents marked them as local.

Apparently they'd overheard. "Shoot, man," declaimed the one nearest the salesman, "don't you know what that is?" The men exchanged amused expressions. "Thought everyone knew Jed."

His companion accepted a draft beer from the bartender. "You told him yet, Ross Ed?"

The laconic Texas shook his head. "Why don't you tell him, Jimmy?"

"Sure!" Turning, the younger man grinned at Siminowski. His clothes smelled of El Paso, but his breath reflected the recent application of expensive deodorizer. "Old Jed there, he's an alien."

"That's right." His slightly older companion slugged his beer. "An alien."

"'Course, he's dead," added the one called Jimmy.

"I see." Siminowski turned back to the bartender.

"That's right, Walter. Jed's a dead alien."

The two beer drinkers were enjoying themselves. "Ross Ed found him. Didn't you, Ross Ed? Right by the side of the road."

"Yeah," chortled Jimmy. "Hitchhiking, wasn't he?" He let out a hoot of self-satisfaction. "Pretty easy with three thumbs. 'Course, we don't really know if he's got thumbs." The young professional turned back to the bartender. "How 'bout it, Ross Ed? Does Jed have thumbs?"

"I expect he does." Ross moved slightly to his left to take an order from a waitress named Doreen. The room was starting to get crowded.

Siminowski took the opportunity to question the two regulars. "So you think it's a dead alien, too?"

"Shoot," declared the first man, "what else could it be?"

"I don't know." The salesman considered. "I've never seen a dead alien before."

"Neither has anyone else, honey." The waitress favored him with a professional smile before melting into the crowd with her order.

Siminowski knew he'd have to leave soon, too, or else he'd have to wait for a dinner table. Like most of his brethren, he avoided room service whenever he had enough time to do so. The predictability of it was mind-numbing.

"Well, I just wanted to know."

"And now you do." Jimmy slid off his stool and gave the stranger a friendly whack on the back. "He can do all sorts of tricks, Jed can. Isn't that right, Ross Ed?"

The bartender replied without looking up from his work. "That's right."

"Make him dance." Jimmy's friend conducted the conversation with his beer. "C'mon, Ross Ed, make him dance!"

The big man seemed hesitant. "I dunno, Jimmy. It's gettin' kind of busy."

"Please." Siminowski was insistent. "That I'd like to see."

"Well, okay." Turning, Ross Ed picked up the strange figure and cradled its anterior region in the palm of his right hand, letting the spine lean against his arm. He handled it as if it weighed nothing. Using his left hand, he began to flip the three legs upward in rehearsed sequence, letting them flop freely. As he did so he whistled an accompaniment.

Siminowski stared intently for a moment, then his expression fell. He sensed himself blushing. One of the young professionals gave him a friendly nudge in the ribs. Both men were having a good laugh, largely at the gullible out-of-towner's expense.

"Pretty impressive, isn't he?" Jimmy chuckled. "A regular alien Fred Astaire."

"Yeah." An embarrassed Siminowski slid off his stool. "Yeah, that's just great. Thanks for the show." He turned to leave, his ears burning. He should've known better. No Texan would pass up a chance to make a fool of a visiting Yankee.

Jimmy called after him. "Hey, don't you want to see him fly?" His companion was laughing hard enough to slosh beer on the floor.

Quietly, Ross Ed set Jed back in his niche on the back bar. It was Friday and the traffic wouldn't let up until closing time. Businessmen just getting off work, professionals on their way home, soldiers from Fort Bliss out for the weekend, and folks on vacation would keep him running until the wee hours. He preferred it that way. It beat standing around cleaning glasses.

The first time one of the locals had asked him about Jed, Ross Ed had simply told the truth. The story quickly made the rounds among the regulars, and after that, they readily participated in what had become a prized local gag. The other bartenders and the waitresses went along. As usual, hotel management was oblivious.

Safe beneath Ross Ed's protective gaze, the alien spent afternoons and evenings entertaining bar patrons and mornings and nights with Ross in the motel. When he went out on one of his sporadic, brief shopping trips Jed went with him, either in the passenger seat or on the floor in back. The system had worked fine for nearly two weeks. Another day or two, Ross Ed felt, and it would be time for him to give notice. He'd saved enough money, but he wasn't the type to run out on management during a busy weekend.

They'd be sorry to lose him. Employers were always sorry to lose him. He did his job efficiently and quietly, and the one time he'd had to back up the regular bouncer the incident had been resolved without damage or bloodshed.

But he hadn't come this far to spend months in another bar,

another hotel. It was time to be on his way. The Rio Grande wasn't the Pacific.

It was crowded even for a Friday night, perhaps due to the big UTEP–New Mexico State game on TV. Occasionally a portion of the now jostling crowd would emit a roar or groan as something significant played itself out on the overhead screens. Mark, the other night bartender, held down the opposite end of the bar. The two men worked well together, each tending capably to their own orders. Behind them Jed took it all in, silent witness to the exotic mass of surging humanity.

None of the waitresses or other bartenders touched Jed because Ross had explained that it was a new kind of kid's space toy and that the electrical system kept shorting out. The result was the occasional nasty shock. It was an explanation readily accepted by his fellow workers, who kept their fingers well clear of the seated figure back of the bar. Not that they were much curious about it anyway.

A hand was waving frantically from the far end of the counter. Someone thirsty, he knew as he ambled toward the semaphoring fingers. On Friday nights someone was always thirsty.

The stocky, well-dressed man seated at the small round table nearest the bar leaned over and spoke to his much younger female companion. "You hear all that, Telita? Dead alien, my ass! Probably got it at Toys 'R' Us and customized it in his garage."

"I'm sure he did, honey." The woman pressed tightly against him, her left arm resting on the shoulder of his expensive suit as she did her best to ignore his breath.

Bending forward, the man lowered his voice to a whisper. "Know what we oughta do, beautiful?"

She smiled and touched one perfect fingernail to the tip of his nose. "Anything you want, honey." The bulge of his wallet allowed her to overlook the rest of him, along with the twenty-year difference in their ages.

"That's for later. I mean now, here."

"No, what?" She feigned interest, just as she'd been feigning interest in everything else he'd said since they'd crossed paths and finalized fiscal arrangements.

"We ought to throw a little panic into Harry from Hicksville. I mean, anyone can buy the Predator or the Alien at their local Sharper Image, and that dorky-looking dummy is the best he could come up with? Who's he think he's fooling?" His eyes glittered. "Let's wait till he's real busy, and then we'll swipe the thing!"

The woman looked uncertain. "I don't know, Jerry. Maybe it's valuable to him."

"Aw, he'll live. We'll just hide it for a while." Malicious mirth stained his words. "Be fun to see the big jerk clomping around looking for it. If he asks us we'll tell him we saw it flying back to Mars, or something."

Telita glanced over at the busy bartender. "Just don't get him mad at us, Jerry. He's pretty big."

"Hell, he can't do anything." Her companion eyed her contemptuously. "Don't you know how these things work? The guy could be eight feet tall and he still can't lay a finger on a customer."

"That depends on whether he cares more about his job or his toy," she pointed out sensibly. "Maybe it doesn't even belong to him. Maybe he borrowed it from a friend."

"Then he'll be in even more of a panic when it disappears." Jerry grinned nastily, enjoying his companion's unease as much as the anticipation. "Look, we're not gonna dump it in the trash, we're just gonna hide it for a little while. No harm done." He snorted and she had to quickly hide a look of distaste. "He probably isn't watching it closely because he doesn't think anybody'd bother something that ugly."

Telita had resigned herself to her wealthy companion's juvenile aspirations. As long as he was conscious, she couldn't avail herself of his wallet's contents. The game had to be played a little longer. "How you gonna do it, Jerry?"

"You go down there. . . ." Pulling her close, he whispered in her ear.

Her eyes widened and she pulled away slightly. "No, Jerry, honey."

"You go down there," he reiterated, his tone darkening, "and distract him." He patted her in a sensitive place and it was all she could do not to flinch. Fortunately, practice enabled her to disengage certain nerve endings.

With an effort she returned his conspiratorial smile. "It won't work. I know his type. He'll smile at me and be polite and attentive, but he won't be distracted."

"You give it your best try, honey." Jerry fondled her again, right there in the middle of the bar. "I have a lot of confidence in you. Tell you what: there's another fifty in it for you, just for diverting the guy. *If* you can do it."

Her apprehension was overwhelmed by greed. She chucked him gently under his chin. "For fifty bucks, Jerry, I'd distract the pope."

"That's my girl." He followed her with admiring eyes as she oozed out of her chair and undulated the length of the bar, drawing admiring stares from every male patron within viewing range.

Amusedly, he observed the scenario which proceeded to unfold at the far end of the bar. Telita had either underestimated her appeal or overestimated the hulking bartender's indifference, because she soon had him engaged in active conversation.

When he was certain the crowd was at its most raucous and the bartender at his most preoccupied, Jerry rose and strolled with studied indifference to the far end of the counter. Ducking lithely beneath the drop-leaf barrier, he found himself confronting the doll.

Up close it looked as if the manufacturer had done a better job than he'd first suspected. There were details in the suit fabric, the chalky color of the skin, and the reflective eyelids that suggested more attention to detail than he'd originally been willing to credit. Even up close he couldn't see how the metal strips and cords were attached to the rust-hued fabric.

He'd sneak it up to the room and hide it there for an hour or so, long enough for the bartender to become more and more frantic. Then he'd hand it back. Or maybe, he thought with a smile, he'd offer to ransom it. How far would the big lunk go to get his toy back? It would be a fun way to start the evening. He already knew how he intended to end it.

A glance showed the bartender still adrift in Telita's charms. He reached for the figure. It didn't look very heavy and he was sure he could manage it. One hand grasped the middle leg while the other reached for the center arm.

The throne on which he found himself was of unusual shape and solid composition but surprisingly congenial to his backside. Both seat and arms were replete with all manner of intricately faceted gemstones and baroque decorations. Bending to inspect several, he saw that they were not gems at all, but rather, astonishingly refractive and beautifully tooled geometries of highly polished metal.

Narrow and deep, the throne would have been inappropriate for any life-form other than his nine-foot-long body. His short, stubby legs barely reached the ground, unlike his slim five-foot-long arms, which easily stroked the floor in the accepted attitude of expectant contemplation. Atop his head rode a frothy farrago of metal strips and wire curlicues like a tiara bent sideways. It hung down over his eyes and was secured somewhere at the back of his long neck. In place of his nose was a foot-long flexible trunk or snout that was no less maneuverable than either arm.

A clutch of similarly fantastic beings crowded the impressive hall in which he found himself. The effect of all the panoply was somewhat muted by the fact that he could see in only three colors. No reds or purples, no oranges or yellows. Everything tended to blue green, gray, or black. As if in compensation, he saw odd glows and light shifts where none ought to exist.

All this he absorbed and digested in an instant as his attention focused on the three figures ritually swaying before him. Though they were naked and unadorned, he did not find their gaunt, angular alien shapes in any way repellent. The tallest of the trio was female, though the means by which he was made aware of this were complex and not at all obvious. So was one of the two smaller shapes. The snout of the minor, six-foot-tall male had not yet developed.

Except for the male the trio was silent. The youngster emitted a steady, high, keening whine that sounded like a set of bagpipes laboring under sentence of death. The young female glared murderously from beneath protective eye ridges. By far the largest of the three, the mature female stared uncompromisingly back at the figure on the throne, managing to convey an opulent snarl of accusation, love, betrayal, and pity.

This is all wrong, he thought to himself. It felt right, but it looked wrong. Or maybe it felt wrong but looked right. Confused, he raised the reed-thin staff clutched in his left hand, startled at the effort this required. He would quickly set things to right.

But before he could make another move or utter a single sound, the trapdoor beneath the trio fell away. The mature female's eyes remained locked inexorably on his until she disappeared from view. Less stoic both by nature and inclination, the two youngsters screamed as they fell.

Shocked and stunned, he started to rise and protest, but it seemed as if the simple act of drawing sufficient air into his lungs required an unaccountably large number of seconds. He could feel his trunk expanding preparatory to ejecting the negatives, but it was too late.

He knew what lay beneath the trapdoors, knew what fate awaited anyone who fell more than a few body lengths in the relentless, crushing gravity. The terrible thirty-foot drop would reduce the supplicants to a pulp of crushed organs and snapped bones, condemning them to a lifetime of excruciating pain if not immediate death. Too late to be of any use, he heard the royal commutation emerge from his snout. The backward blast of air made his eyes ripple and he blinked.

Sweat was pouring down his cheeks and neck, staining the immaculate collar of the handmade shirt, soaking the Italian silk tie, pooling up beneath his armpits. He staggered backward until he hit the inside of the counter. Laughter and helping hands pushed at him.

To her credit, Telita still engrossed the bartender while having enough presence of mind not to look in her "patron's" direction. Steadying himself with an effort, Jerry Henderson found himself staring over the top of a wrinkled sports section at a concerned stranger.

"Hey, you okay, buddy? What're you doing back there, anyway?"

"Nothing. It's . . . nothing, I . . ." Henderson found he couldn't finish the sentence.

As he stumbled out from behind the bar he hit his head on the drop leaf, which did nothing to improve his already seriously impaired equilibrium. This time Telita did notice him. Breaking off her conversation with the bartender, she hurried back as fast as was practical in the outfit she was wearing.

Putting an arm around his shoulders, she helped him to the nearest unoccupied chairs. They fronted a small table squeezed in between the back wall and a silent jukebox. Her concern was genuine. Visions of hundred-dollar bills departing like birds on the wing kept her motivated.

"Jerry-honey, what happened, what's the matter?"

He was looking past her, a bad sign. His expression was

haunted, which was worse. "Wife and kids," he mumbled. "Crystal. Bill and Suzy."

She grabbed his shoulders and shook him hard. It was always risky to lay strong hands on a client, but she didn't care. It was clear that if she didn't do something fast she was going to lose him. What the hell had happened to him?

Then he turned to look at her and she let him go. "Jesus, Jerry, what did you see? What . . . ?"

"Never . . . never mind." Fumbling with his pockets, he brought out his wallet. She did her best to ignore it, even when he shoved a handful of bills into her cleavage. He hadn't bothered to count them, or note the denominations.

"Here. Take this." His voice had gone all high and funny, matching his expression. "A-Louie, Louie, whoa, whoa, I gotta go now." So saying, he rose from the chair and bolted past her before she could resume her grip.

"Telephone!" His desperate words were swallowed up in the boil and babble of the crowd. "Gotta find a telephone!"

Torn between chasing after him and counting the money, she elected to do the latter. The sum was respectable, especially for a few hours of nonwork, but nothing compared with what she'd been expecting. Tens and fives, damn him!

She determined to follow once he'd calmed down. What on earth had gotten into him? Sleazy but sensible, he was the most promising mark she'd scored in weeks. Then in a couple of minutes, poof, he'd gone crazy.

Eventually her attention strayed to the funny doll. It still sat on the back counter, apparently undisturbed. Had it done something to him? Was there a recording inside which had frightened him somehow? Did toy companies make a doll especially for bars which, when handled, blurted out "Hey, asshole, go call your wife and kids!"?

In all probability her carefully laid plans for a night of carefully getting laid were a total loss. Henderson had been clean and rich, two characteristics not often encountered in a mark. Now she was left with bar pickings to choose from, never a pleasant prospect. And it was all the fault of some stupid doll!

Stuffing the small bills into her purse, she rose and walked deliberately around the end of the counter, not even bothering to duck beneath the drop-leaf. Raising the barrier, she strode through and headed straight for her immobile nemesis.

Screw the bartender, she thought. What was the big dumb gringo going to do, manhandle her? She'd scream for help and accuse him of trying to force himself on her. Meanwhile it would be interesting to see how he would react when she raised the doll over her head and threw it into the crowd. After it got good and trampled a few times, maybe it wouldn't be quite so provocative. And she would be on the potentially useful receiving end of much of the resultant attention. If she was lucky, her intercession might precipitate a nice, musky brawl.

Feeling a bit of a fool but too upset to care, she stuck her face in front of the doll's and snarled at it. "What did you do, eh? You think you can spoil my evening? No damn toy spoils my evening, unless it's one I bring with me!" Out of the corner of an eye she thought she saw the bartender, a surprised look on his face, turning toward her, but she didn't hesitate. With her right hand she grabbed the outlandish effigy by its neck.

Her dress was whiter than the snow she had never seen, the starched lace trim like snowflakes standing at attention. She held in her hands a bouquet of mixed red, yellow, and white roses: blood, Texas, purity.

The priest was gently lowering the wrinkled brown larval creature that was her newborn nephew into the baptismal font. As he carefully dripped water on the wide-eyed infant, he chanted softly.

Around her, tears of happiness flowed freely from the visitants, all members of her extended family. Aunt and Uncle Gonzalves had come all the way up from Oaxaca, while Grand-madre Lucinda leaned on her cane as her gray head bobbed like an approving metronome. Telita's mother rested one hand on her daughter's shoulder. Heavier than air, the cheap, strong perfume she'd always favored dominated the lighter fragrances favored by some of the other women.

Telita observed the proceedings closely through bright black eyes whose sight was undistorted by the blue contact lenses she affected as an adult. Drinking in the church, her joyous relations, and the miraculous moment, she remembered how it had been oft-whispered in the family that it was biologically impossible for the child's parents to conceive. How they had prayed hard and in addition made many visits to the best fertility doctor in El Paso. How he had prescribed special medication to go with

Father Aranjez's prayers. How one or the other or both had, to everyone's amazement, worked.

Now here they were, proud Julio and Elena, with miracle baby Hector, whom everyone adored. Preparing to baptize him in the name of the Father, the Son, et cetera, et cetera and no one was paying the slightest attention to her. She couldn't stand it. No one had paid much attention to her since Hector's astonishing and unexpected birth. Was it ever to be so?

So while they ignored her, whereas previously everyone had stopped to remark on her beauty and bearing, she smiled and silently plotted. There were so many things that could happen to a newborn, so many possibilities for turning all that attention back to herself. One of the deadly little spiders with the red hourglass on its abdomen slipped unnoticed into his cradle, or a black scorpion from beneath a deserted rock introduced into his blanket. A malfunctioning heater, bathwater too hot, rat poison accidentally mixed into the formula . . . so many things.

Many noticed her smile, all misinterpreted its meaning. None of them suspected what she was capable of, if it meant regaining the attention that she had come to regard as her birthright.

A rumbling from underfoot, as of a subway train passing. Only, there was no subway in El Paso, none nearer than Los Angeles. As a startled Father Aranjez looked up from his undertaking, a few drops fell in one of the baby's eyes. The insufferable little brat didn't even cry.

The rumbling intensified and the shaking began. Everyone grabbed a friend or relative. Several people crossed themselves and one of the younger women began to moan. Telita's mother gripped her daughter's shoulder hard enough to hurt. Pictures of the saints were bouncing on the walls and dust fell from overhead. Pews creaked as the nails and screws that held them together were unnaturally stressed.

Then the chapel ceiling parted, wood and tile peeling back like cardboard. Women screamed and men threw up their arms or, forgetting where they were, cursed. A shaft of light intense enough to shame a laser pierced the opening. It struck not the ground, not the baptismal font where Father Aranjez stood bending protectively over the baby, but a little dark-haired girl held immobile in the grip of her mother.

She could feel the heat, could smell the ends of her hair beginning to burn like a thousand curly jet-black matches. Her dress shriveled against her as the beads of sweat on her face and arms evaporated in tiny puffs of steam.

She knew what was happening, knew that not even her mother could help her now. She screamed pleadingly at Father Aranjez, but even he was forced to turn from the Eye of God as it penetrated directly to the heart of her evil, jealous feelings. It was time for her to pay for what she'd been thinking, time for her to burn, not even waiting for her to grow up and die, burning her now where she stood. . . .

She screamed.

There were so many people in the bar and so much ambient noise from the crowd and blaring televisions that only those patrons in her immediate vicinity took any notice of the outburst. Seeing that she was standing and in control of herself, they quickly stopped paying attention.

One who did notice her backing wide-eyed away from the doll shape was Ross Ed. He's started forward as soon as he'd noticed her behind the bar. Having touched Jed, she'd quickly drawn her hand back as if she'd been singed.

"Hey there, miss," he called out as he negotiated a path between bar and counter, "what are you doing? You're not allowed back here."

She gripped her right wrist in her left hand, the nails digging into the fine skin. "I . . . I think I burned myself." When she held up her hand Ross saw that it was red but not swollen. Whatever had happened to her wasn't bad enough to raise blisters.

Her eyes were very wide, as if she'd seen a ghost. Or something worse. His gaze shifted to Jed, who sat propped in innocent immobility exactly as Ross Ed had left him. The woman was beautiful, though Ross didn't approve of her attire, a style well known to regular patrons of bars and honky-tonks as Southwestern slut.

Bartenders were not paid to render moral judgments. "We'll put some ice on it," he told her, "but you have to move. Employees only allowed behind the bar."

She bumped up against the drop leaf. Turning, she needed three tries to lift it, letting it slam roughly shut behind her. Before he could call out to her a second time, she was gone, shoving her way through the crowd, a vanishing flicker of silver-and-gray-encased flesh. Her black hair streamed out behind her in sudden and inexplicable disarray.

What had happened? He queried the two men seated nearby.

"Hey, man, I didn't see nothin'," one replied. "Didn't pay no attention when she went behind the bar. I thought she belonged back there. Thought she was one of the waitresses."

"None of the waitresses here that pretty." His companion peered up at Ross Ed. "Me, I was watching the game, man. Turned around when she screamed, though. She looked okay, so I didn't think nothin' of it."

"You didn't see her touch anything?"

"No, man." The first speaker snubbed out his cigarette. "She just squealed and grabbed her hand. You got an espresso machine or something back there? Hot plate?"

"Not at this end of the bar," Ross Ed replied.

"Go figure." The two men returned their attention to the crowd and the game.

Ross considered for a moment before turning to confront his silent companion. Deliberately, he reached out and ran his fingers down the front of the faceplate, feeling of the slightly roughened but perfectly transparent surface. His hand continued down the keellike chest ridge to grasp the middle arm. Faceplate and fabric were pleasantly mild to the touch. Room temperature.

"Hey, big guy," one of the two men was saying, "you ever play any ball?"

"High school." Ross Ed looked back over a shoulder. "Couldn't get out of it. The coaches nagged me unmercifully."

"Yeah, I bet." The man sipped at his drink. "You any good?"

"Not really interested. Kind of slow; did okay, I guess."

"Right." The man gestured at his friend's glass. "Couple of fresh ones, okay?"

"Coming up." Moving down the bar, he drew two clean glasses and set them beneath the tap, filling each one carefully so as to minimize the head. Placing them before the disinterested pair, he collected his tip and returned his attention to his enigmatic companion.

"I don't know what you're doing or how you're doing it," he found himself muttering tersely to the alien figure. "I know you're dead, but if it's just the suit that's doing these things, how come it only affects people once?"

As expected, there was no reply. What did others see when

they made contact with Jed? First the maid, then this woman. Had there been more? He couldn't keep an eye on Jed all the time. Nor would it be a good idea to question everyone in the alien's vicinity. Draw too much attention to himself.

A blustery, red-faced businessman reached out to intercept him as he turned away. With his other hand the man pointed, none too steadily, in Jed's direction.

"Hey, bartender! What is that thing, anyway?"

"Ain't you heard?" volunteered a nearby regular, a machinist at one of the many manufacturing plants that encircled the airport. "It's a dead alien. Name's Jed." He winked at the big man behind the bar. "Ain't that right, Ross Ed?"

"That's right." The bartender shook free and resumed his work.

"That a fact?" The traveler sat back on his stool. "Look's like a damn ventriloquist's dummy to me." Hefting his beer, he shoved the half-full glass in Ross Ed's direction. "Considering how popular that futuristic stuff is these days, I think that's a helluva good idea. You can't get away from it. It's all over the TV and the theaters. Bookstores are full of that science-fiction crap! Perfect idea for a ventriloquist, perfect."

The regular blinked and turned back toward the bar. "Yea-h-h-h. Hey, Ross Ed, how come you never mentioned that before?"

Ross thought fast. Unexpectedly, the half-drunk visitor had inadvertently supplied an all-in-one disguise and rationale for Jed's existence.

"Actually, I'm the dummy and he's the smart one. You know; the brilliant alien from outer space come here to save our civilization? 'Cept he's dead, of course."

Laughter rippled along the bar front as this explanation made the rounds among the knowledgeable.

"Okay," shouted someone farther down the line, "so make him talk, why don't you?"

"I'm not the talker. Jed is." Somewhat to his surprise, Ross Ed found himself entering into the spirit of the moment. He resurrected a mild falsetto he'd once employed on the occasion of a school play. It seemed to please those in attendance. He tried to throw his words toward Jed the way he thought a real ventriloquist might do it.

"I have come," he announced in the artificially high-pitched voice, "to save the Earth from the greatest menace it has ever faced!"

"The president!" someone barked boisterously.

"Naw, just the Democrats," his companion insisted. The laughter turned raucous.

Not only was he surprised at the extent of the response to his modest effort, Ross Ed found that he was enjoying it. As he stood there contemplating his initial unplanned excursion into show business, others standing near the bar urged him on.

"Is that it?"

"Yeah! What's the threat?"

"It comes," Ross Ed found himself saying, "from those who would destroy America's saviors."

"The Republicans! Man, I told you!"

"Aw, shut up!" advised a listener of dissimilar political persuasion.

Other suggestions to fill the void came fast and furious. They ranged from the Sierra Club to Rush Limbaugh.

"You are all wrong," Ross Ed found himself explaining as he served up a Scotch to an appreciative middle-aged woman in severe business dress. "The danger is to that great bastion"—bastion? a part of him thought. Where had he encountered a word like that—"of American culture, the Dallas Coyboys!"

Whoops and roars of amusement vibrated the crowd, punctuated by a few choice remarks from a trio of vociferous supporters of the San Francisco 49ers. This led to the usual loud arguments over the merits of respective home teams.

"It is the Dallas Cowboys who are the true and secret masters of the universe." While declaiming in his high alien voice, Ross Ed effortlessly drew forth beers both draft and bottled. The tips were piling up, and not all in recompense for supplied laughs. Several patrons were showing their appreciation for his deadpan performance.

"My kids think it's the Mighty Morphin' Power Rangers." Halfway down the bar, a construction worker hunkered low over his brew.

"Naw, couldn't be them," insisted someone else. "I hear they're all from California." More laughter lifted above the general chatter.

"Well, that fits those outfits they wear!" another cracked.

As he went with the flow Ross Ed occasionally glanced in

Jed's direction for inspiration. Lines and aphorisms seemed to pop easily into his head just when he needed them. He'd never thought of himself as a particularly funny guy, but the customers seemed to find his quips and responses hilarious. As long as that was the case, he saw no harm in keeping it going.

Meanwhile, his initially amateurish voice throwing continued to improve. He'd heard that some folks had undiscovered natural talents that manifested themselves at odd and unexpected times and places. Perhaps ventriloquism was one of his. Just so long, he thought, as no one asked him to spell it. Certainly it was the perfect cover for Jed.

Hide in plain sight, he reminded himself again.

FIVE

That Friday night would've been the end of it except that Noddy Raskin, head of the hotel's restaurant division, happened to have slipped into the bar while Ross Ed was performing. He'd come for a few moments, stayed for an hour, and made it a point to corner his new bartender subsequent to closing time.

"I caught some of your act tonight, Ross. You're pretty good with that funny-looking dummy. You could be the world's tallest ventriloquist."

"I'm a bartender, Mr. Raskin. I don't have an act. I was just playing around to keep the customers happy."

"And you did that, you sure did." Raskin was short, overweight, and fiftyish, but with a kindly demeanor that endeared him to most of the employees. "Look, I know you're only here on a temporary basis. You made that clear on your job app. We get people in and out of here all the time. Trying to keep good help is a never-ending battle." He put a friendly hand on the big Texan's arm.

"I just wanted you to know that there's always a position for you here. Meanwhile, as long as you're comfortable doing it, keep up the patter. You're right: it is good for business."

Ross Ed considered. "I don't know about that, Mr. Raskin. I really don't want to attract a lot of attention."

The manager didn't hesitate. "I'll give you a five-dollar-an-hour raise."

It was a significant offer, one that would help to ensure he'd be able to sate the thirsty Caddy. Another couple of weeks' work at that rate and he'd be able to go straight through to California and back without having to worry about funds.

"You've got a deal, sir. But remember, I'm not a professional. I tend bar."

"Very well, too." Raskin's right hand fluttered in the other man's direction. "Just keep doing what you're doing. Amuse yourself and you'll amuse the customers. Don't worry about it. You're doing swell."

Before Ross could think of another objection, the manager had turned and headed for the main kitchen.

So Ross allowed the quips and comments to flow. Sometimes he declaimed in terms whose meaning utterly escaped him. Stuff he must have unintentionally absorbed from reading and from watching TV, or bits and pieces of long-forgotten schoolwork. Information stuck in distant recesses of his brain which circumstances and situations unexpectedly brought forth.

Raskin was right. It didn't matter what he said so long as it kept the customers laughing. Customers who laugh feel good, and customers who feel good tend to drink more.

His technique improved without conscious effort, until it seemed he was throwing his voice via Jed without half trying. This ventriloquist stuff wasn't too bad, he told himself. The dummy could get away with saying things that would have precipitated open warfare had they been perceived as issuing from "his" mouth.

Following the manager's advice, he soon stopped worrying about his success. Lots of folks had natural talents. Why shouldn't he have one? Wasn't that only fair? He was reminded of the twelfth grade and Julie Heckerd, who could do math problems in her head that stumped Ross Ed even when he made use of a calculator. Or Evyard Brooks, who could twist his body to make it backward over the high-jump bar. His senior year he'd jumped high enough to finish second in state in his division. Natural talent. Ingrained ability.

Ross Ed had excelled at football and basketball, but only as a consequence of sheer size, not any special skill. Throwing your voice, now, that was something different. Unique. He began to take pride in his ability to bring smiles to the faces of people who arrived drawn and downcast after a hard day's work. His ability, and Jed's, of course.

It was two weeks later or (by another calculation) the second Friday night since the flight of the call girl that things got a little weirder than usual.

An unkempt patron with hair mussed and tie undone was, as so many had done before him, carefully scrutinizing the inhuman shape sequestered behind the bar.

"Hey, if you're an alien, I'll bet you've got a green card!"

Ross responded by throwing his voice with the ease and efficiency of long practice, so that the reply seemed to come directly from the alien.

"No, but I've got green blood."

There were knowing chuckles from the regulars and appreciative smiles from those newcomers within hearing range.

"Is that a third leg," observed the well-dressed, middle-aged businesswoman seated three stools down, "or are you just glad to see me?" A mildly shocked expression on her face, the woman seated on the speaker's right gave her friend a sharp nudge in the ribs.

"I'm not particularly glad to see you," replied Ross Ed smoothly, "but if I was, I can assure you that you'd never forget the experience."

Delighted whoops and a few challenges rose from the woman as well as those seated nearby. Shaking his head at the ease with which they could be entertained, Ross moved to mix the next batch of orders. One of these days he'd have to devote some hard thinking to just how he was able to come up with so many facile, quick responses. As usual, he was too busy to do so while on the job.

A party of young soldiers was seated at one of the near tables, their attention more or less fixed on the overhead television. "Hey, alien man!" a corporal called out as he indicated the TV. "Who's gonna win the game?"

"Who's playing?" Ross Ed asked via Jed.

"Colorado State and Nebraska."

"No contest," insisted one of the corporal's buddies. "CSU shouldn't even be playing the Big Red!"

As usual, Ross replied without half thinking. "Colorado State will come within one field goal but fall short," Jed seemed to say.

"No way!" another soldier insisted disparagingly. "Nebraska's a three-touchdown favorite."

"Analysis of the game as played thus far," Ross Ed heard his own distant voice saying, "suggests that two of Nebraska's three principal backfield performers are playing hurt. Or perhaps they stayed out late last night. Regardless of the explanation, it is clear they are not playing to capability. As a consequence I would expect fumbles to ensue, certainly by the last quarter."

"Yeah, right." The corporal made a good-natured rude gesture which Ross Ed tactfully ignored. With Nebraska up thirty-five to seven, no one minded when the other bartender switched to the much more competitive Oklahoma–Texas A&M game. By tomorrow morning the preceding exchange would be forgotten by all concerned, including Ross. None would remark on Nebraska's remarkably close victory, pulling out the win in the final minutes by throwing Colorado State's quarterback for a safety following a tremendous CSU fourth-quarter rally. It was only another football game.

"All right, *I* got one for you!" One of several businessmen seated at the bar winked knowingly at his associates. "Even a dumb alien should be able to answer this one." Addressing himself not to Ross Ed but to the motionless figure seated on the back counter, he inquired with forced seriousness, "Why did the chicken cross the road?"

"An existential query." As always, Ross Ed didn't wonder at his reply. He just let the words come. It was all that half-forgotten schoolwork, he told himself. As he spoke he added soda to the three drinks lined up neatly before him.

"One would have to begin by assuming that a chicken brain exists that is capable of contemplating such a question. Failing that, it must be inferred that if confronted with such a choice, reaction would be wholly instinctive. Therefore, any actual deeper meanings would be utterly irrelevant from a chicken standpoint. A fowl proposition all around."

The traveler who'd posed the question sat open mouthed on his stool, gawking at the alien corpse as if it had suddenly turned into one of the finalists in the Miss Hawaiian Tropic competition. Then his mouth closed slightly and laughter bubbled forth. His friends chided him good-naturedly and a fine time was had by all.

The night wore on, its path smoothed for those in the bar and restaurant by good food and drink. Ross Ed took his break, returned to resume his duties. Another couple of days and he'd be out of there, back on the road again, heading Pacific-ward. He was anxious to get going.

Three seats at the bar were vacated by vacationers, to be snatched up by a trio of men in their thirties. From their haircuts and attitude Ross suspected that they were officers from Fort Bliss, probably middle and junior grade. He was adept at recognizing all ranks of soldiers as well as civilians, certain tribal features readily manifesting themselves to those with experience in such matters.

"Evening, gentlemen." He offered the usual expectant smile along with the familiar greeting. "What'll it be?"

They placed their orders and he hustled to fill them, seeing that Mark, the other bartender, was momentarily swamped at his end of the counter. Like everyone else who worked in the bar, Mark didn't begrudge Ross Ed his raise. The increased business the act brought in meant more tips for everyone while requiring little additional exertion on their part.

After watching and listening for a while, one of the men nodded in Jed's direction. "Mighty interesting dummy you've got there, mister. Where'd you get it?"

Ross replied while drawing a beer. "I don't think I've seen you fellas in here before."

"We're usually at the Marshal's Club," the man explained. "Or over at the Four Corners. Thought we'd try someplace different tonight. How's the action?"

"Pretty typical for a Friday night." Ross sent the beer on its way.

"Seems mighty busy to me," insisted another of the trio. Ice cubes clinked in his glass as he raised his drink. "Even for a Friday."

"It's a nice hotel," argued the first. "Maybe we should've come in here sooner."

"Been watching you." The third member of the group had a soft yet penetrating voice, with more than a hint of a Midwestern accent. Indiana, Ross Ed thought, or maybe Ohio. "You're good."

Ross shrugged. "It's just something I fool around with. Keeps the work from getting boring."

"No, really." The man sipped his drink. "Like Matt said, your dummy is interesting. That suit . . . what's it made of?"

Before Ross had to invent a reply, the first man interrupted.

"Maybe it's a uniform. Yeah, that's it." He pushed slightly forward, leaning over the bar in Jed's direction. "What's your rank, soldier?"

"I'll only be rank if you open this suit," Ross responded via Jed. "You'd think I stink. Of course, that's what being dead does for you. Nobody makes a deodorant guaranteed for fifty years."

The soldiers guffawed. The middle one finally regained control of his voice long enough to observe, "So you're dead?"

"That's it," Jed explained via Ross Ed.

"You look pretty good to me." Resuming his seat, the first soldier turned back to the bartender. "Come on, where'd you get it? You buy it, or put it together yourself?"

"Bought it. At Geppettos 'R' Us."

More laughter, proving that the soldiers were literate as well as lit. "Does that mean that nose gets longer if it tells a lie?" the second officer wondered.

"That's a third arm, not a nose," Ross Ed explained as a roar erupted from the crowd. On the suspended TVs, Texas had just scored. Any Oklahoma fans in the bar had the good sense to keep silent.

"Hey, I got one for you!" The man who interrupted was almost too drunk to stand, but the seated soldiers agreeably made room for him at the bar. "My kids are always asking me this and no matter what answer I give 'em it never seems to satisfy 'em." When he slugged back beer his head wobbled like a cheap doll in the rear window of an old sedan. "Why is the sky blue?"

"Because it's sad," Ross Ed heard himself replying.

Lowering his head slightly, the man goggled at the figure of Jed while his brain struggled to digest this reply. Around him, the three officers struggled to repress their laughter. Then a smile broke out on the questioner's face and he nodded appreciatively.

"I gotta remember that! The kids'll love that. 'Because it's sad.' That's great, man!" More than satisfied, he staggered back into the milling crowd.

The third officer had placed his beer on the counter. Now he nudged it with a finger. "That's a very interesting answer. Why, pray tell, is the sky sad?" He was speaking to Jed but watching Ross Ed.

"Pollution-ache," came the reply. The soldier pondered this as his two companions turned suddenly to the nearest hanging TV.

"Hey, Steve, you gotta watch this! The Aggies are gonna beat the Okies!"

"Naw," declared his avid companion with certainty. "Oklahoma's just layin' back, playing with 'em."

"No, man, they're gonna beat 'em." He glanced over at the third member of the party. "What do you think, Steve?"

"I haven't been watching," his friend replied.

"Aw, man." In a whisper loud enough to be overheard, the speaker addressed his other companion. "Told you we shouldn't have brought him."

"I know, Rich, but Steve spends too much time in quarters as it is. He needs to get out more."

Steven Suttles ignored both of his colleagues and sometime friends as he waved at the bartender. The big man was there in seconds.

"You want something else, sir?" Ross Ed glanced down at the man's glass. "You haven't finished your beer."

"That's okay." Suttles waved absently. "I'm still admiring your prop. Tell me: what planet is he from? Not Mars, surely." He grinned to show that he meant no harm.

"Of course not, sir." Ross Ed returned the smile. "Men are from Mars; women are from Venus. Aliens are from Hollywood."

Suttles rubbed at his forehead. "I've seen a lot of sci-fi films. I don't ever recall seeing anything that looked like this."

"There are a lot of movies out there, sir. Made-for-cable and direct-to-video as well as the theatrical releases."

"Fair enough. If you won't tell me what planet, how about identifying the relevant solar system?"

"Planning a vacation?" Speaking through Jed, Ross Ed heard himself reciting a series of numbers that meant absolutely nothing to him. He must've retained more of that twelfth-grade math than he thought.

"Those are the requisite coordinates," his voice concluded. "Nice place to visit, but you wouldn't want to live there."

"Why not?" The exceptionally thoughtful officer took another sip of his beer.

"You know the big feedlot just northwest of town?" Ross Ed told him. "Methane. You wouldn't want to live on a world that smells like pig shit."

Suttles considered. "Wouldn't be so bad if you were a pig."

"Then you'd have to wear a different uniform," the alien corpus replied through Ross. Laughter came from those of the bar's regulars within hearing range.

"Must be a long ways off." Suttles debated whether to order another brewski. "What about propulsion?"

"Not a problem," Ross's voice replied from the vicinity of the body. "You get on your bike and ride, baby, ride."

The officer grinned. "I didn't know it was possible to pedal faster than the speed of light."

"Light doesn't have any speed," Ross Ed heard himself saying. "You misperceive the true nature of velocity. It has to do with the real speed at which everything else is moving. Your beer, for example. What you call the 'speed of light' is not only not relevant, it's an irrelevance. Especially if you're trying to get someplace. Your kind makes physics much more complex than it actually is. If you're going to account for actual relative velocity in your travels, it's better to just go around it."

Suttles blinked. "Go around it?"

"Sure." Ross Ed buzzed the kitchen. They were running short on tall glasses. Moving to Jed, he hefted the limp body and began to jiggle it. Arms and legs went flopping in all directions, gangly and unpredictable. "See? Relative velocity of objects in motion is the same, but they're all circumscribed by the same center." He shifted the body back and forth, side to side. "The peripherals don't matter. It's the center that has to be adjusted relative to everything else. That's how you avoid the speed of light. You avoid it and it goes past you. In the interim you've advanced." He snugged the corpse back in its alcove. "Nothing to it."

Those patrons near enough to observe the encounter had giggled readily at the sight of the six flopping alien limbs. Few had paid any attention to Ross Ed's disquisition.

"Any other mysteries of the universe you need solved?" the dummy seemed to squeak.

"Yeah!" Another customer broke in before Suttles could respond. "How can I get this sweet little gal over here to give me more than a smile and a nod?" He indicated the woman seated across the table from him.

"Better forget it," the alien voice declared. "It's the time of the month when she isn't interested. But she doesn't want to tell you that because she's afraid you'll go running after somebody else."

The man looked uncertain, then joined those around him in

laughter. As for his well-lubricated female companion, she looked sharply in the alien's direction, then smiled in confusion at Ross Ed.

Suttles had waited patiently for the byplay to end. Now he leaned slightly toward the bartender, keeping his voice level but low. "How do you let light 'go past you'? What if you can't get up to minimum speed?"

"What's the matter," the dummy chirped as Ross Ed moved his lips, "motion sickness?" A few people chuckled, but for the most part this line of questioning left them uninvolved and indifferent.

"Let's keep it simple." Suttles started in on his second beer. "Suppose I just want to go from here to there as fast as possible." He pointed to the far side of the room.

"Adventurous sort of traveler, aren't you?" Ross Ed recited a rapid-fire series of chemical instructions which Suttles, while appearing uninterested, actually did his best to memorize.

"Of course the trick," the bartender went on in his other-worldly voice, "is to make sure that all of you is involved in the transposition. It can be awkward to have part of you make the jump while the rest is left behind."

"Which part?" queried Matt. The two younger officers howled at their own joke without really comprehending its foundation.

"Excuse me." Suttles slipped off his stool. "Got to go."

"What are you talking about?" One of his companions fumbled at his arm. "It's early yet."

The older man smiled apologetically. "Sorry, guys. There's something I have to check on."

As he turned to leave, his eyes met Ross Ed's. Contact was made and lost in an instant, but there was enough there to put the bartender's nerves on alert. Curiosity he could have pardoned, but there was much more. Real intelligence, and a certain apprehension.

At the entrance to the nearby restaurant Suttles borrowed pencil and paper and hurriedly scribbled out what he could remember of the information the bartender had provided via his ventriloquist's mannequin. Only when he was through did he allow himself to examine it at leisure and with care. This and that, combined so. It didn't seem to make any sense.

Maybe, he told himself, that was the idea.

Since they'd come in Matt's car he was forced to take a taxi all the way back to the base, leaving lights, laughter, and friends behind. No doubt he was embarked on a fool's errand and would quickly come to regret his gullibility. But what intrigued him as much as the cockeyed formula was its source. The only chemical formulae he'd ever heard bartenders spout were pretty basic and involved combining two parts vodka with one part vermouth, add cherry juice, and so on. He glanced at the paper he'd filled with names and equations. It was devoid of allusions to alcohol or its chemical analogues.

Whether it was equally inflammatory remained to be demonstrated.

Suttles was an electrical engineer, not a chemist. Among his many tasks was to ensure that the lights stayed on inside an Abrams tank. But he remembered enough chemistry to be intrigued by what the bartender/dummy combination had deposed.

The cab ride was an extravagance. Now he faced the difficult task of acquiring the necessary equipment late on a Friday night.

SIX

Ross Ed hadn't broken stride. He continued to draw beer, mix drinks, and make jokes. Midnight passed into a new day without anything changing in the bar. But the look on that soldier's face as he'd hurriedly made his exit stuck with him.

He felt bad about leaving the way he did, but Raskin had left hours ago and Ross Ed didn't have his home number. Probably the manager was out with his family anyway. So the short note left on his desk would have to suffice.

Taking off without waiting to collect the three days' pay he had coming to him might look suspicious, but Ross didn't feel he had any choice. The officer might return at any time, with fellow curiosity-seekers in tow. Specialists whose pointed questions Ross might not be able to joke his way out of. He wasn't ready to give up Jed yet. Not by a double shot.

He let Mark close up, tucking the alien under one arm as he made his way through the employee parking lot. The Caddy was waiting for him, hulking and secure.

This late there was little traffic. As for his motel bill, he paid on a daily basis. The bored night clerk didn't bat an eye when Ross Ed informed him that he was checking out.

"Finally decided to leave us, Mr. Hager?" Behind the clerk the printer chattered out a receipt.

"Time I was moving on. You know how it is." Ross remained calm as he periodically checked on the drive-through outside the office.

"Yeah," murmured the clerk, not knowing at all. He'd lived in

El Paso all his life. "Where you headed?" Ross's receipt was extensive and the printer was taking its time. He could have left without it, but that, too, would have looked suspicious.

"Oh, you know. Just traveling around."

"Lucky you. I've got three kids and no money to go anywhere. But hey, that was my choice." Ross Ed felt no need to comment as the man tore off the finished receipt and folded it for ease of handling. "Have a good trip."

Ross accepted the wad of paper. "Thanks. I'll leave the key in the room, next to the phone."

As he prepared to depart he contemplated putting Jed in the trunk. It was spacious, and the night air was pleasant, but in the end the alien ended up back in his familiar place on the passenger seat. Ross Ed knew that if the situation had been reversed he wouldn't have wanted to be stuffed into the trunk like another piece of luggage. The image of Jed driving down the road with a dead Texan slumped in the seat next to him was enough to crack the serious expression that had been threatening to set up permanently on the big man's face.

Pulling out of the lot, he turned down Airway and up the first on-ramp, heading west. Maybe he was being overly cautious, but in any case it felt good to be back on the road again. The slim strongbox he'd picked up at Wal-Mart fit neatly under the passenger seat. It was full of fifties, more than enough to get them to and through California.

He wiped at his eyes with the back of his left hand, checked his watch. The Cadillac's dash-mounted clock was useless, of course, since all General Motors car clocks from the sixties and seventies were purpose-built to fail after a few years' use. It was just after three A.M. He'd drive until his attention started to wander, then find a nice motel and sleep until his system was restored. That should allow him to get well away from El Paso.

In addition to departing in unseemly haste and abandoning his friends, the curious soldier had asked too many calculating questions. Worse, he'd paid attention to the answers. Thinking back, Ross Ed couldn't remember the man laughing, not even once.

Actually, it was kind of surprising that Jed hadn't attracted serious attention before tonight. In that respect Ross knew he'd been lucky. Noticing that the speedometer had crept up to seventy-five, he eased off on the foot feed and let it fall back to sixty-four as he shifted over into the slow lane. It meant that while the majority of traffic would pass him, including the big rigs, any highway-patrol cars in the vicinity would ignore him. He had no desire to repeat the encounter he'd had back at Alamogordo.

The interstate stretched out before him; dark, straight, and promising.

It took Suttles a couple of hours to assemble the necessary materials in a deserted garage on the far side of the motor pool. A couple of humvees stood parked in back, awaiting service. Otherwise the large shedlike structure was empty except for repair gear and supplies. The big overhead fluorescents provided more light than he needed.

Sitting back from the workbench and pushing the magnifying goggles up onto his forehead, he examined the results of an hour's intensive work. The little pile of powder that was the result of his efforts would fit neatly into a thimble with room to spare. It certainly didn't look like much.

Wearily, he glanced out a window. It was starting to grow light outside and he knew he didn't have much time left before the morning detail arrived to begin work. Bearing in mind the bartending ventriloquist's warning, he wanted to conclude the experiment *sans* witnesses. It would also be nice not to have to explain what he was doing in case it proved, as was likely, to be a complete and embarrassing flop.

Devising a suitable receptacle for the experiment had left him stumped until he remembered the stainless-steel thermos bottle he always kept in his work locker. Using a putty knife, he carefully scraped every grain of powder into the thermos before adding two different liquids from a pair of otherwise empty Dr Pepper bottles. Two drops of vinegar completed the foul-smelling concoction.

Sealing the thermos, he placed it upside down on the workbench and stepped back. Feeling more and more like a prize idiot, he stood and stared as the sun continued its inexorable ascent outside. A check of his watch showed that reveille was on the verge of blowing.

And that's about enough of this stupidity, he decided as he took a step toward the bench. Talk about your wasted evenings . . .

A surprisingly deep-throated *bang* stunned his hearing and a blast of air knocked him to the floor. When he finally regained his senses there was no sign of the thermos bottle.

There was, however, a hole a foot in diameter in the middle of the solid steel worktable. Tools and gear had been sent flying in all directions, and indeed, a ball-peen hammer had just missed his head. Stumbling over to the table, he found that he could look through the hole into a depression in the concrete floor seven inches deep.

It took a bit of searching, and he never did find the thermos. But he found where it had gone. He finally noticed the hole in the roof when he tilted his head back to wipe sweat from his eyes. The edges were bent outward, not down, indicating that something had gone up and through. The hole wasn't much wider than the AWOL thermos.

Well now, he mused, isn't that interesting? Just mix up your powder, add vinegar, and wait. If a pinch of the concoction would do that to a heavy thermos, what might a truckload do for a solid-fuel rocket? Very funny, ha-ha, all part of the act.

It was an act he was now thoroughly convinced deserved a much larger and more appreciative audience.

Noddy Raskin was busy and in no mood for company, but his secretary said the visitors were insistent. They were also in full uniform, which didn't surprise him. Visitors from the base usually wore uniforms when making arrangements for the use of civilian facilities. The hotel had hosted many banquets and special events.

He noted one lieutenant colonel among the assembled brass, who filled his modest office to capacity. "Look, if it's about the fight last week, we handled it the way we always do. I'm sorry if there've been repercussions."

All smiles, a young major stepped forward. "Our visit has nothing to do with any fight, Mr. Raskin. We just want to ask you a couple of questions."

Raskin emitted a sardonic snort. "I've heard *that* one before. What are you guys, MPs?" No, he told himself, that couldn't be right. There were no enlisted men in among the visitors, only officers. Come to think of it, that didn't make much sense.

Four of them there were, and not a sergeant or specialist among them. As his initial concerns faded his curiosity intensified. "Won't you please sit down? A couple of you, anyway." What important base function needed catering this time? he wondered.

"That's all right, sir. If you don't mind, we'll stand." The senior officer stepped forward and extended a hand. "I'm Lieutenant Colonel Waltham."

"Nice to meet you." Raskin methodically shook hands. "Listen, I'm always glad to see representatives from the base, but it's Saturday morning and I need to be out of here by noon. So if you'd like to go ahead and ask your questions . . . ?"

"It concerns an employee of yours." The captain who spoke had a soft voice but a penetrating gaze, Raskin decided. "I spent quite a bit of time talking to him last night."

The manager was again on guard. "What's the problem? We don't short our drinks here. This isn't one of the cheap clubs or strip joints out on one-eighty, and we do our best to keep the hookers out."

"Please, sir." The lieutenant colonel made placating motions. "Relax. There's nothing wrong. We just need a little information about an employee, that's all."

Raskin's gaze narrowed speculatively. "Somebody gone AWOL? Surely they wouldn't be dumb enough to get a job here in town, much less this close to the base."

"Nothing like that, I assure you."

Raskin sighed heavily. "All right. Who is it and what have they done?"

"We don't think he's 'done' anything. We just want to talk to him." The captain raised one downward-facing palm over his head. "Real big guy, was working behind the bar last night. Does comedy with a dummy while he's mixing drinks."

If there's nothing wrong, then why are they all so tense? Raskin wondered. You could practically taste it. All the smiles and affability seemed forced. He'd been in the hotel business too long not to know when he was being massaged. Still, he saw no reason to refuse them a reply.

"You mean Ross Hager. What about him?"

"Like I said, we just want to talk to him." The colonel couldn't mask his eagerness.

Raskin leaned back in his chair, his belt straining against his waistline. "Hell, I'd like to talk to him myself. I thought he was happy here."

One of the other officers responded immediately with. "What do you mean 'was'?"

The manager spread his hands wide. "I come in this morning after taking the family to the movies and here's this note sitting on my desk." He sat forward. "Here, I'll show you." He fumbled through the pile of papers before extracting a scrap and waving it at them. "Just like that, he up and leaves. Says it's time he was moving on and he's sorry for taking off without giving notice. Says he knows that I'll understand, which I don't." He shook his head sadly. "One of the best bartenders I've had in years. Did his job, didn't skim the till, and took care of the troublemakers. Too bad."

"He quit? Just like that?" Their expressions were so ardent, Raskin thought, it was almost comical.

"That's what I said. What about it?" He turned wary again. "You guys said there was nothing wrong, that it didn't involve the army."

"That's right," explained another captain. "Mr. Hager is not military. At least, not insofar as we have been able to discover."

"Kind of a hasty departure, wasn't it?" The lieutenant colonel was watching Raskin closely.

The manager shrugged, already tired of the conversation. "Hey, these transient workers, they come and they go, you know? Some of them last a couple of days, some you wish would never leave. But unless they have families with them, you never know." He chuckled at a memory. "That alien ventriloquist act of his brought in a lot of business."

"Yes, it was very well done," agreed the captain restively. "Could you tell us where Mr. Hager was going?"

Raskin shook his head. "Don't have a clue. He never told me and I never asked. Wasn't none of my business."

The four officers exchanged a look before the captain turned back to the desk. "Well then, Mr. Raskin, perhaps you could tell us where Mr. Hager was staying while he was here in El Paso?"

"What the hell, why not?" Turning to a computer terminal, the manager took mouse in hand and began clicking. "You guys will remember this the next time you have a big banquet or conference to schedule, won't you?"

"Yes, of course." The colonel was fairly dancing with impatience.

"Should be right here in the employee records." Windows

changed on the monitor. "Need at least a phone number in case you have to call someone in." He hesitated. "What was it you wanted to talk to him about?"

"It has to do with—" the lieutenant colonel began, but Captain Suttles hastened to interrupt.

"We want to discuss his act." He smiled disingenuously. "I thought it was funny as hell, and we need to find out if he's available to do a major military gathering." He indicated his fellow officers. "We're the organizers, and since everyone has a vote on the choice of food and entertainment, I thought I'd see if we could get him to do a sample of the act for everybody on the committee."

"That's right," the only major in the party chipped in. "If he's as good as Steve says he is, I'm sure we'll hire him on the spot."

"Well then, I hope you find him." Raskin turned back to the monitor. "Maybe he's just gone up to Las Cruces to work for a while. He'd be good with the college crowd. Or maybe he's gone home."

"That would be in your records as well, wouldn't it?" inquired the second captain.

"We'll see."

It didn't take him long to locate Hager's file. He noted with interest the intensity with which two of the officers transcribed the information, whereupon they thanked him profusely and all but fled the office. He looked after them curiously.

They must really want that alien ventriloquist act bad, he decided. Well, that he could understand. Hager had brought in plenty of additional customers. Raskin chuckled as he turned back to his work, remembering the goofy expressions that came over the faces of some of the drunks as they struggled futilely to digest the bartender/dummy's inventive responses to their questions.

There were three of them waiting for him in the sealed conference room. Suttles had expected more, just as he had expected the guard outside the door. No rifle was visible, but the man wore a sidearm at the ready. He knocked, and the familiar voice of General Sykes invited him to enter. The general sounded preoccupied.

Dispensing absently with the usual salute, Sykes gestured for him to take a seat. Not wasting any time, the general proceeded to introductions.

Infantry insignia decorated the shoulders of the others, intentionally noncommittal and uninformative. The woman was blond, very attractive, same early thirties as Suttles himself. As she returned his appraising stare her attitude was one of utter seriousness.

The slightly younger man seated on her right was very tall, perhaps six-four, with a lean but not angular face, small nose and mouth, piercing eyes set close together, one solid eyebrow over both oculars, and the laughing memory of freckles haunting his complexion. His red hair was cut regulation short. He appeared more at ease than his female companion, though he acted at a loss as to what to do with his hands.

"Captain Suttles, meet Captain Kerry"—the woman nodded—"and Captain Robinett." Her associate waved and grinned pleasantly.

All three of us captains, Suttles reflected. Just a coincidence, or a deliberate attempt to ensure that nobody could make any decisions based on rank alone? He expected he'd have an opportunity to find out.

"Captains Kerry and Robinett are with army intelligence," Sykes explained helpfully as he took a seat at the head of the small table.

Which made sense, Suttles knew as he sat down. Kerry wasted no time in launching the subject they'd come together to discuss. "You're the one who saw the alien?"

"Hey, slow down." He smiled. She didn't smile back. "I didn't say it was an alien."

"A dead alien." Robinett studied his agitated fingers. "About three feet tall, looking something like this." From the neat rectangle of papers piled on the table in front of him he held up an artist's rendering of the sort Suttles was familiar with from frequent encounters on the evening news. Someone had produced a remarkably accurate rendition of the alien's head and torso based on the information in Suttles's official report.

"Pretty good," he commented. "The nasal ridge is sharper than that, though, and the central eye is the same size as the others."

Robinett looked at the sketch and surprised Suttles by saying, "I'll fix it. I did the best I could based on what you told us." Now

Suttles understood the reason for the young captain's nervous fingers: they were searching for a pen.

"There's more." He tried not to sound overly critical. "Minor details. I didn't say it was an alien," he reiterated. "*He* said it was a dead alien."

"That's right." Now Kerry smiled slightly, as though it was expected of her. "The bartender."

The somber confrontation in the tiny, windowless room put Suttles in mind of the classic sf/horror films of the fifties. All that was needed was for Kerry to lower her voice and declare in ominous tones that "It's obviously a by-product of the atom bomb." Completing the scene demanded that she change into the standard duty uniform for brilliant young female scientists of that genre: high heels, with skirt and sweater sufficiently tight to slow the circulation of the blood. He suspected that no such nonsense, either oratorical or sartorial, would be forthcoming from the redoubtable and no-nonsense Captain Kerry. Nor was she likely to provide any suggestion of romantic relief.

Times change, he sighed silently.

Already aware that he'd been dropped from the conversational circle, a slightly petulant Sykes rose. "I suppose I'll leave you three to get on with it."

Suttles was about to say to his base commander, "You don't have to leave, sir," but Kerry responded faster. "Thank you, General." Was she just a captain, Suttles wondered, or did the fact that she was army intelligence allow her to give orders to a senior officer?

Looking uncomfortable and ill at ease with the entire proceeding, Sykes departed. Only when the door closed behind him did Robinett speak up again.

"You're sure it was dead?"

"I'm not even sure it was an alien." Suttles replied more sharply than he intended. These two weren't making him feel at ease. "It could've been nothing more than a toy or a clever mock-up, a ventriloquist's dummy. He was a damn good ventriloquist."

"Sure," snapped Kerry. "Just your average oilfield-roughneck Edgar Bergen. I'm sorry, but that's one dual career I've yet to encounter."

Suttles blinked. "How'd you know he was an oilfield worker?"

"We've already run the usual preliminary checks." Robinett

looked apologetic. "Wasn't difficult. Social security number, unemployment insurance records, workmen's comp. No bank-account records, though. A true son of the Texas soil." He sniffed.

Kerry picked up the thread. "Ross Edward Hager: born and raised, Abilene, Texas. Played high-school . . . these details are incidental and you can be filled in later."

Suttles shifted in his seat. "When I put together the report I wondered if anyone would believe me. Why did you? I don't think I would have."

"You supplied corroborative proof in the form of the formula for advanced thermos-bottle propellant." When he wasn't smiling, Robinett's expression was difficult to read. "You also had the good sense to place that at the top of your account, and the source of your inspiration near the end. The introduction made your conclusion a lot more palatable. I used to make bottle rockets myself when I was a kid. But they didn't punch holes in steel roofs and concrete floors. They also had a tendency to come back down."

"So nobody's found it yet." Suttles contemplated the import of this revelation.

"We've searched, but we've had to be subtle about it. We can't have legions of reward-seekers searching the vicinity for an ordinary thermos bottle. Someone's liable to get suspicious and call a reporter."

"'U.S. Army will pay one hundred dollars for return of used thermos bottles, possibly dented, to be found in the general vicinity of greater metropolitan El Paso.'" Kerry smiled thinly. "That's a bulletin I don't think we'll be putting out anytime soon. We'd love to have it back, of course."

"What convinced you?" Suttles wanted to know.

"Analysis of powder fragments left behind on the workbench you used to concoct the propellant." She made a face. "It had been cleaned off since you used it, but we found enough to be conclusive. The results were impressive enough to unsettle people who are normally difficult to excite. More importantly, your results were reproducible."

"You might be interested to know," Robinett went on, "that your bartender's propellant works just as well in small rockets as in thermos bottles."

"How well?"

Robinett scratched his nose. "We'll know if and when we can find the small rocket. You might say that we lost track of its tracker. My own hypothesis is that both thermos and rocket got going so fast that they burned up on reentry, but no one else is willing to subscribe to the theory that a motor-pool captain in El Paso has become the first person in history to orbit a thermos bottle." He turned sharp blue eyes on Suttles. "Yet."

"Of course, this wonderful material could be terrestrial in origin," Kerry argued. "If not domestic, then Japanese or European. It's the source that has us excited." A hint of real excitement broke through her habitual reserve.

"You walk into a local bar and chat with the bartender, a manual laborer from Texas whose actions in no way betray signs of hidden intelligence. In the course of your visit this otherwise ordinary-looking gentleman displays the abilities of a Vegas-quality ventriloquist and through his 'dummy' gives you the formula for a new type of high-energy dry fuel, suitable for use in rockets. In the light of these unprecedented circumstances the possible existence of an actual dead alien being must be viewed with an open mind.

"What we don't understand is why anyone in possession of what might well be the most valuable single article on the planet would choose to keep it a secret."

Robinett leaned over the table. "His boss at the hotel where he was working couldn't tell us where he was going. I don't suppose you'd have any idea, Captain Suttles?"

"I'm afraid not. Frankly, I didn't know he'd left."

"Actually, we just missed him. Not that it matters." Kerry waved absently. "We know what kind of car he's driving and we have the license number."

"He could be anywhere by now," Suttles pointed out.

"No, not quite anywhere." Again that thin, predatory smile. "We've moved very fast on this. He doesn't know anyone wants to talk to him and he's not on the run. We'll find him. We've been in touch . . . quietly, of course . . . with highway-patrol headquarters in a dozen states. When his car is located we'll arrange to pick up him and his 'baggage.' Everything will be handled with the utmost discretion." She looked to her companion.

"Army intelligence having broken this discovery, we'd kind of like to keep it to ourselves," he explained. "At least until we know what we have."

"If there is anything to be had," Kerry added. "Until we're sure one way or the other we want to keep the CIA, FBI, NSA, and other government acronyms out of it. So we have to find this Hager person ourselves."

"What's my status in all this?" Suttles looked from one expectant face to the other. "When we're finished here do I resume my normal duties?"

"I'm afraid not," Robinett informed him. "As of right now, we're assigned to you and you're assigned to us. The orders have already been cut. Since you're our only actual contact with this Hager, it was felt that your presence might be useful when we pick him up. He might feel more comfortable talking to someone he's met before. Texan to Texan, if you will. Our accents," he added dryly, "might inspire something less than confidence."

"Do you have a problem with that?" Kerry asked bluntly.

"Not at all, Captain."

"It should be more interesting than your usual duties." Robinett was trying to put him at ease, Suttles felt. "Don't you read mysteries?"

"Not any that center on Texas roughneck ventriloquists with dead aliens for company."

The younger man chuckled. "No, I have to admit this is the first time I've encountered that particular setup. I expect we'll be the first."

"It very likely is something other than a dead alien, you know." Suttles was a bit taken aback at the pace of events.

"Very likely," Robinett agreed. "However, the possibility that it just might be what the bartender claims opens suggestive windows. You must be interested in finding out yourself or you wouldn't have tried that formula."

"You're sure it's dead?" Kerry's impatience dominated her disposition.

"It never moved or breathed or opened its eyes." Suttles was emphatic. "If it was once a live thing, it's certainly deceased now. I had ample opportunity to study it and I was as close to it as you are to me now."

Robinett in particular looked disappointed. "I don't understand. From what we've been able to learn about this Hager person, he doesn't seem to have any money. Why isn't he on a TV talk show by now, or charging people three bucks a head to have a look at his discovery?"

It was Suttles's turn to smile knowingly. "This is just a good ol' country boy you're dealing with here. I know hundreds of guys like that, both military and civilian. Plenty of them aren't obsessed with big bank balances. It's not that they're indifferent to money; it just isn't something that rules their lives."

"We'll persuade him that turning over his discovery is in the national interest." Robinett turned wistful. "Antigravity, now, it would be nice to get an answer from the dummy on that."

The more skeptical Kerry made a derisive sound. "Why not immortality, while you're at it?"

"Now, now, Captain. You know the routine. Physical sciences first."

"No," she corrected him as she rose. "Before you can make any wishes you have to confront the genie. Even if it's a dead one."

On the way out Suttles tried to hold the door for her, but she beat him to it.

SEVEN

Ross Ed awoke to find the sun setting. He'd pulled into Lordsburg around six A.M. and checked into the motel, tired but happy to be back on the road. Having slept through the day, he felt rested and alert. A good supper and he'd be ready to go again. As for driving after dark, that had never bothered him. He'd driven plenty of rig trucks and other oil vehicles through the Texas night, often on roads that were little more than game tracks.

Besides, if someone *was* looking for him, it wouldn't be a bad idea to sleep during the day and do his driving at night.

Unfolding himself from the bed, he ran through a few wake-up calisthenics. These were a necessity, as he'd learned from hard experience that sleeping in cramped, too-short motel beds always left him aching and sore when he woke up.

While he worked out the stiffness in his muscles, he hailed his patient companion. Jed sat in the room's single chair, between the round table and low dresser. His eyes remained shut and he looked neither to left nor right nor, for that matter, straight ahead.

"How 'bout it, Jed? You sleep okay?" The alien did not move or reply and Ross Ed smiled to himself. "I'll take that as a yes."

Parting the cheap curtains, he found himself with a partial view of the setting sun. Anxious as he was to continue on his way, he knew it would be wise to have something solid to eat before returning to the shrouded monotony of the interstate.

Problem was, this was his first time in Lordsburg, and other than the usual international fast-food suspects, he didn't have a clue where a man might find a decent meal. From what he'd seen of the town on his way in, the "burg" portion of the name certainly fit. He wasn't sure about the "Lord" part. Travels through Texas and Louisiana had taught him early on that small-town restaurants might offer you the best meal of your life . . . or an early death.

Stepping into the tub-shower, he hunched over in the usual gnomish position and did his best to come clean. The effort left him feeling much refreshed and ready to drive. But first, something to eat.

After packing the car, he checked out and inquired after a good local restaurant, uttering the usual long-distance traveler's silent prayer that it wasn't some ptomaine palace which happened to be owned by the motel clerk's uncle Og.

"What kind of food you like?" the young man asked in return.

Ross shrugged. "Pretty much anything's fine with me, so long as it's reasonable, filling, and wholesome. Don't mind a little grease." He was, after all, a Texan.

The clerk directed him to an out-of-the-way Mexican restaurant on the north side of the railroad tracks. All concrete bricks, wrought iron, and raucous music blasting from the adjoining bar, Ross Ed immediately identified it as a local hangout. It was plenty crowded, and the food proved to match the spirit. He never would have found the place without the clerk's directions.

More than satisfied, he followed his number-eight combination plate with homemade pie and a last glass of iced tea before taking the bill up to the register. The waitress rang him up with a smile and bade him a cheery *buenas noches*.

By the time the remnants of the red chili chimichanga reminded him of its presence, he was already out in the dimly lit parking lot heading for the Caddy. As usual, he'd parked it a little ways from the next nearest vehicle to preserve it from careless dings and scratches.

Intent on calculating the next leg of his interstate odyssey, he didn't notice the clutch of young locals until he'd unlocked the car. That's what they'd been waiting for, he realized as they materialized around him. To see if he was the vehicle's owner, and to learn if the Caddy was protected by any kind of custom alarm system.

"Nice car, man."

He turned to confront them. There were half a dozen, all in

their early to mid-twenties. Two or three he might have handled, but not six. Then he saw that even two would have been too many because they had their hands in their pockets. They might have been holding nothing more lethal than short-stemmed screwdrivers, but it was a chance he couldn't take. It went a long ways toward explaining the strutting bravado of the much smaller individual who was addressing him contemptuously. The guy acted like he had high-caliber backup.

His black hair was cut short and a fragmentary mustache struggled to survive beneath his nose. His jeans were new but dirty and the only iron his long-sleeve western shirt had ever seen was wrought. Instead of boots he wore the kind of fancy sneakers hyped by overpaid basketball players. Their presence didn't surprise him. He'd often seen three-hundred-dollars sneakers on the feet of men who didn't make three hundred dollars a month. The economics of such relationships were best not questioned.

None of them were smiling, not even sarcastically. They were all business. The shortest and heaviest of the group, who very much resembled a deeply tanned beach ball, stood well behind his compadres, keeping an eye on the rest of the parking lot lest their business be disturbed by wandering kibitzers.

"Mind stepping around to the other side?" In case Ross Ed didn't get the idea, the man gestured sharply.

"Look, guys, I don't know what you've got in mind, but I'm just on my way out of town."

"Do it *now,*" the swarthy speaker reiterated impatiently. One of his companions gestured pointedly with the bulge in his jacket.

Ross complied, dropping the car keys into his pocket as he did so. There was an old Ruger stuffed under one of the backseat cushions and he tried to think how he might reach it without triggering a possibly fatal reaction.

He stopped by the rear right door and turned. "All right, what d'you want? I haven't got much money." He hoped they wouldn't find the slim metal box shoved under the front passenger seat. It contained everything he'd saved from his sojourn in El Paso.

The younger man sniffed derisively. "Come on, man. We don't want no trouble. We don't want to hurt you. Just give us your wallet, man, and the keys, and you won't see us no more, okay?" He stuck out an expectant hand, palm up.

"Hey now, wait a minute." Ross raised and spread both arms. Given his impressive wingspan, it was a gesture sufficiently alarming to make his antagonists tense. "Take it easy. Look, you can have the wallet. There's about a hundred and fifty bucks in there. Let me take my license out and leave me my car, okay? I've got to get to California. There's a job waiting for me there," he lied, "and if I don't make it on time they'll give it to somebody else. You take the car and I've got nothing."

The leader of the pack shrugged indifferently. "I'm really sorry, man, but it's such a *nice* car, you know? A classic."

"Come on, I know what they like over the border." Ross gestured at the Caddy. "This ain't no Chevy Suburban or Camaro. Besides, man, it sticks out like a beached whale. Where you gonna hide it?"

"Let us worry about that. Besides, who said anything about taking it across the border? I kind of thought we might keep it in the neighborhood, you know? Tell you what, man. We're not bad guys." Turning to his friends, he added something in Spanish. Ross Ed possessed a passable command of the language and caught the joke, but it didn't make him smile the way it did the others.

"You say you got a hundred and fifty bucks in your wallet? We'll leave you fifty. Me, I think that's pretty generous of us. Greyhound comes through here twice a day, you can get a ticket back to someplace useful."

"I'd rather keep my car. Got a lot of sentimental value, you know?"

"You'll get over it, man. It's not like it's new."

The one with his hand shoved inside his jacket stepped forward unsmilingly. "That's enough talk. Give us the keys."

Ross Ed nodded at the bulge. "You let that thing off and everybody in the restaurant will be out here in ten seconds."

The young man pulled what he was holding and Ross saw that it was no screwdriver. "Don't mess with me, man. These little twenty-twos hardly make any noise at all. Besides, they've got the jukebox going in the bar. Nobody in there can hear nothing."

"A twenty-two's not going to stop me," Ross Ed replied, stalling as best he could.

"Maybe not one shot, but there's eight in this clip. I put a couple in your face, man, and you won't care. Is that worth an old car? Me, I don't think it's got that much sentimental value to you."

"All right, all right, you can have it." Slowly he turned toward the Caddy. "Can I just get a couple of personal things out?"

"Sure, man." Now that the issue had been decided peaceably the first speaker could afford to be magnanimous. "Give me the keys first." A reluctant Ross Ed tossed them over.

His tormentor moved past him to unlock the car, grinning as he did so. "Don't want you pulling any surprises out of the glove compartment or from under the seat. You tell me what you got to have and I'll get it for you." He pulled the passenger door open.

The little shit knew what he was doing, Ross Ed had to admit. There was no way he could slip past him to get at the money box or the gun in the back.

"Hey, *mira este,* you guys!"

"Look at what?" The pistol holder strained to see without coming too close to Ross Ed. "I don't see nothing. C'mon, man, I'm getting nervous. We been here a long time."

"Relax," the speaker snapped at his buddy. "Nobody's coming out here." Straightening, he looked back at the tall Texan. "What is this thing, man?" Reaching into the car, he put a hand on a cold alien shoulder.

Ross twitched, but nothing happened. The young hood gave no indication that anything out of the ordinary had occurred. He eyed his quarry expectantly.

"It's a ventriloquist's dummy," Ross Ed heard himself saying. "It's an act I do sometimes when I'm tending bar. Helps break the monotony. Good for a few extra tips."

"No shit?" Reaching into the car, the speaker picked up the body. While Ross sweated, the figure of Jed was held out for all to see. "Look at this ugly sucker!"

A couple of the onlookers chortled. Others made rude remarks.

"Hey, man, you think those are all legs?"

"Shit, the dude that made that was *on* something!"

"And he didn' stop in time. Made too many arms and legs."

"Can I have him back?" Ross strove to sound both deferential and desperate. "I'd hate to lose the tips." Every time the speaker swung the body around Ross flinched, envisioning fragile bits of suit and body snapping loose.

Smirking unpleasantly, the hood looked up at him. "Sure, you can have it, man. Here, catch!"

So saying, he held the corpse out in front of him with both hands and drew back his right leg.

"No!" When Ross took a step forward he abruptly found both guns aimed at his chest. There was nothing he could do. As attached as he'd become to the deceased alien, it wasn't worth dying for.

Ross's tormentor betrayed his North rather than Central or South American origins by bringing his right foot straight up and forward instead of sideways soccer-style. The expensive sneaker made solid contact in the vicinity of Jed's posterior region. Ross Ed prepared to lunge at the alien to keep it from striking the ground, but something intervened.

Several somethings, in fact.

At the instant the grinning young man's foot connected with the body there was a blinding flash of green light. It overwhelmed Ross's vision. He felt a damp, stinging sensation, as though he'd been hit in the face by a gallon of electrified moss. A sharp burning smell filled his nostrils.

As his sight returned he saw that the would-be vandal's body was encased in brilliant green. It twitched and jerked, as if under attack from a malevolent aurora. At the same time something struck Ross in the chest and he reflexively threw out his arms to catch it. A hasty examination revealed that Jed was undamaged and unchanged.

Precariously balanced on his left leg, each short black hair sticking straight out, eyes bulged and mouth wide in a soundless scream, the kicker vibrated and shimmied. Smoke rose from his hair and the tips of his fingers.

Then he toppled slowly over onto his right side, arms and legs frozen in position. Smoke continued to rise from his extremities as if from dozens of incense sticks.

"Mierde," mumbled one of the unfortunate's companions, his eyes as wide as those of the freshly baked corpse. Together with his friends, he rushed forward to inspect the body.

Bending on one knee, one of the young men gingerly touched the knee of the deceased, only to draw it back sharply. "Jesus, he's hot!"

"He's more than hot, man." The stunned commentator looked slowly over at the silently watching Ross Ed. "He's *muerte.*"

"Fried." The fat boy who'd been serving as lookout was also staring at the tall Texan. "That thing fried 'im."

"It don' make no sense." The speaker's face twisted. "You son-of-a-bitch, you killed Roberto!" He raised the barrel of the shiny little .22.

Holding on to the alien with one hand, Ross Ed took a step back and raised the other. "Hold on now, I didn't kill anybody. I don't know what happened any more than you do." He held up the six-limbed figure. "I ain't even sure what Jed here is."

"Jed?" The gunman's eyes narrowed. "Yeah, that's what done it. What the hell is that thing, man?"

"I told you." Keeping his eyes on the gun, Ross pleaded his case. "I don't know."

"It ain't no dummy, man. You're the dummy, for letting it kill Roberto." Without another word, he fired.

Ross Ed flinched. The pistol utilized .22 shorts. He knew they were .22 shorts because he could see the bullet clearly. It had stopped about an inch from Jed's faceplate, Ross Ed having instinctively raised the alien corpse in front of him for what meager protection it might offer. The bullet hovered in midair, neither advancing nor falling to the ground. So heightened by the situation were his senses that he could make out the grooves in the side of the slug.

More jaws dropped. A couple of the muggers started forward to examine the inexplicable phenomenon more closely. As they did so the bullet pivoted a hundred and eighty degrees and returned at speed down the line along which it had been fired, with the result that it entered neatly into the barrel of the pistol and blew up in the gun's chamber.

The gunman let out a startled yelp and dropped the red-hot weapon. As its flowered barrel fell away Ross Ed could see blood dripping from the man's hand. He was lucky he hadn't been packing a larger-caliber gun or he would've lost fingers. As it was, he bled copiously.

"Work of the devil!" someone shouted.

"Come on, man, let's get out of here!" Another had put his arm around his injured compadre and was urging him away.

The second gunman continued to gape at Ross Ed, his own weapon gripped shakily in his hand. Ross swung the alien body around to face him.

"Come on, want to shoot at me, too?"

"Hey, no, man, not me, man." Flinging the pistol aside, all bravado gone, the youth started backing away.

A low-rider Monte Carlo screeched to a halt behind him, scattering dirt, and the ex-gunman promptly piled into the backseat. He was followed rapidly by the others. As they dug out, Ross Ed felt something vibrating in his hands. It was Jed, or Jed's suit. A soft, pale green glow emanated from the material. Several embedded wires and devices throbbed with energy.

A bolt of lime-colored lightning leaped from the center of the suit to strike the fleeing car. There was no recoil, no sound. The alien's eyes remained closed and its limbs limp. The shaft of crooked light went up the Monte Carlo's tailpipe. Yelps and screams sounded from within as a green glow spread over the entire vehicle.

Ross Ed winced as the engine blew, sending the smoking hood flying end over end to crash into a nearby dusty field. The engineless, hoodless car weaved crazily until it came to a halt not far from the road. Bodies piled out, smoke rising from their clothing, which they proceeded to rip off and cast aside with inspired enthusiasm. Their howls and complaints were of the climatically challenged rather than the mortally wounded. The only fatal casualty was the Chevy, an innocent mechanical.

Mostly naked now, the five survivors vanished into the field on the far side of the road, still flailing frantically at smoking hair and blistered body parts. Ross Ed would have laughed, except that the body lying in front of him gave no sign of rising up and walking away.

When the last outraged yelp had faded from hearing, he walked over to the body of the unfortunate would-be mugger and removed the Cadillac's keys from his pocket. Returning to the waiting car, he carefully placed Jed in his familiar seated position on the passenger side, then hurried around in front and slid in behind the wheel.

While the engine idled he sat and tried to make sense of what had just happened. When he found that he couldn't, he wisely decided simply to accept it.

Knowing it couldn't hear him, he glanced sideways at his diminutive passenger anyway. "Thanks." Feeling foolish, he continued on. "I know you're dead, Jed, but something in that suit of yours ain't. Some kind of protective mechanism, or shield. Whatever it is, I'm glad it's still working. Without it, this could've gone down real bad."

Away from the restaurant he drove through absolute blackness until he crossed the tracks back into the more built-up part of town. Signs led him back onto the familiar confines of the interstate. Taking the Caddy up to seventy-five, he held it there while he deliberated where to make the next stop. With the Arizona border looming near, he considered pushing at least as far as Tucson, maybe even trying for Yuma. There was no need to extend himself, he knew. He wasn't on a fixed schedule.

No car, police or otherwise, was following him. Probably his tormentors hadn't stopped running, much less decided whether or not to notify the local police. By the time they did he'd be long gone. Besides, even if they sought political intervention, no one would believe their story. Ross Ed had witnessed it all, and he didn't believe it either.

He'd have to be more careful in the future. He was so used to his size keeping him out of trouble that he'd grown careless. That wouldn't work, he knew, in a bad area of a big city any more than it had in the dusty parking lot of a small-town restaurant. Also, there was no gauging the potential of the alien suit's defensive mechanisms and he had no intention of pushing its limits to find out.

He flipped the radio on and music filled the Caddy's spacious interior. "What else can you do?" he heard himself asking the alien corpse. "I mean, suppose both of them had tried to shoot me at once. Could you have stopped both bullets? Suppose they'd just jumped me. Would you have let 'em beat the crap out of me, or what?"

As usual, there was no reply. Motionless and voiceless, the slack figure gaped blindly at the windshield.

EIGHT

Robinett rejoined Suttles and Kerry in the unmarked white government sedan which had been parked next to the equally inscrutable van, the latter having been set up for use as a mobile field headquarters. Aware that putting tanks and Bradley fighting vehicles out on the road would have instantly destroyed their anonymity, they had opted instead for the cooperation of local authorities. Besides, it was considered unlikely that much in the way of firepower would be required to apprehend one meandering bartender-cum-ventriloquist.

The interstate rest stop was a perfectly logical place to halt and inspect passing vehicles. Regular travelers along this section of I-10 were used to Border Patrol roadblocks. Once Robinett had gotten the inevitable crack about apprehending illegal aliens out of the way, they had been able to devise and implement procedure.

Neither the Border Patrol nor the Arizona Department of Public Safety had been informed of the real reason for the action. They'd been told only that it was a matter of national security, and that all they had to do was apprehend one easily identifiable and probably unarmed fugitive. Once the individual in question had been turned over to the military, their involvement would be at an end. None of the intelligence officers' superiors back in Washington had seen any need to further enlighten the locals, a policy with which the trio on site fully concurred.

The roadblock hardly slowed traffic, since everything was waved through. There was no need to search individual vehicles since they knew exactly what they were looking for, and this late at night there was minimal traffic. A white 1972 Cadillac Fleetwood would stand out among the swarm of smaller, newer cars like a termite queen in an egg chamber.

They knew their man was on this section of interstate because he'd been tracked as far as the Chevron station on the western edge of Las Cruces, where he'd bought gas. There was no guarantee that he wouldn't get off somewhere before the isolated rest stop, perhaps take one of the numerous state highways that ran north and south, but Robinett and Suttles considered it unlikely. Their target didn't know anyone was after him, and if he was heading west, the interstate was the fastest and most practical way to go, particularly in an older vehicle.

If they were wrong, they'd backtrack until they found him. Hopefully they'd guessed right and could wrap things up tonight; quietly, without fanfare, and before the media came sniffing around.

Once the Border Patrol stopped his car, they'd escort him over to the rest-stop parking lot, which had been closed to public access for the night. Out of sight of the freeway, they could then convince him that it would be in his best interests to cooperate. It had all been thought out very carefully. No one anticipated any trouble, and Suttles had assured them that for all his size their subject didn't seem the type, but they were prepared for it nonetheless.

Kerry checked her watch. It was dark and they were tired, but everyone was too excited to rest. "You really think he'll come through here?"

"I don't see why not." Suttles leaned back against the side of the car. "If he was going to panic he'd have avoided the interstate from the start, maybe run up one-eighty toward Carlsbad. The fact that he's stayed on I-10 at least as far as Las Cruces shows that while he may be concerned, he's not frantic."

"I know, I know. I just want to get this part over with."

"And we're anxious to see the thing." Robinett was trying to relax in the backseat and doing a poor job of it.

"I hope he sees the light and agrees to help us." Kerry was toying with her watch, which boasted more buttons than Suttles's home stereo. "He's the only one who's familiar with the artifact and he could save us a lot of time."

"I agree," murmured Suttles. "It would be awkward if he were to get shot."

"Yes, it might—" She broke off and eyed him disapprovingly. While amply endowed in other areas, the captain was sorely deficient in the humor department.

The steady stream of cars and trucks continued to filter through the roadblock. None of the drivers saw or suspected anything unusual. The gray van, white car, and other nondescript vehicles lined up at the rest stop were invisible from the road, as was the Apache attack helicopter parked behind a low, scrub-covered hillock.

It was a little after nine when the call they'd been waiting for finally came through. The Border Patrol had made positive identification on the vehicle they were looking for as it passed through the Arizona–New Mexico agricultural checkpoint. Furthermore, the officer who'd made the ID had matched the car's driver with the official description of their quarry.

According to plan, nothing had been done at the state border to detain or restrain the driver, who had been allowed to pass through freely. It was twenty miles from the agricultural checkpoint to the isolated, silent rest stop and its attendant roadblock. As word was passed that the Cadillac was finally on its way, a heightened sense of excitement permeated both military and local officials.

"The woman at the border who identified him said he appeared relaxed and at ease." Suttles nervously fingered the cellular phone attached to his belt.

"What about the creature?" Kerry wanted to know.

Suttles shook his head. "She didn't see it. Like all the other officers at the checkpoint she'd been instructed not to do anything that might make our man nervous. She felt that bending over and trying to see inside might qualify.

"She did report that there appeared to be an object on the passenger seat, but she couldn't see clearly enough to make out details."

"Imagine." Robinett had to smile. "Carrying something like that around in the front seat of your car, where anybody and everybody can see it."

"Why not?" Suttles was staring toward the interstate. "There are no procedures for storing or preserving alien bodies. Maybe sunlight and fresh air is good for it. When it was propped up behind that hotel bar, I don't remember noticing any overt signs of degeneration."

"I hope he cooperates." Kerry didn't have to add that if he didn't they were prepared to take whatever steps might prove necessary, from sedating the Texan to shooting him. Discreetly, of course.

On a hill several hundred yards down the interstate from the roadblock a spotter equipped with night-vision binoculars and a closed-channel two-way would give a signal the moment the Cadillac came into view. Instantly, military police in civvies would assist the Border and Highway Patrol officers in strengthening and raising the roadblock beyond what would normally be employed to check traffic. No one expected this Hager to try to run it, but army Intelligence wasn't prepared to take chances. There would be a brief flurry of activity that might pique the curiosity of a few passing drivers, but that would have to be risked. For a couple of moments, the entire westbound portion of I-10 would be shut down.

"Hopefully when he's confronted he won't do something stupid like threaten to set the body on fire," Kerry murmured.

"He didn't strike me as stupid," Suttles commented. "Not real bright, pretty laid-back, but not stupid. I've had plenty like him under my command. Not all of them from Texas, either."

Robinett nodded knowingly. "He was smart enough after that encounter with you to pack up and run."

"We don't know that my questioning was what prompted him to leave. That's still just a supposition."

"Agreed, but you have to admit it makes for a curious coincidence."

"I know." Suttles straightened as an enlisted man approached. "What is it, Sergeant?"

"Just got the word from the spotter, sir." The noncom jerked a thumb in the direction of the roadway. "He's on his way in."

"Right." Kerry emerged from the sedan. "Let's get ready."

They formed a line alongside the car, waiting for the Cadillac to be escorted into the rest-stop parking lot.

Out on the interstate, the handpicked team of rangers was helping to heave the extra barriers into position. Traffic slowed immediately, prompting audible grumbles from delayed drivers. A couple of eighteen-wheelers were allowed to pass, followed by a van, a Corvette, and several compact cars. Behind trailed a station wagon full of family and a brand-new Eldorado encapsulating an irritated elderly couple. The police hurried them along.

Suttles was listening on his phone. "Here he comes," he whispered.

Out on the freeway, traffic stopped. A single Border Patrol officer approached the oldest car in the line, tipped his hat, and spoke politely to the driver. As she engaged him in conversation three military police in civilian clothes moved up to form a circumspect line separating the Cadillac from the Ford next to it.

"Come on, come on," Robinett was muttering under his breath.

"He's turning off," Suttles announced with relief. "He's coming in." He clipped the phone back to his belt.

They could see it now, a massive old hunk of cream-colored metal rolling slowly toward them. Half a dozen rangers hefting automatic weapons jogged along on both sides, boxing it in. Out on the interstate the roadblock was removed as rapidly as it had been put up, allowing traffic to flow freely once again.

Suttles let out a deep sigh. The hardest part of their task had been accomplished. Now the course of events could move from confrontation to interrogation.

"You'll get to see it now," he told his companions. "Don't expect too much. Visually, it's not very impressive."

"Spoken like someone who's already seen it." Robinett was fairly shaking with excitement.

It was Suttles who, according to plan, walked up to the Fleetwood when it braked to a halt and greeted the driver. Sparing a glance for the passenger's side, he saw that the alien shape was indeed seated there. In the dim light it reminded him of a sleeping child. Otherwise it looked no different from his first glimpse of it back at the hotel bar. Similarly, the driver looked just as Suttles remembered him. It was nice to be able to address the much bigger man while he was sitting down.

"Good evening, Mr. Hager." The Texan didn't blink. Considering the lateness of the hour, he struck the captain as awfully alert, almost as if he'd just awakened from a rejuvenating nap.

"Evenin'." The driver frowned speculatively. "Have we met before?"

"Once. In El Paso." Suttles ventured what was intended as a reassuring smile.

Unable to restrain themselves, Robinett and Kerry had left their position to approach the car. Both were leaning over and peering inside. Kerry all but had her face pressed up against the passenger-side window as she strove to take the measure of the diminutive figure seated there.

Doing his best to occupy the Texan's attention, Suttles continued. "I came into the hotel one night when you were tending bar. Asked a few questions?"

The driver nodded slowly, gazing thoughtfully at the captain. "Yeah. Yeah, I remember you now. Had a hunch you might come looking. Could tell by the kinds of questions you asked and the look in your eye when you left. You pushed off in a hurry." His expression fell. "Thought I'd lost you."

"Hey, it's nothing personal." Suttles tried to reassure him. "I'm just doing my job here. So are all these other people. Mr. Hager."

"How come you know my name?"

"We do our research." He fought to contain his impatience. "Ever since that first encounter I've been curious to have a closer look at your dead alien. So have some friends of mine."

The driver considered this. "I don't reckon it would do me any good to refuse."

"We don't want any trouble. Nobody's mad at you, Mr. Hager. But my friends are pretty determined."

"Uh-huh. I don't want no trouble either." He sighed heavily. "Okay, but just keep in mind that Jed's *my* dead alien."

"Nobody's disputing your proprietary rights, Mr. Hager." *Not yet, anyway.* "You named it Jed?"

"That's right."

Wearing a look of anguished impatience, Robinett had straightened and was staring over the roof of the Caddy. "Could you get him to roll down the window, maybe? It's dark, the glass is dirty, and we can't see very well."

"Just a minute." Not wanting to rush things, Suttles threw him a warning glance. There was no need to hurry, not with their quarry finally secured. For one thing, the subtle byplay Suttles had observed between the big Texan and the alien corpse needed to be studied in much greater detail, and that would be difficult to do without Hager's cooperation.

"You've made what some people think might be a very important discovery, Mr. Hager. Important to the government of the United States. We're very interested in what you've learned."

Ross Ed jerked his head in the direction of the parked trucks. "That the reason for the army? Jed don't have any military value."

"Just a precaution, Mr. Hager. May I call you Ross?"

"Nope."

This time Suttles had to force the smile. "I hope that will change. How did you come to develop your ventriloquist's act with the alien, Mr. Hager?"

Ross shrugged. "Started bringing Jed to the bar, folks noticed him, and they commented. I smart-mouthed 'em back and it just grew from there. The customers liked it. So did the boss."

"You smart-mouthed me some pretty interesting formulae. Have you ever taken any advanced chemistry courses, Mr. Hager?"

The Texan turned away from his interrogator. "Don't really recall. Been out of school some time now."

"*Very* advanced chemistry," Hager added, pressing him.

"Sometimes things just pop into my head."

"Do they?" Suttles looked past him, at the motionless alien form. "Does Jed have anything to do with that? If he does, then I'm sure you can understand our interest. Him being dead and all. I assure you, Mr. Hager, that no harm will come to you if you cooperate with us."

"Wasn't worried about me."

His guts knotting with repressed excitement, Robinett joined in. "Surely you can understand how important it is not to keep a discovery like this to yourself, Mr. Hager?"

"Yes," added Kerry, "that would be very selfish of you."

Ross Ed eyed them through the closed window before turning back to Suttles. "Who're they?"

"Captains Kerry and Robinett." Lowering his voice, he looked for a way to establish some rapport. "Captain Kerry is the good-looking one. By the way, I'm Steven Suttles." He extended a hand.

The Texan shook it automatically. "Can't say as I'm pleased to meet you, Mr. Suttles." Thick fingers withdrew. "I know this is probably too important to keep to myself, but I kind of wanted to break the news about Jed in my own way and in my own time."

"I guess I can appreciate that. But you know, while you're waiting, bad things might happen to"—he hesitated only for an instant—"Jed. He could suffer irreparable damage, or be lost, or even stolen."

Ross Ed shook his head. "I don't think so. I know he won't be stolen." This was stated with such conviction that Suttles didn't attempt to dispute it. "And I know he won't be misplaced. As far as damage, well, he's been dropped a few times and he don't seem none the worse for wear."

"Must be a pretty strong suit he's wearing." Suttles squinted past the driver. "There are some people who'd really like to have a closer look at that suit."

"I bet."

It was about time to put an end to the small talk, Suttles knew. Not only were Kerry and Robinett having a silent fit, but their superiors were anxiously awaiting a report. He took a step back.

"I know we can come to some sort of mutually satisfactory arrangement regarding Jed, Mr. Hager. Why don't you step out of your car and we'll discuss it." He gestured toward the featureless van. "There's hot coffee and doughnuts inside."

"Not hungry, thanks." For the second time Ross Ed gestured in the direction of the truck. "If everything's okay and nothing's going to happen, then why all the guns?"

"Like I told you, just a precaution. Now that I know everything's okay, I can take care of it." Straightening, Suttles barked an order. Immediately, every soldier within range put up his or her weapon. "There, feel more comfortable now?"

"A little; not much. Nobody's put anything away."

"Please, Mr. Hager. It's vital that we have your help and cooperation. Won't you please get out of the car?"

Ross weighed his choices. "And if I don't?"

Suttles didn't like the turn the conversation had taken but was compelled to follow through. "I'm afraid you really don't have much choice, Mr. Hager. Neither do I. You're not under arrest or anything, but it really is imperative that you come with us. Preferably willingly." Turning, he showed how army vehicles and troops had blocked both the entrance and the exit to the rest stop.

"As you can see, you can't leave. I'd be personally upset if you were to try."

The Texan eyed him evenly. "You mean I'll get shot."

Suttles considered before replying. "Probably not. To be brutally direct about it, no one wants to risk hitting the alien.

These are very, very good marksmen and they're under strict orders. If you try to run, they'll shoot to disable your vehicle. I don't doubt that they'll succeed."

"And if I get out and try to leave on foot, they'll shoot to disable me?"

The captain was distinctly unhappy. "Like I said, they're very good marksmen."

Ross Ed smiled thinly. "Well, that just makes me feel warm and welcome all over."

Suttles was not above pleading. "Nobody wants anyone to get hurt. All I'm asking is that you step out of the car so we can talk." He gestured at the sandy, scrub-covered knoll that rose behind the bathrooms. "There's a helicopter waiting behind that hill to take all of us into Tucson. From there we'll go by plane back to New Mexico."

"Back to New Mexico?" Ross's expression turned wry. "To Alamogordo?"

"No." Puzzled, Suttles wondered what had prompted that supposition. "To Sandia National Laboratories. The folks there can ask better questions than I can. They very much want to have a look at your friend."

"I bet they do. Probably like to cut him out of his suit, too. Open him up and take pictures of his insides, maybe his brain."

Suttles made placating motions. "They won't hurt anything. Why would they damage that which they want to study?" Besides, it's already dead, he wanted to add, but didn't. Something in the big man's attitude told him the comment wouldn't go over very well.

The discussion was interrupted by a tapping on the opposite window. Bending, Suttles could see Kerry staring in at the driver.

"Mr. Hager, are you a good American? Don't you want to do what's best for your country?"

"Sure I do," he told her before returning his attention to Suttles. "I also kinda want to do what's best for me and what's best for Jed. Don't that make me a good American?"

"Of course it does," Suttles responded soothingly, "but we also—ow!"

Ross Ed blinked. "Mosquito?"

A confused Suttles straightened and shook his wrist. "I don't think so, I—hey!" This time he jerked and grabbed at his head.

Something was rattling on the pavement, a staccato drumming

that steadily increased in violence. Ross Ed thought he recognized the sound. Leaning out the window, he watched as the hail bounced madly off the asphalt. Funny kind of hail, though. Gray instead of white, it left black streaks on the pavement where individual pellets struck at an angle.

The size of the pellets increased slightly. Being from Texas, where storms occasionally produced hailstones the size of grapefruit, Ross wasn't impressed. But when one smashed into a concrete curb and left in its wake a gaping hole, he allowed as how this particular storm just might exceed any in his previous experience. It was, in point of fact, a meteorological disturbance in every sense of the word.

Something plowed into the restroom roof, spraying bits of broken tile all over the parking area. Another hailstone left the satellite antenna mounted atop the parked van looking like something you wouldn't pay five bucks for at a garage sale. It continued on through the roof of the van, tore out the side, and left a neat twelve-foot-long furrow in the solid pavement.

Now *that* was a hailstone, he reflected. Even for Texas.

The downpour continued to pummel vehicles, structures, and the surrounding terrain. Only the Cadillac seemed immune, an island of serenity in a deluge of destruction. Stones fell in front of it, behind, and all around, but not on. Baffled, Ross Ed turned to his only companion.

"What is it this time?" Jed the dead did not reply.

The three captains were running for cover, any cover, trying to protect their heads with their hands. Two of them stumbled toward the rest rooms while the one who'd been talking to Ross Ed threw himself into a parked car. He was forced to abandon it when a stone the size of a cantaloupe crashed through the windshield. Trailing glass shards, he joined a cluster of soldiers who were making a dash for the bathrooms.

Seeing as how his car was undamaged and unattended, Ross Ed turned the key in the ignition and put it in drive. Nobody emerged from under cover to challenge him. Easing off on the brake, he headed out of the parking lot. Stones began to strike the spot where he'd been parked, but the Caddy received not so much as a scratch. It was as if a giant umbrella had been opened over the car, shielding it from the downpour.

The heavily armed rangers and military police who moments earlier had been manning barricades had fled in search of safety.

Nudging the wooden barriers aside, Ross eased the Fleetwood through and accelerated down the on-ramp. Most highly localized of storms, the tempest raged behind him but did not follow.

The night was clear and cloudless as he reentered I-10 and pushed the Caddy up to seventy-five. There was no longer any point in driving slow to avoid attention. They knew what he looked like, and what his car looked like.

He debated how soon to abandon the interstate. If he could just make Tucson, he might have a chance to lose himself in the maze of city streets. The more he thought about it, the less likely it seemed that they'd give him that chance. A high-speed car chase through a major urban center would be a poor way of maintaining secrecy, which they had obviously gone to some length to preserve. He was sure they'd do anything to prevent him from reaching the city. Therefore he would have to exit as soon as possible and try to lose them in the countryside.

The officer he'd spoken to had been up-front about their intent. Certainly that had been equally clear to Jed. There was no question in Ross Ed's mind that the alien (or at least the built-in defensive mechanisms in the alien suit) was responsible for the delivering deluge.

"Thanks," he told the corpse. "Come too far to start backtracking. Need more time to decide what to do." Jed chose not to argue the point.

When the appalling downpour finally ceased, the military contingent trapped in the rest stop cautiously emerged from shelter to inspect their surroundings and regroup. Robinett was the first to notice that the Cadillac was gone. Somehow Suttles wasn't surprised.

Not a desert plant had been left standing. Every vehicle, including the trucks, had been badly damaged. Certainly none were in drivable condition, much less capable of pursuit. Trashed along with windshields, engines, tires, and instrument panels was a lot of very expensive electronic surveillance and communications gear. The van in particular looked like it had taken direct hits from a couple of rocket-propelled grenades. It and the two cars were so full of holes they appeared to have been used for target practice.

Which they had been, Suttles reflected. By the heavens.

Reaching up, he felt a trickle of blood running down his right temple. No one had escaped the battering. Exposed skin had been bruised, clothing shredded. It could have been worse, he reflected. They had suffered a thousand minor injuries and not a single major one. Intent, coincidence, or luck?

"What the hell happened?" Robinett was cradling a badly banged-up left arm.

"It wasn't hail." Suttles decided that in spite of her bruises and scratches Captain Kerry was more alluring in tattered attire than tailored. Wrapping a length of torn cloth around her fingers, she reached into one of the million holes that now pockmarked the rest stop and picked up a tiny chunk of gray material.

"It's still hot." She showed it to her companions, rolling it between her fingertips so it wouldn't burn through the material. "Heavy, too, for its size."

"What is it?" Suttles squinted at the nondescript granule.

"Isn't it obvious? It's a meteorite. Smaller than some of those that hit, larger than a lot of others." Flicking it aside, she indicated his ripped shirt. "Some primitive societies will launder with pumice, but this is ridiculous."

"That's crazy," he retorted. "No way. How come we're only scratched and cut, while the vehicles have been totaled?"

A bemused Robinett was kneeling to examine some of the debris. "I guess as meteor storms go this one was highly selective. Most of the big stuff didn't fall until we were under cover. It didn't want to kill us, just put us out of commission." He turned slightly to eye Kerry. "Want to bet that the first person to take a hike over the hill finds nothing but used helicopter parts scattered across the desert?"

There was no need to take the bet, as a couple of the rangers had already left to check on the chopper's status. Taking a seat on a decorative boulder noticeably scarred by the storm, Suttles glanced down as the remaining bits of his cellular phone trickled away into the dirt, leaving only a slab of plastic and a few dangling capacitors clipped to his belt. Not surprisingly, there wasn't a single intact piece of communications equipment to be found among the dazed and befuddled company.

"He's gone." Robinett nodded toward the far end of the parking area, where the wooden barriers had been pushed aside to allow a large vehicle room enough to pass. "And we're stuck without any means of calling for help."

"Let's get out on the interstate," Kerry suggested. "We'll flag down someone with a car phone, or a trucker with a CB."

Suttles trailed behind his two colleagues. "I'm afraid it won't be that simple. If I were out driving in the middle of the night, I *might* stop for someone in a uniform. Even a trucker might not pull over for a bunch of beat-up, gesticulating maniacs dressed in rags. *I* wouldn't stop."

"We'll find somebody. People are curious." She glanced down at her muchly revealed self. "If necessary I'll go stand in the middle of the slow lane. That ought to make a trucker or two blink."

Don't overestimate your attractions, Suttles murmured . . . but only to himself.

On one point they agreed: sooner or later someone would pull over to find out what had happened. He peered back over his shoulder, in the direction of distant Tucson. The question was, how long until that happy moment arrived? How far would their long tall Texan have traveled by then? They didn't even know what direction he might be heading. Unless he was a complete fool he'd get off the interstate fast, whence he could continue in any conceivable direction. He might even now be heading for the international border at high speed. If he made it into Mexico before they could cut him off, they'd have a hell of a time getting him back. Sealing the border must be their first priority. Keep him in the country and they'd run him to ground sooner or later.

Robinett was staring skyward, his voice full of wonder. "How do you order up a meteor storm, keep it confined to an absurdly small area, and moderate the impacts? Thousands, we must have taken thousands of hits. Surely they couldn't *all* have been individually guided?"

"The suit." They both looked back at Suttles. "The alien may be dead, but his suit is still active. It contains mechanisms we don't understand. A logical function of such a piece of equipment would be to preserve and defend its owner."

"So you bomb your perceived enemies with micrometeroites." Kerry snorted in disbelief.

Robinett rubbed his injured arm. "Some of them weren't so micro. I took a couple of hundred hits myself, yet I'm still walking around." He nodded off to their right. "Meanwhile the big brothers of the pinheads that were pelting me were punching holes in army trucks. I can't even conceive of that kind of precision."

"All the more reason why we have to get ahold of that suit and its contents." A thoroughly frustrated Kerry kicked an uprooted cactus aside.

"Yes." Robinett turned thoughtful. "I wonder what other tricks it has in its repertoire? Maybe next time it won't be so careful."

"We'll take precautions." Skin gleaming through her torn clothing, Kerry topped a low rise and started down toward the interstate.

"Against micro-manipulated meteor storms?" Robinett sounded something less than confident. "We're going to have a hell of a time bringing this guy in."

"We'll get him." Sand slid beneath her shoes. "If nothing else, he has to sleep *sometime*."

"That's so," agreed Robinett, "but dead aliens probably don't."

"Then you're convinced that's what it is?" Suttles asked him.

"I wasn't before. I am now. At least, I'm convinced that it's an alien. I'm not so convinced that it's dead."

"I told you; it's the suit that's doing everything."

"You're sure? You're absolutely positive it's dead? I won't be convinced until the autopsy's been run."

Remembering the Texan's concern for the bodily integrity of his discovery, Suttles felt guilty. "I saw it up close. It's dead."

"Right. And form follows function. There's dead and then there's dead. Read your Egyptology."

Behind them officers were beginning to give orders to their demoralized troops. Equipment salvage commenced in the hopes of finding something capable of communicating with headquarters. The effort proved futile.

Almost as futile as the captains' attempts to flag down passing traffic. Vehicle after vehicle ignored their frantic gesturing. A few slowed slightly but then sped up again, their occupants no doubt discussing and probably having a laugh at the expense of the trio gesticulating by the side of the road. The operator of one eighteen-wheeler slowed long enough to favor Kerry with an appreciative whistle, but didn't stop.

Recognizing that this might take a while, Suttles found himself a comfortable patch of sand and sat down. Eventually they would be missed and others would come to check on the operator's status. That could take some time.

With every car that shot indifferently past, with every truck that rattled the road without slowing, their quarry was receding farther and farther into the cool, clear Arizona night.

NINE

On the crumpled map, Tucson loomed tantalizingly near, but the longer he thought about it the less sure Ross Ed was of his ability to avoid the attentions of the military there, much less the local police.

The Fleetwood was the problem. Instead of a generic world car he was cruising the highways and byways of the Southwest in a veritable boat, a land yacht in a sea of canoes. He was too easy to spot.

It was all very unfair. He was no criminal. He'd set out from home to see the Pacific, and by God, he was damn well going to see the Pacific! Army or no army.

Though he wondered how harshly his would-be captors had suffered from the violent storm, he wasn't about to go back and check on them. He might not be so lucky a second time. He did hope no one had been seriously injured. It was evident that their capabilities had been crippled because the lights in his rearview remained distant. Until they recovered he would continue to put miles and speculation between them.

Having cornered him once on the interstate, it was reasonable to suppose that they might try to do so again. Certainly the Caddy would be easy to spot from the air. Therefore it would behoove him to get off and make his way on less traveled byways.

He considered Mexico. It was close, and possibly safe. But the roads south were few and easily reconnoitered. Besides, if he thought of it, it was likely that the military would, too. Still, it was a tempting thought. If only he knew how much time he had before pursuit resumed, or if they had managed to contact additional help by now. The sooner he made a decision, he knew, the better his chances of retaining his freedom.

He thought back to the confrontation. The officer who'd done most of the talking had seemed to mean well, but while friendly enough, he'd been plenty insistent. They wanted Jed, and they wanted him. There'd been no mistake about that. Sure, Ross was an upstanding, proud, patriotic citizen, but that could and frequently did mean different things to different people.

At the moment the democratic principle that seemed to be most in question was the matter of personal property rights. Though it was hard to think of Jed as property, he'd found the body, and until a court stated otherwise, the body was his. Not the army nor anyone else was going to take his dead buddy away from him without his consent.

Probably the best way of ensuring his rights would be to hightail it into the nearest real city and wake up a newspaper editor or two. Surely the discovery of a real, genuine, honest-to-Mars alien body ought to rank right up there as news with the president's personal peccadilloes and the outbreak of the latest fighting in Bosnia. Of course, it wouldn't outrate the O.J. trial, but Ross Ed was nothing if not a realist.

He frowned. While tempting, he decided to hold on to the idea and keep it as a last resort. He didn't much like the idea of playing Kato Kaelin to a dead body. Essentially a private person, the notion of having his face splashed all over the tabloids was one that held very little appeal.

No, what he wanted more than anything else was to be left alone to sort out his options in his own good time. That meant no deals and no publicity. After all, what if despite everything he'd seen and all that he'd been through, Jed still turned out to be the product of an elaborate hoax, some eccentric billionaire's idea of a joke not only on Ross Ed but on the military and the rest of the government? He'd wind up looking like a champion idiot. Better, as his daddy always said, to take things slowly. Do that, and you're less likely to step in a mess of rattlers, or something even more unpleasant.

The sign swelled in his sight until he could read the numerals "191." A quick check of the map revealed that it ran south to the border and north into the mountains. It seemed as good an exit as any. Besides, he was getting hungry, and it was hard to think on an empty stomach.

The map showed a few towns strung out along the highway, but a quick glance gave no indication of comparative size. He'd just have to take his chances.

No one exited behind him. At the bottom of the off-ramp a sign pointed toward Safford, 35 miles. Turning right, he headed up a signless, structureless country highway. Away from the interstate it was black as the intestines of an abandoned coal mine. A good place to stage an ambush or an abduction, but first they had to find him.

"What d'you think I should do, Jed?" Leaning back against the still-plush leather seat, the stiff-necked, limp-armed alien did not reply. "I wish I knew how you're doin' all this. How'd you make those rocks fall from the sky? How'd you help me come up with all those jokes back in El Paso? Oh, I know you are responsible for that. See, I'm smart enough to understand I ain't smart enough to figure it all out on my own."

Jed did not respond, his lifeless eyes contemplating the dark road before them, his tiny, oddly formed mouth eternally mute. Neither did he offer comment on the nocturnal inhabitants of this little-populated region when one happened to skitter madly across the pavement, or remark on the brilliance of the stars overhead. The ideal passenger, he was content simply to ride.

His vacation sure had grown complicated, Ross Ed mused as he drove. Of course, it didn't have to be. All he had to do was stop and make one phone call and within an hour the burden of worrying about Jed would be lifted from him. They might even fly him out to the Pacific. He badly wished to know what the alien wanted him to do, but Jed was dead, all judgment fled.

So it was up to him. When in doubt, keep driving, which is what he did.

One thing he was pretty certain of by now: as long as he remained close to the alien, the circle of protection that shielded it would enclose him as well. Lordsburg was proof of that, with the events of the rest stop offering additional confirmation. What if he walked a mile away? Would he still be protected? He decided to stick close to Jed at all times. They were going to see the sea, and no one was going to stop them.

While laudable, such resolution did nothing to mollify his stomach, which rumbled incessantly.

It wasn't a Texas truck stop, but the homey restaurant whose neon signature proclaimed it the Saguaro Café had the one sign in its window he'd been looking for: OPEN 24 HOURS. Beneath this was the smaller legend, *We Never Close (Well, Hardly Ever).*

Lights within indicating that tonight was not the proverbial Hardly Ever, he pulled into the dirt lot and cut the engine. Around the café, the town slumbered. Farther down the highway/main street a convenience store cast garish lights on grateful moths. Aerosmith whispered from a pickup parked out front, doing sonic battle with crickets. While the music was louder, the insects had the advantage of numbers.

Upon leaving the interstate, the highway had climbed steadily. It was nice to see trees again instead of just low desert scrub. Pausing thoughtfully for a moment, Ross Ed walked around the front of the Fleetwood and opened the passenger-side door. There was no response to this overture, but he didn't care.

"You know, Jed, I bet you're pretty tired of sittin' in the car. How'd you like to see how humans eat?"

Reaching in, he hefted the corpse and tucked it sideways under his right arm. After locking the car, he turned and entered the café.

The long front room faced the parking lot and the highway beyond. There were hints of a back room, closed at this hour for lack of customers. Booths beneath windows looked out on the lot, while stools fronted a counter like so many mushrooms standing at attention. The café boasted the usual accessories: stainless-steel milk dispenser, multiple milkshake mixer, display rack of miniature cereal boxes, glass-fronted cooler holding pies and cakes on white doilies, all common to countless such establishments from sea to shining sea.

There were the expected local touches: deer heads high up on the walls, one nice elk, a javelina, cheap paintings of regional scenery by local would-be artists, a glass souvenir case beneath the cash register offering a desultory selection of Genuine Indian Jewelry! for sale. No black velvet paintings, which boded well for the food. Like an ancient hunter stalking game, Ross Ed knew from experience what spoor to look for in a small-town restaurant. So far, the Saguaro Café measured up.

In the farthest booth, a young man and woman were sharing piles of bacon, pancakes, and syrupy kisses. They were as oblivious to Ross Ed's arrival as they were to the rest of the nonedible, nonkissable cosmos. The tall, broad-shouldered man seated at the counter wore a battered cowboy hat and beard along with an air of general indifference. He did take a moment to glance toward the entrance, but Ross was careful not to meet his eyes and the diner silently went back to his meal. Her back to the booths, a statuesque woman in shapeless clothes sat at the far end of the counter and sipped coffee.

Choosing a booth, he was delighted to discover that it was big enough for him to relax in without having to stick his legs out into the aisle. Uncommonly, his knees didn't scrape the gum-encrusted underside of the table. Taking the laminated menu from its metal holder, he squinted out at the car. The cafe's blinds were down, which didn't make much sense given the hour. Probably lowered in expectation of early-morning sunshine, he decided. Occasionally (very occasionally) the lights of a passing car or truck could be seen making their patient way up or down the strip of highway outside the restaurant.

The waitress must have been in her sixties, at least. Her skin was burned by the sun and wrinkled with experience, but her eyes were young. Thin, parchment-hued arms seemed held together by steel wires laid in just under the skin.

"What'll it be, hon? You need a minute to look at the menu?" Ever so slightly, her eyes strayed to the alien shape seated across from the big customer. Obviously dying to ask about Jed, she was too professional to do so. At least, not until she'd brought Ross some food.

He knew women like this, who'd been waitressing all their lives and couldn't imagine doing anything else. Forty years of waiting on tables taught one when to ask questions and when to hold off. Her restrained curiosity tickled him.

"Coffee." His eyes ran down the menu. "Denver omelette, pancakes on the side, maple syrup, whole-wheat toast . . . no, make that a bagel and cream cheese."

Her eyebrows lifted slightly as she scribbled. "Didn't figure you for the bagel type."

He grinned. "One of the first thing you learn if you do a lot of traveling is that when you're hungry, one bagel can fill you up near as much as a fourteen-ounce porterhouse. They both take up about the same amount of space in your stomach. Once worked with a Jewish guy on a rig near Odessa who told me that's how the Jews got through the forty days and the forty nights. Forget all that stuff about manna, he said."

Without missing a beat, she aimed her pencil at Jed. "Nothing for your friend?"

Ross kept calm. It was unlikely this woman held down a second career with U.S. Army Intelligence. "You hear him ordering?"

That brought forth a grin that took twenty years off her overworked face. "I guess not."

He watched while she walked back behind the counter and stuck the ticket into a clip on the revolving order take. The cook swung it around and inspected it mechanically. He looked relatively awake, so maybe the omelette wouldn't be too greasy. It was the only order up.

She came back with the coffee and left the pot on his table. About the time his food arrived, the midnight cowboy rose from his stool, paid his bill, and left. Ross Ed attacked the dripping platter with enthusiasm.

The waitress wasn't surprised when he ordered apple pie à la mode. "Full pie, or just a slice? You look like you could handle a whole pie."

He patted himself in the general vicinity of his belt. "Not after that omelette. Just a slice, please."

The pie proved the equal of the rest of his meal. He was half-done, the ice cream melting faster than he could finish it, when he happened to glance through the blinds. Another car had pulled in. No surprise there, except that with the entire lot to choose from, it ended up right next to the Caddy. When the headlights dimmed he was able to see the faint, irregular outlines of two or three people within. He took another mouthful of pie and vanilla.

Before he could swallow, a second car drew up on the other side of the Fleetwood. Observing this, Ross Ed began to linger over his food. It might be quite a while before the opportunity arose again to eat in a country café. When no one emerged from either car to enter the restaurant and do something normal like order food, he was sure of it.

He could only nurse the dessert and coffee for so long. Wanting to keep everything quiet, they'd wait awhile for him to emerge. From their standpoint it would be better that way. No noise, no fuss. No witnesses. Two large trucks pulled into the parking lot of the motel across the street, one behind the other. There were no markings on their sides and no one emerged from them, either.

He wanted to urge Jed to slump lower on the other side of the table. Actually, the alien's helmeted head was below the window line and probably invisible from outside. The blinds obscured the diners from view anyway, he suspected.

"Well, Jed, I reckon this is it. Unless you got more tricks up your sleeve. You got an extra sleeve, anyway."

They sure had found him fast, he thought, despite his leaving the interstate. Apparently even state country highways were too easy to cover. Had some cop waiting silently for speeders noted the Caddy's description and license and called it in? It was unlikely he'd ever know.

Probably ought to have turned around and headed back toward El Paso, he decided. Well, it was too late for recriminations. They wanted him and Jed awfully bad, and it looked like they were going to have them.

He recalled what he'd read about the Roswell Incident. Was Jed about to be reunited with his lost shipmates? Were there three-armed and three-legged frozen alien bodies lying in cold storage far beneath some super-secret military base? He didn't think they'd allow him to go on the talk-show circuit and discuss it.

The restaurant entrance stayed closed. No need for them to hurry, he knew. They had the Caddy hemmed in, figuring he had to be inside. When he stepped out to reclaim his vehicle, they'd grab him. Silently and with a minimum of fuss, but they'd grab him. Nor did he think they'd wait forever. Certainly not until morning, when the before-work breakfast crowd would start to trickle in.

"Got a problem?"

Looking up, he saw that the tall woman who'd been seated at the far end of the counter had left her stool and come over to inspect him. He'd been so intent on the activity outside that he hadn't noticed her approach.

Big girl, he thought. Heavyset throughout but well proportioned. Broad smile, intensely blue eyes, blond shoulder-length hair that ended in soft curls. The simple beige dress she had on had been cut more for comfort than looks. She stared straight at him, too, not demurely off to one side. There was nothing subtle in her query, her gaze, or her stance.

"What makes you think I've got a problem?"

"I've been watching you. When you came in you were pretty relaxed. Now all of a sudden you've gone tight. I like watching people." She gestured at Jed and grinned. "Think your friend'll mind if I sit down next to him?" Without waiting for a reply, she slid into the seat opposite. "Wish I could say he's kinda cute, but he's actually sorta ugly." To further illustrate the point, she opened her mouth and shoved her right index finger partway inside.

"That's okay. Jed handles criticism better than most of the people I know. See? Your comments don't bother him at all. 'Course, it helps to be dead. Just don't touch him," he added when she made a move to lift one of the alien's arms.

"Why not?" Her fingers hovered.

"Just don't. If you do, I can't be responsible for the consequences."

"Aw, that's all right. A little guy like this wouldn't hurt me. I can tell."

Before he could make a move to stop her, she'd slipped an arm around the body and cuddled it close, like a favorite childhood doll rescued from the dump.

"There, you see? He doesn't mind." She examined the triangular face. "Is it a 'he,' or should I just think of it as an it?"

Ross eased back against his side of the booth. First contact with Jed had initiated all manner of reactions these past weeks, but contact with this woman didn't seem to inspire anything. The alien simply leaned limply against the tall female shape, a situation not to be despised.

"I think of him as a he," the Texan explained softly. He was not looking at her.

She frowned slightly. "Why are you looking out the window?" Leaning to her left, she tried to peer through the blinds. "Cops after you?"

He jerked around sharply to face her. "What makes you think the police are after me?"

She made a face. "Are you going to answer all my questions with paraphrases?" She gestured toward the parking lot. "I can see all those cars out there. They're full of people not going anywhere. That says to me that they're waiting for something, or for someone."

"The cops aren't after me." He debated whether to explain further before deciding, whatthehell. "It's more like the army."

For the first timer she evinced real surprise. "You don't look like the deserter type. Wrong haircut, for one thing. Your posture isn't military, either."

"I'm not. I'm just a guy from Texas."

"Oilfield worker." She indicated his left hand. "You're missing your third and fourth fingers. Roughnecks are always missing body parts. We get a few of them through here." Again that engaging smile. "Roughnecks, not body parts."

"Why don't you just go back to your coffee? You don't want to get involved." He returned his attention to the preternaturally active parking lot, trying to decide what to do next.

"What's the matter, don't like my company? Besides, if I want to 'get involved,' it's none of your business. If I should take a notion to jump into the ocean, ain't nobody's business if I do."

Her singing voice was much higher than the one she used for speaking. Almost girlish, he thought. He winced as she squeezed Jed close, but there was still no reaction from the alien or its suit. He eyed her with a mix of curiosity and astonishment.

"I'm Caroline. I don't much like cops. I don't know enough about the army to dislike it, but if they're after you, then I don't think I like them, either."

"You don't know anything about me," he replied briskly.

"Sure I do. You're big, polite to an old waitress, you've got one hell of an appetite, you're not so bad looking . . . not great, but not so bad . . . and you run around with a funny friend." She turned to study the alien. "It's pretty soft. What's it made out of, anyway?"

"Old cheese, for all I know," he grunted. He didn't think they'd wait outside much longer. "I found him. Named him Jed. He's an alien. A real alien. Dead, but real."

"Well hell, any fool can see that. Pretty well preserved, too. Must be the suit." She fingered the material. "Wonder what this stuff's made out of?"

"I haven't a clue. All I know is that the army's real interested in him, and in me."

"I bet." She squinted through the blinds. "That your Cadillac they've got sandwiched?"

He nodded. "I figure they're expecting me to walk out when I'm through eating, so they're holding off picking me up until they can do it with no witnesses."

"Makes sense. How long have you been keeping one step ahead of them?"

Keeping his voice low, he leaned over the table. "You know, I'm probably gonna be on my way pretty quick here to some super-secret laboratory or government installation. I don't need any sarcasm from you."

"Why not?" she replied innocently. "You're not going to find any in the army." As she spoke she wagged a finger in his face. "Now, according to what you say, as soon as you step out that front door, they're going to hustle you into one of those waiting cars or trucks, is that it?" He nodded, wondering where she was going with this.

He soon found out.

"Then why don't you and your friend come with me?" She glanced over her right shoulder. "There's a back door, for employees. I know because I've been eating here fairly frequently and they let their regulars park out back."

Now she had his full attention. "You've got a car out back?"

"Sort of. It's a nice, nondescript, late-model Ford van. If they hold off for another half hour we can put a lot of miles between you and them."

Despite the fact that he had little time to waste on rumination, he did so anyway. "How do I know you're not with them? Maybe you're just trying to get me out of here voluntarily so I won't have the chance to make a scene."

"Because if I was with them I wouldn't have said what I've said. I'd be saying something like, 'Please, Mister'—what did you say your name was?"

"Hager. Ross Ed Hager."

"I'd be saying something like, 'Please, Mr. Hager, won't you step outside voluntarily and not make a scene?' There'd be no need for me to suggest slipping out the back way. Besides, what've you got to lose?"

"At this point, not much." Lips tight, he nodded in the direction of the lot. "Hate to leave the Caddy behind, though. I've had that car a long time. We're old friends."

"Think they'll send it to Washington, or wherever, with you? They'll probably take it apart."

"I guess. I shouldn't worry about it. It's just a car."

"From now on, I'm your witness, your corroboration," she told him. "Anything happens to you, I'm there to make a note of it. You're sure you didn't steal this little guy from a government repository or something?" She gave the alien a brisk shake, to which it continued not to respond.

"I told you, I found him."

"Why not? I find stuff all the time." Her tone became urgent. "Look, are you going to let me help you, or are you just going to be one more name for me to jot down on the roll call of my life?"

"You talk funny." Sliding out of the booth, he remembered to leave a good tip. "Let's get out of here."

"I'll go first." She turned toward the kitchen. With no new customers to attend, the elderly waitress had stepped in back to chat with the cook. At the moment neither of them was watching the front.

"Come on."

Tucking Jed under one arm, he followed her to the end of the aisle, turning left past the sign that announced the location of the two rest rooms. Another door led through a back storeroom piled high with food and janitorial supplies, past a work sink, and out through the promised rear portal.

There were three vehicles in the small back lot—the cook's, the waitress's, and his blond savior's dark blue van. A three-quarter-ton, it boasted a raised roof with black plastic windows embedded in the rear. Otherwise the side panels were intact, offering plenty of privacy to anyone within.

Loping around to the passenger side, he climbed in through the unlocked door and gently set Jed down alongside the captain's chair. As Caroline climbed in behind the wheel he registered a made-up foldout bed, several storage cabinets, a small sink, a built-in microwave oven suspended from a cabinet above the sink, and assorted other unspectacular and thoroughly prosaic built-ins.

Backing up and keeping her headlights off, she pulled out of the lot and onto the secondary road which paralleled the highway. After less than a mile the highway curved westward, but the road they had taken continued north. Leaving the last commercial buildings behind, they found themselves in an outlying neighborhood of isolated homes and tall trees.

"They're not stupid, you know." Ross Ed couldn't keep

himself from continuously checking the rearview mirror on the passenger side for signs of pursuit. "They'll figure out that I left with you."

"Maybe not." She spoke without taking her hands off the wheel or her eyes off the road. "Nobody saw us leave together. I've eaten in there a lot without striking up long-term friendships. Usually I'm not there this late. I didn't know that waitress, and she doesn't know me."

"What were you doing in there?"

"Bad case of the midnight munchies."

He checked the rearview again. "Can we go any faster?"

"Take it easy. You want to attract attention, speeding along in the middle of the night? You'll notice there's not a whole lot of traffic to blend in with." She slapped the wheel, fairly bouncing in her seat. "Damn! This is the most fun I've had in weeks!"

He made himself settle into the comfortable, high-backed chair. "You live in Safford?"

"Have been for a while. Working as a checker at the Safeway."

"Won't someone start asking questions when you don't show up for work?"

"They'll wait awhile. Assume that I'm goofing off, or out with a boyfriend, or something. It'll be a few days before they check on me. By that time we're long gone."

The van struck a dip and Ross Ed's head threatened to dent the ceiling, an all-too-frequent hazard he faced in the majority of vehicles. "You can just walk away from your apartment and job like that?"

"What apartment? You're in it. As for my job, it's not like I was running the production line at Boeing. They'll just replace me. I mean, don't get me wrong. I don't do this sort of thing on a regular basis. Usually I give notice. I just got the feeling you were in kind of a hurry, that's all." She grinned over at him. "*Carpe diem,* and all that."

"Beg pardon?"

"Never mind."

By this time Ross Ed had decided that this was a woman it would be nice to Get To Know. What he had at first taken for flirtatious playfulness masked a streak of genuine independence. He had the feeling she didn't much give a damn if she was picked up by the army or not. In that event, he felt it would not be out of place to feel sorry for the army. Anyway, who was he to be questioning her? She'd just saved him . . . or at least prolonged his freedom.

"By the way, thanks."

"You're welcome." She chuckled. "They don't know what kind of car I'm driving, which way we've gone, or when you left." She checked the rearview on her side. "Still nobody back there. I wonder how much longer they'll sit around waiting on you?"

"Hard to say. If they think I just ordered, they might hold off an hour or more."

"That's the spirit. Meanwhile we'll put lots of Arizona between us."

"Where we headed?"

She eyed him expectantly. "Where'd you want to go? Do they know where you were heading?"

"No. I haven't told anyone except a few friends back home, and they just know I want to see the Pacific."

"So they'll have to search from Canada to Mexico. That ought to give 'em pause." She considered. "We could cut up and over on Highway 70 through Globe into Phoenix, or east and down to Lordsburg."

"No," he countered sharply, "not Lordsburg. I've been to Lordsburg."

"Me, too. Can't say as I blame you. Okay, how about we get back on one-ninety-one and head for Clifton? Although if they managed to track you to Safford, they might block the road up that way, too." She wrenched hard on the wheel and Ross fought to keep his balance in the chair as they began bouncing up a narrow dirt road.

"Since I've been working in Safford I've done a lot of camping around here. There are dozens of roads that cut through the San Carlos reservation. It'll be a little rocky, but we can take our time and work our way northward without having to worry about roadblocks. We'll pick up pavement again outside Fort Apache."

"There's really a town here called Fort Apache? I thought that was just a movie title."

"Nope, it's a real place. From there we'll head on into Show Low. If they're not waiting for us there, you can bet your ass against a pig's hindquarters that we'll have lost them. From there we'll hit Holbrook and get on Interstate 40. Then we'll head west again. You want to see the Pacific, we'll damn well go see the Pacific. I don't see them trying to monitor *both* interstates. Cause too much comment."

"I dunno. They really want me. And Jed, too, of course."

"Too bad for them. By the time they figure out you're not in the immediate vicinity, we'll be a couple of hundred miles to the north. When they decide to start checking the other interstates, we'll be in California. And they still have to identify the transportation you're using."

"I'm sold," he told her gratefully. "I'm going to have to leave it up to you. Until this trip I'd never been further west than Hobbes, and I don't know this part of the country."

"I do. The mountains are magnificent." She checked her console. "Only problem is, do we have enough gas to make Fort Apache? There won't be anything open there, but there will be in Show Low, and it's not much farther. We'll do the best we can." The bottom dropped out of the van for a moment, sending him careening off the sidewall. "Sorry. Plenty of ravines and potholes out here. If we run empty, maybe we can buy some gas from somebody who's out camping.

"Now that that's settled, tell me about yourself. Who are you, and what's with the dead alien?"

His deceased companion was bouncing around on the carpet like an abandoned rag doll, but otherwise appeared none the worse for their close call. "Jed seems to like you."

"Yeah? How can you tell?"

"You know how it is. After you've spent some time with someone you get to know their moods."

"He's alien, he's dead, and he has moods?"

"Sure. I can just tell. He likes you."

"I'm so flattered. Tell Jed I like him, too, as long as he doesn't start to decompose in my van."

Having long since left the last ranch house far behind, they bumped and banged northward, continuing their steady climb into the mountains.

TEN

Suttles was the first one into the café, followed closely by Kerry, Robinett, and a pair of massively muscled military police. No one entered armed. The last thing they wanted was any kind of wild shoot-out. Not out of concern for the safety of those inside but lest the priceless alien be damaged.

Hurriedly the captain surveyed their surroundings: counter, stools, booths, kitchen in back smelling of old grease and singed shortening, a single young couple at the far end now turning to gaze curiously at the handful of intruders.

The waitress emerged from the kitchen to greet them. She reminded Suttles of his paternal grandmother. "Can I help you? You want something to eat? We don't have a booth big enough for five, but I can put a chair on the end of a table."

"We're not hungry." Anxiously, his eyes scanned the interior. "We're looking for someone."

"A friend," put in Kerry unnecessarily . . . and unconvincingly.

"Big man, about six-five, six-six. He may have been carrying an object with him. Something like a large doll, or a ventriloquist's dummy."

Peering past the three officers, the waitress could see half a dozen high beams playing over the parked Cadillac. Both hood and trunk lid were up and these areas were likewise receiving their fair share of attention. A small-town old-timer she might be, but she wasn't dumb.

"Come on; you aren't friends of this gentleman."

"We just want to talk to him, ma'am." Suttles threw Kerry a

warning look. Somewhat to his surprise, she got the message and kept quiet.

The elderly employee pondered the request. "He didn't look like a bad sort. I know people. That's one thing you learn in this business; people. You say you just want to ask him some questions?"

"That's right, ma'am." Flipping open his billfold, Robinett displayed his identification. "United States Army Intelligence. We don't want to hurt him and he hasn't done anything bad."

"I'm glad to hear that. He was a nice young man. Good tipper, too."

Kerry couldn't restrain herself. "You don't happen to know where he is, do you? That's his car out front."

"I guessed, seeing the way you people are going through it. What're you looking for? Drugs?"

Suttles chafed at the delays, but he suspected if they lost their temper with this particular senior citizen, she'd simply clam up and refuse to talk to them. "No, ma'am."

"Didn't he go out front?"

"No. We've been watching the front. He hasn't come out that way."

"Well then, I expect he went out the back. Unless he's in the can expressing his opinion of our cooking."

At a word from Kerry, a cluster of military police hustled in the direction of the rest rooms. "How long since you've seen him?"

"Heck, I don't know." The waitress jerked a thumb toward the kitchen. "Jericho and I been talking. This time of night it gets pretty slow around here. I don't write down when customers arrive and when they leave. All I care is that they pay their tabs and leave a little something for the old lady."

"When you *were* speaking to him, did he seem nervous at all, or upset?"

"No, but you're right about one thing: he did have a funny-looking toy with him. Put it right there"—she pointed to a booth—"on the seat opposite. I just glanced at it. Didn't really take a good look. Figured it was for some kid."

Having gone with the search party, Robinett now rejoined his companions. "Bathrooms are empty. We're searching out back."

"Footprints?" inquired Kerry.

The slim officer shook his head. "Gravel parking lot. Maybe

on the other side, if he ran and the ground's moist enough. Guy that big ought to leave footprints." His expression was downcast. "Wonder how much we missed him by?"

"This isn't a big town." Kerry was thinking furiously. "Maybe he knocked on somebody's door and asked for shelter. Maybe he's sleeping in somebody's garage, or behind a woodpile. He can't have gotten far."

"Unless he managed to hitch a ride out back, or stole a car," Robinett pointed out. "It's worth checking out. I'll get in touch with the local police and we'll establish a confinement perimeter." Pulling a cellular phone from his belt, he began dialing as he walked away.

"I don't understand," murmured the elderly waitress. "What's this young man done?"

"Like we told you; nothing." Suttles put on his best public-relations smile. "He just needs to answer some questions. It's not something you need to worry about. You sure there's nothing else you can tell us that might be useful?"

She shrugged. "Only that Jericho makes the best hash browns this side of Santa Fe. You sure you don't want something to eat?"

Actually, Suttles would have killed for a plate of bacon and eggs, but they didn't have time. Not yet, not now. Turning, he accompanied Kerry to the entrance. Robinett rejoined them moments later.

"What do you think, Geoff?" he asked the taller officer.

Robinett shook his head dolefully. "The police are ready to cooperate, but as to where we go next, I don't know. I'm kind of new at this sort of thing. Materials science is more my line."

"If he's been gone more than thirty minutes he could be anywhere." Kerry was chewing on her lower lip, an activity that oddly enough did nothing to mute her attractiveness. "If somebody's hiding him there's not much we can do."

"I really doubt that's the case." Suttles sounded confident. "Would you let a stranger that size into your house in the middle of the night, no matter how convincing a sob story he told you?"

"No, I wouldn't," admitted Robinett, "but small-town people can be more empathetic than smart."

"It's too soon to start panicking." Kerry took a deep breath. "Probably he's still around here. If so, we'll pick him up tonight or tomorrow. The forest service can help. He can only hike so far without food or water."

"We need to check out all the commercial Dumpsters in town, to," Robinett suggested.

"That's the spirit." She clapped him on the back. "It's not like he's slipped away from us in Phoenix or, God forbid, Los Angeles. The road checks are already in place and both the Arizona and New Mexico highway patrols have been alerted to be on the lookout for anyone matching his description. We'll get him."

"I know," muttered Suttles. "It's just that the longer he's on the loose, the greater the likelihood that he might do something stupid, like dump the alien in a trash can or bury it with an eye toward coming back for it later."

"The greatest scientific discovery of the last couple of hundred years," she grumbled, "and it's in the hands of some dumb oilfield grunt from Texas."

Robinett grinned sardonically. "He may be an oilfield grunt and he may be from Texas, but I don't know how dumb he is. So far he's managed to elude *us*."

It was an observation for which the restive Kerry had no ready retort.

Ross Ed squinched back and forth, trying to find a comfortable position in the passenger chair. Behind him, the alien body lolled gently back and forth each time the van hit a dip or bump in the road.

"If you don't my asking, Caroline, what were you doing in that café so late?"

"Working graveyard at the grocery. After I punch out I usually go get something to eat. You get tired of eating supermarket deli. Except for the fast-food joints, the Saguaro's the only other place in town to do that. Then I crawl into the van and fall out."

Set on high beam, the headlights cut through the forest ahead. Several times she had to brake while deer made up their startled cervoid minds which way to bolt, and once a majestic bull elk stalked regally across their path.

The creeks they crossed varied from empty to full, but the larger were spanned by old wooden bridges that rattled beneath the van's big tires. Caroline drove like she knew exactly where she was going. After the past couple of days it was pure bliss to have someone else doing the driving.

"I couldn't live in a van," he told her, trying to make conversation.

"I agree. You wouldn't fit. They must want you real serious." She shifted into low as they rattled up another grade.

"I'm just an accessory. What they're really after is Jed." He indicated the six-limbed corpse flopping around on the carpet beside him.

"We're on reservation land now. Apache."

He squinted out the window at the dark forest. There'd been no formal gate or barrier. Either she knew the spot well, or they'd rumbled past a sign visible only from her side.

"Tell me," she asked him, "what do you do with 'Jed' when you're not hiding him from the government?"

"I've been tending bar in El Paso. Got the idea of using him as kind of ventriloquist's dummy, to loosen up the customers. Brought in real good tips."

"I bet. 'E.T., phone your wife. You know she doesn't like you hanging out in bars with low-life humans.' "

He smiled politely. "Something like that. After a while I got the patter down pretty good. It just seemed to flow." He glanced down at the inanimate object on the floor. "I think Jed kind of inspired me."

"I'm sure he did. Look at me: I can't stop laughing."

His expression turned serious. "Not everything that Jed sparked turned out to be a laugh riot. There were serious moments, too. Enough to get the army interested in him, anyway."

The rear wheels threw dirt as she spun the wheel to make a tight curve. "What're you going to do when we lose your happy soldier friends?"

"First thing," he replied with unwavering determination, "I want to see the Pacific. After that . . . I haven't decided yet. I've worked hard all my life. Dirty, dangerous work. Don't seem able to save anything. Seems like there are always friends and cousins and nieces and nephews that need a few bucks. My daddy never had any money, but when he died, three hundred people came to his funeral." He paused long enough for one hard swallow.

"I think Jed's probably worth some serious money to the right people. I just want to do the right thing where everybody's concerned, including him."

"Hollywood's near the Pacific," she suggested. "I bet you could find some interest there."

"No!" The sharpness of his reply surprised him. "I don't want anything to do with those people. Read too much about 'em, heard too much on TV."

"Well then, what about taking him to a newspaper, or better still, to one of the big universities? I bet their science departments would bid against each other for the right to study him. I mean, he's got three arms and three legs."

"If they are arms and legs." He eyed their compliant passenger. "I admit that's what they look like, but we can't be sure. I've never tried to take him out of that suit. Fact is, I ain't so sure that'd be a good idea."

"Taking him out of his suit?"

"No. Trying to."

"Why not? At least you'd learn something about his anatomy."

"Caroline, I don't think the suit would let me."

"I see." She grew quiet. Something with bright eyes materialized briefly in their headlights before vanishing, unidentified, into the night.

"Those strips and pieces of metal and porcelain that look that they're part of the suit? Sometimes they glow, and even hum softly. I've seen light pass right through them."

She considered. "So like, the suit's more valuable than its owner?"

"Maybe. In any case, I'm not about to try and cut him out of it. In addition to defending him, it may also be the only thing that's keeping his body from disintegrating.

"So now you know about me, and about Jed. It's your turn, Caroline. Tell me about you."

"Me? I've been in Safford going on four months."

"And before that?"

"Tulsa. Left a good job there, mediocre home, bad husband. Number two. Just decided to work my way west. Unlike you, I don't have this killer desire to see the ocean, but I've heard that San Diego's pretty, not as overwhelming as L.A., and a good place to look for work."

"We can head that direction," he told her. "It's all the same ocean. There is one thing I'm curious about, though."

"What's that?" She kept her attention on the meandering dirt track.

"You've accepted me and my story without a lot of fuss. If I was eating supper and noticed that the police and the military were after *you,* I'm not so sure I would've picked you up."

"Sure you would have. I'm much prettier than you." Her tone turned earnest. "Look, Ross Ed, I'm not doing this because I buy your story completely, although if that's a fake dead alien it's a mighty good one. I'm doing this because I took a liking to *you.* Like I said before, I know people. I saw how you treated that poor old waitress, and I watched your face in the dessert-cabinet mirrors. You've got a real good nature. Good-natured men are hard to find. Believe me, I know. They tend to be quiet and reserved and don't announce themselves, which makes it hard for us gals to find them. Me, I've been looking for a good-natured guy for quite a while."

"You don't know me," he replied. "I'm told I can be pretty disagreeable when riled."

"That's all right. I'd rather be around a good-natured man who throws an occasional tantrum than someone like my last husband, who was always angry and threw an occasional smile. If it comes with the rest of the portfolio, you can even be a little crazy." She smiled across at him.

"See, I'm just your average gullible gal, Ross Ed. We automatically go for the guys who are dead wrong for us. Something in our makeup. A malfunctioning gene that leads to malfunctioning jeans."

"You helped me out of a tight spot. I'll try to be as nice as I can."

Reaching over, she patted his leg just above the knee. "I don't think it'll take much of an effort for you, Ross Ed. I think niceness comes natural to you."

She patted him just the way he would have patted a dog. Except that he wasn't a dog and she hadn't patted him on the head, although that might have something to do with her inability to reach it.

Not only did their remaining gas last through the night, they still had some showing on the gauge when they finally pulled into the sleepy outskirts of Show Low. Nevertheless, both expressed silent gratitude to the manifold deities of Detroit when the convenience store and its welcoming pumps hove into view.

Situated high in the eastern Arizona mountains, Show Low was a gateway to fishing and camping territory, much of which they had just passed through. In addition to gas, the attached country store sold everything from refrigerated bait to hand-tied flies to butane capsules for camp stoves.

While Caroline filled the van, Ross Ed did some cursory shopping. He missed the steel strongbox under the passenger seat of the Cadillac, but enough bills remained in his wallet to keep him from feeling like a freeloader. Though sleeping bags lined a high shelf, he ignored them. The van was tight and warm and the carpeted floor bed enough.

The fiftyish owner answered Ross's questions readily and with interest while his wife stacked cans of tuna and sardines on a shelf. When Caroline called out that the tank was full, the amiable gray-haired gentleman stepped outside to check the air in their tires.

While working on the front, he happened to pass the open door on the driver's side, which Caroline had left open to allow the van to air out. For just an instant he had a clear view of the interior—cabinets, storage racks, carpet, living supplies, dead alien. Then he moved on to the last tire.

"All up to thirty-three psi." He let the retractable black air hose slink, snakelike, back into its hole. "Eighteen and a half gallons of unleaded." A hand extended in Ross Ed's direction. "Cash or credit?"

"Cash." Before Caroline could protest, Ross handed over a ten and a twenty. Despite her protests, he'd pay his share as long as he could.

"Thanks, son. I'll have your change in a jiffy." The owner jerked a thumb back at the van. "Nice-lookin' dead alien you've got there."

Ross Ed blinked. "I beg your pardon?"

Pivoting, the older man walked back to the van and raised up on tiptoes to peer through the passenger-side window. Not knowing what to do, Ross Ed did nothing. Out on the street in plain sight he couldn't very well tackle the man and drag him away.

"Yep, that's a dead alien, all right." Resuming a normal footing, the store owner turned back to the tall Texan. "Not the way I'd have pictured one, though."

Caroline moved to insert herself between the man and the van. "I don't know what you're talking about, mister. That's my son's toy. One of the villains from the Mighty Morphin' Power Rangers. Don't you watch TV?"

"Not that show," the man replied. "Mostly Ted Koppel and Louie Rukeyser." Raising his voice, he shouted toward the store. "Hey, Martha, they got a dead alien out here!"

Glancing around nervously, Ross Ed made quieting motions with both hands. "Please, could you keep your voice down?" Other cars were pulling in and out of the station, most making use of the self-pay feature on the pumps.

"Why?" The oldster was grinning through his neatly trimmed spade beard. "Afraid some kid'll try and steal her son's toy?"

Before Ross could comment, Caroline spoke up resignedly. "Okay, mister, you got us dead to rights. It's a dead alien. See, we're part of a crew that's been shooting a low-budget sci-fi flick down near Fort Apache. Frank and I, we were extras. They finished with us yesterday. My boyfriend there"—and Ross Ed started slightly at this—"was hired to play one of the ravenous invading aliens. 'Cause of his size, see?" She looked back at the van.

"When moviemakers finish with props they don't need anymore, they just dump a lot of them, and I thought the little alien would be a good one to take to my kid. Pretty neat looking, isn't it?"

"Almost as neat as your story," the owner avowed. "But I still think you folks have come across a real dead alien. I know they do remarkable work in Hollywood these days, but that ain't no computer graphic denting your carpet, and I don't think it's no prop, neither. Martha! Get yourself out here and have a look at this."

Ross Ed stepped past him. "Sorry, but we really have to be on our way."

"That's right," agreed Caroline. "See, we're on our way to . . . to Denver. I've got a modeling job up there and my boyfriend—"

"Is going to join me inside. Just as you are, young lady." The revolver he'd pulled from a shoulder holster shone as bright, clean, and efficient looking as anything the army had pointed in Ross's direction.

Sure am seeing a lot of handguns here lately, Ross Ed mused, remembering Lordsburg.

"Now just a minute . . . !" Caroline took a step forward, halted when the weapon's muzzle swung in her direction.

"You can have all the minutes you want, missy, so long as you do as I say. That way nobody'll get hurt. I don't *want* anybody to get hurt." Gesturing with the pistol, he herded them toward the store. As he complied, Ross Ed raised his hands.

"You crazy?" The owner gestured a second time with the weapon. "Put your hands down. You want to attract attention? How'd you two happen to come across a dead alien, anyhow?"

"It's his," announced Caroline, abruptly passing the conversation to her companion.

"It's a long story," Ross Ed began. "No, actually it's kind of a short story, but there are a lot of details."

"Save it. You'll make a full report later. I really don't want to shoot either of you, but I will if you force me. This is too important to play around with. See, I've been waiting more than thirty years for something like this to happen. Traveled quite a bit in search of it, too, and then it ups and presents itself to me right here in my front yard. Sometimes the fates are kind."

"Kind of loony," Caroline quipped.

Ross was shaking his head slowly. "I don't know what you're talking about, mister."

"You will." Again he yelled toward the store. "Martha, dammit, get out here!"

"Hold your water, you old fart! I'm coming." Emerging from within, the woman Ross Ed had seen stacking canned seafood hustled over to the van, opened the door, and peered inside. She spent a long time looking. The twelve-gauge Mossburg riot gun she held in one hand hung loose from her fingers.

"That's a dead alien, all right. A real one. Knew somebody'd find one someday. Just didn't expect it drive in here and ask for gas, as it were."

"So what now?" snapped Caroline. "You've found what you say you've been looking for for thirty years. What happens next? What happens to us?"

The owner smiled at her as they resumed their escorted march toward the entrance. "Nothing unpleasant, as long as you cooperate. Where are the keys?"

"In the ignition."

He nodded, shouted back over his shoulder. "Keys are in the ignition, Martha! Be sure and lock it up good."

His wife's voice drifted over to them. "I'll just move it around back, Walter." Moments later Ross Ed could hear the Ford starting up.

"Step on inside and we'll have us a chat." The owner gestured with the impressive handgun. "Don't let me forget, son: I owe you change out of that thirty."

"Don't worry, *Walter*." Ross Ed glared back at their captor. "I won't forget any of this."

"That's it," Caroline whispered, nudging him in the ribs. "Put him at ease, make him feel better about this."

"Sorry," he muttered. "I'm not feeling real accomodatin' right now."

"Then don't worry about accommodating him. Just accommodate the gun."

As his wife entered through a back door Walter directed them to a couch surrounded by fishing gear and gaudy boxes of candy and cookies. "You need to make some phone calls, dear. Is the fax working?"

"I'm sure it is." Setting the riot gun down but keeping it close at hand, the woman slid into a chair fronting a computer and monitor. Her fingers danced on the keyboard and the screen changed. Ross Ed squinted but couldn't make out the readout.

"Who're you calling?" Caroline asked.

"Just some friends who think the way we do and share similar interests. It's sort of a club."

"Then you're not calling the police?" Ross Ed eyed her husband uncertainly.

"Should I?" Walter chuckled softly. "Most likely they'd help themselves to your alien. Is that what you want?"

"No."

"Us neither."

"Oh, so you want it for yourself!" Caroline declared accusingly.

Ross Ed leaned close. "That's it. Put him at ease, make him feel better about this." She glared at him but said nothing.

"I wouldn't put it quite like that, missy. Can I get you something to drink? Coffee, a soda? I have to help Martha with the calls. We don't want to waste any time."

"Oh, surely not," Caroline agreed sarcastically.

"Nothing for me, but thanks." Ross settled down into the old, overstuffed couch.

"You're welcome." The owner turned to his other captive. "Missy?"

"I'll have a soda. Any kind of cola is fine, so long as it has caffeine and refined white sugar."

"With ice?"

"If you don't mind."

"Not at all." He headed for a tall, glass-faced refrigerator. "Please don't make a dash for the door. I'm a very good shot, and if you're lying on the floor twisting in pain, you won't enjoy your soda as much." He winked at Ross Ed. "Don't worry, son. I'll take it out of your change."

Instead of replying, Ross yawned helplessly. Returning with the cold can, which he passed to a grateful if wary Caroline, the owner regarded his heavyset guest.

"You look all done in, son. When's the last time you had a decent sleep?"

"Not that long ago." Unable to stop himself, he yawned again. Instinctively, Caroline mimicked him. "It's just that my system's kind of out of whack. I've been driving at night and sleeping during the day.

Walter nodded. "I guess we can fix that." He indicated a rear door. "We've got a couple of bunks in back, for visiting friends. Why don't you go lie down?"

Too tired and confused to argue, Ross decided he might as well comply. After a decent nap he'd try to think of something. It would also be easier to come up with a solution to their present predicament if he had some idea as to just what the hell this charming country couple was up to. But as he escorted them toward the back room, Walter simply grinned and offered vague promises of incipient revelation.

"You're sure you're not going to call the police while we're asleep?" Gingerly, Ross tested the springs on the bunk. They creaked, but held.

"Now, wouldn't that be stupid? They'd have no conception of what you've found, no clue as to its import. On the other hand, Martha and I do. You'll see. You'll thank yourselves that you stumbled in on us." He gestured with the pistol. "Sorry about the gun, but you're a big fella and I didn't feel like taking chances." He backed toward the doorway. "We'll call you if we need you."

The door shut behind him. Unsurprisingly, the action concluded with a distinctive *click* as a lock was slipped home.

"What do they want with Jed?" He lay down on the bunk and stared at the ceiling. "I hope they don't do anything stupid, like trying to pry him out of his suit."

"Well, if they do, we should be pretty safe in here." Sitting on the other bunk, she rapped her knuckles on the all-too-solid wall. "What's it capable of, anyway?"

"I try hard not to think about it." He rolled over to face her. After the jouncing, spine-jarring ride through the mountains, the bunk felt like his grandmother's feather bed.

Shortly thereafter, he wasn't feeling much of anything at all.

ELEVEN

It was past noon when he finally woke. If not completely relaxed and at ease, his body at least felt like it was back on a normal daytime schedule. In fact, he felt better than he had at any time since his hasty departure from El Paso.

The sole abnormality consisted of a heavy weight pressed up against him. Looking down, he saw that Caroline had dragged the other bunk over next to his and had snuggled as close as was possible. He tried to rise quietly, a procedure which for Ross Ed Hager was somewhat akin to trying to drive a dyspeptic steer up a loading chute without making any noise. She blinked, stretched, smiled, and then impulsively kissed him full on the mouth. He flinched slightly before relaxing, leaving it to her to finally pull away.

"What was that for?"

Rolling back onto her bunk, she straightened her hair and grinned mischievously. "Sorry. I thought you were my first husband."

"The hell you did. You were wide-awake."

"So I lied." She sat up and yawned deliciously. "What are you going to do about it? Punish me?"

"That's right. I'm going to make you do that again." And he was about to when a gentle knock on the door interrupted them. He found himself saying automatically, "Come in," even as he realized that as virtual prisoners, the knock signified the granting of still another unexpected courtesy. It didn't make any sense. If their captors were a music genre he'd have to call them Cutthroat

Country. He felt like they'd been captured by the Mayberry Militia movement. It was all very disconcerting.

It was the owner's wife, all muffin smiles and bucolic vibes. "Good morning! Or I guess I should say, good afternoon. You two slept well."

Uncertain whether her intent was to feed them, shoot them, or recruit them into the local quilting bee, Ross Ed rubbed sleep from his eyes. "Like we told your husband last night, we've been running on a nighttime schedule." He blinked at her. "Where's Jed?"

"Your little alien?" She reminded him of his ninth-grade English teacher, Mrs. DeWeese, who no matter the circumstances was forever smiling and chipper. Many's the time he'd dreamed of strangling Mrs. DeWeese, slowly and with great pleasure.

However, unlike his teacher, who'd never employed anything more lethal than a yardstick, the owner's wife cradled the threatening shape of the Mossburg lightly under one arm.

"Unless he's suddenly come to life and learned how to jump-start a 1988 Ford van, I imagine he's where you left him, on the floor next to the front seats. Don't worry. Walter parked it in the shade. There's a big carport out back we use for storing recreational vehicles."

"So you operate this place as a garage, too?" Caroline had put her feet on the floor and turned to face the woman.

"Not officially, but Walter's pretty handy and there's always folks who pull in needing this or that minor problem fixed. Your van'll be perfectly safe back there. Things are happening, you know. Our friends are starting to arrive."

"Friends?" Ross was watching her carefully. What had they fallen into? "What sort of friends?"

"Members of our little organization. You'll see."

Caroline wasn't sure she wanted to. "Unless you want to get yourselves involved in something over your heads, you'd better let us go now. U.S. Army Intelligence is after us."

"Really? Oh, I doubt they're after *you*. Your alien, now, that I can believe." She laughed gaily. "My goodness, dear, do you think we worry about such things away up here? This is Arizona, young lady. We like to think of ourselves as more independent than folks back east. Maybe because we're so much better armed." She wagged a schoolmarmish finger at them. "You know old Ben Franklin's saying: 'A little target practice each day keeps one healthy, wealthy, and wise.'

"If these army people haven't found you by now, then I don't think they will for a while yet. Meantime we will be able to have a formal meeting of our group. Oh, there's big things happening, there are!" She stepped aside. "Why don't you come out and meet some of our friends?"

The captives exchanged a look. Together they rose from their respective bunks and followed the woman out into the store.

A couple of snack tables were piled high, and half a dozen people milled about, chatting and laughing. Ross Ed looked for but couldn't find the husband. He did, however, notice that the blinds had been drawn on the windows and that the "Closed" sign had been put out.

"Attention, attention please, everybody!" Conversation faded as all present turned to Martha's direction. "This is the young man who found the alien we now know as 'Jed.' "

Abruptly Ross found himself surrounded. His avid audience was a diverse lot, from wrinkled oldsters who made the store owners look like teens to bright-eyed couples in their twenties. Too bright-eyed. One perfectly tanned, prosperous-looking pair wore the same perpetually eager expression as his aunt Florene's pedigreed cocker spaniels. As to the multitude of questions they threw at him, he was for the most part at a loss to come up with answers.

It was Caroline who pointed out the multiplicity of accents. Some were distinctively Deep South you-all while others bore the sharp twang of lifelong New Englanders. An Oriental couple chattered together in a language he didn't recognize. They looked tired, as if they'd come a very long way in an extremely short time. But while their energy might flag, their enthusiasm matched that of their colleagues.

"Our friends have come from many places." Turning, Ross found himself once more confronted by the owner, who'd entered via another back door. "Not everyone could make it on such short notice, but we'll have a representative gathering."

"Gathering for what?" Ross asked curiously.

"You'll find out tonight. Everything's being taken care of."

"No one's come asking for us?"

"Nobody."

Martha went up to her husband and put a comforting arm

around his waist. She still carried the Mossburg, like a prized piece of jewelry. "He says army intelligence is after them."

"Can't say as I'm surprised. But they won't find them. You have my word on that one, son." He gave Ross Ed a friendly nudge. With his elbow instead of the big .45.

"Look, who are you people? What's going on here? What do you want with us and with Jed?"

"Tonight," the man replied firmly. "Although I suppose I could tell you."

"Oh, don't, Walter." His wife nuzzled him affectionately. "You'll spoil the surprise." She beamed at Ross, Mrs. Cleaver with a gun.

"You must be famished," the store owner decided.

Caroline spoke up immediately. "Didn't I see a nice coffee-house when we drove in?"

"Now, young lady, you know I can't let you leave the store. You might do something stupid, and then I'd have to shoot you. But help yourselves to anything at the counter, and if you want to look in the phone book, we can send out. How about a nice steak and fries?"

Less than a hour after phoning, their lunch arrived, hot and country-sized. It was served to them in the back room, where they were allowed to enjoy the meal in private.

"If people didn't keep sticking guns in my face, I could almost enjoy this." Ross Ed shoved in a couple of french fries. "Who are these crazy people?"

"How should I know?" It wasn't often Ross Ed encountered a woman with an appetite to match his own.

"Well, you're from this area."

"This area?" She shook her fork at him. "Do you know how far we are from Safford? This is another world up here. All I know is how the roads run." She sawed at her steak. "They seem harmless enough."

"Harmless people don't threaten you with forty-fives and shotguns."

"They do where I come from. You might as well try to relax, Ross Ed. There isn't anything we can do. Mr. Walter has your alien and my van keys."

"I could swear I heard one couple speaking Japanese. At least, I think it was Japanese. I didn't know you could get here from Japan in half a day."

She considered. "Maybe they're from Topeka. Eat your steak."

Nobody bothered them for the rest of the day. They were not allowed out, but any requests they made were fulfilled promptly, politely, and to the best of their hosts' ability. Throughout, they were treated with a combination of the utmost courtesy and firmness.

"You'll see tonight," was all they were told.

It was with a mixture of trepidation and anticipation that they counted off the hours. Brought back into the store, they watched as the visitors left in twos and threes. One by one, cars and vans and trucks pulled out of the once-crowded parking area in front of the building. Others departed from across the street. The organization these people belonged to might be secretive, but it wasn't paranoid. Plenty of townfolk were witness to their comings and goings.

Then maybe they weren't about to be sacrificed by a coven of clean-living devil-worshipers, Ross decided with more than a modicum of relief.

Much later and long after everyone else had left, Walter looked up while Martha escorted the captives around back. It was reassuring to see the old van parked between rusting junkers and a retired Winnebago.

Ross Ed checked his watch. "It's going on near midnight."

"I knew it was late," Caroline commented. "I didn't realize it was *that* late."

"More night driving," he groused. "Just when I thought we were back on a normal schedule."

As it turned out, neither of them had to do any driving. It was Martha who slipped behind the wheel and shoved the ignition key into its slot. Seating the captives on the foldout bed, her husband rotated the passenger chair until it faced rearward. The .45 dangled loosely from his right hand. Untouched, the alien body lay on the floor exactly as Ross had left it.

The van started up smoothly and Martha pulled out of the lot. Through the windows Ross saw scattered mountain homes quickly give way to solid forest.

"You be careful with my van." Under the circumstances, Caroline's warning carried little weight. "It's not only my transportation, it's my home."

"And very nicely done up it is, dear." Martha glanced

rearward. "Although those back windows could really do with some new curtains."

"I don't concern myself with the decor," Caroline shot back. "I'm not really the domestic type."

"It doesn't matter." Walter was waving the pistol in small, lazy circles. "After tonight you won't have to worry about such things anymore."

Ross Ed tensed. "What's that supposed to mean?"

"Not what you think, son. Nothing's going to happen to you. Leastwise, nothing bad. I'm not going to do anything to you, nor is Martha, nor are any of our friends. But what *they're* going to do, well, I imagine it's going to be pretty wonderful. Whatever it is, they'll do it to us as well, so we're all in the same boat, you see." He sucked pine scent. "This is a momentous evening. Not only for you, and for us, but for all mankind."

"I still don't have a clue what you're talking about," Ross responded irritably. "I miss my own car, I'm tired of being chased, and I'd like some real answers to my questions."

"Yeah, you owe us. No more cryptograms."

Ross eyed his companion admirably, wishing he could use words the way she did.

The store owner seemed about to respond, but once again his wife dissuaded him. "Come on now, Walter. They've waited this long. Let's not spoil the surprise."

There was nothing the two discouraged captives could do but sit and wait as the van bounced its way down the poorly maintained forest road.

"I don't much like surprises." Ross Ed lay down on the bed, his long legs draped uncomfortably over the end.

"Well, you'll like this one, son. I guarantee it."

Another hour's casual driving brought them to a turnoff which was little more than an overgrown track. Broken stems and branches showed where many vehicles had preceded the van. With high reeds blocking the view off to their right, it was impossible to see anything that looked like a real road, but Martha seemed to know exactly where she was going.

The reeds opened up to reveal a silvery shimmering: a mountain lake bordered by more cattails and high ponderosa pines. As they turned toward the gleaming body of water, Ross thought he could make out lights bobbing in the darkness. The unfulfilled moon helped.

A few headlights showed where the others had parked. The weaving points of illumination he'd seen from the van were produced by flashlights and lanterns of varying strength. Martha pulled the van in between a late-model Lincoln and a big Dodge ramcharger.

"Well, we're here." Her husband slid forward, opened the side door, and stepped out. "Let's go." He was staring off into the darkness. "I think James and Jenny brought our outfits. Sorry we don't have any for you two."

"Yes," agreed Martha as she came around the front of the van to rejoin them. "I'm afraid we wouldn't have anything to fit you anyway, young man. But if you stay in the background there shouldn't be any problem." She'd brought the shotgun with her, Ross noted.

"I'll be back in a jif." Her husband disappeared in the direction of the lake.

His wife gestured with the riot gun. "No last-minute heroics, please. Gunfire here would spoil everything."

"Take it easy." I ain't the heroic type." Feeling a hand on his arm, Ross looked down to see Caroline batting her lashes at him.

"Aw, c'mon, I bet you could be if you had to."

"Well, I don't have to. Can't you be serious for a moment?"

"If I strain real hard I can sometimes manage it," she told him, clinging tighter to his arm.

"That's the spirit, dear. Really, you have nothing to worry about." She looked off to her left. "I see they're setting up."

Between lake and forest was a low grassy area; too muddy to qualify as a real meadow, too dry to pass for lake bottom. The store owners' numerous and oddly assorted friends were milling about there, well away from their cars. Thanks to the abundant artificial light, Ross Ed could see that they were all dressed alike, though he couldn't make out any details.

Walter returned carrying two sets of neatly folded and pressed clothing. While his wife looked on he donned a satin overcape with billowing sleeves. Bright gold, it wrapped around and snugged at the waist with a silver sash, the combination an odd mix of the ultramodern and medieval. Unrecognizable insignia and designs had been woven into the overcape with brightly colored thread. His head remained unadorned, which allowed Ross Ed to relax. He'd been half expecting a tall, pointy cap of some kind.

Taking the shotgun from his wife, the store owner kept watch while she slipped into her own identical outfit. After they traded back, he climbed into the open van and reemerged with Jed cradled gently in his arms. The six limbs hung limp but the head and neck, as always, remained stiff and perpendicular to the spine.

"Who are you people, really?" the uneasy Texan demanded to know.

"Why, we are the Circle of Knowers." The woman gestured cheerfully with the Mossburg. "Hurry up, now. We're almost ready." There was an excitement, a tension in her voice that Ross Ed hadn't noticed before.

"Knowers of what?" Caroline inquired as they were marched toward the near-meadow.

"Why, the visitations, of course. Honestly, the information that the so-called news media conceal! Sometimes I think no one else besides the Knowers know how to read between the lines. Don't you see the images on your television set that They don't mean for you to see?"

Though it was difficult in the darkness, Ross Ed tried to count flashlights and forms. He estimated between thirty and forty overcaped supplicants had formed a crescent-shaped line near the back of the scruffy meadow, facing the lake. Their vehicles were parked well away from this staging area.

"I guess not," he finally replied. "I don't read the papers or watch the news on TV much. Too depressing."

"Well, I do." Caroline flipped her hair back, not wanting to miss anything. "I'm so 'up' most of the time that I need an occasional dose of depression to bring me back to Earth."

The woman chuckled unexpectedly. "'Bring you back to Earth.' That's very good, dear. Very appropriate."

"So what are we doing here?" Caroline pressed the woman. "Let me guess: it's the local midnight-fishing derby. The big mouth who catches the biggest bigmouth gets another star sewn on his or her cape."

Her sarcasm didn't faze Martha in the slightest. "You're righter than you know, dear. We are sort of going fishing, but not for bass. You see, it's well known that the Visitors will come to rescue any of their kind that they know to be in trouble."

"Rescue?" Then the dawn of realization broke over Ross Ed,

and it was no less cloudy than these folks' thinking. He knew enough to recognize a cult when he saw one.

"So that's it. Y'all are a bunch of saucer nuts!"

"And you're worried that *I* might provoke them." Caroline shook her head slowly.

The woman took no umbrage at the undiplomatic judgment. "We don't really think they use flying saucers. We have no knowledge of the true nature of their ships' shapes, since no one's ever made a proper picture or recording of one. But as to their presence and motivations we have no doubt."

"Because?" Caroline prompted.

The woman smiled. "Because we are the Circle of Knowers."

"There you are." Caroline spread both palms upward. "*Quod erat demonstrandum.*"

"Don't mock, dear. It doesn't become you. Especially in Latin. Yes, we are the Knowers, working silently, gathering our tiny bits and scraps of information, hoping each day to learn a little more, to one day perhaps even make contact. And then you two happen along, with your priceless cargo. Drive right up to our place you do, and if Walter hadn't happened to peek inside your van, we never would have known. Of course, he knew right away what it was. Walter's been a Knower for nigh on thirty years."

"This little midnight soiree." Caroline indicated the gathering. "Ever done this before?"

"Oh yes! Each time we thought we had a real alien body, or a piece of one, but each time it turned out that we were mistaken." She lowered her voice. "Of course, you know that the real alien bodies are in an underground cryogenic vault at Sandia. We've tried for years to get one of our people in there but without any luck. Their security is very good."

Sandia. Where had he heard that name before? Ross wondered.

"They were picked up after the crash at Roswell," the woman went on. "The Russians are holding two themselves, in a converted chromium mine in the northern Caucasus. It's so sad. They don't know what to do with them, so they keep them frozen and under cover. They're afraid of the Visitors, who simply want to make contact. In order to convince them to do so, we have to provide a suitably strong reason. Offering them the body of one of their own should be sufficient." She looked after her husband, who had lengthened his stride and moved on ahead.

"Personally, I expected them to be slimmer, with larger eyes and heart-shaped skulls. The extra limbs are a surprise, too."

Linking hands, the supplicants began to chant wordlessly as Walter reverently set the alien corpse down on a crude metal altar. It was about four feet high and nicely made. Probably welded in somebody's garage, Ross mused. At least the assembled weren't bowing and scraping, which would have dirtied their nice, clean capes.

As the last flashlight was turned off Walter stepped back from the altar and raised his hands and eyes heavenward. Over the monotonal chanting he launched into a hysterically solemn invocation which reminded Ross Ed of similar paeans to absolutism frequently espoused by uncritical enthusiasts of many stripes, usually in taverns. Being woefully ignorant of the True Realities and pitiably uninformed (not to mention improperly dressed), he and Caroline were kept out of sight at the far end of the line.

In the absence of anything resembling a bullhorn or amplifier of Promethean proportions, Ross wasn't exactly sure how Walter and his buddies expected their hokum to be heard by the heavens. And indeed, Jed's immobile presence notwithstanding, the heavens so far seemed inclined to treat the gathering with monumental, if not cosmic, indifference.

Ross Ed's only concern was that when nothing happened, the frustrated cultists might choose to take out their disappointments on the bearers of false idols, meaning him and Caroline. Not to mention what they might do to Jed. The deep, concealing lake was all too conveniently close. Leaning over, he murmured of his misgivings.

"Can you run?" he finished by asking her. Martha was too busy chanting to pay much attention to them.

"If I have to. But they've been so nice to us. Why would they turn violent now?"

"Because they're nuts, and my daddy always told me you can't talk sense with nuts."

"An observation not in line with current mainstream developments in mass psychology, but to the point," she conceded.

"I hate it when you talk like that."

"Sorry."

The chanting and invoking continued for another hour. When Ross next checked his watch he saw that it was after two in the morning. Time was running out on the Visitors and a few of the Knowers were starting to show signs of wilting. As yet there was no muttering in the ranks, but Ross Ed could see it coming.

Was he never going to get back to a normal daytime schedule?

Caroline interrupted his reverie. "At least they're only sacrificing Jed and not us."

"Don't applaud yet. They're not through. Have you been listening to our friend Walter?"

"I've been trying not to. Interspatial bullshit." She winced and shifted her stance. "Wish I could sit down. The grass looks comfortable. But I don't think they'd consider that a properly reverential position."

"You could ask. It's not like we're going to try anything."

She pursed her lips. "Why, Ross Ed Hager, were you thinking of trying something?"

"I didn't mean that. I just . . ." Recognizing that certain smile, he chose another tack. "All I'm saying is that they're taking this business pretty seriously. It's all nonsense, of course, but it's dangerous to spit in somebody else's holy water."

She shook her head. "You need to chill, Ross Ed. They're nuts, sure, but they don't strike me as homicidal nuts."

"Remember that when they finally decide to call it a night without having accomplished anything."

She made a face, listening. "If I was an alien, the racket they're making would send me warp-factoring in the opposite direction. Even for an amateur choir, this bunch could do with a few music lessons."

"Poor Jed." Ross Ed stared at the altar and its immobile burden. "He can't even put his hands over his ears. Assuming he has ears."

"See how they've cut the grass and reeds down by the water?" She pointed. "That's where the 'Visitors' are supposed to land."

Somewhere on the far side of the lake a frog commenced to croak, its insouciant *burr-upp* a mocking counterpoint to the dreary chant, some of whose perpetrators were beginning to exhibit unmistakable signs of waning enthusiasm. Ross Ed considered joining in but decided not to. Where the unseen amphibian could get away with mocking the ceremony, he could not.

Tilting back his head, he surveyed a truly magnificent night sky. In the clear mountain air thousands of stars were visible, including the denser swath of the Milky Way. While it wasn't Texas, the cool scent of pine and cedar lent a pungency to the atmosphere that was every bit as refreshing as mesquite. As a true Texan, it put him in mind of certain thoughts, certain feelings. He looked back down at the expectant Caroline.

"I could really use a beer."

Pushing out her lower lip, she nodded understandingly. "Sure. Let's get a couple of lawn chairs and we'll set ourselves up here with a cooler and a portable TV. Our 'hosts' would appreciate that, they would."

He found himself checking his watch again. It was coming up on two-thirty. "How long d'you reckon they can keep this up?"

"I don't know, but by the looks of them I'd say more than a few are about ready to pack it in."

"That's what I was thinking. What I don't understand," he continued, "is what they expect from Jed. I mean, even if he was alive, I don't know what they think he could do. But he ain't. He's plain demised."

"Well, according to what you've been telling me, he's done all right looking after you."

"That's just the suit. It reacts to threats." He scrutinized the line of cultists, several of whom were sounding distinctly hoarse. "This is just irritating, not threatening. You touched the suit and nothing happened. Hell, old Walter there picked Jed up and *carried* him, and nothing happened."

"Maybe whatever part of the suit that was handling protection finally gave out," she suggested. "Maybe its batteries, or whatever, finally ran down. Maybe they're as dead as Jed."

Well, maybe not quite.

A soft amber light had begun to suffuse the apex of the altar.

TWELVE

Caroline crowded close to Ross Ed. "Maybe," she whispered, "these people know something we don't."

As they looked on, the yellow-gold glow slowly intensified, until it grew bright enough to obscure rather than illuminate the now hazy outlines of the alien body. A concerted murmur of repressed excitement rose from the rejuvenated cultists, who thus inspired, redoubled their efforts. Their muddled mantra rose higher than the treetops, violating the sleep of innocent woodland creatures struggling to stay secure in their dislocated slumber.

I'll be damned, Ross Ed thought silently, if they haven't activated something.

"See!" Martha's expression reflected her elation. "We who are the Initiates *know*. We've known the truth all along. If given reason enough, the Visitors will come." She was serene in her assurance, confident in her knowledge, and most important at all, still secure in her grip on the Mossburg.

Putting an arm around Caroline, who clung tight without being intimidated, Ross watched in silence as the body of his inhuman dead companion grew in brightness until the light completely obscured his silhouette. Jed was now enveloped in a ball of golden efflorescence that was almost too intense to look upon.

They heard the object before they could see it. Faint at first, the low whine sounded like a dying refrigerator compressor. By the time it had grown to a sirenlike wail, several of the more prosaic cultists had begun to whisper among themselves. Signs of mutiny appeared in the hitherto solid ranks. One man broke for the parking area, only to be gently but firmly restrained by his neighbors.

Then they saw the ship.

Ross Ed knew what it was the instant it came sliding into view above the trees on the far side of the lake. Not because he was an expert on extraterrestrial vessels or avionics design, or even because he'd seen his share of speculative films, but because it quite obviously couldn't be anything else. It wasn't saucer-shaped, nor did it resemble the rockets that launched from Cape Canaveral. As it drew near, wailing insistently, it took on the appearance of a jumble of dark purple cubes, like square grapes. Some joined their neighbors at perfect right angles while others bulged and grew from otherwise flat surfaces. Except for a few orange stripes painted or seared onto several of the larger cubes, the vessel was featureless. Notable for their absence were any glowing lights. A few pinpoints of bright red seemed to dart around the end facing the chanters, like remoras clinging to the lower jaw of a shark.

It was not Ross Ed's admittedly limited idea of a spaceship.

As the cubist collage hovered a hundred feet above the lake, the cultists bellowed their nonsense with inspired vigor, sounding not unlike a big-city train station at rush hour. Coming to the abrupt realization that what they were experiencing was real and that there might be more to membership in the group than periodic participation in a friendly fraternal organization of like-minded wackos, several of the chanters who couldn't take it anymore bolted for their vehicles, frantically shucking off their capes as they ran. Their eyes were very wide. Those who remained filled in the resultant gaps without missing a beat.

A big late-model Seville and a Toyota pickup ground to life, only to have their ignitions crash. Instead of emerging, their terrified owners chose to hunker down inside. Ross Ed heard the insistent *clack* of power door locks engaging. If their vehicles had come equipped with sheets, he reckoned, right about now those inside would be pulling them over their heads.

His own first reaction was to imitate their example, but Martha and her Mossburg were still close, the chipper PTA lady still too alert. Besides, if there was any way to recover him, he didn't want to abandon Jed. He knew Caroline would go along with whatever he chose to do.

The nearer it came, the bigger the cube-ship grew. Larger than a 747, it filled a respectable portion of the night sky. The red lights flitting around the front end reminded him of giant fireflies. They emitted a tinkling sound which slowly became audible above the whine-wail of the ship itself.

The front end extended twenty feet or so over the meadow as the giant craft settled toward the lake, halting just above the water. Like burgeoning blossoms, additional cubes erupted from the fore underside of the spatial apparition. One made contact with the damp soil and stopped.

The surface facing the onlookers irised open to highlight nearby grass and reeds with a pale pink effulgence. Chanting ceased. The forest seemed to be holding its breath. Even the obstreperous frog was cowed.

The wail-whine died. Towering above the tallest pines, the awkward-looking but incredibly impressive craft continued to hover a foot or so above the water.

Ross Ed whispered to the woman snugged close to him. "Be ready."

"Be ready?" She frowned up at him. "Ready for what?"

"I dunno. Just . . . be ready."

"Is that music coming from those little circling red lights?"

"Sounds like it. I suppose it could be music. Or it might be their version of landing sirens. You've seen too many movies, Caroline."

"I know, but there was nothing in any of them like this."

A number of the cultists had produced photographic equipment and were busily shooting away with everything from 35mm disposables to elaborate compact digital camcorders. One optimist cursed the slowness of his cheap Polaroid. The noise of so many devices clicking, advancing, and whirring all at once generated a sound more alien than anything coming from the giant craft.

Caroline raised her voice and her hand simultaneously. "Something's coming out."

Shapes and shadows were distorting the pink glow that poured from the opening. As Walter and one of the other cultists moved forward, Ross Ed saw that they now wore caps surmounted with wire mesh. Little balls rotated within the wire. There were no tiny propellers, but somehow the effect was the same. Mindful of the shotgun's proximity, he was careful not to laugh.

He strained to see clearly. What would Jed's people think

when they saw their comrade's corpse? How would they react, not only to the body but to the decidedly eclectic human welcoming committee? He looked forward to finally learning how Jed used his three legs for locomotion.

Two aliens emerged from the open cube. They looked nothing like Jed. Each was nearly seven feet tall and constructed along far more massive lines than the diminutive alien he'd come to know so well. Assuming their bulk was of terrestrial proportions, each must have weighed in the neighborhood of three or four hundred pounds.

Neither wore helmet or faceplate. Both legs were thick, muscular, and jointed front and back at the knee. Far slimmer arms reached the ground, giving the arrivals an incongruously apelike posture if not appearance. Blocky, rectangular skulls composed a third of the total body length. The two eyes were oval instead of round like Jed's. Wide, down-curving mouths were located directly beneath the ocular orbits. While there was no indication of nostrils, the ears were external and high-set, looping up and over to meet atop the skull. At least, he assumed they were ears. They looked distinctly eary.

In the absence of recognizable hands, each arm split at the end into a dozen flexible digits eight to nine inches in length. Pale lavender shirts and shorts crossed with diagonal black stripes hid the remainder of their anatomies.

Tubes running from large backpacks ended in cuplike cones. At periodic intervals the visitors would place the latter over their mouths and appear to inhale deeply. Or exhale. Given the distance, Ross couldn't tell. Smaller packs clung to the back of each massive leg. When one considered the length of those arms, the arrangement made sense.

Walter and his companion approached slowly but without fear, occasionally pausing to bow or bless with upraised palms. Halting a couple of yards in front of the two aliens, who had observed this overture silently, Walter spread both arms wide and launched into a florid invocation of welcome. What he could hear of it didn't make much sense to Ross Ed. It was impossible to know what the aliens were making of it.

Walter turned occasionally to variously point at the crescent of awed spectators, the sky, the forest, the ground, and not infrequently or immodestly, himself. After several minutes of this the two aliens exchanged a look. If they spoke, their speech was inaudible to human ears, or at least Ross Ed's.

Walter shut up and his companion started in, exhibiting an equal amount of enthusiasm and energy. Again the two aliens exchanged a glance. Then the one nearest the humans drew back his right leg and promptly kicked the more-than-a-little-startled speaker right between his legs. It was impossible to know whether this was due to a detailed knowledge of human physiology or simple chance. In any event, it did not matter to the erstwhile greeter, who with great alacrity reacted to this First Contact between mankind and another intelligent alien species by ceasing his blabbering and crumpling wordlessly to the ground. On the spot Ross Ed made a decision not to apply for the position of ambassador to whatever world these particular aliens happened to call home.

Employing half a dozen digits on its left arm, the second creature removed from a leg pouch a device which most nearly resembled a tapered gallon jug. The narrow end was promptly raised in the direction of the assembled cultists.

The ground in front of them exploded, sending clumps of torn grass and heavy clods of dirt flying. There was hardly any noise. Instantly, all thoughts of chanting departed the minds of the assembled. With shrieks and shouts the line broke and scattered, some running for their cars, others melting into the woods.

Caroline was tugging at his hand. "Ross Ed, come on, we've got to get out of here!"

He hesitated. "I can't." She couldn't budge him. Three women couldn't have budged him. He started forward. "I've got to get Jed."

"Are you insane?" Dirt flew over them as the alien continued to sweep the meadow with the weapon, or portable excavator, or whatever it was.

Meanwhile its companion had picked up Walter and was shaking him violently. Disdaining marital vows in favor of common sense, Martha had abandoned both Mossburg and husband in favor of making a run for it. She was nowhere to be seen.

Kicking and squealing, Walter was lifted into the night air. For his part, at least, it was not necessary to enter into a debate as to whether or not there had been a breakdown in interspecies communications. As he picked his way toward the altar a hunched-over Ross Ed could hear him pleading with his captor.

By this time the second alien had put down its jug gun and picked up the unfortunate greeter he'd booted in the 'nads. Holding the man at arm's length, it began to slap him back and forth across the face, using its dozen or so flexible digits like a handful of tiny whips. As he raced onto the meadow Ross Ed could hear the methodical *slap-slap* of tentacle on skin.

Caroline was shouting after him. "Ross Ed, dammit, if you get yourself killed I'll never speak to you again!"

"Get the van!" he yelled back at her. "I don't think they want to kill anybody. If that was what they had in mind, they'd have done so by now."

"Maybe they're just bad shots!" Seeing that she couldn't dissuade him, she turned and ran toward the Ford.

Ross had to dodge a wave of panicked cultists and, in one instance, actually shove someone out of the way. As he drew nearer he saw that the glow from Jed's suit was beginning to fade. Frequent sideways glances showed that the two aliens hadn't moved from where they'd stopped. The second had finally put down his human, who was presently engaged in trying to evacuate the scene by crawling away slowly at the maximum speed he could muster.

Having been shaken until his eyeballs felt loose inside his head, Walter hung flaccid in the other alien's digits. It was impossible to tell whether he'd been knocked out or had simply fainted. With what sounded like a disgusted belch, the creature tossed the unconscious store owner aside. Reaching into a leg pouch, it extracted another of the jug-shaped devices.

Together, the pair resumed venting their opinion on the surrounding countryside. A pair of sixty-foot pines came crashing down. More inoffensive meadow erupted skyward in comparative silence. The only time Ross Ed winced at the bloodless carnage was when a beautifully restored 1957 Ford Thunderbird became the focus of alien destruction. Taking a direct hit from one of the jugs, it shuddered like a movie critic at an Italian made-for-video film festival before exploding in a shower of fiery metal fragments and expensive restoration parts.

Preoccupied, the aliens ignored Ross as he darted forward, snatched Jed from atop the crude altar, and broke into an end run for the parking area. Cars continued to blow up in front of him.

All were unoccupied, confirming his hypothesis concerning alien intent.

He'd expected the suit to be hot to the touch, or at least tingly, but the intense glow it had generated left no aftereffects. It felt the same as always. As he ran he took a moment to study the alien visage visible through the faceplate.

"I wish you could tell me what that was all about!" Unsurprisingly, Jed chose not to reply.

A compact Chevy went *poomph* as it heaved cheap upholstery moonward. Except for the carnival of exploding vehicles, the parking area was rapidly emptying. Ross Ed wondered at the nature of the aliens' weapons but felt no overriding desire to linger in the vicinity to conduct a detailed analysis.

As the van screeched to a halt next to him, he wrenched open the side door and unceremoniously dumped Jed inside. Following a moment later, he squeezed himself through the opening and yelled, "Go, go!"

"What d'you think I'm trying to do? Thromp the brake?"

Hunched over and moving forward, he was nearly thrown into the dash as she slammed into reverse. After taking a moment to secure Jed, he fought his way into the passenger chair and sat down hard, gripping the foldaway armrests.

"Got him!" he told her triumphantly.

She wasn't impressed. "Sure is a lot of trouble to go through for a *dead* alien." Her voice rose as she abused a Honda. "Get going or get out of the way!" Off to their left another couple of trees came crashing down.

One after another, those vehicles still in operating condition bounced, raced, or flew up the track in the direction of the main dirt road, their frantic drivers handling them as if they were trying for the checkered flag at Indianapolis.

Leaning out the window and looking back, Ross Ed saw puffs of haze rise as owners brought out fire extinguishers to cope with minor incapacitating blazes. The explosions seemed to have ceased. Those cars which weren't burning and hadn't been blown up were filled to overflowing with squawking cultists.

Grabbing at him, Caroline indicated the view out her side. "Look, they're leaving!"

Ross turned just in time to see the two aliens reenter their cube-ship. The pink glow vanished as the strange doorway irised shut and the wail-whine promptly built to a complaint of stentorian proportions. Majestically, the great vessel lifted above the lakeshore.

He was distracted by a knocking on his door. The young couple that was running alongside couldn't have been out of their twenties.

"Please, mister, let us in! Our car's gone, blown up."

"I dunno." He considered the distraught duo.

"Come on, Ross, let them in." Caroline smiled reassuringly. "It won't be any trouble. We can drop them somewhere." She eased off on the accelerator and the van slowed. The exhausted pair quickly climbed in back.

"There it goes." She leaned into the wheel so he could see.

The cube-ship was accelerating. Soon it was a drifting piñata pinned against the stars, then a blocky smudge, and at last it was gone.

"Hey!" The woman, who was Hollywood pretty, lifted her legs off the carpet. "There's the thing that caused all the trouble."

"Oh no." Reaching back, Ross Ed scooped up the alien body and cradled it protectively. "It wasn't Jed's fault."

"So that's what it's called." The husband eyed the corpse speculatively. "Walter told us it had a name." He leaned back, resting on his elbows. His overcape was torn and filthy, with the everyday clothes beneath in not much better shape. The shoes he wore would have cost Ross several days' pay.

"What d'you think went wrong, Sues?"

"I don't know." The woman was on the verge of tears. Ross supposed she was entitled. "Everything was going so well." Turning, she hugged her husband close. "At least now we know for sure that they're out there, Bobby."

"Yeah, and they can *stay* out there." Ross Ed shifted the uncomplaining Jed to the other side of his lap. "What the hell happened?"

"I don't know." The husband was inconsolable. "Maybe the Circle chose the wrong chant. Perhaps the phase of the moon had something to do with it." He gestured at Jed. "Maybe that's not a real alien after all."

"But what about the glow from the presentation pod, Bobby?" his wife objected. "What caused that, if not the alien?"

The young man's face twisted. "Walter and Martha always struck me as pretty slick customers. They could've rigged something up to fake it."

She pulled away from him. "Well, they didn't fake that ship, or those horrible mean creatures who came out of it!"

"That's true." The husband inclined his head back, as if he could see through the roof of the van. "There are aliens out there, all right."

"Uh-huh," agreed Ross Ed, "and we sure learned one thing from them tonight."

Lightly shadowed blue eyes regarded him expectantly. "What's that, mister? That interstellar travel is really possible, or that there are more than one intelligent species out there?"

He scowled at her. "We learned that they don't want to be bothered. I figure that when Jed started up that light he must've also sent out some kind of signal that traveled farther. Maybe it interrupted the other aliens' flight plan, called 'em off course somehow. Or maybe it just ruined their TV reception. Who can say? All I know is that you can't just go around shooting off messages and signals and disrupting communications all over the place and expect folks to react with happy talk and big smiles. I don't know where the hell they came from or how they found this spot and Jed, but I do know that they were mighty damn angry about it."

"Angry, sure, and so they delivered a lesson." The woman was too optimistic to be unrepentant.

"Angry, my ass." Caroline glanced back at their passengers. "Somebody could've been killed! *Everybody* could've been killed."

"Me, I'd say that was a pretty stern warning," Ross contended. "You'd better be sure who you're contacting and how you go about it. Next time they might blow up more than trees and cars. There are some things mankind isn't meant to understand."

Caroline frowned at him. "You really believe that, Ross Ed?"

"Well, no. But it sure makes sense when they say it in all those films that turn up on the *Late Show*."

"I wonder what they were?" Once more the woman curled up close to her husband. "Besides ill-tempered, I mean."

"Let somebody else find out." The young man eyed Ross hopefully. "You'll take us back to Show Low? I'm positive that from there I can wire my parents for airfare home."

"Yeah, sure. Why not?" Ross settled back in the captain's chair. "We'll drop you off in town. It's on our way to Lubbock anyway." He winked at Caroline and then, wondering exactly how the hell it popped into his head, he added, "They were Ceryutians." She gaped wordlessly at him.

"Yes, Ceryutians. I'm certain of it. Fourth planet out from the eighth star in the L'Sariax Sector."

"Is that a fact?" The husband's reply was challenging. "And just how do you happen to know that?"

"Hey, if you'd seen a Ceryutian before you wouldn't have to ask. They're famous for their tempers. It was bad enough to draw them off course, but the fact that it was to a backwater primitive world like Earth made it much worse."

"Why, that makes perfect sense." The wife giggled. "Tell us another one, mister." When Ross Ed didn't reply, she turned solemnly to her mate. "I told you we shouldn't have gotten involved with the Circle, Bobby. We should have listened to the Swami Rajmanpursata. Why, I was near his meditation center in Brentwood just last week and—"

"All *right* already." Her husband dropped his head into his hands. "So the Swami was right. As soon as we get back home we'll discuss the whole business with him and see what he has to say."

"That's my Bobby-guy." It grew very quiet in back.

They were back on the main forest road when Caroline looked over at Ross and inquired, "Ceryutians? Eighth planet of the fourth star?"

"Fourth planet of the eighth star. L'Sariax Sector." He spread his hands helplessly. "Hey, I just call 'em as I see 'em."

"Uh-huh," she replied slowly. "Ross, have you ever stopped to think *how* you see them?"

"Not really. Sometimes stuff like that just sort of comes to me." He grinned infectiously. "Guess I've got a good imagination."

"Sure you do. You've also spent several weeks in close proximity to a real, genuine, dead alien. Ever think the two might be connected?"

"I try not to think about this whole business to much. Hurts my head."

"Hey, the camera!" exclaimed a voice from the back. Glancing rearward, Ross Ed watched as the woman withdrew an exceedingly compact Nikon from her brassiere. She checked one of the windows on top and beamed excitedly. "Twenty shots! I've got twenty shots. Wait till the skeptics at PSYCOP see these!"

"Way to go, Sues." Her hubby beamed.

Ross Ed didn't join in the celebration. Something told him the woman was the proud possessor of twenty clear, sharp-toned pictures of a grayish-blue fog bank. So were all the others who'd escaped with their equipment intact, including the videographers. Hours and hours of tape of dense, impenetrable, unremarkable, and decidedly unalienistic fog. Not all the illumination propagated by aliens dead and alive was as straightforward as streetlights. Several emitted on wavelengths that were more than a little unkind to photographic enterprises.

How he knew that he couldn't have said. It just sort of seemed to make sense.

One conclusion anyone could have made: whatever he was, Jed was not a Ceryutian. Not even a distant cousin. He was no more related to the long-armed stompers than Ross was to the longhorn on his uncle Bucklin's ranch. Probably less so. Having witnessed a demonstration of Ceryutian manners, Ross Ed felt good about that.

It just went to show that if you insisted on phoning home, you damn well better make sure you didn't get a wrong number and inadvertently agitate some perfidity. Evidently there were some badass beings out there.

THIRTEEN

The sun was showing itself through the trees when they finally dropped their passengers off outside the main market in Show Low. As they disembarked, the couple was arguing about whether to make the first call to his parents, her parents, or their swami.

From Show Low, Ross and Caroline continued north on the highway toward Interstate 40. There'd been no sign in town of inquisitive army types, but having been cornered once, Ross didn't want to take any chances by lingering over breakfast. With Caroline in agreement, they whizzed through the local McDonald's and McBreakfasted their McButts out of town as quickly as possible.

When they finally reached the interstate without incident, Caroline broached the idea of sticking to the back roads, just to add some insurance. Impatient as he was to reach the coast, Ross Ed reluctantly conceded the efficacy of her suggestion (though he didn't phrase it quite that way . . . as he readily conceded, she was the smart one).

Passing through Holbrook, they disdained the interstate in favor of State Route 77 north.

"We can swing west through the Navajo-Hopi reservation." With little traffic and a straight road ahead Caroline was able to relax behind the wheel. Outside, the last pines had given way to spacious vistas of ruddy sandstone and distant mountains. "There's nothing up here but tiny towns and local police. We'll take two-eighty-four over to one-sixty and swing down by the

Canyon. That way we can lose ourselves in the tourist traffic and not have to take I-40 until we're well past Flagstaff. If they were going to establish a checkpoint on the interstate, that's where it would be: this side of Flag or the other. Either way we'll bypass it." She looked over at him.

"It's either that or keep heading north."

"There ain't no ocean in Utah."

"I know." Reaching over, she placed her right hand on his left. "Salt Lake City's a long way from San Diego."

Reacting to the van's approach, a cottontail leaped off the road and into a culvert. Red-tailed and Swainson's hawks patrolled the pavement in search of fresh roadkill.

"This country makes west Texas look lush," he observed.

"Pretty, though." Raising her hand, she pointed to her right. "The Painted Desert is off that way somewhere."

As they drove they were confronted by a living history of the American pickup truck, either hurrying in the opposite direction or speeding up to pass them from behind. From time to time isolated homes and house trailers poked satellite dishes above the rugged hills, spying on ESPN, CNN, HBO, and their fellow entertainment acronyms from sites in gullies, washes, and miniature plateaus. Many of the new homes were partnered with a stumpy hogan, their entrances facing the rising sun in the traditional manner.

The deeper they traveled into the reservation, the more isolated they felt. For the first time since he'd fled El Paso, Ross Ed began to feel at ease. This was one place where he didn't expect the army to come looking for him. With luck, the military's neatly dressed, excessively polite representatives would be hunting for him in the vicinity of Tucson, hundreds of miles to the south.

He was anxious to head west again. Continuing in the direction they were going would take them to the ocean, all right: the Arctic Ocean. He didn't much care for cold country.

"Will you relax?" She gave him a friendly punch in the shoulder. "We've lost them. Can't you tell? They don't even know what kind of vehicle you're traveling in, or if you're on a bus, or a plane, much less where you are."

He divided his attention between her and the relentlessly spectacular scenery. "You didn't meet these people. I did. They're not going to give up. If any military base managed to track or record what happened up in the mountains last night, sooner or later connections are going to be made with Jed. Right now they're trying to keep it quiet, but if the story breaks wide, my face will be in every paper and on every evening newscast within an hour."

"And a very nice face it is, too." Her trivializing of the situation was disarming. "You really think anyone's going to take those saucer people seriously?"

"I suppose not."

"Then calm down, Ross Ed. Enjoy the ride." She grinned and nodded toward the back. "Take a lesson from your friend."

Indeed, there was no disputing that of the three occupants of the van, the alien was by far the most relaxed. An unfair comparison, Ross knew, because in Jed's case it was a permanent condition.

An hour later they pulled over so Ross could take the wheel for a while. He flinched when she picked the body up and set him in her lap, arranging the three arms in a kind of tripartite fold. Crossing the three legs was more difficult; left over center, center over right. The result left Jed looking like a spurious fugitive from *Sesame Street*. The intimate, repeated physical contact had no visible effect on her.

"Don't you think you should put him back on the floor? What if somebody seems him?"

"What if they do?" Raising one alien arm, she let it flap loosely at a passing car. "What do they see? A man and a woman cruising along in their van, enjoying the scenery. If they look real close they might see that the woman has a very strange doll or a real ugly baby in her lap. I feel sorry for poor Jed. How'd you like to ride all the way to California lying on the floor? Just drive, Ross Ed. We're not going to stop any traffic up here."

By unspoken mutual agreement they let the radio occupy the conversational space for a while. Eventually Ross turned back to her. "You know, Caroline, you've been awfully good to me throughout this whole crazy business."

"Don't think I don't know it. I told you why."

"I'm not looking for any kind of long-term relationship."

"Ever had one?"

He told her about his own two marriages.

"Naw," she decided when he'd finished the distressing recitation, "you never have. You can be married to someone without having a real relationship. I know; I've done both."

"Just the same, don't get any ideas. I like you, Caroline, and I don't want to see you get hurt."

"What, *moi,* get ideas?" Her eyes widened as she placed her fingers over her cleavage. "Why, Ross Ed, I would never think of such a thing. I'm just helping you make it to California."

"Just so long as we understand each other."

"Right." The van banged as they hit a pothole. "You know, you give me a funny look every time I touch Jed." Holding the alien by the shoulders, she turned it toward her. "Doesn't he?" Shaking it back and forth, she managed to induce in the head and neck a passable imitation of a nod.

Ross clenched his teeth. "Don't *do* that."

"Why not?" She was honestly bemused. "What's the problem?"

He couldn't forget the night in Lordsburg: the gun and the addlepated bullets. "When people . . . touch . . . Jed, they sometimes see things. Other times, stuff happens."

"Is that all? Look what happened last night."

"No, not like that. I mean, *personal* things. Your surroundings don't act natural. Pictures form in the mind."

"Are you talking about telekinesis and telepathy? That's fantasy. Besides, he's dead." Her eyes were inches from the alien's own. They didn't stare back.

"I don't reckon it has anything to do with Jed. Obviously, he can't do anything. But the suit's another matter."

"Well, I've picked him up, turned him around, bounced him in my lap, played with his limbs, tossed him in back, and I haven't felt or seen a single thing out of the ordinary."

"I guess he, or his suit, likes you. Or at least doesn't see you as a threat. Or maybe, just maybe, there's no rhyme or reason to it. Maybe sometimes the suit reacts to contact and sometimes it doesn't." He told her about Lordsburg.

"That's quite a story." Her attitude had become less flippant and she regarded the alien in her lap with new respect. "Maybe you're right. Maybe it only reacts to certain people. Something in their brain waves, or their movements. Personally, I think both Jed and his suit are comfortable with us. Can't you see how he's enjoying the scenery? He's hardly taken his eyes off the road." Her cheeks dimpled.

He studied the console. "I'd feel better if we had some coolant along. It's getting hot outside."

She was shaking her head slowly. "There's a whole gallon in the back right storage bin. You really don't know how to relax, do you?"

"Yeah, I do," he objected. "Guess I might as well, since you seem to have thought of everything."

"Coolant, jumper cables, spare fan belt, tools. Dead alien. Your name it, I've got it on board." She jiggled Jed on her lap. "Oversized testosterone unit who doesn't know when he's well off. Oh yeah, I always travel properly equipped."

He could only grunt by way of response, unselfconsciously confirming her evaluation.

As they slowed to pass through small towns with unpronounceable names, no one looked at them twice. Thousands of tourists made the look-see loop through the reservations and the locals were accustomed to strange vehicles and their even stranger occupants.

When the road finally turned west toward the great unbroken gash in the earth known as the Grand Canyon, Ross Ed's energy level rose perceptibly. Eventually they'd swing south to pick up Interstate 40. If they weren't confronted there he suspected that it would be clear sailing all the way to California.

Exhausted from the previous long, late night, they stopped early at a motel in Tuba City. Ross checked in while Caroline struggled to squeeze the van into one of the few shady parking spots.

The clerk who checked them in spared him the embarrassment of trying to decide what sort of accommodations to request by announcing regretfully that every room in the motel came equipped with twin beds. The formalities concluded, they found their room, cranked the air-conditioning to the max, and did what little unpacking was required.

The clerk, whose name was John Qaannasqatszi, watched through one of the heavily tinted office windows as the newcomers moved in. They seemed to have no luggage at all. Not that it was any of his business. The switchboard buzzed as other guests demanded his services.

It was while switching in an incoming call for number thirty-four that he noticed the big Texan transferring something large and bulky from the van to the room. It had arms and legs and a funny-shaped head.

It couldn't be, he told himself. A brief glimpse wasn't enough to support anything but rank speculation. Still, he found it impossible to banish the image from his thoughts. Pondering, analyzing, he debated how best to proceed based on what he'd observed.

He'd seen it before. Not, as Ross Ed might have suspected, posed on the front of a tabloid beneath screaming absurdities, not on television or in a theater, but in multiple, reproducible form. It wasn't one of his tribe's more common kachinas, of which there were hundreds, but there was no mistaking the long, central snout and the planting stick held between the legs.

Kachina reproductions could be bought all over the Southwest. Most were churned out by factory-style operations, others were the product of long-established family businesses, and a few were the result of long hours and painstaking effort by truly talented artisans. The best were hand-carved and painted. Sizes varied from thumbnail collectibles to life-size dancers in full ceremonial regalia weighing over a hundred pounds. True collectors usually started with someone like Watermelon Man or Hoop Dancer, advancing gradually to the less common and more esoteric members of the Hopi pantheon.

What were these two blatantly non-Hopi doing with such a large, well-made, and rare representative of the sacred line? Where had they acquired it? He'd have to take a closer look.

On through the rest of the afternoon and into evening he checked travelers in and a very few out. As he did so he kept an eye on the big blue van.

It was around eight when the couple finally left the room, climbed into the van, and headed out. Dinnertime, he told himself. Clerking at the motel was a dead-end job, which he had occupied for several years now. Could it be that luck was about to break his way for a change?

He waited another ten minutes to make sure they'd gone for something to eat and hadn't just run up to the drugstore or convenience station. With the desk quiet and curiosity consuming his insides, he took one of the passkeys, put out the "Back in Fifteen Minutes" sign, and headed with deliberate casualness down the concrete walkway. Number ten yielded willingly to his key and he stepped inside, making sure to shut the door firmly behind him. There wasn't much to see: the usual female accessories neatly laid out next to the sink, towels still in place, the shower-tub unused. Even the remote for the TV hadn't been disturbed. But both beds had been slept in.

The room was no suite and it didn't take long to find the kachina. It was sitting up in the otherwise empty closet, facing out. Articulated kachinas were rare, but someone had obviously lavished a great deal of care on this one.

Turning on the light over the sink, he knelt for a better look. The figure seemed to have three eyes instead of two. He tried to remember if that fit the description for this particular kachina, but he wasn't sure. When he was young he'd paid very little attention to the instructor.

The oddly keeled skull was different, too, as was the helmet-like headpiece. Certainly an extremely rare type of kachina and without a doubt very valuable. How could he gain possession? He could offer to buy it, of course, if only he'd had some money.

This was no cottonwood carving but a sculpture fashioned with careful deliberation from bits and pieces of multiple materials. Behind the protective glass the flesh of the face was extremely lifelike. Many traditional markings were missing, but perhaps whoever had made this hadn't been given enough time to add the appropriate paint and final decorations. These were omissions easily remedied.

Decidedly odd, but still a wonderful and valuable piece, he concluded. One he had to have. Numerous possible explanations for the kachina's disappearance sprang to mind. The simplest thing to do was declare it stolen and file a police report. Meanwhile he could take a couple of days off, drive over to Gallup, and quietly price his new acquisition. He knew the right dealers for such a surreptitious enterprise, having previously pulled similar scams with more pedestrian items such as the camera equipment and jewelry which guests unaccountably left unguarded in their rooms while they went out to eat, shop, or sightsee.

How much was it worth? Did the absent guests have any idea of its true value? He would follow his usual routine of donning cleaning gloves and trashing the room to make it look like a real burglary. On the end table between the beds was a cheap watch he could pocket to spice the scenario. Altogether the operation would take less than five minutes. Nor was he motivated by any racial concerns. He was equally happy to steal from the occasional Indians who stayed at the motel while visiting friends or relatives.

Verily it was the strangest kachina. He didn't know them all, having been shamefully inattentive during the relevant lectures in school, or when his grandfather had been talking. But what else could it be? It was no child's toy, and in any case no children were traveling with the couple. The transparent faceplate, he'd decided, was an add-on to protect the delicate carving of the face, and could doubtless be removed for display purposes.

Certainly it was no more grotesque than several of the clown kachinas. Not that its appearance mattered, because he had no intention of taking it home and putting it up on a shelf in his ratty apartment. His intent was to turn it into ready cash as quickly as possible. If he was lucky he might get several hundred bucks for it.

Rising, he walked over to the window and eased the curtain aside. Still no sign of the van. He'd shove the sculpture into a motel laundry bag and stow it in one of several favorite and secure hiding places until the police finished their check of the premises. After the guests checked out, he'd head on over to Gallup. They'd file their report and leave. No one hung around Tuba City any longer than necessary. The attractions in the vicinity were impressive, but limited.

He considered how best to pick it up, wondering how securely the movable limbs were fastened to the body. Reaching under the right arm, he slipped his own hand around the back and lifted . . . pausing only long enough to adjust the breechcloth which barely covered his nether regions.

It was all he wore, except for the band around his head which kept his long hair out of his eyes. The deerskin strip was soaked through with his sweat.

Rising from his crouch, he drew his hand back from the kachina and turned to survey his surroundings. The high plateau of Third Mesa shimmered in the evening light. It had been a good day. They had suffered no serious casualties in beating off the attack by the strange white men who had come seeking to steal their possessions and souls. The crazy white man claimed to have been looking for something called the Seven Cities of Cibola and had stumbled into the land of the Hopi instead.

A voice hailed him and he moved to the edge of the plateau. Peering over the sheer drop, he saw that the hunting party which had gone out after the battle was now returning, making its patient way up the steps cut into the bare rock. One of the men had an antelope slung over his shoulders. His family and relatives would eat well tonight. Everyone would eat well. There were many reasons to celebrate. In addition to beating off the white men, the rains had been good this year. It was time to give thanks to the gods.

With the setting sun at his back he turned and headed for the village. Not even stupid white people who threw thunder and lightning from their fingers would dare to try scaling the towering cliffs of the mesa in the dark.

The women had the fires going already and their cheery glow pointed the way. His children would be waiting with wide eyes and baited breath to hear the details of the battle, while his wife would have begun preparation of the evening meal.

As he jogged along the trail which skirted the edge of the cliffs, he found his thoughts drifting back to the strange white people who had foolishly believed they could drive the Hopi from the sacred mesa. They had come searching for cities paved with gold and pots overflowing with jewels. Instead of talking like civilized people, they had indiscriminately thrown thunder and lightning. But the gods, and the great cliffs, had protected the village, and the invaders had been driven away with arrows and spears and stones. He didn't think they'd return.

In his mind's eye he saw them still, a thin line of bedraggled men and animals wending their way southward. They would find no gold in that land; nothing but relentless heat and searing death. Their hunger for the yellow metal he could not understand, not when there was game and water and corn and squash to be had in plenty.

His children came running as soon as they espied his lithe form loping up the trail. He gathered them to him as he approached their apartment. Shumaqui, his beautiful wife, waited to greet him in the approved fashion. He was a lucky man, he knew. Not a leader of men or a shaman, but one whose modest abilities as a hunter and warrior were respected by others.

Lifting his youngest under her arms, he placed the laughing, giggling girl on his shoulders, where for a few moments she could lord it over her brothers. Tomorrow he would take them on the horse and ride into the trading post. He very much wanted to show his family the new machine the trader Williamson had just acquired.

It was called an aut'o'mobile, and it made as much noise as ten thousand chickens. Personally, he didn't see the sense of it. In order to make it work, you had to feed it a special expensive drink. It smelled bad and didn't always go where you wanted it to. Unlike a horse, it couldn't find its own way home if you were lost, and its droppings were useless for fertilizing the fields. But it certainly was interesting to look at as it bounced and rattled its way down the road toward Flagstaff.

He thought that Williamson, who was a good and kindly man, might take the children for a ride around the trading post. If he would do that, John would give him one of the small silver-and-turquoise rings the white man seemed to prize so highly.

The big Packard ran smoothly as it carried him south toward the city. From there he would travel by bus to the training camp that had been set up near Phoenix. Many of his friends and relatives were already assembling in Flag, waiting for him and a few other laggards to join them before departing. Navajo, Hopi, Havasupai, Hualapai, Zuni: members of all the northern tribes had rushed to enlist.

Some of the elders had been less than enthusiastic. It was the white man's war, they insisted. Why should they volunteer to fight people they did not know who lived in places they had never seen who had never caused them any harm?

Because despite the frequent prejudice they had to endure, the young men had replied, this was their land, even if they no longer had as much voice in its affairs and its running as had once belonged to them. Besides, were they not warriors, descendants of a long line of warriors? This was a chance to show what they could do, and certainly more exciting than anything else that had come alone in some time.

So along with innumerable cousins and uncles and friends, John, too, had signed up, not waiting to be drafted, wondering as the driver guided the Packard down the bumpy dirt road whether Germany in the summertime would be as hot as Arizona.

Except that he hadn't wanted to fight, didn't see what they were doing there, in the damnable stinking fetid hell of Southeast Asia. Only the support and similar skepticism of the friends he'd made helped him survive toward the end of his hitch. 'Nam was an equal-opportunity brutalizer that took no account of race, color, or creed.

How had he come to be in the steaming, hostile jungle, where branches became the muzzles of AK-47s and roots triggered mines that at the very least would blow your leg off? Far, far way, Gloria and the kids lingered over every letter he managed to send, sweating out his return.

One of the lucky ones, he was nearing the end of his tour of duty with his body intact and no visible scars. There were plenty of the latter, but they were all tucked away upstairs, where only he could see them. He knew they would never heal, but with luck he would be able to keep them from everyone but his patient and understanding wife.

When the children gathered outside the trailer he told them as much as he dared, much as his ancestors had told stories of their hunts and their wars. He was of a long line of warriors rich in tales of great triumphs and narrow escapes, of desperate survival and elaborate mythological wonders. All these tales he told, while the children regarded him raptly out of awestruck eyes as their parents sat nearby. Occasionally an elder would nod approvingly and John would continue, encouraged.

"They went this way." He drew lines in the air with his hands. "And so we went that way. Into the swamp, holding our rifles over our heads, ignoring the leeches and the mosquitoes and the snakes. We did it to get behind them, and we did. They never knew what hit them." His right arm completed a wide, sweeping movement.

To press firmly against the back of the kachina.

He did not blink but simply stared at those three vacant, lightly reflective, inhuman eyes. Very glad he was that they were not open, not gazing back at him, because if they were he was afraid they might see all the way to his soul, a component of himself of which he was not at the moment particularly proud. They were more eloquent in death than most eyes were in life.

What death, what life? It was a carving, a sculpture. Wood and clay and artist's sculpy, nothing more. It had never been alive.

Drawing his arm back, he felt a terrible cramping pain in his legs and sat down hard, his head bumping off the wall. The painful tingling grew worse as the muscles straightened and he struggled to massage it away. How had he come to be kneeling in the same position for such a long time?

A quick glance revealed that the room was still empty. It was exactly as he'd entered it . . . forty minutes ago, according to his watch. He'd been kneeling and staring at the kachina for forty minutes. No wonder his thighs and calves were killing him.

In that forty minutes he had beheld a personal history spanning several hundreds of years. He'd seen himself as his father, who'd fought in Vietnam. His grandfather, who had battled the Nazis in World War II. More ancient of days still he'd seen, all the way back to the time of Coronado and the first Spaniards to visit the country of the people.

Temporarily unable to walk, he rolled over onto hands and knees and crawled away from the closet, away from the vacant, accusing eyes that saw farther into him than he had ever dared look himself. When he reached the door he used the handle to pull himself to his feet.

Forty minutes. The big Texan and his lady might be back any minute, could be driving into the parking lot even now. He had to get out.

Feeling was returning to his nether regions. When he felt he could walk without falling, he turned the knob and stumbled out of the room. He had enough presence of mind to make sure the door latched behind him.

As he staggered toward the office he considered what had happened to him. Not for a moment did he doubt the reality of it. A kachina of real power, he knew. Through it he had relived his entire recent family history, viewed ancestors who were noble and brave. There hadn't been a thief among them. All had married and raised fine, respected children.

Except him. Except John Qaannasqatszi. He had neither wife nor children, had nothing except a crummy job in a cheap motel. All those good people who had gone before, who had survived war and drought and disease, only to see the culmination of all their striving in . . . him? His very existence did shame to their memories.

That was going to change, he vowed. Now, and forever. The forty minutes he'd spent crouching and holding the kachina had given him back something he was sure he'd lost forever.

His honor.

So it was that Mrs. Patricia Thurwood of Grass Valley, California, was mildly stunned to receive in the mail several weeks later an unsolicited postal money order for two hundred and twenty-six dollars. There was nothing to indicate who had sent it or why, except that it matched an amount she had lost in the course of a vacation a number of years before.

Not long thereafter Mrs. Bea Davis of Des Moines, Iowa, found among the usual bills and letters a gift certificate made out in her name which entitled her to visit any branch of a nationwide jewelry-store chain and pick out a new ladies' watch worth not more than five hundred dollars.

Others letters and missives, certificates and greetings, went out in their own good time. None bore return signatures, but all had Flagstaff postmarks.

None of this was known, either at the time or later, to Ross Ed and Caroline, who returned to their room full of satisfying if not gourmet-quality food. A different clerk checked them out in the morning, a perfectly normal state of motel affairs which caused them not even a millisecond of afterthought. It had been a blissfully uneventful night, which was exactly what they had sought.

FOURTEEN

Ross Ed looked forward to seeing the Grand Canyon. It wasn't a component of his original itinerary, but seeing as how they were going to have to skirt the rim, it seemed foolish not to make the slight detour and have a look.

Heading south through Cameron, they soon found themselves among crowds of sightseers from all over the world. The park itself was crowded, but less so than it would have been on a holiday or weekend. The summer trams weren't in operation yet and it was possible to take your own car along the south-rim drive.

Inquiring at the main office, they discovered that a couple of cabins had just become available at Phantom Ranch, at the bottom of the canyon.

"What do you think?" Ross Ed asked her as the reservations clerk helped someone else with a backcountry hiking permit.

"I think it'd be wonderful, Ross. We've lost the army, so why not have some fun? Hiking could be a nice change from driving, and if I get tired, you can always carry me."

Deliberately, he let his eyes travel the length of her. "I dunno about that, Caroline. You're a pretty big girl."

She executed a little pirouette. "Me? Why, I'm light as feather. A six-foot feather, from a giant roc."

"Rocks don't have feathers," he countered. She patiently explained.

Since they would be spending the night at the ranch, they had no need to carry anything but some snack bars and sufficient water, which they purchased at the busy park convenience store. It was chilly when they started out the next morning, but they were informed it would be thirty degrees warmer at the bottom of the canyon.

Among her possessions Caroline found a daypack which, with straps extended to the maximum, just did fit on Ross Ed's back. Into this they packed the food bars, water, and one uncomplaining dead alien. A light blanket covered Jed's head and upper torso, which stuck out of the top of the pack. No way, Ross declared, was he going to leave his deceased friend overnight in the van in a public parking lot, where inquisitive saucer nuts and army types might find him. The little alien wasn't heavy, and in any case, Ross was used to toting far heavier loads.

"Besides, the ranger said not to leave any valuables in your car." As they started down the Bright Angel trail he shortened his stride so that Caroline could keep pace without straining.

"Well, if they break into my van they won't find anything valuable." Artfully, she stepped around one of the ubiquitous piles of mule dung which decorated the trail. "I know what valuables *are,* of course. I can comprehend them theoretically."

"Tell me what you'd consider a theoretical valuable, Caroline."

As they descended they discussed dreams of what she'd never had. Once they passed Indian Gardens they left the last of the day hikers behind and the overwhelming solitude of the Canyon closed in around them. Thus far they'd encountered elderly couples in astonishing physical condition, Scandinavian students clad in shorts despite the crisp air, folks burdened with rods and gear who gave new meaning to the phrase *dedicated fisherman* (or indubitable idiot), and a few solo travelers who shared an interchangeable faraway look. None of them in the slightest resembled incognito police or U.S. Army Intelligence operatives.

Maybe we really have lost them, Ross concluded. He put a little spring in his step . . . but not too much, lest it send him careening over the occasional thousand-foot drop.

The canyon was more magnificent than either of them had anticipated, one of those rare tourist attractions that actually lived up to all its hype. Their rustic cabin at Phantom Ranch was charming and private. The only problem was with the beds, which did not fit Ross Ed. Nor could he put the double bunks end to end to achieve his usual solution. For that matter, they barely fit Caroline. But both of them coped.

Leaving Jed propped on an upper bunk with his empty eyes facing a profusion of canyon wildflowers, they walked in leisurely fashion to the main dining hall. There they enjoyed a hearty western-style steak dinner in the company of fellow travelers who were too tired to spare the jumbo-sized couple more than a sideways glance or two.

"How about a walk?" Caroline suggested when they were through. The ranch staff was preparing for the second dinner sitting and the inner canyon, with the sun having already slid out of sight behind rocks as old as the earth, was rapidly cooling down.

"Good idea. Just what I need after an all-day hike: a walk. But we have to go back to cabin and get Jed."

She gave him a wry smile. "What for? It's our cabin. Afraid of Jed-snatchers coming in by army helicopter?"

"Actually, I'm more concerned about a maid or somebody showing up to check the linens, or something." His tone asked for understanding. "I just feel better when I know where he is."

She shrugged. "As long as you're the one hauling him around and not me."

Once again the alien body was stuffed into the day pack and the light blanket tucked over its head and upper body. Reassured, Ross Ed caught up with Caroline on the lower portion of the trail. Together they started down to the river, passing backpackers and tenters. Some had arrived late and were still setting up their gear.

Below the last camping area they turned west along the river trail, the ruddy Colorado roaring on their left, the rumble of its waters echoing off the walls of the inner canyon. They saw no one else. Everyone was preparing, eating, or digesting their supper. People did occasionally hike the canyon trails at night, but for the moment they had the little spur which paralleled the river path all to themselves.

Eventually it dead-ended at a lovely vantage point a few yards above the high-water line. A couple of crude wooden benches knocked together by the Park Service offered surcease to tired travelers. They were more level than the surrounding rocks, but not much softer.

As the first stars began to emerge they sat down side by side. To Ross Ed it seemed perfectly appropriate (indeed, required in such a place) that he put his arm around Caroline. She edged a little closer, and not just for warmth.

"I've been thinking," she began.

"So have we," asserted a voice.

They turned sharply. Squinting in the gathering darkness, Ross thought he recognized the couple from the dinner seating. Elderly and nondescript in appearance, they had been at the next communal bench over from his. The woman was plump and pink-cheeked, the man taller and well built. They appeared to be in their early or mid-sixties. Typical travelers, utterly unremarkable in any way.

Neither carried a pack. Both were clad in jeans, hiking boots, and flannel shirts. The only difference in attire lay in their respective accessories: her gun was much smaller than his. Alongside the magnum her husband hefted, her little snub-nosed .25 seemed barely adequate.

Caroline slumped. "I guess army intelligence comes in all sizes and shapes."

"Army intelligence? Did you hear that, luv?" The woman smiled at her companion. "She thinks we're army intelligence." The man chuckled.

Ross Ed experienced a sinking feeling of the sort usually reserved for those times when wildcatters' accountants failed to show up come payday.

"If you're not army intelligence, then who are you working for? The FBI? CIA?"

The man ran the fingers of his free hand through his shock of snowy-white hair. The muzzle of the magnum remained absolutely steady. "No, no, my boy. We're strictly freelancers. We work for ourselves. I'm Gennady Larkspur, and this is my wife, Miriam."

"I do alterations," the kindly little old lady explained helpfully. "You know; take in sewing? Gennady pretty much runs the dry-cleaning business by himself." She gave her husband an admiring look. "Gen's very efficient."

Caroline's gaze narrowed. "You sure you're not from some super-secret government agency that we've never heard of?"

"No, we're from Indiana." The woman looked past them. "It really is pretty out here. Quiet, too."

"What is it you want from us?" Afraid he knew the answer all too well, Ross Ed still felt compelled to go through the formality of asking the question.

"I think you know that, young man." The grandmotherly figure gestured with the .25. "We want your alien corpse, of course."

"Oh, great," muttered Caroline. "More saucer people."

Gennady Larkspur corrected her firmly. "You misunderstand us. We're not part of or party to any organization or cult. We are strictly independent."

"We've been tracking you ever since you left El Paso," the woman explained, "waiting for just the right opportunity to relieve you of your luggage. Those army people you're so concerned about kept getting in the way. Clumsy, aren't they? Everyone's always in such a rush these days, unwilling to wait until the right moment. Like those unfortunate young men you encountered in Lordsburg, and then those poor, deluded saucer folk."

"Localized meteorite storms, telekinesis or something like it we have no name for, and then the appearance of real, if cantankerous aliens." The man's eyes sparkled. "Yes, indeedy, we're very impressed with your deceased little companion.

"We thought our chance had come when you left it behind while you went out to dinner in Tuba City." The woman frowned. "But for some reason, as soon as you left, the night clerk went into your room and didn't come back out until you returned. Gen and I could have gone in anyway, but our success all these years has been predicated on protecting our anonymity and avoiding confrontation whenever possible. So we restrained our impatience and continued to shadow you after you checked out the next morning."

"Actually, it was fun following you down here." He looked pleased. "Gen and I are great walkers."

"I thought we got the last cabin," Ross Ed remarked.

"You did, my boy, but I'm sure you won't mind letting Miriam and I use it." The man's voice was flat and matter-of-fact.

The color had drained from Caroline's face. "You . . . you're not going to *shoot* us?"

"Why, luv, what do you think these guns are for?" The woman was apologetic. "Besides, fit though we are, I'm not sure Gen and I could keep pace with you two going *up*hill."

Ross Ed started to fumble with the pack straps. "You don't need to do that. We'll give you the alien."

"Yes, you will, sonny." Again she gestured with the pistol. "'Jed,' I believe you call it."

"I don't understand. How do you know all this?"

"We have our sources." Gennady Larkspur smiled thinly. "In Washington. Even in the army. Whenever anything crops up that they think we might find interesting, they let us know. As to how we've managed to keep in touch with you, well, when appropriately modified, cellular phones are wonderful tools for listening in on other folks' conversations."

"We have to get out once in a while," his wife added. "As you can imagine, dry cleaning and sewing doesn't make for a very exciting life."

"It doesn't pay as well, either." Her husband shifted the heavy pistol to his other hand. "You'd think the IRS or someone would ask how we can afford the town house in Zurich and the condo in the Caymans, but they never have. I guess they're too busy prosecuting the poor schnook down the street for his last hundred-dollar underpayment.

"Gen is very efficient," his wife reminded them.

"But why do you have to kill us?" Looking from one elderly face to the other, Caroline found intelligence and wisdom, but no sympathy.

"Oh, all right, I suppose we don't." Gennady Larkspur might as well have been discussing a stained shirt collar with a customer. "Though if you don't do exactly as we say, I promise you that we'll do exactly that. Both Miriam and I have killed before."

In the increasing darkness they no longer looked so kindly, Ross Ed decided. Ghostly now; ghoulish even, their Midwestern twang fraught with menace.

"If you shoot us, the campers at the ranch will hear your guns," Caroline pointed out.

"I don't think so, luv. Why do you think Gen and I waited until you hiked over here? That was very thoughtful of you." She glanced to her left. "Just listen to that river! Isn't that magnificent? And loud. You could fire a rocket-propelled grenade down here and no one would hear it back at the ranch." She gestured with her free hand, indicating that it was time for Ross to hand over his inanimate companion.

Caroline nudged him. "Go on, Ross Ed. There's nothing we can do. I'm sorry."

Resigned, he resumed fumbling with the pack. "If you're going to shoot somebody, shoot me. Leave her alone. She has nothing to do with this."

"Why, she has everything to do with this, luv." Miriam Larkspur pursed her lips. "Like you, she's seen both our faces. But we're inclined to be compassionate, Gen and I. What are you going to do? Go to the police and tell them that a pair of senior citizens from Indiana held you up at gunpoint and stole your dead alien? I don't think so."

Ross Ed had the pack off his shoulders and was removing the thin blanket. Gennady Larkspur leaned forward slightly, tense with expectation.

"Doesn't look like much, does it, to have caused so much consternation in Washington and Langley?"

"Kind of scrawny," his wife agreed.

Removing Jed from the backpack, Ross Ed worked to gently unravel the tangle of limbs.

"Quit stalling." Holstering her pistol, Miriam Larkspur extended both arms. As Ross Ed took a step forward, her husband gestured warningly with the magnum.

"Just throw it. I don't want those big arms of yours anywhere near the missus."

"Okay, just take it easy." Ross prepared to pitch Jed to the waiting woman.

A burst of light flared from the suit and he promptly did something he'd never done to Jed before: he dropped him.

"Ow . . . dammit!" Tucking both hands under his arms, he tried to squeeze away the pain.

Gennady Larkspur raised the pistol warningly. "No tricks, now!"

"Tricks, hell!" Shaking both hands, Ross blew repeatedly on his fingers. "Look how red they are. The damn thing burned me! Lousy, stinking, ugly alien mummy!"

"You're not being funny, son." Larkspur gestured with the magnum. "Pick it up and toss it to my wife."

"But I'm telling you, it *burned* me! You think I'm making it up?" He held up his right hand, which was indeed a flushed, angry red. Blisters were already visible, forming beneath the skin of his palm and fingertips.

The dry cleaner hesitated, then glanced at his wife. "Keep them covered, Miriam." She nodded and once again drew down on their prisoners with her tiny but highly efficient pistol.

Removing his flannel shirt, Larkspur wrapped it around his right hand and approached the alien body. He was bending and reaching for it when the laser-bright bolt of light exploded from the suit. The bolt was dark on one side and bright on the other, as if half the beam had been painted black. It was unlike anything Ross Ed had ever seen before. He had no explanation for it, but needn't have felt inadequate. No dozen physicists on the planet could have explained it, either.

It temporarily blinded the Larkspurs. A second, much more powerful bolt lanced from the suit to the river. This was accompanied by a voice speaking in English. Reverberant and profound, it vibrated the air.

"Behold! This I do for my people!"

Where the beam struck the water, the river curled backward in a vast reverse wave, as if it had suddenly slammed up against a great and invisible dam. The result was a clear path across suddenly exposed riverbed. A few flopping fish and marooned soda cans floated in isolated eddies.

"Go now!" thundered the voice. "Sinai awaits. Ye of evil intent, be warned! Do not attempt to follow my people!"

Gennady Larkspur had fallen to his knees and was rubbing at his light-shocked eyes. "Forgive us! We didn't know. We—"

"For heaven's sake, Gennady, get up!" Equally dazzled, his wife was tugging futilely at his arms.

"Come on!" Picking up the alien body and shoving it into a dumbfounded Ross Ed's arms, Caroline urged him toward the dry cross section of river bottom.

"But . . . but it can't be. Didn't you hear? It's . . ."

She shoved him hard with both hands, nearly knocking him off his feet. As long as he was stumbling, he decided he might as well stumble with her.

"Just move your big Texas butt!"

Together they clambered over boulders and driftwood until they reached the waterline. The backward-arching wave towered above them, an ominous, rumbling shape looming over their left shoulders as they started across.

Somewhat less than overawed, Miriam Larkspur had abandoned her mumbling husband to his shocked recriminations.

Taking aim with both hands, she fired at the fleeing couple. But while she was an excellent shot, the combination of increasing darkness, distance, and the impossible wave caused her to miss badly. The Texan and the woman ducked their heads and kept running.

"Woe unto those who would disobey My Word!" the voice pealed.

She turned back to her husband and smacked him hard across the face. "Dammit, Gennady! You stupid old man, get up!"

"But, Miriam, don't you hear it? Don't you hear the Voice?"

"They're getting away!" She pointed toward the river. "Where they've gone we can follow. This time I'll put a bullet in each of them."

"Don't you remember the story?" At her continual urging he rose, but shakily. "When the Red Sea was parted and—"

"Red Sea, schmedsea!" she interrupted him. "Don't you recognize that voice?" She slapped him again. "Get a hold of yourself, Gennady."

"The voice?" Dazed, he looked down at her. "It has to be the voice of—"

"It's Charlton Heston, you idiot! I don't know how the alien got a recording of it. Must have picked it off a television station showing his old movies, but I'd recognize it anywhere."

"Those who pursue are lost!" the voice declaimed unctuously.

"See? Limited vocabulary. You think a deity would speak today in a Hollywood variant of Old Testament rhythms? It'd be more direct. It's the alien suit that's doing it. *The suit!*" She reached up to smack him again but this time he forstalled her.

"Yes." Realization struck home, uncomfortably. His expression hardened. Gennady Larkspur didn't like being made a fool of, not by his fellowman nor by an alien corpse. "Yes, of course." Drawing the magnum, he followed his wife toward the river.

"Hurry! We can't let them get too far ahead of us." She picked her way nimbly over and through the rocks.

Upon reaching the waterline, he paused to look up at the mighty reversing wave. "I don't know, Miriam. Are you sure about this? Maybe it would be better to go back and pick them up somewhere else."

"Are you crazy?" She'd already started across. "If we lose them here and they switch vehicles, we might never catch up to them again. Or the army might nab them first. I'm going." Her voice was cold as ice. "All I need is one clean shot."

Reluctantly, he followed her out onto the damp sand, warily eyeing the massive wall of dark water off to their left. There were times when he felt that despite the boredom and the comparative poverty they should have stuck to the dry-cleaning business.

But that would have meant spending their entire lives in Indiana. The thought gave him strength.

Making use of the residual light from Jed's suit, Ross Ed and Caroline picked and scrambled their way across the river bottom. Once, Caroline tripped and nearly fell over an enormous stranded catfish, but managed to recover to stumble on.

"I wonder if Moses had a dead alien to help him." Ross kept glancing to his left, at the boiling, dancing wall of water. What would happen if he stuck his hand into the aqueous anomaly? He decided this was no time to find out. They needed to keep moving. Powered by Jed's suit, the incredible hydrological diversion certainly couldn't hold forever. Besides, the water was ice-cold.

Looking back over a shoulder, he thought he heard another shot. With the entire pent-up force of the Colorado hollering in his ear, it was impossible to tell for sure. In any event, nothing nasty whizzed past him.

They were near enough now to the south shore to see the outlines of the rocky bank. "You think they're following us?"

Caroline looked back. "I don't know. I can't see anything behind us. They'd have to be pretty stupid. Or avaricious."

"What?"

"Greedy."

He nodded to himself. "Then they're following us. I wouldn't put anything past those two. And I don't think they'll be so polite if they catch up to us again. What's that?"

A thunderous, reverberating *boom* was rolling up behind them.

"The wave!" she yelled. "It's collapsing behind us!"

"Come on, move it!" A glance revealed that the glow from the dead alien's suit was beginning to fade. The force that had been holding back the water was starting to fail. Frankly, Ross Ed was surprised it had held this long. The suit had shown itself capable of many minor miracles, but even advanced alien technology had to have its limits.

Running hard and looking back, he could both see and hear the water crashing down behind them as the river reclaimed its course. Had anyone else witnessed the incredible phenomenon? He doubted it. People didn't hike the river at night and the occurrence had taken place well downstream from the nearest campsite and the two pedestrian bridges which spanned the gorge. As for the noise, well, the rapids-rich Colorado was always noisy.

With the angry, surging water lapping at their feet, they reached the far bank and began to climb. Caroline got her feet wet, but otherwise they were safe and dry above the waterline. They'd made it.

On the opposite bank, a soaked and shivering Gennady and Miriam Lurkspur sprawled out on the flattest boulder they could find. They were in danger of being swept downstream when Gennady, clinging to his sputtering mate, had managed to reach out and grab a piece of driftwood projecting from the bank. Their weapons were now so much scrap tumbling and banging along the river bottom.

The loss didn't concern them. In Arizona you could buy a .44 magnum in a drugstore. But the uncontrollable shivering was another matter.

Arms wrapped around her chest and shaking violently, Miriam Larkspur rose to her feet and chattered at her husband. "Come on, Gennady. We've got to get some coffee or hot lemonade in us or we're going to catch our death out here."

"I kn-kn-know." He was trembling with the cold as he squinted at the restored river. It was hard to focus and he could see no sign of their quarry. "It was the alien, of course. How do you suppose it did that little trick?"

"I don't know." His wife wrung river water from her long hair. "But the more I learn about it, the more I want it. We could retire, Gennady. We could name our own price. No more spying for the French, no more industrial espionage in the dairy business."

"I know."

"We'll find them again." She sneezed explosively. "You'll see." She started up the rocks toward the viewpoint and the trail. "Let's gid bag to their cabin and pile the blangids on before we catch pneumonia."

Of course, they already had, but it would take a day for the symptoms to fully manifest themselves. It would put an end to their hunt in a manner neither they nor their quarry could have imagined, and without any further intervention on the part of dead aliens.

FIFTEEN

On the far side of the river, Ross Ed and Caroline were becoming chilled. Though they had escaped the water, nighttime temperatures at the bottom of the canyon were still cool this time of year.

Ross Ed pointed upstream. "Let's head for the bridges. Once we find the trail we can follow it up to the South Rim. I don't think those two will be in any mood to follow us, even if they're in any kind of shape to do so."

But the intervening rocks and boulders proved difficult to surmount, nor was Jed's suit inclined to shed more light on the matter.

"This is crazy. If we don't wait until morning someone's going to break a leg stumbling around in the dark." Caroline began a search of the surrounding slope. "Find a soft rock and we'll try and get some sleep until it's light."

"I don't know if we should hang around here, Caroline." Her companion was trying to see across the river. "After a night's rest, those two might decide it's worth trying to find us again."

"I'm sorry, Ross, but I'm not going floundering through these rocks in the dark. Don't worry. We'll lose them tomorrow."

They found a piece of high, sandy beach sheltered from the occasional breeze by surrounding boulders. The ground still held some of the heat it had soaked up during the day. Leaning Jed and his backpack up against a suitable rock, they stretched out side by side on the sand.

Tentatively, he took her hand. Together they regarded the stars.

"I wonder which one he's from?"

She slid closer. "Pick one, Ross Ed. Pick one and wish on it."

"I'm not real good at that sort of thing, Caroline. You do it."

"I have to think." Beneath the starlight, she smiled. "Don't want to waste my wish. You know, lying here, in this place, by using a little imagination it's possible to believe that we're the only two people left in the world." Turning on her side, she looked deeply into his eyes. It was one of those perfect moments that can never be planned, cannot be predicted. Even Jed looked on favorably, or at least offered no disapproving comment. Their mouths eased inexorably toward one another.

"Hey, look there!"

Parting almost as violently as they'd hoped to come together, they rolled in opposite directions. Sand and desire went flying.

The voice belonged neither to Gennady Larkspur nor his murderous mate, but to a young man with a radiant and intrusive flashlight. A very young man, they saw as he came nearer. Ross Ed guessed him to be in his mid-teens. And he had company.

In response to his cry, half a dozen additional lights emerged from the rocks like so many crazed deep-sea denizens. Together, they provided enough light to illuminate the bodies as well as the faces of their owners. The former were for the most part lanky, the latter openly curious.

"What are you guys doing down here?" inquired the eldest, without a hint of sarcasm. He *might* be twenty, Ross Ed decided.

Rising slowly, he brushed sand from his clothes. "I might ask you the same question." A more demure Caroline turned her back on the nocturnal newcomers while she cleaned herself off.

"We're from Phoenix." The eldest of the young men straightened proudly. "Troop Four-Oh-Four, on a special merit-badge camp-out. Snicks thought he saw movement down here."

The boy who'd first shone a light on them nodded. "Thought it might be a couple of mating cougars, but it was only you guys." He sniffed pointedly. "Shoulda known from the absence of any musk."

Ross Ed had the grace to blush, though in the subdued light it passed unnoticed.

"We decided to investigate." The neatly dressed youths crowded closer. "You two all right?" They ranged in age from the leader's twenty to a gawky stripling of fifteen.

"We're fine, thanks." Caroline spoke a little more sharply than she'd intended. Musk, indeed. She made shooing motions. "You can go on now. We'll be all right. Go back to the ranch."

"We're not staying at the ranch, ma'am." One of the other boys gestured across the river. "We've been camping on the north side, up by the falls. We're on our way out, now."

Ross Ed frowned. "In the middle of the night?"

The leader grinned proudly. "Special merit badge. A night hike's part of our training. That's why all the flashlights."

"It's great!" insisted one of the younger boys. "There's nobody else out and we've got the trail all to ourselves. Also, you get to see some neat animals that don't come out during the day."

"Like cougars, maybe." The boy who'd discovered Ross Ed and Caroline was still disappointed.

They exchanged a look. "Would we be imposing," asked Caroline sweetly, "if we came with you? Just sort of tagged along? We wouldn't hinder your training."

The leader stood a little taller; almost as tall as Caroline. "You're more than welcome, ma'am. You sure you're okay?"

A shout came from one of the other boys. "Hey, what's that?" The beam from his light was focused squarely on Ross Ed's backpack and its extraterrestrial contents.

Ross Ed replied without thinking. "That's my ventriloquist's dummy."

The leader's face twisted uncertainly. "You take it hiking with you?"

"You a ventriloquist, mister?" wondered one of the other boys. "Proper!"

"Yeah, show us, mister!"

Besieged by requests, Ross Ed could do naught but comply. Besides, it allowed him to ignore the troop leader's more pointed queries.

"Go ahead, Vegas Ed." A smirking Caroline urged him on. "Show 'em your stuff." Once again she trained her penetrating smile on the still-hesitant leader. "I don't suppose you boys would have anything to eat or drink?"

Instantly she was offered half-full canteens, fruit juice, power bars, tropical chocolate, cookies, marshmallow munchies, trail mix, and in one instance, piroshki.

The leader was dubious. "We can't hang around here, guys. We're supposed to be back on the rim by daybreak."

"Don't sweat it, Mark." The second oldest had hopped down

off the rocks and was bending over to stare at Jed. "Dude, it looks like some kind of *alien.*"

Ross Ed artfully stepped between them. "Don't touch him. He's . . . the work is pretty delicate and he needs some repairs." He hefted the pack in both arms.

"What's his name?" someone asked as they started up. Caroline regretfully bade the beautiful pocket beach good-bye.

"Jed." Reaching down, Ross took one of the three limp arms and made waving motions with it. "Say hi, Jed." His alien voice complied.

"Cool!" Two of the youngest boys flanked the Texan on either side, gazing wide-eyed at his burden. They seemed to flow over the rocks, not missing a step.

Ten feet above the beach they struck a narrow trail. In their exhaustive attempts to hike upstream, Ross Ed and Caroline had missed it completely in the dark.

"There are lots of side trails down here," the leader explained. "Most of them just parallel the river for a short distance. You have to know where you're going."

Caroline put a hand on his shoulder. "I'm sure *you* know the best and fastest way up." By this time their guide had completely forgotten about the incongruousness of finding a ventriloquist's dummy at the bottom of the Grand Canyon, and his inquiry was not repeated.

"Come on, mister, make him talk some more." The kids were persistent.

Ross Ed sighed. He hadn't done this since El Paso, but the routine came back to him effortlessly.

"All right," the alien shape seemed to say, "what would you scouts like to know?"

One of the boys frowned. "His lips didn't move. Hey, mister, how come his lips don't move when you make him 'talk'?"

"That's easy," Ross replied. "If you'll look closely, you'll see that he hasn't got any lips." He tilted Jed toward the questioner.

"See, kid?" "Jed" said. "Ain't got no lips. No external flesh flaps framing the oral cavity. Can't blow no trumpet. Call it an evolutionary retreat from peripheral prehensibility." The boy's face screwed up in an expression of uncertainty.

"He means he doesn't need them," Caroline explained to the boy. She continued to whisper periodically to the troop leader, keeping his thoughts focused on getting them out of the canyon as fast as possible and away from what she and her companion might have been doing down there. She succeeded in this to the extent that he virtually ignored his younger companions.

With their powerful lights to illuminate the way, they soon intersected the main Bright Angel trail. Climbing became simpler, though no less exhausting. Ross Ed was glad they were doing it at night instead of during the heat of the day. That was something else their pursuers from Indiana would have to cope with, provided they were in any kind of shape to follow. Occasional glances back down the trail revealed no sign of movement. Neither the Larkspurs nor anyone else was tracking the troop.

The boys were full of questions, laughing and chuckling delightedly as they analyzed the "alien's" responses.

"Cool voice you've given him, mister." The teen loped along effortlessly just in front of Ross Ed. "Can he do anything else?"

"Sorry," Ross told him. "I've got to save my breath. Throwing your voice can be pretty tiring when you're trying to hike out of a place like this."

"Aw, come on." The youth brightened. "Make him talk alien."

"He is talking," Ross Ed replied.

"No, you're having him talk English. Make him talk *alien*. You know: his own language."

"I don't know . . ." Ross Ed considered, then shrugged. Why not give it a try? The results would be amusing, and he could hardly be criticized for inaccuracy.

What emanated from his mouth when he next parted his lips was a spew of sound so extraordinary that even those no longer interested in the dummy looked around sharply, Caroline included. No one was more surprised than Ross Ed himself.

"Wow." The teen regarded Ross with new respect. "What did that mean?"

Ross was wondering much the same thing himself. How had he produced such sounds? "Hey, how should I know? It's alien, after all."

"What kind of alien?" another boy asked.

Ross looked down at him. "If you don't know where the Grand Succession of the Three Worlds lies, and the depth of its phenomenological development, it wouldn't mean anything to you. So don't sweat it, kid." He blinked. "You can see it from here, though."

"Oh yeah? Where?"

Tilting back his head, Ross Ed selected seemingly at random a cluster of bright stars that decorated the canvas of night almost directly overhead. "Right there. See? Just to the left of the Banded Nebula."

Another boy sounded uncertain. "I don't see any nebula."

"Well, it's there. Use your imagination. A very nice place it is, too. The Grand Procession is actually one world orbited by a moon the size of your Earth and another moon which circles the first."

"A moon circling a moon circling a world. That's pretty neat." One of the older boys came closer. "If there are oceans on the worlds, how does having two moons affect the tides?"

Ross Ed found himself explaining without knowing quite what he was saying, but it seemed to satisfy his youthful and scientifically inclined interrogator. Other questions followed, including one about faster-than-light travel. His answer set several of the scouts to arguing among themselves, allowing him to give his throat a rest.

Questions helped pass the time as they surmounted the Devil's Corkscrew, passed Indian Gardens with its sleeping campers, and started in on the final miles. Throughout, the trail behind them remained clear. He was beginning to feel hopeful that they'd really lost their tormentors.

"What's he made out of, mister?" That was a question that hadn't come up yet.

"Oh, you know," Ross replied disingenuously. "The usual stuff. Wood, plastic, paint, glass."

The boy looked dubious. "Doesn't look like plastic to me." Before Ross Ed could intercept him, he'd reached up and touched the alien faceplate.

An intense, fuzzy blue glow immediately sprang from the faceplate, spreading out in waves from the center. It washed across the boy's fingers until it enveloped his entire hand, stopping at the wrist. With a yelp of surprise, the kid drew back his arm. The glow continued to cling to his fingers like a live thing.

Holding his wrist with his other hand, he stared at the gently pulsating azure while his companions crowded close.

"Hey, check it out!"

"Is it hot?"

"Does it hurt?"

The boy held his luminous palm up to his face. "No, it doesn't hurt. It's kinda cool-like. Like my dad's aftershave." Bringing the glow nearer, he sniffed. "It *smells* like my dad's aftershave."

One of the other youths turned to Ross Ed, his attention focused on the alien body. "Can I?"

Ross shrugged. The first boy was suffering no ill effects. Anything for a break from their constant questioning. "Sure, why not?"

The second youth touched the faceplate. Streaks of dark blue lightning instantly swarmed his fingers and palm. Drawing back his hand, he eyed the blueness wonderingly.

"Awesome!"

Swinging his arm in a wide arc, he created a fiery blue pinwheel. Excepting their leader, the rest of the troop crowded their tall guest, each clamoring for his dose of azure.

Shortly thereafter, luminous blue hands helped flashlights show the way up Bright Angel Canyon.

"What makes it do that, mister?" one of the boys finally thought to ask.

Ross replied with a stream of what sounded to him like perfect gobbledygook but which appeared to satisfy the older boys. They in turn attempted to explain it to their younger comrades. It was full of references to things like segregated ionized gas fields and pocket auroras, none of which made any sense to Ross Ed.

One of the scouts discovered that by flinging his hand sharply skyward he could send miniature bolts of blue lightning flying from his fingertips. The consequences were inevitable. Devoid of the necessary equipment for a water-balloon fight, the boys eagerly entered into a vigorous and noisy light fight, tossing harmless blue streaks at one another accompanied by much laughter and good-natured juvenile cursing. More than a little taken with Caroline's company, their leader did not intervene.

Within half an hour the glow began to fade from the boys' hands. Touching Jed's faceplate failed to recharge their dimming fingers. No one complained, choosing to flick their last bits of azure fire at rocks and plants instead of each other.

"Batteries are running down." That was an explanation even Ross could understand. Much to his relief, they didn't question him further.

They staggered out onto the Rim just as the sun began to show itself on the eastern horizon. The few hardy tourists who braved the hour to view the sunrise ignored the weary troop of youngsters and their two adult companions.

If nothing else, Ross reflected, hauling a dead alien around the country sure played havoc with orderly sleep habits.

They bade farewell to the helpful scouts, who marched spiritedly into the Bright Angel Lodge in search of the adults who would drive them home. Caroline gave thanks and bade farewell to their leader with a kiss that instantly ruined him for the college girls he usually dated. Ross Ed admired him for not staggering off the walkway as he led his charges into the building.

Caroline's van waited where they had parked it, undisturbed and as far as they could tell, free of surveillance. Nevertheless, they approached with caution, half expecting men in sunglasses and coats to rush them from half a dozen different directions. All they encountered was a sleepy family of five and a couple of white-tailed does looking for an early-morning handout.

Unlocking the driver's side door, Caroline boosted herself into the seat. The van was unoccupied. Taking the seat opposite, Ross Ed removed Jed from the backpack and settled the lumpy body onto his lap. There was no reason to do so, of course, but in a perverse way he felt that the little alien was entitled to a view.

"Hey," he told Caroline in response to the look she gave him, "he spent all that time bouncing around on my back and didn't make a single complaint. I can't just dump him on the floor."

"Oh, to be sure." The engine turned over smoothly and she let it warm a moment in the cool morning air. "That's all right, Ross Ed. I like my men a little crazy." She patted him fondly on the shoulder, then did the same to the alien corpus. "My aliens, too."

He tensed slightly, but once again Jed failed to respond to her touch. There was no rhyme or reason to the alien suit's reactions and he knew he ought to stop worrying about it. Some people it affected, others it ignored. Predicting how it was going to react was something that was clearly beyond him.

They kept a look out as Caroline pulled out of the lot. As near as they could tell, no one was following them. Leaving the park, she accelerated down the long, dull straightaway that in an hour or so would link up with Interstate 40.

Morning was clear and calm. Caroline suggested that instead of turning west on the interstate and heading immediately for

California, they go through Flagstaff and down into Oak Creek Canyon.

"I've always wanted to see Sedona," she explained. "While I was living in Safford people kept telling me how beautiful it is."

"Never heard of it." Ross Ed shifted the alien body on his lap.

"We have to turn south sooner or later anyway if we're going to San Diego."

He shrugged. "It's your van, Caroline."

Her expression turned somber. "I know, but they're your troubles, Ross Ed. I wouldn't make any decisions without your okay."

He smiled appreciatively. "Let's do it."

Oak Creek Canyon was a south-running green-veined slash in the surface of Mother Earth. The small river at the bottom was lined with giant sycamores, oaks, and all manner of lush vegetation that belied the alpine landscape which covered the spectacular surrounding buttes. When the canyon finally opened out into a vast spray of carmine, russet, and vermilion cliffs and pinnacles, the sight was truly breathtaking.

A small restaurant calling itself Shugrue's Hillside served up a fabulous view and the best food they'd had in days. The location also let them keep a simultaneous eye on the van and the single highway running through town. There was no sign of any pursuit; no solemn-visaged military types in mufti, no wide-eyed saucer fruitcakes, no homicidal grandparents from the heartland. For the first time in a week he felt comparatively safe.

Although they knew it would behoove them not to linger in any one place for too long, they let the waiter convince them that they simply must drive up to the local airport. Scraped out of a flat-topped mountain, it afforded the most sublime view in town.

After Caroline finished her second fresh raspberry mousse in a summer basket made of chocolate meringue, they made the short drive. Following the waiter's directions, they parked in the airport motel lot and started along the trail which led to the designated overlook, Ross Ed once again not trusting Jed to the locked van and packing him on his back. The rock beneath their feet was the color of powdered rust.

Though it was a brief hike, they were still surprised to find half a dozen visitants of varying age and gender seated on bare rock in a neat semicircle facing the sweeping panorama of mountains and town. Clad in low-cut fringed buckskin, beads, sandals, and a headband straight out of the sixties, the young woman in her late twenties who had been sitting cross-legged facing the semicircle rose to greet them.

"Sweet blessings attend you." Instead of shaking Ross Ed's hand, she bowed slightly. "I am Sharona."

"Uh, nice to meet you. I'm Ross Ed, this here is Caroline."

Sharona turned and gestured with her right hand. "Please, won't you join the circle? We were just on the verge of invoking."

A dubious Caroline noted that the five figures who formed the semicircle were now holding hands. "Just a second. What kind of 'circle' is this?"

The woman smiled beatifically, an expression which seemed permanently affixed to her face. "Why, it is the circle of contemplation of the Great Mysterium, of course." She made an effort to conceal her condescension, but not much of one.

"Sure it is," Ross Ed acknowledged.

"It may be that as strangers you do not know that Sedona is one of the seven great power centers of the planet Earth. There are many vortexes here. Meditating atop one can improve one's health, state of mind, and financial prospects, as well as providing insight into the Great Mysterium. On such a journey it is useful to have a guide. I am such a guide," she concluded, without becoming (or any other sort of) modesty.

Twitching as if he'd just spotted a rattler coiled beneath the bush in front of him, Ross Ed started to back away. It was an instinctive reaction (not to mention the pertinent one), but a curious Caroline restrained him.

"Hold on now, Ross Ed. It's a dynamite view, and a little contemplation of the Great Mysterium certainly won't hurt you."

"I dunno about that." He'd always been leery of people who joined hands in semicircles. But she was right about the view. Besides, what harm could it do? They could enjoy the scenery while studiously ignoring the contemplating.

Putting her palms together in front of her, Sharona blessed their presence while Ross Ed took the occasion to meditate briefly on the surging cleavage her pose revealed. Maybe it was no Great Mysterium, but it was sure worth a moment's contemplation.

Additional blessings were shared among the assembled as the guide resumed her yoga stance opposite. Resting her palms on her knees, she closed her eyes and began chanting. Now more than ever, Ross Ed's natural instinct was to get up and run.

Caroline, however, was holding his left hand along with the right of the man next to her as she and Ross extended the semicircle. He leaned over and whispered.

"What the hell am I supposed to do?"

"Breathe deeply." Eyes shut tight, Sharona proceeded to demonstrate most impressively. "Close your eyes. *Feel* the forces rising from within Mother Earth. Let them flow *into* you, *through* you. Be suffused with the energy so that you may leave here a better person than when you came!"

Ross whispered again to Caroline, who had her eyes shut. "I've got this corn on my big left toe. Think this'll get rid of that?"

"Hush!" She squeezed his hand. "You're not giving this a fair try."

Several responses sprang immediately to mind, all of which he sensibly repressed. "How about you? Feel any energy rising?"

"If you can't participate, just look at the view," she hissed at him.

"Can I do that? I'm supposed to have my eyes shut."

"So cheat a little. You're not entering into the spirit of the occasion anyway."

"Is that the force of the vortex, or your fingernails I'm feeling?" he asked. She didn't reply.

They sat like that for some time, until Ross Ed had had about all the meditation, contemplation, energy vortex force, and view he could stand. At last Sharona broke the silence, her eyes still shut.

"Speak to us, O voices of Gaia! Speak to our innermost longings. Show us the True Path to the Inner Light."

"Okay," said a disembodied voice.

Several of the seated blinked. It was to their credit (or something else) that the others kept their eyes closed. One man started to rise, but those flanking him gripped his hands tightly and held him in place.

Unable to resist the opportunity, Ross Ed was throwing his voice again, making it sound as if it originated from Jed. He wasn't sure how he came up with some of the things he said, but as usual it all seemed to fit together appropriately.

A well-dressed woman in her early sixties spoke up from the

far side of the semicircle. "O Voices of the Earth, tell me: will I be young and beautiful in my next reincarnation? I, who am the many-times distant great-granddaughter of Neraiep of Mu."

Ross Ed heard his Jed voice replying. "You're not the many-times distant great-granddaughter of Neraiep of Mu. You're the many-times distant great-granddaughter of Edwinna, daughter of Wentworth, a farmer in the Cotswolds. She wasn't particularly comely either, but it doesn't matter, since there's no such thing as reincarnation. So you'd better enjoy this life while you can, because when you're dead, woman, you're dead. You can't even come back as a puppy."

Mercilessly skewered by this response, the outraged matron opened her eyes to stare murderously at Ross. She was about to offer a rebuttal when the attractive woman in her thirties who was seated in the middle of the semicircle interrupted.

"Speak to me, O Voices! I am a miserable trader of stocks and bonds. Will the market steady and rise over the next six months?"

Eyes still closed, Sharona commented disapprovingly. "That is not a query worthy of the Great Light. Here we decry crass materialism. Here we—"

The Jed voice overrode her protestations. "It doesn't matter, because unless you move your ass right quick, Hendricks is going to find out about the six hundred thousand you've siphoned off the Baxter and Rozensweig accounts. Unless you can find a way to restore the missing funds, the only Great Light you're going to be seeing in six months will be the kind that's filtered through metal bars."

Dropping her hands and opening her eyes, the stunned stockbroker gawked at Ross. He, however, had his eyes shut and was to all outward appearances meditating ferociously. The smile on his face was a decent approximation of the guide's.

"How did . . . ?" The woman scrambled to her feet, nearly falling in the process. "Excuse me, I have to make a phone call." Thanks to her two-hundred-dollar walking shoes, she was out of sight in minutes, racing toward the airport motel.

Sharona sighed reluctantly. "Close the circle. The path must not be broken." Complying with her directions, the remaining supplicants edged close enough to reform the chain of hands. "Please. No more inquiries unless they are worthy of the Forces and the True Spirit of the vortex."

No one said anything for several minutes, until a portly gentleman could no longer restrain herself.

"Tell me, O Voices, of my daughter. She died last year, aged eleven. Cancer." His voice, Ross Ed thought, was remarkably even and controlled. "Why do such things have to happen? Will she ever come back to me? Will I meet her again in the Afterlife?"

"The Afterlife," an uneasy Ross Ed heard himself replying in alienated tones, "is a question of such profound uncertainty that no positive reply can be given. But if your offspring lived her brief life as truly as she could, and was given honest love in return, then that is sufficient to justify any existence and ensure that the memory of it will be forever enshrined. In such circumstances, the highly debatable nature of the physics of an Afterlife pale to irrelevancy."

While the bereaved father sobbed silently to himself Sharona found she could not longer remain aloof. "Tell me, O Voices, how may I best learn the True Way? How may I let the full force of the Mysterium into my being so that I may better guide others who seek the Path? Let the full energy field of the vortex flow through me!" She stiffened slightly.

Ross's alien voice replied without hesitation. "There is no Mysterium, no True Way, no Path, and no vortex. You're squatting on a pile of Kaibab sandstone that contains nothing more enlightening than a few simple invertebrate fossils. There's no inner light, no energy in crystals, no power in triangle reinforcement or any of the other pseudo-superstitious baloney you're dreaming about. If you really want to improve yourself and help others, then dump this ludicrous psychobabble, get a few good books, and rejoin the natural universe. Profound cogitation doesn't work real well if the body's on fast forward and the brain's always in pause."

Her composure more than a little shattered, guide Sharona dropped her hands and opened her eyes. "Of all the nervy, sarcastic, insulting . . . !"

"The truth is often insulting," Ross Ed responded via Jed.

She climbed to her feet and dusted off her buckskins. "Come, people. After opening our hearts and circle to these newcomers, it is evident they have not the necessary will to clear their minds for new ways of perceiving."

"Not at all," declared the disembodied alien voice. "Self-delusion is a common method of 'perception' among the less advanced species. It offers a comforting refuge from thought. Like any advanced being, I simply choose not to make use of it. Incidentally, if you would but take the time to examine them, you would find that the rules by which the cosmos actually does operate are far more sublime and enlightening than the pablum you propound as a substitute. Chanting is no substitute for calculus, crystals no surrogate for cosmology.

"Of course, they're harder to comprehend, but that's the beauty of it. You get out of cerebration what you put into it. And settle down. You're leaking bad karma all over the place."

The agitated members of the circle stomped off in the wake of their guide, following her toward the parking lot. Only the man whose daughter had died remained behind. He looked long and hard at the alien body and at Ross Ed before shaking the latter's hand, solemnly and firmly. Then he, too, departed.

When they were out of earshot Caroline turned from the magnificent panorama to her tall companion. "Well, you certainly livened up that little get-together. How did you know some of those things?"

"I just make 'em up as I go along, like I told you before."

She was eyeing him intently. "Pretty specific invention, if you ask me. How'd you know that stockbroker was an embezzler?"

"Aren't they all?"

"You named accounts and an amount."

He looked away. "I'm not sure she heard the details, Caroline. The accusation was enough. It was a lucky guess."

"Yeah, sure. If you've seen enough red rocks, let's go."

SIXTEEN

They recognized the woman standing athwart the trail as one of the two members of the semicircle who had not asked a question. Early forties, stocky but attractive, she wore her auburn hair cut short and fashionable. Caroline saw her makeup as sparse and expensive. Signs of a recent, expertly executed face-lift were barely discernible. She didn't strike them as the vortex-sitting type.

"Aren't you leaving with the other true believers?" Caroline inquired. "Or did you lose your way?"

"I'm no true believer. At least, not in this blarney." Her voice was strong, her words clipped and forceful. She extended her hand to Caroline first, making an instant friend of Ross Ed's companion.

"Name's Teal, LaFerenella Teal. Friends call me Tealeaf." She turned to shake hands with Ross, her grip as firm as her speech. "I'm just sort of taking a break here, a mini-vacation. Got a friend who owns a house down on the creek. I thought it would be a kick to see what one of these vortex circle sessions was like. Now I'm glad I did." She nodded at the figure riding loosely in Ross Ed's backpack. "You make that dummy yourself?"

"I reckon you could say that I'm responsible for him."

Nodding, the woman raced on. If she'd been speaking Castilian, the breathless pace would have seemed perfectly normal. "That's one of the best ventriloquist acts I've ever seen. And your answers . . . well, let's just say that I'm impressed, and I don't impress easily. What's your name?"

"Ross Ed Hager. This is Caroline." He jerked his head slightly to indicate his smaller companion. "This is Jed. He's dead."

"Jed the Dead. I like that, I like it a lot. Do you have professional representation, Ross Ed?"

His brows drew together. "Representation?"

Caroline stepped in. "What are you, some kind of theatrical agent or something?"

"Actually, I'm a producer."

"And what, exactly, is it that you produce?"

The woman grinned. "Anything I can, sister." Her gaze switched back to the slightly bemused Texan. "I take it from your confusion over my query that you do *not* have representation. In that event, I would like to take you on."

"I thought you said you weren't an agent." Caroline was watching the woman carefully.

"It's kind of a gray area. 'Ross Ed and the Dead Alien.' Oh yes, I like that. Edgar Bergen and Charlie McCarthy it ain't, but then this is the nineties, not the thirties. I got a question for you, big fella."

Ross Ed waited. The woman's thoughts seemed to move as rapidly as her speech.

"Can you sing?"

"Passably, I guess. I sure never tried to—"

"Rock?"

He was apologetic. "I kind of prefer country-western."

She waved it off. "Doesn't matter, doesn't matter. That can be fixed. It's the ventriloquism that's a natural. How long you been doing this act?"

"Not very long," he confessed.

"Well, you could never tell it by me. I think you're absolutely fabulous, sweetie. But what are we standing out here in the sun for?" Pivoting, she started back toward the parking lot, assuming they would follow. As that was their destination anyway, they did so.

"I'm telling you," she rambled on, "you've got a great future ahead of you, Ross Ed. You and Jed there." She chuckled knowingly.

"I don't know that I know what you're talking about, ma'am. I don't know that I'm interested in the kind of 'real future' you have in mind."

"Call me Tealeaf, please. You've done this act before?"

He thought of El Paso. "A few times, but I'm not sure I want to take it on television."

"Who said anything about television? First we've got to get you up on a stage, get you some proper backup people." She made a face. "Need to do something about those clothes, too. I want you to sing through your dummy. An alien dummy. I'm telling you, Ross Ed, it'll be a sensation!"

"But I don't think I'm that good a singer," he protested.

"Since when did singing ability have anything to do with the success of a contemporary band? It's the gimmick that's critical, Ross Ed. The hook, the difference, the next outrage. A singing dead alien: it can't miss. That otherworldly voice you do is perfect for CD. How d'you manipulate your throat like that?"

"I guess it's a talent," he replied, not knowing what else to say.

"A natural! I knew it the first time I heard it."

Abruptly, he stopped. "Look, you're being very nice about all this, but I think you should know that I'm no performer. I'm just an oilfield roughneck. The business with Jed, well, that's just kind of a hobby. I'm not sure I want to do it in front of a big audience."

She gaped at him. "Not do it? Are you crazy? You can't just squash a natural ability like that. It's not fair to all the no-talent performers who make it. Once in a while you have to give them something to aspire to."

How does one say no to this woman? he found himself wondering. He suspected that not many people did.

"Okay, but you should know that army intelligence is after us."

Turning away, she waved disarmingly. "Don't tell me, don't tell. I don't care who's after you, I'll take care of it. I have friends who can fix anything. The important thing is to place a unique talent like yours before the public so that they can make their own decision. Understand?"

"I think—"

"Good!" They were almost to the parking lot. The members of the circle, having missed out on the True Path, had climbed into their cars instead and taken the one which intersected Highway 69 a couple of miles down the hill. "Now tell me: when was the last time you had to worry about these people who are after you?"

Ross glanced at Caroline. "It's been a while."

"Doesn't matter, doesn't matter. You'll give me the details and I'll handle it. Imagine trying to suppress a natural talent like yours! Nobody has that right; not the police or anyone." Her gaze narrowed slightly. "You haven't killed anybody, have you?"

Ross Ed remembered Lordsburg. He hadn't laid a finger on anyone. The suit had done it all. "Nope."

"Then you have nothing to worry about. Not that I couldn't have fixed things anyway, but this makes it a little easier." Putting her left arm through Ross Ed's right and her right arm around Caroline's waist, she urged them forward. "So tell me: how did you get to Sedona?"

Caroline pointed. "That's my van."

"That van." Tealeaf managed to make it sound vaguely loathsome, like something you'd spray under the refrigerator for. "Okay, all right. We'll drive it down to my friend's house. He has plenty of garage space. Nobody'll find it there."

"I don't think you understand." Ross Ed gently disengaged his arm. "The people who are after me are real smart, and real persistent."

She stared up at him. "I've been twenty-six years in the Business, bubalah. I'm telling you that there's nothing I can't handle. You know the O.J. trial?" She leaned over and whispered even though there was no one around for a hundred yards to overhear. "I represent half the legal counsel. Both sides. Half of 'em. Book rights, movies, you name it." She patted him on the arm. "You just leave everything to me. We're gonna go back to L.A. and I'll set up some meetings."

"But we wanted to go to San Diego," Caroline protested.

"What are you, zoo freaks? Sea World converts? Hey, no problem. I'll let you use one of my cars, you can go anywhere you want. But we can't hang around here. When an opportunity presents itself you've got to pounce on it with both feet, pin it down, and hang on."

Caroline pursed her lips thoughtfully. "Sounds like you're getting ready to kill something."

Tealeaf shrugged. "Business metaphor. Listen, we'll fly back in my plane and—"

"Your plane?" For the first time Ross Ed was more impressed than wary. Where he came from, only oilmen and big ranchers had their own planes.

"Sure. What d'you think, I drove myself here in a Geo or

something? The desert's hot, that's why it's a desert. Once we get home you can stay at my place, there's plenty of room." She reminisced briefly. "I don't *think* Tomo's still staying there. No, I kicked him out last month. You guys can have his room. Or one of the others if you prefer, I don't care. You want to see San Diego, we'll see that you get to San Diego. You want to see the ocean, you can do that from my house. I'm in Malibu."

Caroline expressed fresh interest. "I've heard a lot about Malibu. Is there anything left of it?"

"Fire, flood, mud slide, earthquake, riot: it doesn't matter. It's like a perennial: comes back every year. Malibu's not a place anyway, it's a state of mind."

"You can't sleep in a state of mind," Ross Ed insisted.

"In Malibu you can. Anyway, don't worry, my house is still standing. It's right on the beach. Nice and private, big eucalyptus trees, you'll be real comfortable there. You want to drive your van and meet me there?" She waited for an answer.

Ross Ed looked at Caroline. "What d'you think?"

She took a deep breath. "If anything's going to throw them off your trail, garaging the van and flying the next six hundred miles in a private plane ought to do it."

"I expect you're right." He was still reluctant. "I don't know about this, ma'am . . . Tealeaf. You're moving awful fast for me."

"That's how you stay alive in this business. Look, you've got a unique gimmick, talent, stage presence . . . well, size, anyway. The rest can be taught, or covered. You don't like the way I do business, you don't like the way things are going, you just walk. I'll fly you back here and you can pick up your van and go on your merry way. What do you say?" Again she extended her right hand, this time first to Ross Ed.

He hesitated. "Do I have to sign anything?"

"Not yet, but you will. Don't worry; you want lawyers, I'll get you lawyers. Remember, I represent the best."

Turning to his right, he gazed at the distant Bradshaw Mountains. "I'm about ready for the Pacific, and Caroline's right about the plane."

"Of course I am! I'm right about everything. Most of the time, anyway. As for the police, don't worry about them. Hollywood's full of people the cops have been after for years. Thieves, embezzlers, adulterers, arsonists, drug dealers, professional liars and cheats, and some of them don't even work in the business." On the ever-wary Caroline she bestowed a warm, maternal smile that was at least half-genuine.

"I promise that you'll get to San Diego. I'll get you passes to any place you want." Hard and sharp, her eyes flicked back to Ross Ed. "Well?"

Somewhere a raven cawed, having been momentarily out-jawed. Ross Ed took Tealeaf's hand.

"I'm sick of driving, and I miss my car anyway."

The trip to Los Angeles in Tealeaf's twin-engine Beechcraft was no bumpier than the average commercial flight. Setting down in Santa Monica, they picked up her garaged Mercedes and made the drive up the coast to Malibu.

Her house boasted three levels, two decks, the promised enormous eucalyptus forming a pale green barrier between the house and the access road, and on the second level overlooking the sand, a hammock of white cotton rope big enough to hold four people. The sun was already beginning to set somewhere in the vicinity of Japan. Ross Ed half expected to wake up and find he'd been cast in a commercial for the local chamber of commerce.

The whirlwind who was hosting them roared through the house, checking fax and answering machines, before leaving for her Santa Monica office. She managed to do all this while simultaneously holding down at least three conversations on her cellular phone, which must have been surgically attached to the side of her head. In her wake they found spotlessly clean rooms, fresh flowers, and a fully stocked commercial-grade refrigerator large enough to hold an entire steer carcass. The freezer alone contained four different brands of premium ice cream, all in pint containers.

Despite this largesse, Ross Ed still wasn't sure he liked Tealeaf, but he had to admire her. She talked, moved, and reacted three times faster than anyone he'd ever met. It was impossible to imagine what might happen if she touched Jed and the alien's suit chose to react to the contact.

Given the run of the manse, he and Caroline investigated the place like children. Warm California sunlight poured in through the photosensitized windows, gilding everything inside from furniture to flowers.

"What the hell's a spring roll?" As they explored he munched on an assortment of snack foods scavenged from the gigantic fridge.

"Beats me. Is it any good?"

"Too small to tell. Want to take a walk on the beach?"

"Sure. As soon as I figure out how to operate these doors."

Attained at last, the Pacific was not entirely as Ross Ed had envisioned it. The beach sloped sharply down into the bay and the waves were small and choppy. Instead of turquoise blue, the water was a dark pea-soup green, its mysteries hidden. It was cold and full of stringy vegetation. Kelp, Caroline called it. Probably some of it in the ice cream they'd seen in the freezer. As they hiked barefoot along the gritty sand she proceeded to explain how that could be.

He was more than a little disappointed. Gulf-coast sand was pure white and soft, the water warm and if not turquoise blue, at least semitransparent. Out beneath the oil rigs fish swarmed in abundance and you could see well down into the water. Where were all the caroling surfers and giggling girls in high-tech bikinis? Perhaps it was the wrong time of year. Or day. Or beach.

They did encounter other afternoon strollers; a young couple holding hands, a schoolteacher and his wife on break, a couple of boogie boarders looking for breaking surf, Robert Redford, and a painter searching for inspiration in the farrago of pitching sea and moody overcast. Reaching a narrow breakwater, they turned and began to retrace their steps.

"Well, you made it." Caroline bent to pick up a fragment of driftwood. Put a woman on a beach, he knew from experience, and she'd return home with pockets full of stuff she'd never look at twice anywhere else. "So what do you think of the Pacific Ocean?"

"So far I'm not impressed." He gazed out over the green waters. "It sounds nice. Waves in the Gulf are pretty small. But the water there is warmer, clearer, and cleaner. As for swimming, give me a Texas lake anytime. Maybe it'll be nicer down near San Diego."

"We'll see. Tealeaf promised." A check of her watch showed that it was later than they realized. "She said she'd be back in time for a late lunch."

Indeed, at the appointed half hour their hostess burst into the house and effusively embraced each of them in turn. "Ross Ed, Caroline! Did you have a good morning?" Without giving either of them a chance to answer, she swept past, making a beeline for the fax machine. She'd changed at her office into something light and flowing, halfway between a Paris gown and a Sears bathrobe.

Moments later the door rang, or rather, symphonied, and she rushed to admit three visitors. These she escorted into the den, with its expensive but meaningless modern sculptures, thick carpet, and impressive, filtered view of the sea.

A short, skinny guy with black hair cropped and thinning to match plopped himself down in one of the oversized couches and was nearly swallowed up. He did not removed his dark sunglasses. Buoying him up by sitting down on the other side of the couch was an older man whose haircut would have cost Ross Ed the equivalent of a week's salary. There wasn't a patch of skin on him that wasn't perfectly tanned. Though probably in his mid-sixties, he had the body of a healthy man twenty years younger. Completing the trio, a large woman with a deep, booming voice positioned herself gracefully in one of the big, framing armchairs.

As their hostess directed Ross Ed and Caroline to the couch opposite, Sunglasses leaned back against a cushion, crossed his legs, and announced to anyone who might be interested, "They don't look like much."

Their female companion had focused on Ross. "Let's hold the snap judgments. He's big, anyway. In fact, they're both big."

Sunglasses ignored the admonishment. "I don't see anything here to get excited about."

Tealeaf smiled encouragingly at Ross Ed. "Go and get your friend, won't you?"

"Are you sure about these people?" Ross enjoyed the way the two men tensed in response to his query. On Tealeaf's reassurance, he rose and recovered Jed from where they'd placed him in an empty closet.

When he returned, the newcomers were picking at a tray of hors d'oeruves Tealeaf had set out. It was piled high with sandwiches the size of silver dollars. Was all the food in California miniaturized? he found himself wondering.

Sitting back down near Caroline, he positioned the alien corpse on his left knee. Sunglasses eyed the otherworldly form dubiously.

"Not your usual ventriloquist's dummy."

"Didn't I tell you?" Tealeaf enthused.

The large woman spoke up. "If this doesn't go, you could try them with the World Wrestling Federation. He's big enough. He could do a Frankenstein, claim the alien was controlling him."

That brought forth the first smile from Sunglasses. "Not a bad idea. Call them the E.T. Texans, do 'em up in matching spandex, and match them against Bam Bam Williams or Haystack Carfax first time out."

"We will not," Tealeaf countered. "Although it's not a bad idea, Max."

"All my ideas are invariably good," Sunglasses allowed, without a hint of false modesty.

The senior tanning poster spoke up. "You spoke of a music career. Can the guy sing?" He was eyeing Ross Ed the way the butcher back home used to size up a fresh side of beef.

"Does it matter?" asserted Max, thereby confirming what Tealeaf had said back in Sedona. "Forty years ago, sure. Not now."

Suntan ignored Sunglasses. "You said he was a ventriloquist with a twist, Tealeaf." He smiled hopefully at Ross Ed. "So don't make us ask, kid. Ventriloquize."

"Yeah, throw your voice." Max chuckled.

"Where do you want me to throw it to?" Ross Ed responded in his alien voice, which as always seemed to come from the vicinity of Jed's head.

The big woman sat up straighter. "Hey, that's pretty good!"

"No, it's damn good." Suntan's expression hadn't changed, but his pint-sized companion actually removed his shades, thereby revealing sharply focused, deep-set black eyes resting atop bags that spoke eloquently of too many long nights out supported by periodic overdoses of proscribed pharmaceuticals.

"I swear I didn't see your lips move, kid. Do that again." The older man leaned forward intently.

Ross Ed complied. The man whistled appreciatively, Max nodded, and the heavyset woman broke out in a wide grin.

"Can't you see it?" Seizing the moment, Tealeaf stepped into their midst. "Him doing a concert and making it sound like it's coming from the dummy? Talk about a new approach!"

The blond-maned man hadn't taken his eyes from the tall Texan. "How about it, kid? You can throw your voice. Can you throw a song?"

"Can you play an instrument?" the woman wanted to know. "Guitar, kazoo, anything?" From the hors d'oeuvres tray she selected a sculpture of fresh pumpernickel, Iranian caviar, and imported sesame seed. It put Ross Ed in mind of friends back home who occasionally did not have enough to eat.

"I'm moderately handy with a harmonica."

"A harp player. Excellent!" The AARP poster boy looked to his left. "Max? Who can we put him together with?"

Having redonned his dark shades, the younger man turned thoughtful. "How many sides you want to go with? Two, three, four?"

"Four. He's new at this and we need to make sure he's well covered. The singing we can work on."

"Sure," agreed the big woman. "Remember Rex Harrison? Never 'sang' a lick in *My Fair Lady*."

"Bring him to the Melrose studio tomorrow." Taking pad and pen from an inside pocket, Max scribbled a note and passed it to Tealeaf. "Eleven o'clock. I can get the boys together before then, but I can't get them up."

"They need to be good," Tealeaf warned him.

He offered a wan smile by way of reply. "All my people are good. Don't worry, we'll pull it together. Things are slow and there are some fine people looking for gigs. He'll be righteously backed. Guitar, bass, drums, maybe keyboard. That's all anybody needs."

"What about material?"

"No prob." He adjusted his shades. "We got tons of sheets lying around. Nobody cares about words anyway. Thrash, metal, grunge, industrial, techno, Manchester United; crank it up enough and it all sounds the same from the back of the clubs."

"I'll have to take your word for it, Max. You know I can't stand that stuff."

"Maybe he can throw the voice around the club," the blond man suggested. "What about contracts?"

"Don't you worry about that. I've got my people working on it."

He eyed her without smiling. "That's why I'm worried."

"Gustav, have I ever cheated you? Max? Sophia?" When no response was forthcoming, she simply ignored the implications. "We need to put Ross Ed and his act out there fast, before somebody else comes up with the idea. Once the word gets out on the street there'll be alien bands all over the place."

Curious to see how Tealeaf's guests would react, Ross decided to toss a little truth into the brew. "It's not a gimmick. Jed is a real alien, you know."

The blond man smiled. "Yeah, sure, kid, sure. Hollywood's full of 'em."

Tealeaf escorted her guests out, her patented patter rising above their still-querulous but now mildly excited voices.

"What do you make of that?" Caroline tried one of the tiny sandwiches, frowned, and delicately spat it out into a napkin.

"Hard to say. It sure went fast." Picking up a remote control from a nearby end table, he switched on the sixty-inch TV and leaned back on the couch, flipping channels in search of something mindless and entertaining.

"You ought to try this." She offered him something round and red from the tray. "I've had them before and they grow on you."

He eyed the doughnut shape and its pink topping warily. "What is it?"

"Bagel, cream cheese, onion, and lox."

"I've had bagels before. This smells like dead fish."

"It *is* dead fish."

"You eat it all together like that?"

"How else?" Demonstrating, she popped it in her mouth and chewed. Several minutes later she was still chewing.

Looking over his shoulder, he considered the ocean. "I wonder if you can find a good chicken-fry around here?"

"This is Los Angeles. I bet you can find anything."

He pointed excitedly at the screen. "Hey, look. Must be one of the *Star Wars* films."

Though he boosted the volume on the enormous set, the horde of battling spaceships made no sound. Bursts of energy beyond human ken flashed on screen, not unlike the conversation which had just concluded. Only when the view cut to the interior of one of the warring vessels did the noise and confusion of combat become audible.

He fiddled with the remote. "Damn sound keeps going in and out."

"Maybe it's in the broadcast." She tried to calm him. "Can't do anything about that. Neat special effects, though." She blinked at the screen. "I don't remember any of the ships in the *Star Wars* films looking like that."

"Now there's a *good* alien," he declared as something lethargic and legless lumbered into view. "Much better than Jed."

Numerous tentacles emerged from the lump of gray protoplasm, which was clad in swirling bands of bright red and yellow. Silvery cilia propelled it across the deck. In the background a knot of identical creatures clustered over a table or bench. They were soon joined by a hunched-over giraffelike being equipped with two sets of prehensile lips in lieu of hands. More neat special effects hung from its long, muscular neck, within easy reach of the double lips.

A series of eyespots ran around the upper quarter of the gray domers, as Ross Ed named them. It spoke through a device attached to its upper body by an encircling band of metal, bellowing and barking at others of its kind.

"Doesn't look like any of the aliens from *Star Wars,* either."

"Sure they do," Ross Ed insisted. "Don't you remember the cantina scene from the first movie? That was full of aliens, some of whom you only saw for a few seconds."

"I don't know. . . ."

As the perspective shifted it became possible to view the ferocious altercation through wide circular ports. Other aliens walked, slidded, or scuttled in and out of view. Wholly into the film, Ross Ed decided to try one of the bagel-and-lox combinations. Unlike anything he'd ever eaten before, the combination of flavors exploded in his mouth. He swallowed and helped himself to another.

Just as he was coming to the realization that bagels with cream cheese and lox require a longer period to digest than, say, aluminum foil, the gray domer which had dominated the foreground view turned toward them. Contracting its full compliment of cilia, it nearly leaped off the floor. Responding to this outcry, the giraffe creature ambled over and filled the screen with its head, blocking out nearly everything else. Its two eyes were bright red, the pupils tiny and black.

Withdrawing, it conversed with the gray domer. Other domers began to edge near, peering between the disputants in the direction of the screen. Several equally curious and uniquely distinctive aliens joined the growing assemblage. All variously pointed, gestured, or gesticulated in the direction of the screen.

Several argued vociferously enough to come to blows and had to be separated by others of their own kind.

"I don't remember any of this, but it's great!" Ross Ed leaned forward. "They make it look like that domer in the middle is staring straight at you."

As he finished, the alien in question pointed something that looked like an empty peanut-butter jar filled with scraps from a machine shop directly at the screen. One tentacle nudged a transparent switch.

Caroline screamed as the big-screen TV exploded, sending shards of faux wood and electronic components flying. Ross Ed threw up his hands to protect his face.

When he dropped them there was nothing left of the set but a smoking base from which occasional sparks fizzed and sputtered. Waving away the smoke, he made sure Jed and Caroline were all right before stumbling over to the wall to pull what remained of the plug from its socket. The house, at least, seemed undamaged.

Meanwhile Caroline had opened a window to let the sharply acrid smoke out. She turned back to him, coughing.

"Well, that was interesting."

"Pretty strong film. Set must've had a bad short inside. Maybe I turned the volume up too much."

"I don't think it was a short, Ross Ed." She was staring, not at the ruins of the TV, but at where an alien corpse lay motionless on the couch. The suit wasn't glowing, and that certainly wasn't a smile on the keeled, inhuman face, but she suspected what had happened nonetheless.

"Jed did it," she declared firmly. "I don't know how, or why, but he's responsible." She turned back to the demolished big-screen. "That wasn't a movie, Ross Ed. We were looking at real aliens, engaged in a real battle, and they finally started to look back at us. I don't think they liked being spied on."

"So what you're saying," he replied slowly as he considered her words, "is that Jed pulled in a channel that's not on local cable."

"You could put it that way."

A voice from the hall reached them, followed by its flabbergasted owner. "Hey, what have you two been up to?"

Without thinking, Ross Ed pointed at his smaller companion. "Wasn't us. It was Jed."

"Oh right, sure." Tealeaf shrugged and smiled, irrepressible as ever. "No matter. It's probably still under warranty. I get one every year when the new models come out." She waved at a puff of smoke. "What were you watching?"

"Interstellar war." Caroline didn't smile. In the course of their unexpected insight she'd seen too many "special effects" blown to smithereens.

"Well, I hope your alien takes it easier on Maxy's gear. The equipment professional musicians use these days costs a fortune." Walking over, she put a friendly arm around his waist. "You've got a huge career ahead of you, Ross. You, and your clever dummy, and your friend, too, if she wants to be a part of this."

"Sorry." Caroline shook her head. "If it's all the same to you, I'll just watch."

"Whatever you want, sweetie." Tealeaf was clearly relieved that Caroline did not insist on participating. It would simplify contractual matters.

"Now then," she continued, letting go of Ross Ed's belt line, "everything's set for Saturday at the Nosh Pit."

His expression twisted. "Nosh Pit?"

"It's a combo restaurant-club. Real popular, up on Sunset. Just down from Tower and the Whiskey. I know it seems that things are moving fast, but you'll do fine. All you have to do is step out on stage, move around, speak or sing through your dummy, and have a good time. Maybe play a little harmonica. Your backup will be so loud nobody'll notice any discomfort or problems anyway. Don't worry about clothes. We'll take care of that tomorrow."

"You really think this will work?" he asked uneasily.

"Do I know what I'm doing or do I know what I'm doing?"

"I don't know, Tealeaf. *Do* you know what you're doing?"

"Always, *bubalah.* Remember, what matters is who your backup is, how you look, how much PR you've got fronting you, where you can get a gig, and what the reviews are like." She winked. "Just remember that the people who are after you aren't likely to look in the Nosh Pit. They're probably all bouncing off themselves somewhere in the middle of Arizona. So you owe me one performance, anyway."

"Shouldn't I rehearse seriously with these musicians first?" he wondered.

"Why? They're professionals. Just improvise and they'll follow you. That's their job. That's what they get paid for."

He made a face. "Somehow that doesn't seem very honest."

"Sweetie, we're talking the *music* business here. Don't worry about it. Let me do the worrying." She smiled cheerily. "That's what *I* get paid for." Her attention shifted to the motionless body on the couch. "Now just for Auntie Tealeaf, make him say something. Go on, anything at all. I'm going to be too busy setting things up to watch you work."

Ross Ed retreated until he was standing alongside his dead companion. "I don't know what to say," he said, immediately following which he heard himself declaiming through Jed, in his best alien voice, "You're a scheming, conniving, ruthless, amoral example of your poor, benighted species who does absolutely nothing for anyone around you without the prospect of personal gain. You have no real, true friends, including the three recently departed so-called business associates.

"You think Gustav is a pompous ass who's made millions foisting dreck on a gullible public, that Sophia is an overweight slob who doesn't know her butt from a hole in the ground but happens to be the daughter-in-law of the head of one of the most powerful agencies in town, and Max is a drug-dealing slimeball who if he wasn't working in the music business would be out cleaning high-school toilets while pandering meth to students on the side.

"None of which matters because you're having the contracts drawn up so you can control everything and cheat everyone out of what you think is going to be the biggest novelty act to hit popular music since 'Ahab the Arab' was a number-one hit. You haven't got an honest bone in your body, you swindled your own brother out of his share of the family inheritance to get enough money to start your business, and you'd sleep with anything on two or four legs if you thought it would give you a leg up in contract negotiations, except that nowadays you have to pay for that sort of thing."

Caroline couldn't breathe and Ross Ed looked horrified, but their hostess didn't bat an eye. "Hey, that's *very* good! Maybe that little sucker really is a real dead alien."

"You . . . you're not offended?" He kept waiting for the explosion. It never came.

"Should I be? Everything you said about my 'friends' is true.

So is pretty much everything you said about me. You want to survive in this business, you learn to ignore the truth. It's not really a problem because there isn't much truth in this town that has to be ignored." She tucked her arm in his and patted it reassuringly. "Nothing to get upset about. Now, you kids finish up this snack tray or I'm going to have to throw it out." She scrutinized the still-smoking ruins of the TV.

"No fire damage. There are four more sets scattered around the house, so it's not like we're going to have to go without a television." Stepping back, she wagged a finger at him. "Just watch what channels you tune to in the future, *bubalah.* I'll get somebody in to clear up this mess." She started searching end tables and cabinets. "Now where did I put that phone? I'll be right back."

Ross Ed watched her go. "You talk to anybody back home like that and guns start to come out."

"This isn't Texas." Caroline dug into the remaining hors d'oeuvres. "Talk about your alien cultures."

"I suppose." He turned to Jed. The alien body lay exactly as he'd placed it on the cushions. "I don't know why I said all that stuff, much less how."

"You told me you don't know why you say any of it. Didn't seem to bother her much." She popped a triangular tidbit.

"I wonder if it's possible to insult *anybody* here."

"Try these little green things; they're wonderful. I think they like being insulted, Ross Ed. They're so used to underlings agreeing with everything they say, I think they must enjoy it when somebody talks back to them."

"Maybe so.." She was right; the green unidentifiables were delicious. "I just wasn't raised to speak to people like that."

"Tealeaf told you not to worry about it. Just concentrate on what you're going to do Saturday. If we're lucky, it'll be fun. Then we can go to San Diego."

He eyed her speculatively. "You're enjoying all of this, aren't you, Caroline?"

She sat back on the sumptuous couch, one hand full of tiny sandwiches. "I may not be that old, Ross Ed, but I've learned to go with the flow. This flow is full of free housing, free food, and free entertainment. So I'm going with it. You should, too. Try to relax and enjoy yourself."

SEVENTEEN

The couple of casual rehearsals Max had set up prior to Saturday went smoothly enough. The three musicians who had signed to back the new act looked bored and tired, but went through their paces with studied professionalism. Ross Ed played the harmonica a little, joining in as best he could. New songs had been selected from a rotating file, and while he didn't agree with all the words or sentiments, he wanted to please his sponsors and so did his best to mouth them in what he hoped would be an acceptable manner.

Since his presence wasn't required for the rehearsals and because everyone concerned wanted to keep the unique nature of the group under wraps until the last possible moment, Jed remained back at Tealeaf's house. Ross Ed wouldn't utilize him until the actual performance on Saturday. He didn't think it would matter. The backup music was so loud and the drummer and lead guitarist so forceful with their own vocals that nobody would be able to hear him anyway.

A couple of songs were dumped and one more added before Tealeaf and Max pronounced themselves satisfied. Showtime Saturday was ten P.M., when the new group Live Texans and Dead Aliens would follow a well-established local band onto the stage.

When they arrived at the club late Saturday afternoon, it proved to be something of a disappointment. The walls were flat, square, and included op-art depictions of everything from passenger pigeons to flying whales to exploding drum sets.

Dozens of spotlights and smaller bulbs clung to the ceiling like hibernating bats, throwing their light through intervening scrims onto the scarred wood and linoleum floor. Tealeaf thought it was wonderful.

Passing the bouncer, who wasn't much bigger than Ross Ed, she introduced them to the club manager. He favored Ross with a quick once-over, grunted, and gave them the nickel tour.

With the introductory formalities concluded, Tealeaf took them to dinner at an expensive local restaurant whose portions wouldn't qualify as appetizers at any truck stop between Fort Stockton and the Louisiana border. A double dessert was all that stood between Ross and outright hunger.

After dinner their hostess took them to a mall to kill the rest of the evening while they waited for showtime. Ross Ed looked on disapprovingly while Caroline made zealous use of Tealeaf's assortment of credit cards. It was a side of his companion he hadn't seen before. Maybe he was being too hard on her, he told himself. She'd had nothing when he'd met her. All women, he knew, possessed the sometimes dormant but never missing "S" chromosome to go along with the X and the Y. "S" standing for Shopping, of course.

With the trunk full of frivolous purchases which nevertheless delighted both women, they raced back to Malibu, unloaded, picked up one deceased alien, and returned via Sunset Boulevard to the club.

"I can't wait." Though she appeared permanently preoccupied, Tealeaf was an excellent driver. Being a native Angeleno, she'd absorbed the rudiments of driving before she could walk. "You're going to be great, Ross. You can throw that voice all over the club, bounce it off the walls, make it sound like it's coming from different members of the audience. This is going to be a huge success, I know it! After the show we'll fine-tune any problems, and tomorrow we'll turn the reviewers loose for a look at you."

"Reviewers?" He turned in the seat to look back at Caroline. "You mean my picture's going to be in the papers and on TV?"

"If everything goes well. Don't worry. Making you and Jed public figures will fix it so that no government agency will dare snatch you off the streets."

"What if these reviewer people want to ask questions about Jed?"

"Not a prob. I have suitable answers already written up. Also the questions. You won't have to actually converse with anybody." She reached over and patted his leg. She was a great patter, he'd noticed. "Just hang in there on stage for an hour or so and leave everything else to me. Don't let the audience get to you. Hollywood crowds are pretty out there. Given your size, I don't think anyone will try to bother you. If they do, just kick 'em off the stage."

Caroline leaned forward. "Isn't that assault?"

"In L.A. we call it performer-audience interaction, sweetie. Trust me, they love it. If you have any personal problems just walk backstage. I'll be there with refreshments at the ready."

"Walk backstage?" Ross Ed wasn't sure he understood the proper procedure. "You mean, while the performance is going on?"

"Sure. Nobody'll notice. If anything, they'll applaud louder. You can have a drink, make love, go to the can; whatever you want. The band'll carry you. That's the way it works." She smiled sympathetically. "This really is all new to you, isn't it?"

Feeling slightly inadequate, he looked straight ahead. Sunset Boulevard came at him in a blur of headlights and expensive homes. "It's real different from the oil business or tending bar, that's for sure."

Club roadies were removing the first group's instruments from the stage and setting up for the next set. Meanwhile Ross Ed, Caroline, Tealeaf, and the members of the band waited backstage. Hearing the crowd milling noisily around out front, Ross started to grow nervous. What was he doing here, trying to convince hundreds of people he was a musician and stage presence? Playing ventriloquist for the occasional barfly was one thing: singing to a sophisticated big-city audience something else.

"Just relax." Tealeaf was smiling and reassuring and pretty high on something that didn't require water for ingestion. "Don't worry about the crowd. There's a full house and the floor is packed. Go out there and have fun. Prance around the stage and kick a few people in the teeth."

He looked solemnly down at her. "I can't do that, Tealeaf. I was raised proper."

She waved it off. "Well then, spit on them, or something. You don't want to disappoint your fans, do you?"

His eyebrows lifted. "I have fans? I haven't done anything yet."

"What do you think publicity's for, sweetie?" She grinned through her pharmacologically induced haze.

"Let's do it, man." Roger, the lead guitarist, clapped Ross Ed on the back and headed for his waiting instruments. Roger was from Blackpool, in England, and most of what he said was quite incomprehensible. He made an ideal backup singer.

The rest of the band followed, settling themselves into position. His mane of black hair reaching below his shoulders and covering his eyes like a sheepdog's, the drummer donned a grotesque latex alien mask, all rubber drool and painted-on blood. Live Texans and Dead Aliens had been airbrushed onto the big drum in front of him, the letters green and pustulant. A few amputated rubber tentacles dangled from mike stands. Downcast, Ross pointed it all out to Tealeaf.

"I'm sorry," she apologized, "but it was the best we could do on such short notice. Once we set up a tour we'll have a regular special-effects team." It wasn't what he was referring to, but given the brief window of opportunity he chose not to comment.

As both guitarists tuned their instruments, the crowd set up a howl out front. It was an appropriate unearthly sound, unlike anything Ross Ed had ever heard before. Caroline wished him luck with a whisper and a kiss.

Resigned, he removed the silent and unprotesting Jed from the venerable backpack and cradled the body in his right arm. The lumpy alien form felt neither lighter nor heavier than when he'd first removed it from the depths of its New Mexico mountain cave. How long ago had it been? He couldn't quite remember.

On the other side of the drop curtain someone screaming loud enough to injure an untrained human throat was making an introduction. Ross Ed thought he heard his name mentioned but he couldn't be sure. The noise from the band, as his backup swung into action, was acute enough to kill flies.

Up went the curtain and an unseen hand shoved him forward, sending him stumbling out on stage. Apparently this was an accepted mode of entry, because the crowd roared at his appearance. Backed by an incomprehensible rampage of sound, he stared out at the mob. The club was a milling sea of expectant faces, outrageous hair, and enough pierced body parts to do a tribe of nineteenth-century Papuans proud.

The combination of deafening music and braying crowd sounded like a well blowout on hold. He tried to say something to the bass player, without success. The man was wearing industrial-strength earplugs and didn't acknowledge him. Helpless, he turned to the seething, boiling mass of postpubescent humanity. Tealeaf was right; it was the standard packed-house Hollywood crowd: riot-in-a-box, with applause the coupon on the back.

He wasn't sure the activity many of them were engaged in could be called dancing. Certainly it was a long way from doing the cotton-eyed Joe. Glancing into the wings he saw Caroline smiling encouragingly and an anxious Tealeaf gesturing for him to do something, anything. Caroline had on a new outfit, he noticed. It looked expensive.

Taking center stage, he pulled out his harmonica and began playing. Though he wondered how they could possibly pick out the homely hum of the harp from the background bellow, the crowd noise immediately ratcheted up a notch.

Something soared past his head to land in the vicinity of the drummer, who kicked it aside without missing a beat. Not especially familiar with feminine hygiene products, Ross Ed was unable to identify it. Without waiting for him, the band launched into another song. Though he didn't know it, it was actually quieter on stage than out front beneath the towering obelisks of gigantic black speakers. Occasionally a member or two of the audience would pause to caress the speakers in a pantomime reminiscent of a particularly famous scene from a well-known movie.

Ross Ed thought about trying the harmonica again. Instead, he found himself looking down at Jed. How anyone could hear anything he said in his alien voice he couldn't imagine, but Tealeaf was waving frantically and pointing at the crowd. Caroline smiled encouragingly, fingering the new necklace that adorned her neck.

He couldn't just sit there, he knew. Settling Jed on his knee, he did his best to improvise.

Something must have engaged because the suit began to glow. This time the light was pale green. Axing away, the lead guitarist grinned at him. Ross found himself mumbling the words to a favorite old song. Results were immediate.

The hundred or so kids who found themselves actually

dancing on the ceiling didn't miss a step, but it did slow the band for a minute. Mattress the drummer kept pounding out the backbeat rhythm, however, and the two astonished guitarists soon picked up where they'd left off.

As for the dancers, they weren't fazed in the slightest. Progeny of a technologically sophisticated society, they embraced the inversion of natural law as readily as they would a new ride at Disneyland, to which the more thoughtful members of the mob were already comparing the experience.

Experimenting, Ross Ed soon had them bouncing off the walls, ceiling, and floor simultaneously. Dance moves were tried that had previously existed only in fevered imaginations as the club scene was subsumed in a mad Einsteinian jitterbug. "Swing your partner" took on meaning that country had never intended.

The stage remained relatively inviolate. Why climb on stage to throw yourself back into the audience when you could bang your head on the roof? It was advanced moshing of a kind that made Samoan fire dancing look like the fox-trot.

Shrieks of delight and screams of pleasure rose above the roar, inspiring the band to even more frenzied riffs in which Ross Ed's alien song-speak was submerged but not lost. He amused himself by trying to separate the males in the crowd from the females. Given the variations in attire, hair, and bodily adornment it proved an impossible task, a result which would have delighted the participants.

There was no panic. The youthful audience adapted to the gravitational alternations as if they'd been doing so all their lives. Some of the spins and gyrations they invented were wondrous to behold. Occasionally Ross Ed or one of the band members would have to fend off overly exuberant dancers by shoving their flying bodies back into the seething maelstrom of the audience, much to the latter's delight.

When Ross changed to another song and the crowd gently drifted back to earth, there were a few shouts and howls of disappointment. These vanished when the monsters began appearing among them and started choosing up partners.

Not really monsters, some of them were simply monstrous in appearance. They were other aliens, in a remarkable plethora of sizes, shapes, and colors. Another of the suit's miraculous defensive mechanisms had been deployed, he decided. How it had determined that the dancers were a threat he couldn't imagine, unless one considered a wild-eyed, madly gyrating seventeen-year-old girl clad mostly in buckles, braces, and leather a danger.

Marvelously detailed and possessed of more than a little solidity, the aliens included males, females, neuters, and a couple who were a walking education in reproductive adaptation. He wondered how many the suit was inventing and how many it had dredged up from some vast stored memory of images. If the latter, then the universe included a great many more intelligences than anyone suspected, some sufficiently outrageous as to skate believability. Not one looked remotely like Jed.

Caroline was enjoying the show from the wings while Tealeaf tried frantically to talk on her cellular phone. Even with one hand over her other ear the colossal din must be making it impossible for her to make herself understood to the party on the other end.

While the band managed to preserve its equipment, the crowd started to take the club apart. Feeling themselves invulnerable and super-invigorated, they began with the lighting fixtures and moved on to tables and chairs. Confronted by a raging mob of rampaging aliens and teenagers, the outnumbered bouncers sensibly sought refuge in the comparative safety of the manager's office.

A first cousin to the giraffe thing Ross Ed had seen on Tealeaf's television kept bumping its head into the lower light fixtures. Sparks and electrical flashes flew, adding to the general air of uncontrolled celebration. There wasn't much he and the band could do except play on. It sounded like someone was banging a derrick on the roof.

A girl with rings in most visible parts of her body leaped up on stage. Throwing her arms around Jed, she planted a big fat kiss on the transparent faceplate. Ross Ed started to push her away.

"Look, hon, I don't know if that's such a good—"

There was a scintillating, actinic flash. Every hair on the girl's head, of which there were a fair number, promptly stood straight out. Remarkably, so did the hair of her eyebrows and for all he knew, any hair that remained anywhere else. She was wearing a lot of metal, which he suspected had aided in conducting the charge. There was also a certain amount of heat involved, because the lipstick had melted right off her mouth. It ran in a purple streak down her face and onto her chest.

Arms and legs spread wide, she staggered backward, eyes

staring straight ahead, and tumbled backward into the crowd. It accepted her with a roar, like some vast, amorphous, carnivorous animal. Her expression as she was swallowed up was a mixture of shock and divine delight. Someone put her back on her feet and Ross saw her blink, reassuring him that she wasn't dead.

Her shocking experience precipitated a rush toward the stage by every young woman within twenty feet. Many were dressed as if they'd failed metal shop in school, and had decided to make projects of themselves.

As they threatened to overwhelm the stage, they suddenly smashed together in a great writhing mass of female confusion. When one girl tried to pull herself free, she found herself immediately snapped back into the pile. Nose rings, earrings, and innumerable other rings, together with an astonishing assortment of additional objects metallic in origin had suddenly become magnetized, silver and copper as well as steel.

Stumbling, screaming, and staggering, the compacted mass of adolescent feminity staggered about until it fell back into the crowd, still stuck together. As a defense mechanism it equaled or exceeded anything the alien suit had exhibited thus far.

Though it seemed impossible, the noise level inside the club had intensified. In the distance he saw people from off the street, who having heard the joyous cacophony, were trying to force their way inside through the single narrow entrance. That sort of cramming would bring the fire department and close on their heels, the police, neither of which Ross Ed wanted to have to deal with.

In fact, he'd reached the conclusion that if this was what contemporary show business required, he much preferred the kind of simple, low-key ventriloquist act he'd perfected at the bar in the El Paso Sheraton. Rising, he determined that he and Jed had just given their first and last onstage performance.

The light from the alien suit shifted from green to a deep, ominous purple. As it did so, the air in the club began to change. Sensitive high-tech equipment for atmospheric analysis wasn't necessary to detect the shift. The atmopshere was thickening, as if the cavernous room was filling with a pale mauve fog.

At first it didn't affect the dancers, who continued to thrash and mosh energetically. While the exotic mist thickened around them, sucking up the alien arrivals, the air remained clear and fresh on stage. Then, without warning, the giddy celebrants began to slump where they were standing. There was no coughing or hacking, no gasping for air. People simply keeled over; sometimes in tandem with their partners, more frequently by themselves. The more resilient crumpled atop those who had succumbed first. To a one, all wore the look of the happily high.

That's when Caroline burst from the wings. "Ross Ed, don't you see what's happening? You've got to make it stop!"

"Don't reckon I can, Caroline. Shoot, I don't even know what's going on."

Wearing a murderous scowl, one of the managers was charging the stage. He didn't quite make it before the fog caught up with him. His expression underwent a shift startling in its suddenness, from the homicidal to the sublimely stupid, as his eyes rolled back in his head and he fell over in a heap of customers.

Only when none were left standing did the band finally pack it in. No one made any obvious jokes about "laying them in the aisles" or "knocking 'em dead." For one thing, no one was dead. As proof of this a loud whine filled the club's interior. Instead of the sound of ten hands clapping, it was the drone of a hundred throats snoring, interspersed with the occasional semicomatose giggle.

Drumsticks dangling from one hand, a perspiring Mattress put a comradely arm around Ross Ed's shoulders. The band members hadn't thought much of him at first, him not being a musician and all, but the prematurely terminated show had changed their opinion.

"Too cool, dude. Like, when's the next gig? Imagine doing this at the Forum, or like, Anaheim Stadium!"

Ross Ed politely disengaged himself and took Caroline's hand. It had an unnatural feel to it. Looking down, he saw that it was newly adorned with rings. He tucked Jed higher under his other arm.

"Let's get out of here."

Behind him, the lead guitarist wiped hair and sweat from his face. "Hey, man, you be at the studio next week?"

"Sorry, guys, but I think I'm out."

"What!" The leader of the backups cursed and threw his instrument down on the stage. "You can't quit on us now, man! Look at what you've done!" He gestured at the slumberous audience.

"That's why I'm leaving."

"Sweetie baby darling, you can't do this!" It was Tealeaf, her phone back in her purse. "What happened out there, anyway?"

"I told the guys, I don't know. I only hope I didn't hurt anybody."

"You didn't hurt anyone." She pointed. "See?"

Ross Ed turned. People were starting to rise. Many put their hands to their heads. Others inhaled deeply. A few wandered about wide-eyed but blind, bumping off the walls and each other. Those who returned first from the fog into which the fog had put them began to clap. Several cheered, feebly but with becoming enthusiasm.

"You see?" Tealeaf was at her encouraging best. "They love you. They want more. Our contract with the club calls for you to—"

"Screw the club." Caroline locked her arm firmly in Ross Ed's. "We're going back to the beach house."

The diminutive producer eyed them appraisingly. The woman was implacable, the Texan immovable. "All right, you go ahead. I know this has been rough on you. Overnight success is tough on everybody. Get some rest. I'll deal with management. But I'm warning you: when word of what happened here gets out, I won't be able to cope with the offers. You're going to be a very rich, very famous oil worker, Ross Ed Hager."

"C'mon, Caroline." Unsure whether he wanted to be very rich or even a little bit famous, Ross guided his two companions, one more alive than most and the other exceedingly calm, toward the backstage exit.

Behind him, wild cries of "Encore!", "Bravo!", and "More!" came increasingly from the crowd. Coming from a gathering whose usual stage-directed commentary ranged from the unprintable to the unperformable, it was a remarkably sedate demonstration. The purple fog had mellowed the mob in ways still to be determined. Throughout the greater Los Angeles basin later that night, numerous households would tremble to the stunned looks of astonished and bewildered parents. The alien suit's method of coping with the unruly and potentially dangerous crowd was to utilize a soporific fog to affect a permanent change in their individual psychological makeups. They would stagger back out onto the streets no longer a threat to themselves or anyone else.

Never mind the music or the ventriloquist act, a stunned Tealeaf realized as she took stock of this mass sea change. If they could bottle the purple fog they could rule the world. Every parent on the planet would buy it.

The car their hostess had loaned them was waiting in the parking lot. As Caroline slid behind the wheel Ross Ed gently placed Jed in the rear seat.

"Think you can find your way back? This place is even bigger than Houston."

"Sure." She started the engine. "You head west until you hit the ocean and then you go north." She pulled out onto Sunset, burning rubber while dodging two cars that were uncommon even in their country of origin.

Still concerned, Ross Ed turned to gaze through the rear window. "You really think everyone back there is okay?"

She kept her eyes on the street. "Okay? Hell, they're better than they were when they came in! Freaks into Fauntleroys."

"This isn't for me, Caroline. That woman talked so fast I didn't know how to say no. Now I do. I'm not doing that again."

Caroline blasted around a loafing Lexus. "Tealeaf won't give up. She'll cajole, threaten, cry, do anything she can to get you back on stage."

"It won't work." He folded his arms. "Just because she's giving us room and board doesn't mean I'm obliged to her for anything more than that. I know how to deal with that kind of people. There are a lot of 'em in the oil business."

"It doesn't matter. You didn't see her face when you were working your magic or cyberstuff or whatever it was you were doing out there. I did. She won't leave you alone."

"Then we have to get away from here."

Clubs and record stores and restaurants gave way to the lavishly landscaped four-lane road which ran through Beverly Hills. Traffic thinned. All they had to watch out for now between there and the sea were joggers lost in the susurrations of their multihundred-dollar Walkmen and renegade poodles desperately on the prowl for an unlicensed coupling.

"Don't worry, Ross Ed. And don't be too hard on her. After all, she did get us to the Pacific. I've got my own credit card." She patted the fanny pack she always wore. "Whenever you're ready we can rent a car and head south."

"Tomorrow, when she's out of the house." He brooded while

Caroline swept the car around twists and curves. "You know, I really do prefer country-western."

She grinned. "Maybe you ought to give that a try. Can you do an alien Garth Brooks? Or is Garth Brooks really an alien in disguise? I've often wondered."

As always, she'd made him smile. The least he could do was respond in kind. " 'Often'?"

"Well, maybe once."

"Caroline, I don't want to be anybody but myself, and I'm no performer. Tonight showed me that. Once was a hoot, and it was also enough. Besides, I don't think I like these people." He checked the silent presence occupying the backseat. "Give me a dead alien for company anytime."

EIGHTEEN

He admired how effortlessly she found her way back to the beach house. It wasn't that he had an especially poor sense of direction himself: you couldn't survive in Texas with a bad one. It was just that they'd hardly spent any time at all in the sprawling, unfathomable city.

"I've lived in a lot of places, a lot of big cities as well as small towns." She didn't elaborate. "I'm used to finding my way around in strange places."

The built-in gate opener admitted them to the circular drive which fronted the house. A similar device attached to the key chain granted entry. Motion sensors turned on the interior lights.

A couple of shouts produced no reply. Evidently Tealeaf was still working her contacts. Ross Ed wondered when the woman slept. Well, all her entreaties and calls were a waste of time. He'd had his one showbiz fling, and was done with it.

The house echoed around him; prohibitively expensive, over-decorated, trendy, and cold. If these were the rewards for success in Hollywood, he'd take Albany. Albany, Texas, that is.

Caroline opened a back door. "It's nice out. Let's go for a walk."

"Sure. Just let me get Jed. After what I said about quitting, I wouldn't put it past Tealeaf or one of her friends to try and swipe him."

Once again the sturdy backpack was put to use as Ross swung it and its alien contents onto his shoulders. Together they left the house, walked down toward the water, and turned north.

The night was damp but warm as they headed for the Malibu pier, a long skeletal wooden arm stretching straight out over the water. A few lights illuminated the walkway. Dense fog hovered just offshore, a common spring occurrence along the Southern California coast. Most of the multimillion-dollar homes that lined the beach were dark, their owners away at work, play, or home asleep.

From time to time they passed another couple, or a nocturnal jogger, or someone walking a dog. Once they encountered a handsome middle-aged woman walking her cat. The immaculately groomed feline acted perfectly at home on the sand. Except for the constant complaint of the waves, it was very quiet, the noise of Pacific Coast Highway smothered by intervening slopes and trees.

Reaching the pier, they climbed the steps which led up from the beach and sauntered lazily toward the oversized gazebo that marked the far end. As the fog continued its inexorable onshore crawl couples enjoying the romantic location began to take their leave in search of warmer climes. The heavy wooden planks creaked beneath their feet, sounding more like the passing of ponies than people.

Glancing down between the boards, Ross Ed discovered he could see the dark water surging beneath his boots. Rather than the crisp, cheery sea of so many films, the Pacific he had found was a dark, solemn entity whose mournful lullaby he found soothing if not inspiring.

By the time they reached the open-sided, conical-roofed shelter at the end, the rest of the pier was deserted. Somewhere far out at sea, a melancholy buoy clanged its rhythmic warning at passing boats. High up in the eaves, ubiquitous house finches huddled silently in multiple nests. Among the feathers and twigs, down and bits of cotton, Ross Ed made out a torn tag with the name Gucci prominently displayed. He had to smile. Only in Southern California.

The fog closed in around them, turning the naked bulbs strung along the pier railings into magical will-o'-the-wisps. It swallowed up the houses that lined the beach and obliterated the lights of distant Palos Verdes. He felt as if he were adrift on an empty ship.

Well, not quite empty.

"You wanted to see the Pacific." Caroline snuggled close. "You're standing on it. Over it, anyway. What d'you think?"

"It smells. Stronger than I thought it would."

"That's the kelp," she explained helpfully. "Kelp, and salt, and fish, and other things. Like it?"

"I'm not sure."

She inhaled deeply. "To me it's like perfume." She leaned over the railing. "Look, I think I see barnacles."

For long minutes they inspected the invertebrate life which clung to the outer pilings, watched only by the fog and the dead alien. Above them, finches slept. For them, nocturnal visitors were an every day occurrence.

"If it wasn't for you, Caroline, I don't think I could've made it this far."

"Now don't go using me for an excuse." The fog softened her face, giving her the pasteurized patina of a teenager. "You did it yourself. If I hadn't helped you, someone else would have. You're just a likable sort of guy, Ross Ed." She nodded at his extraterrestrial burden. "Where do you think Jed's going to end up? With the government, a foreign power, in private hands, on national television, or what?"

"I'm not sure," he told her honestly. "All I know for certain is that I don't want somebody else telling me what to do. That's how I've run my whole life. Maybe for the worse, but it's who I am. Whatever happens to Jed, I want to be the one to decide it."

"He's glowing again," she informed him.

Sure enough, a glance over his shoulder revealed that a cool, soft pink light was emanating from the suit. Ross frowned. "I don't get it. We're not being threatened."

"Feel anything? Maybe it's overheating."

He shook his head. "Doesn't feel any different. If it's putting out any heat it's not noticeable."

"Damn, and I was starting to get cold."

He extended a long arm. "Then you'd better get a little closer."

"Closer than this?" She moved nearer, teasing.

"As close as you can." He grinned back. "You don't want to get chilled out here." His arm wrapped around her.

Illuminated by Jed light, they searched the fog for passing ships. Some were out there, as evidenced by the occasional querulous *blatt* of a foghorn, but the mist was too thick to see through.

"You sang for that club crowd," she remarked softly. "How about you sing something for me, Ross Ed Hager?"

He pondered the couple of ballads he knew reasonably well, finally selecting the one he thought most appropriate to the situation and surroundings. Hesitant yet resonant, his voice drifted out into the fog.

Not too bad, he told himself. His audience might be small, but it was appreciative.

It soon grew larger.

The eerie, wavering reply which boomed out of the mist startled him. "What the hell is that?"

Caroline's eyes were wide. "Keep singing. I think you've got an audience. A *big* audience."

She was right. There were only three of them, but together they unarguably constituted a big audience. Whales were common along the coast of California that time of year, migrating from the Gulf of Alaska south to Mexico and the Galapagos. Usually they were grays, but occasionally they were joined by some of their larger cetacean cousins.

The trio of humpbacks that clustered around the end of the pier had just enough water under them to support their massive bodies. Keeping time in its haunting falsetto with Ross Ed's country-western lament, one immense female rolled over on her side and waved lazily with a flipper that towered over the wooden cupola. This whale-lice-encrusted metronome gleamed whitely in the light from Jed's suit.

Between vocalizations the humpbacks exhaled in powerful *whooshes,* reminding Ross of pistons at work on a rig. He wanted to stop and just listen to their haunting whoops and hollers, but Caroline urged him to continue. So he did so, even though he knew it was the alien suit and not his singing which was most likely responsible for drawing the congenial leviathans up from the deeps.

Not only were they louder than he, they could carry a tune better, too. What old Preacher Williams wouldn't have given, he thought, remembering his Sunday-school days, to have had them in his choir.

Damned if they didn't applaud, too, those great flippers smacking together wetly when he finished the song. Suitably inspired, he chose another and started in, his voice carrying out over the water. One cow decided to show her gratitude by rubbing up against the pier, her fifty-ton bulk causing the sturdy structure to groan momentarily. Jed's suit was now blazing orange and pulsing in time to the music.

Two ballads later Ross Ed decided he'd had enough. When the whales realized that the improbable, improvised quartet had sung its last, they breached simultaneously while emitting a final, farewell wail. Falling back, they sent water cascading over the railing. Only by turning and retreating rapidly to the far side of the cupola did Ross Ed and Caroline manage to avoid a soaking.

Together they stared into the fog until the rhythmic moaning frayed to a final pianissimo. The last, lingering chords gave Ross Ed a start of recognition.

"Hey, that's Patsy Cline. I didn't sing any Patsy Cline."

"Maybe they picked it up from a passing boat."

"You reckon? I'd heard that some whales sing, but I didn't know they could mimic human songs."

"Mimic? I'd say that was an improvement."

He threw her a sharp look. "You can't improve on Patsy Cline."

The orange refulgence was fading from Jed's suit. "Maybe we should go back. Tealeaf's liable to panic when she finds her car home but not her guests. We don't want her putting out an all-points on us." She hugged herself tightly. "Besides, it's getting kind of chilly."

It wasn't the chill, he knew. It was the damp; little fingers of ocean that snuck slyly up your pant legs and down your back, working their way into your muscles. Putting his left arm around her shoulders and hefting Jed in the other, he turned to go.

However, despite the lateness of the hour, the fog, and the rising dank, they were no longer alone on the pier. Nor was the couple waiting to greet them spooning teenagers or retired celebrities out for their evening constitutional.

"Hello, Mr. Hager."

It was the quiet-voiced but determined army captain from El Paso. Flanking him was the lady officer Ross Ed had first encountered at the roadblocked New Mexico rest stop. They wore uniforms this time. When a third figure stepped out from behind a tall piling, Ross recognized their lanky companion. He held what looked like a fishing pole. Closer inspection, surprisingly, confirmed it.

They didn't appear to be armed. Captain Suttles spoke softly, casually, as though relating an ordinary day's happenings. "You ran us quite a race, Ross Ed, but even the fleetest deer leaves a trail. For example, we ran into some of your saucer people in New Mexico."

"They're not *my* saucer people," Ross protested.

Suttles chuckled. "They think otherwise. They feel they have a proprietary interest in you. We enlightened them, of course. We didn't believe everything they told us, but there was enough to more than whet our interest. Especially after what your dead friend, or your dead friend's defense mechanisms, did to us south of Safford.

"After that we lost you for a while, until one of our units received a copy of a report from a very distraught motel manager in a place called Tuba City. Seems he's confined to a hospital because he's suffering from persistent hallucinations. He claims to be the reincarnation of a sixteenth-century Hopi medicine man named Saqaatska." The captain was momentarily distracted as Robinett cast his line into the water.

"Then there's the story we wrested out of a couple from Indiana whom the government has crossed paths with in the past. At that point we thought we were closing in on you, but you lost us again. Lost us completely, until we heard about what happened in Los Angeles." He was almost apologetic. "There isn't much out of the ordinary that happens in a city as thoroughly monitored as Los Angeles that one government agency or another doesn't hear about. Computers make intelligence sharing a lot easier than it was in the past. You should consider yourself honored, Ross Ed: you've been hypertexted.

"Considering the way our luck had been going, I was half convinced that when we arrived here you'd already have left for someplace else. I can't tell you how relieved I was when we saw you and your lady friend standing out here on the end of the pier." He leaned to his right to peek curiously around the big Texan. "Were those whales I was hearing a little while ago?"

Caroline growled at him. "What if they were?"

"Just curious. Please don't be angry with us. Try to understand our position. We're just doing what we think is not only right, but necessary. I still don't know why you ran from us back in New Mexico, but I want to personally assure you that you'll be given the best of treatment. And no hard feelings."

Ross Ed eyed him solidly. "What happens now?"

"You'll be handsomely compensated for your discovery and given proper recognition and credit." Suttles tried his best to inject some levity into what was a tense situation. "The army doesn't even plan to charge you for the damage that occurred to their vehicles and equipment back in New Mexico."

"What if I told you I wasn't interested?"

When Kerry broke in, her manner was impatient and brusque as ever. "What *are* you interested in, Mr. Hager?"

"I haven't given it a whole lot of thought." It was his turn to smile. "You folks haven't given me much time to think things through. I guess I just want to make sure that whatever I end up doing with Jed, it's the right thing."

Robinett barely looked up from his fishing. "Now *there's* a radical notion. I'm not sure the government has a procedure for coping with that. I'm curious, Mr. Hager. To your way of thinking, just what would the right thing be?"

"I told you, I don't know yet. Whatever's best for me, and Caroline, and Jed, too, of course."

"Nothing personal, Mr. Hager," murmured Suttles gently, "but I think that your alien friend long ago left behind any concerns about what is right, wrong, or best. He'd dead. We only want to have a look at him. And his wonderful suit, of course."

To his irritation, Kerry once again injected herself into the conversation. "Just in case you're entertaining any thoughts of making a run for it, Mr. Hager, you need to have a look at the parking lot between the end of the pier and the Sandpiper restaurant."

Ross Ed and Caroline peered into the hovering mist. Clad in civilian clothes but leaving no doubt by their actions as to who they took orders from, armed men and women were lined up in a semicircle facing the far end of the pier. Others had advanced to guard the stairway which crooked sideways down to the beach. Behind them were the vague outlines of squat Humvees and a large truck. Ross couldn't be sure, but thought he saw where at least one heavy machine gun had been set up on the sand.

Like the laconic Robinett, the soldiers on the beach carried long, thin objects. Ross Ed didn't think they were fishing poles.

"We don't want any trouble, Mr. Hager." Suttles did his best to mute Kerry's bellicosity. "The troops you see are all armed with tranquilizer rifles. Nobody wants you to get hurt. But we really can't allow you to get away from us again. Chasing you around the country is expensive, time-consuming, and makes us look bad.

"Besides, we want your help. It's obvious that the suit has somehow imprinted on you, perhaps because you were the first human to come in contact with it. We really don't know, and that's one of the things we urgently want to find out. You're more familiar with it and the body it contains than anyone else. Your cooperation could save us a lot of time and money.

"So you see, much as I would personally like to, we can't let you go gallivanting around the country by yourself with something this valuable." He hesitated only briefly. "You do have some idea of how valuable it is, don't you?"

"If you mean financially, yeah, I have a pretty good notion."

"As Captain Suttles said, you'll be well paid for your cooperation, Mr. Hager." Kerry was staring so hard at the diminutive figure stuffed in the Texan's backpack that she was trembling.

"There's nothing more you can do with the alien, Ross Ed." Robinett made a face as he reeled in his line and saw that he'd caught only kelp. He continued talking as he cleaned the hook. "You've had him for a while. Why not give the experts a chance? Fair's fair. Are you worried that we're going to damage the body? Do you really think we'd be so careless with the discovery of the millennium? Or is that you think our intentions are bad, that we want to learn the secrets of the alien suit so we can use them to help us build super-secret super-weapons?"

"Don't you?" snapped Caroline.

"Wouldn't be averse to it," Robinett admitted, "but that's a small part of the knowledge we hope to gain. A very small part."

"As sworn soldiers, the defense of the United States is our responsibility." Kerry drew herself up. "I work for the United States Army, not the Los Angeles Department of Sanitation or Aunt Jennie's Bakery back home in Greensboro. When Captain Suttles told you that we were just doing our job, he was doing no less than telling you the truth. You wouldn't want your alien and his miraculous suit technology to fall into the wrong hands, would you? It's impossible to keep this sort of thing secret from other governments for very long. We know, for example, that the Russians and the Japanese already have an inkling of what's been going on out here."

"None of which matters." Reluctantly, Robinett set his pole in one of the metal holders than were spotted along the seagull-stained railings. "Because this is where it ends, Mr. Hager. You can't get off this pier." He indicated the dark green waves rolling in beneath their feet. "The water's cold, it's deep here, and sharks like to feed at night. I wouldn't chance it." His eyes met Ross Ed's. "Besides, aren't you tired of running? Why not just do the sensible thing and come with us? I promise you that everyone will end up happy. I've seen the tranquilizer darts. Getting punctured by one doesn't look like it'd be a lot of fun."

"We've made friends here in Los Angeles." Caroline was emphatic in her half-truth. "They could make a lot of unfavorable publicity. You wouldn't like that."

"No, we wouldn't," Suttles admitted, "but we'd live with it."

Ross Ed drew himself up to his full, impressive height. "Nobody's taking Jed until I'm good and ready." Reaching up and back, he swung the backpack around until it was resting against his chest. Carefully he removed the alien corpse from its carrier. Robinett sucked in his breath as he got his first clear, full-length view of the body. Kerry's eyes glinted.

"I claim my rights as an American. Jed stays with me until I say otherwise." Advancing on Robinett, who bravely held his ground, Ross suddenly turned and extended both arms over the railing. "If you won't let us leave here quietly, I'll drop him in the ocean."

Robinett twitched. Kerry started forward and Suttles had to put out an arm to restrain her. "Easy now, let's everybody just take it easy. You don't want to do that, Mr. Hager. You don't want to trash something you've spent so much time protecting."

"Don't fool yourself." Robinett considered making a grab for the alien, which was only inches from his grasp. "I'm a strong swimmer. Throw it over and I'll be right behind, even if it is cold down there. It won't hit the water much before I do."

"What if he sinks?" Ross Ed continued to dangle Jed precariously over the roiling water. "What if he goes straight to the bottom? This suit's pretty solid. It's dark down there."

"Be reasonable." With a great effort Kerry kept her emotions in check. "Do that and we'd have a team of specialists out here in minutes."

"Me, I don't know if that'd be fast enough." Caroline's

expression was stern. "Like Ross Ed said, the water's dark. There are waves, and tides."

"We'd recover the body promptly. Make no mistake about that."

"I reckon you would," Ross conceded, "but in what kind of shape? No telling how old this suit is. I wonder if it leaks? Seawater might contaminate it right quick. Might even dissolve poor little Jed's whole body."

"You argue plausibly." A visibly distraught Robinett took a step forward.

Ross Ed effortlessly retreated a comparable distance. "Back off, mister. Have you forgotten what happened the last time you tried to take him away from me?"

"We haven't forgotten." Kerry was rapidly running out of patience. "But it's a chance we'll have to take."

"For everyone's sake, please try to look at this rationally." Suttles glanced back over his shoulder. "There are forty rangers on the beach, more in the lot behind the restaurant. They have heavy weapons and their commander isn't as sold on talking as we are." He did his best to empathize. "You can't get away, Mr. Hager. It's over."

"More like a stalemate, I'd say." Caroline stood close to Ross Ed. "Rush us and we dump the alien in the water. Stand there talking and Ross Ed's arms get more and more tired."

Kerry's voice was hard. "I think you're bluffing. This is the second time I've seen you with the artifact. You've grown attached to it. It's downright unnatural. I don't think you can speak so sympathetically about it one moment and consider abandoning it to the ocean the next."

Ross Ed's response took the form of a thin, infuriating smile. "Well, ma'am, you know how to find out."

"I'm not leaving this pier without it."

"Why not just put it down while we're talking?" Suttles urged him.

"So some sharpshooter can put a bullet in him?" Caroline hugged the Texan. "Don't do it, Ross Ed."

"This is a matter of national security!" By now Kerry had advanced from simple frustration to outrage.

"National insecurity, you mean." Ross Ed's determination was unshakable. Unfortunately, his arms weren't. Slowly, so as not to panic the three officers into trying something desperate, he set

Jed down on the railing, resting him in his familiar ventriloquist's dummy posture. It was eerie to see him sitting there, practically of his own accord, the fog-diffused light shining moistly off the unearthly suit, the multiple limbs dangling loosely. Ross kept the body from tumbling off the railing by clutching a fistful of suit fabric tightly in his right hand.

Caroline's comment had started him thinking about long-range scopes and infrared sights. Were there crosshairs trained on his head and hers even as they argued with the three officers? He made sure to keep Jed balanced precariously on the edge of the weathered wood so that if he was shot, the little alien would go spinning into the sea.

The one called Suttles was right, he knew. He *was* tired of running. And if they'd managed to find him here, they'd find him and Caroline anywhere they tried to flee. Next time they might decide to shoot first and talk later, even if only with tranquilizer darts. It was pretty clear that it was simply a matter of time before they caught him asleep or off guard and snatched Jed away. He turned to his left.

"What do you think, Caroline? What d'you think I should do? Jed's turned bullets before, but I ain't sure I want to count on him doing it again." Instead of replying, she looked over her shoulder and frowned. Frowned at the sky and the fog. "What, what is it?" He followed her line of sight and saw nothing.

"Don't you hear that?" Terse determination had given way to puzzlement and uncertainty.

He squinted into the mist. "What is it, more whales?"

"No. Not whales."

"Excuse me?" Suttles took a step forward. "Remember us?" But the big Texan and his statuesque companion ignored him.

The light was faint at first, too dim to be seen from shore. As it drew nearer it split into several distinct sources. All thoughts of fishing forgotten, Robinett stepped away from the railing.

"Chopper," decided Kerry curtly. "The Grandparents of the Damned from Indiana, or worse. Somebody get on the phone, quick."

"It's not a helicopter." Robinett was backing up slowly.

Between the end of the pier and the land, the fog bank remained solid and impenetrable. From the cupola westward a vast globe of mist simply evaporated, as if scooped out by a giant hand. In its place hovered a disk-shaped artifact a little larger than Disneyland and slightly smaller than Burbank. A very few faint lights showed along the edge facing the pier as it whispered of faraway places and inconceivable technologies.

Tearing his gaze away from the fantastic aerial apparition, Ross Ed noted that Jed's suit was not glowing. What that portended he did not know, but he had a feeling they were going to find out.

He found himself telling Caroline that everything was going to be okay. She was less than completely convinced.

"How do *you* know it's going to be okay?"

"Isn't it obvious?" he found himself saying. "It's Jed's folks come to recover his body."

"How do you know that? How do you know it has anything to do with Jed's people? Remember the cube-ship in the mountains?" She was flinching slightly, as if that would make any difference should the gigantic object choose to close the intervening space between its underside and the surface.

"Yes I do, and this doesn't look anything like it. Who else would just suddenly show up like this except someone looking for Jed? We didn't perform any kind of ceremony and his suit isn't glowing or reacting defensively. We didn't send any kind of signal." He nodded in the direction of the monstrous ship. "Whoever's in there came looking for *him*. Has to be."

"But how did they find him?"

Ross shrugged. "Maybe his suit's been putting out some kind of undetectable signal ever since he's been here and it was blocked until I pulled him out of that cave." He glanced back at the three awestruck officers. "Pretty good timing."

"If they're here for Jed, then what are they waiting for? Why don't they take him? It's like they're looking us over."

"If you're not going to use that phone," Kerry hissed at Robinett, "let me have it."

"What for?" The tall scientist-soldier stood gaping at the ship. "Who you gonna call, alien-busters? Looks like we've been outflanked."

"We can't just let him go," she argued desperately.

"Can't we? Tell you what," Robinett told her, "*you* run over there and try wrestling him away from good ol' Ross Ed. But let me get off this pier before the aliens see what you're up to."

"What makes you think they're watching us?" Her usual conviction was lacking.

"You think this ship's here to take on a load of kelp?"

Before she could reply, Ross Ed had lifted the alien body off the railing and thrust it skyward, holding it high over his head.

"Here he is!" he yelled. "I've been looking after him for a while, but now I guess it's time to take him home for a proper burial!" Or whatever it was Jed's kind did with their dead, he reflected.

A shaft of palest blue light emerged from the leading edge of the vessel, bathing in its luminescence the dead alien, Ross Ed Hager, and Caroline Kramer. All three, together with the section of the pier on which they were standing and the upper three feet of water in which it was resting, promptly vanished. A soft whistle accompanied their departure, followed by an ear-tickling *pop* as air rushed in to occupy the volume thus displaced.

Suttles found himself staring at a gap in the pier some ten feet long. The cupola at the end had become an island. As he leaned out over the freshly cut edge, he got drenched when the occupants of the ship dumped the seawater they'd inadvertently sucked up back where it belonged. The mass of planks and pilings extracted from the pier followed, just missing him.

"Well, that's that." Robinett aided his friend and fellow officer in his attempts to dry himself off. "I think we can stop wondering about whether technologically advanced life exists elsewhere in the universe."

"Advanced, hell," groused Suttles as he tried to wring out his sopping sleeves. "They could've missed me."

"What do you mean, 'that's that'?" Kerry had advanced to the edge of the gap. "Use your phone, man! Call the air force."

"And tell 'em what?" Hands in pockets, Robinett sauntered forward to join her. "That there's a spaceship the size of the Pentagon sitting on the end of the Malibu pier? Even if they believed me, what would you expect them to do? Try to force it down? Somehow I don't think that would be a good idea." He nodded toward the ship.

"Whoever's in there has already shown that they can manipulate matter and gravity. All the air force can manipulate are small things that go boom. If whoever's up there isn't interested in saying hello, let's at least try not to tick them off. We've already lost the chance to return the corpse to them. Let's not lose something else as well. Like maybe Los Angeles."

"You're assuming they're hostile."

"I'm not assuming anything. I just don't happen to think that throwing F-22s at them is a good way of signaling our honorable intentions."

Momentarily displaced by nonmeterological forces, the fog was beginning to return, closing in around the vast bulge of the alien vessel. The isolated lights dispersed as the entire gigantic specter seemed to melt into the mist. Then it was gone.

Robinett heaved a sigh. "I guess we might as well go, too."

"No, let's hang around awhile yet." Suttles was leaning cautiously over the gap in the pier, eyeing the cleanly sheared-off planks and pilings that were floating in the water below. "They didn't need the piece of pier they grabbed so they dumped it back. Maybe they'll decide they don't need the Texan or the blonde either and they'll toss *them* back."

Kerry nodded approvingly. "I'd rather have the corpse, but at this point I'll settle for a chat with our perambulating roughneck."

Suttles eyed Robinett. "There's a use for your phone. Get a hold of the Coast Guard. Tell 'em we need a couple of ships out here to look for, um, a man and a woman who may have fallen overboard. Just in case they get disposed of farther out at sea."

"Good idea." The other captain removed the unit from his belt and began dialing.

"For a first contact," Kerry remarked somberly, "that wasn't handled too well."

"Don't blame yourself." Turning away from the hole in the pier, Suttles put an arm around her shoulders. She allowed it to remain. Together they gazed out into the fog, which on this night concealed far more than wandering albatrosses and migrating whales. "It's not like we were allowed any input. I can handle arguments and disagreements, but it's tough when you're just ignored."

NINETEEN

There were half a dozen aliens waiting in a domed chamber no larger than a decent-sized apartment. Somehow Ross Ed had expected something grander. While the floor was a milky, opaque white, the curving walls and ceiling were composed of some vitreous green substance that allowed one to see into it for some distance. The complete absence of any right angles was disconcerting and gave their new surroundings a vaguely organic feel. Ross Ed felt as if they'd been transported to the interior of a giant lime-flavored Gummi Bear.

Squiggles and arcs of solid color seemed to swim within the walls. Some pulsed with life and light while others stayed dark. A few exhibited malleable borders which shrank or expanded as he watched.

None of the assembled aliens, who were eyeing the recent arrivals intently, resembled Jed in the least. Nor were they as massive and overbearing as the crew of the cube-ship who had treated the Arizona assemblage of saucer adherents so indelicately.

Barrellike bodies were supported by four surprisingly gracile yet strong legs, the front pair of which were longer than the rear. No arms, hands, tentacles, or other recognizable manipulative digits were visible. Set atop a long, flexible neck, the flattened skull boasted two stalked eyes set well out to the sides, like the sideview mirrors on a sports car. A flap of pinkish, flexible skin formed a forward-facing crest that ran from the base of one stalk to the other. Several of these crests were streaked with gray, others with black. Ross Ed imagined a single, oversized ear. With necks held erect, they were roughly Caroline's height. Ross estimated the heaviest of them at about three hundred pounds. Their clothing was cream-colored, with a line of black spots running down the front across the chest. Feet or hooves were hidden within short, black leatherette-look booties.

Even more remarkable than the head was the single ropelike, flexible tail. Slightly longer than the entire body, it split at the tip into half a dozen flexible, super-strong hairs. As two of the creatures left the group to adjust several of the devices drifting through the walls, the visiting humans were able to observe how fluidly the arrangement worked. The tail-hairs had great range and delicacy of touch, while with their two-foot-long necks the aliens were able to look straight back along their spines to supervise the work.

Nothing he saw shouted "Gun!" at Ross Ed, but that was no guarantee weapons weren't present. Initially prepared to hand Jed over to the first alien they saw, he now kept the diminutive body close. Whoever these beings were, none could be accounted the tripedal corpse's first cousin.

The second largest of the four who continued to confront them stepped forward. As it addressed them, mouth movements revealed double rows of grinding teeth set within the long, flattened jaws. Though far more complex and melodious, the speech unaccountably reminded Ross of a frustrated bulldog's barking.

When the speech finally concluded, he looked at Caroline and together the two of them spread their hands wide and shook their heads. They had no way of knowing if the gestures were understood, but two of the creatures promptly came forward and made fumbling motions with their tail hands in the direction of his backpack.

"Hold on there." Ross Ed put up both hands and stepped back.

The one who had delivered the barking greeting yipped something else and the two fumblers obediently abandoned their efforts. As the apparent leader, or officer in charge, or teacher, or whatever it was advanced, Ross Ed was put in mind of a heavyset deer. Eyes moving independently like a chameleon's, it studied the taller biped. Then it chirped at the two underlings, who promptly galloped off down a distant corridor.

There followed several long, awkward moments which alien

and human spent inspecting each other. Ross Ed allowed the creature to walk completely around him so long as it made no move toward Jed. When it was finished with him it repeated the inspection with Caroline. Occasionally it would reach out with the unique tail-hand to caress this or that part of their bodies. The touch was featherlight.

When it was satisfied, it stepped back. Caroline leaned over to whisper to Ross. "What do you make of all this?"

"I dunno, except that they sure want to get their tails on Jed. But they're not willing to force the issue. At least, not yet."

"We can't do anything to stop them. Even if there was a door in the floor, I have a feeling it's a long drop to the ocean."

"I ain't big on swimming anyways. What I'd really like to know is what their interest is in Jed. Obviously, these ain't his people." He glanced over his shoulder at the figure riding high on his back. "Shame he can't tell us."

Clip-clopping softly on the creamy white floor, the two aliens who had departed in haste returned with several devices loaded on their backs. Using his tail-hand to remove one, the alien in charge advanced on Ross Ed. More than a little short on choices, the Texan decided to hold his ground.

Turning his left flank toward the human, the quadruped held out the studded strap and shook it vigorously. It was clear Ross was supposed to take it and do something with it, but what? For the second time he spread his hands helplessly.

Grunting softly, the alien demonstrated by slipping the strap over its head and tightening it beneath its jaws. It then selected a second and offered it to Ross.

"Reckon we're supposed to put these on."

Caroline hesitated. "You think it's safe?"

He shrugged. "You think we've got a choice? They're not forcing them on us, and I expect that's a good sign. I don't see how we'll gain any points by refusing."

Reaching out, he took the strap and slipped it over his head. It was smooth under his jaw and didn't cut or pinch. Binding pressure was gentle but firm. Caroline considered tying a bow in her own but decided it might comprise the device's function.

Satisfied, the alien stepped back and regarded them thoughtfully. "Since you fortuitously utilize spoken communication, we have been able to calibrate these inductive translators for the dominant local language. Can you understand me?"

When Ross Ed replied, barks and yips seemed to issue from his mouth. While the process was confusing to him, the aliens were obviously well pleased.

"What do you want with us?"

"With you, nothing." The tail-hand flicked away an imaginary fly. "I am Frontrunner Uroon and we want the Shakaleeshva."

Ross Ed blinked. "The what?"

"I'm sorry, but we seem to be fresh out of Shakaleeshvas at the moment." Caroline smiled in what she hoped was a winning manner. "But if you'll put us down in Beverly Hills, we could look for one for you. I've been told that you can find almost anything you want in L.A."

Tail-hand and head gestured in tandem. "I refer to the individual you carry on your back."

"You want Jed?"

"'Je'ed.'" Uroon mimicked the Texan's pronunciation. "What is a Je'ed?"

"It's the name I gave him."

"Very well then. If it will facilitate communication, we will employ your nomenclature. Please pass me the Jed. It is important that we talk with him."

"Talk with . . . ?" Ross Ed turned to Caroline, who for a change shrugged at him instead of the quadrupeds. "You can't talk to him. He's dead."

"We'll be the judges of that, if you don't mind." The tail-hand flicked lazily back and forth.

"What could you possibly want to talk to him about?"

Bright pink eyes bobbed on their short stalks. "What does it matter to you, human? We are the Culakhan and we have our reasons. You will comply. Without wishing to appear impolite, I must point out that you can be made to comply. But we have no quarrel with you. We do not harass simple animals."

"Hey, watch it. Just because we don't build giant spaceships and beams that lift people off the ground and headbands that translate different folks' speech and instruments that float in the wall and . . ." He hesitated. "Okay, so maybe we are a little simple. But we're not animals."

Caroline jumped in. "That's right. We're sort of in-between, I guess."

Turning to an associate, Frontrunner Uroon muttered something Ross Ed's translator band didn't pick up. When his head swung back, it dipped slightly. "We have no desire to be discourteous. I am simply relating the facts." The tail-hand extended. "You will now transfer the Jed."

Ross's natural inclination was to retreat, except that a glassy green wall was barely a few yards behind him. "Look, why don't you tell us what's going on here and what you want with Jed?"

"Time burns," the quadruped muttered. "We could simply take him and return you the way you came . . . without the use of the lifting beam. However, we are constrained by our own Code of Conduct, which prohibit where avoidable the abuse of ignorant life-forms."

"There you go again," chided an exasperated Caroline.

"Apologies." Uroon gestured with the tail-hand. "The being that rides upon your back, the Shakaleeshva you call Jed, is wanted by the Culakhan for a long litany of crimes."

Ross gaped. "What, Jed? I don't believe it."

Caroline gazed up at him. "Why shouldn't you believe it? You don't know anything about Jed. He's dead. And since he's dead he can't talk to them anyway, so why worry about it?"

For the first time the alien body weighed heavily on the Texan's shoulders. "I can't believe I've been carrying around an extraterrestrial criminal for the past couple of months."

She kept her response gentle. " You can't disbelieve it, Ross."

"We will prove it to you." Uroon stepped forward. "Pass him over. In return, you may remain for the opening of the interrogation."

"This is nuts. He's *dead.* I mean, I may not know how to fly a ship like this or speak your language without the aid of this headband, but I know when something's dead. I'm from Texas, for God's sake! Roadkill's a way of life down there."

"'Roadkill'?" The Culakhan affected confusion. Apparently certain concepts were beyond the capacity of the remarkable headbands to literalize.

"Besides, even if Jed did do something wrong, he's past paying for the offense."

Uroon and a couple of the other Culakhan were fiddling with their headbands. "There is some difficulty with comprehension. Please pass him to me."

Fresh out of options as well as ideas, Ross Ed could only think to say, "You'll really let us be present when you do whatever it is you're going to do?"

"We will commence the questioning here and now." Uroon dipped his head a second time. "Such is the task I am charged with."

"Well, all right, then. As long as you promise." Reaching up and back, Ross swung the pack onto his chest and gently removed Jed. Uroon and an associate accepted the corpse, handling it with care if not reverence.

Ross Ed watched uneasily as a pair of aliens clad in red appeared in the corridor. They had pink patches running down their chests. Between them they hauled two backpacks full of instruments.

A portable inclined bench was unfolded and set up on the deck. Jed was laid across it and strapped in place, arms secured at his side and front, legs near the base. An elaborate assortment of devices were attached to his suit and headpiece.

Another technician wheeled a large, complex console up behind the pinioned alien and began manipulating unseen controls. Indicator lights flashed and blinked.

"This is ridiculous." Some time had passed and Ross had discovered that he was getting hungry. "I told you, he's dead. Can you bring back the dead?"

"Of course not." Uroon stood nearby, commenting occasionally to the preoccupied technicians. "The revivification of the deceased is a task that exceeds the capability of any science we are familiar with."

"Well then, what the hell . . . ?" A hand slipped around Ross's waist. A real hand and not a tail-hand.

"Take it easy," Caroline whispered. "They're going to do what they're going to do, and nothing you can say is going to stop them. Obviously Jed's suit can't stop them, either. It won't do any good to make them mad. Let's just watch. We might learn something." She cast a suggestive look in the direction of the depression in the floor behind them.

"What I don't understand is why they don't just chuck us out that lock. They've got what they want."

Uroon overheard. "As I mentioned earlier, the actions of all Culakhan are constrained by the Codes of Conduct. Unlike the despicable Shakaleeshva, we have immutable values."

Two of the technicians stepped back from the bench-bound body, making room for Uroon. Approaching, he took up a position directly in front of the corpse and sat back on his haunches. The Culakhan behind the console studied his instrumentation intently. Ross Ed had the distinct impression that the walls were watching.

"I am Uroon, Frontrunner and Commendidar of the vessel *Trestasia,* of the Culakhan Combine," the quadruped barked sharply. "You are the Shakaleeshva known to these humans as 'Jed.' "

"All right, so you've caught up with me. So what?"

The reply emerged from some kind of artificial larynx which had been attached to the little alien's headpiece. It was a fine, confident voice, though Ross Ed had no way of knowing if it was an accurate reflection of Jed's actual speaking voice or simply a by-product of the device relaying the words. He'd been watching closely and there'd been no sign of lip (or any other kind of) movement behind the transparent faceplate.

Caroline piped up alongside him. "Will somebody please explain to me how he can talk if he's dead?"

"Do not interrupt!" Codes of Conduct or not, Uroon wasn't above showing impatience.

The conversation which ensued between Frontrunner Uroon and the dead Shakaleeshva was long, tedious, and dealt with many concepts and terms unfamiliar to the two stunned humans. It frequently exceeded the ability of the translator headbands to keep up.

Unable to stand it any longer, Ross Ed stepped forward. "Look, this isn't fair. Jed can't move, he can't run away, and he can't object to the terms of the discussion."

"Of course he can object," replied Uroon. "Kindly also keep in mind that unlike the rest of us, he does not have to eat, drink, or deal with the by-products of those processes."

"But dammit, I don't *understand.* Is he dead or not?"

"It is true that the body has failed, and in that sense he is dead, but the Shakaleeshva's special, and very expensive, biosuit succeeded in preserving specific cognitive processes against the chance of future reactivation. This we have accomplished. Only the mind is functional and capable of restoration to full activity, and only a portion of it at that. Neuromuscular motor and all related physiologic functions are indeed 'dead.' "

"So he's half-dead?" Caroline asked.

"More than half, if you go by body weight. Less than half, if you regard the mind and its memories as paramount indicators of life. The distinction is more social and philosophical then biological. You may be interested to know that even as we are speaking, his suit is being properly recharged. Except for its defensive functions, of course, which we suppressed upon contact and have subsequently disengaged. Having come this far to find him, we have no intention of losing him now. We intend to seek restitution from what survives." The tail-hand fluttered in Jed's direction.

"Lamentably, the Shakaleeshva is not being very cooperative. This is to be expected. It is not easy to persuade the dead, much less effectively threaten them, but in this instance ways will be found. In any event, you are relieved of any responsibility or concern in this matter."

Caroline's earlier bravado shrank in proportion to her voice, which dropped to a whisper. "What . . . what are you going to do with us?"

"According to the specified portion of the appropriate Code, the relevant thing." Uroon elected not to elaborate on this enigma. Starting at the back of his neck, a quiver ran down the length of his body. "For the moment I am tired. It has been a stressful time. The initial period of interrogation is now concluded. We will resume following the prescribed period of rest."

So saying, the Culakhan barked commands at the others. In single file they clip-clopped off down the corridor. A translucent green panel slid down behind them, preventing anyone from following. Not that Ross Ed or Caroline was so inclined.

Ross examined the nearly deserted chamber. Lights still glistened within walls and shone from the peculiar console. Others enveloped Jed's body in a colorful cocoon, giving him the look of an abandoned Christmas ornament. Resting on the inclined bench and encased in a tangle of instrumentation, he looked little different than from when Ross had dragged him out of the New Mexico cave. The expression on his funny, triangular face was unchanged.

Crossing his legs, Ross Ed sat down next to his alien companion. Caroline joined him. Starting at the three feet, he let his gaze travel up the length of the alien corpus until he found himself staring at the immobile inhuman face.

"You talked to them. Can you talk to us as well?" He didn't really expect a reply.

"Sure. Why the hell not?" declared the artificial larynx from its location atop the headpiece. The peculiar-shaped mouth didn't move, the eyes didn't twitch. "How you doin', Ross Ed?"

"I . . . I'm doing okay, Jed. That Uroon fella tried to explain, but I still ain't sure I understand how you're doing this. Are you dead or not?"

"Well, yes and no."

Caroline nodded sardonically. "I'm glad we finally got *that* cleared up."

It was uncanny to hear so lively and active a voice emerge from so utterly motionless a body. "I guess you would say that I'm dead except for my mind. Don't try to understand. I don't, not entirely."

Ross frowned. "Your suit preserved your memories and you don't understand how?"

"Hey, you watch television. Can you give me a detailed technical explanation of how it works?" Ross Ed had to admit that he could not. "I was comatose until you activated the relevant suit functions by hauling me out of that cave. On contact with another intelligence, the suit reactivated my mental functions. But without the necessary additional specialized equipment, there was no way I could contact you directly. Not knowing your language, I couldn't exactly spell out an explanation in the sand. Also, I was forced to function minimally except when a defensive reaction was called for."

"You know that I watch television. How could you know that if you can't see me, if your eyes aren't working?"

"Aural functions are operative, and there are ways of perceiving you can't imagine that go beyond simple rods-and-cones vision. Let's just say that I don't have to open my eyes to see. You lose a lot of color saturation and depth perception that way, but the dead can't be choosy. This gear I'm currently hooked up to helps a lot. The Culakhan are as inventive as they are persistent."

"They've been very polite," Caroline noted.

"Don't kid yourselves. If they find a hole in their revered Codes of Conduct that'll allow them to get rid of you without violating any precious precepts, they'll throw you out the nearest hatch. And since they've disconnected all my suit's defensive functions, I won't be able to do a thing to stop them."

"Oh." Her gaze strayed once more to the depression in the floor.

"You're the first dead person I've ever talked to," Ross Ed commented. "It ain't easy."

"You think this is a snap for me?"

The Texan shifted his position on the slick floor. "So you're a Shakaleeshva. Whatever that is. What's your real name?"

"How about we just stick with Jed? It's short, easy, and I've grown kind of fond of it over the past several planetary revolutions. it has no rhythm to it, no music, but it's possessed of a certain coarse efficiency."

Ross Ed scrutinized the immobile alien face closely. "So what you're telling me is that you've been aware of everything that's happened since I found you in the mountains."

"That's right."

"The ventriloquist act. You put all those words in my mouth."

"Sure. It was ventriloquism at its best, only the roles were the reverse of what people thought. You were the dummy. I couldn't talk myself, but I could influence your speech. Used a lot of power, but it was good therapy. Please don't think too meanly of me. It got pretty boring just lying around."

"I can imagine," murmured Caroline.

"I enjoyed your company, Ross Ed Hager. Your protective instincts commended you to me, and I did my best to help out where possible. I can't move my dead arms and legs, but thanks to this suit I was able to influence my surroundings by other means. Within limits, I could not only protect myself, but those around me."

"I know." As Ross Ed reflected, memories came flooding back.

"Once they located me by homing in on emanations from my suit, I couldn't do anything to keep the Culakhan from picking us up. Don't think I didn't try, though."

"How'd you happen to end up in that cave, anyway?" Ross asked.

"My ship went down close by. Nothing astonishing. Just your usual mechanical foul-up. Spaceships aren't perfect instruments either, you know."

"Then there *was* a UFO crash near Roswell! All those old books were right."

"Roswell, Roswell . . . let me look at your thoughts for a minute, Ross Ed."

The Texan's jaw dropped slightly. "You can do that?"

"Of course. How else do you think we worked the ventriloquist act so smoothly? Hang on. Just a moment . . . there, that's it. Let your mind go nice and blank, the way it usually does."

"Thanks," Ross mumbled.

"Only a little deeper . . . there, that's got it. It's just like searching one of your primitive computers. Access the soft drive. When you get right down to it, any memory is nothing more than stratified electrical impulses.

"Oh, now I see. So *that's* what got sucked into the spatial displacer. A 'weather balloon,' whatever that is. Fouled me up good, it did. I didn't put down very smoothly. Got out of the ship before the molecular bonds disengaged and managed to crawl into that cave. Long-term survival programming took over from there. Unfortunately, the suit couldn't preserve more than my mind for very long, so it began shutting down noncritical functions. Extremities go first, then the internal organs." Caroline made a face. "If you hadn't found me, Ross Ed, I'd have died completely in there. Within another of your planet's five years there wouldn't have been even this much of me left."

"I'm sorry about what happened to your ship." Ross uncrossed his legs, relieving the cramp that had uncomfortably announced itself. "Our people are always shooting stuff up into the sky."

"Don't feel so bad. I *wanted* to put down here. That's why I came in a ship designed to self-destruct. I wanted to crash on your world. It's just that I planned on having a little more control over the process. I'm afraid I wasn't paying full attention during approach and survey, preferring to leave the details to the automatics. Anything substantial they would have detected and avoided. This weather-balloon device was apparently insubstantial enough to be overlooked yet solid enough to cause problems."

"You *wanted* to kill yourself?" Caroline stared at the motionless form.

"No, no, no! I said crash, not kill. There's a difference. Damn, this is frustrating, not being able to support words with gestures! I have in mind several the Culakhan wouldn't appreciate.

"It was my intention to crash just hard enough to engage the ship's self-destruct sequence, which is designed to prevent advanced technology from falling into the hands of primitive species, but not so violently as to injure myself. A recordable crash sequence would hopefully convince any who might come after that I had perished in the debacle, with the result that I would be left alone." A hint of irony corrupted the artificial speech. "I'm afraid my incompetence has rendered the scenario all too likely. With my suit's life-support functions fully recharged, my mind and thoughts will live for another fifty of your years, although it is not my health and well-being that interests the Culakhan."

"You know, I've been meaning to ask you about that." Ross Ed leaned forward to stare into shuttered eyes. "I can't tell if you're telling the truth, so I'm going to assume that the Shakaleeshva code of conduct is at least as binding as the Culakhan's. Go ahead and read what I'm thinking."

There was a brief pause before the synthetic voice responded. "No, I'm not a criminal, Ross. Rather the contrary, in fact."

"Then why would they say such things about you?"

"Understand that the Culakhan have their own reasons for wanting to make an example of what's left of me. It's all quite complicated and the details need not concern you. I'm not sure what they intend to do with me except that it will be unconventional. After all, they can't exactly threaten to kill me." Something not unlike a chuckle drifted out of the mechanical larynx.

"I'm going to take you at your word." Ross Ed rose and surveyed the chamber. "I've stuck with you this long. I guess we're together to the end."

"Uh, hello? Excuse me a minute, here?" Caroline tugged at his pant leg until he gave her a hand up. "I haven't agreed to stick with anybody, and I'm not real interested in being dead. If there's another option I'd sure like to hear it."

Ross considered. "Maybe we can play on this Code of Conduct of theirs."

"I wouldn't count on that," Jed told them. "Besides, being dead's not so bad. It's just kind of slow."

Caroline loomed over the motionless, instrument-laden form. "I'm a slow kind of person. If there's any chance of getting out of here in a state of not-dead, I'd like to take it."

Ross Ed had walked back to the edge of the depression in the floor. "If we could get this door, or hatch, or whatever it is open, I wonder if we could survive the drop to the ocean."

"What makes you believe we're still over the ocean?" Jed queried. "You think the Shakaleeshva are still hanging around fifteen feet above the end of the Malibu pier? I haven't sensed the mind distortion that goes with the activation of spatial displacement, so we're still in your atmosphere, but our altitude could be anything from ten feet to ten miles."

"Um. Well, it was just an idea." Caroline had come up alongside Ross Ed and he put an arm around her. "At least we're together."

Putting both hands against his chest, she shoved hard. "What the hell's that supposed to mean? Haven't you been listening to me, Ross Ed? I don't want to die here, not with you or anybody else. I still haven't been to San Diego. I love you, but I draw the line at mutual-death scenarios. They're too friggin' gothic."

"It doesn't matter. We're stuck until they find a gap in their manners that lets them kick us out with a clear conscience."

"You're overwrought," Jed insisted. "The Culakhan are relentless bastards, but they pride themselves on what they consider to be their gentility. When they're finished their observations they'll *probably* put you down somewhere. You're representatives of an ignorant, primitive species, you see, and therefore it would be demeaning to kill you."

"Then we can relax," Caroline declared hopefully.

"In all likelihood."

Ross Ed wasn't satisfied, the whole situation rankled, and he wasn't used to feeling helpless. "I wish we could do something for you, Jed."

"I can't imagine what. As you can see, at the moment I'm not real mobile. Give me some time to cerebrate. I still haven't had an opportunity to properly analyze the instrumentation they've hooked me up to."

Ross started to nod before he remembered that Jed wouldn't be able to see the gesture. Could he perceive it? "Whatever happens, it's nice to finally have been able to say hello."

"Pardon me if I don't shake your hand." The voice had grown distant, contemplative.

After being assured it could not harm them, they were given protein substitute to eat and water to drink. It did nothing for their taste buds but did assuage the growing hunger in Ross Ed's stomach. Soon thereafter the interrogation resumed. He and Caroline were ignored, which both supposed was all to the good. Despite Jed's reassurances, they weren't quite convinced that Uroon's ultimate intentions were entirely benign.

TWENTY

According to Ross Ed's watch, two days had passed and yet another interrogation concluded when the Frontrunner unexpectedly turned to them and announced, "It has been decided. You are to be returned to the surface to live out the remainder of your simple lives."

Caroline could hardly control herself. "That's great, but why?"

"Because we have no further use for you here. You have nothing more to contribute to our deliberations. We assent to this because it is—"

"I know; part of your Code of Conduct."

"Not entirely." Looking straight back over its spine, the Frontrunner gestured with three of its prehensile tail-hairs. "The Shakaleeshva has deferred to compliance provided we return you safely to your world. I confess myself surprised at his interest, which we know to be out of keeping with his true character.

"We can compel response, but it will be easier for all concerned if his assistance can be gained. There are significant questions in quest of resolution which cooperation would facilitate. Hence our accession." The Culakhan turned back to them. "Where would you like to be set down?"

"How about right where you picked us up?" suggested Caroline.

"No." Ross's expression was set. "Texas would be better. I've got family in the Corpus Christi area. I've been promising to drop in on them for some time. Think you could land us there?"

"If you will but supply coordinates we shall put you down anywhere on the surface."

He grimaced. "Coordinates, huh? Yours or mine? How bout if I just draw you a picture?"

Caroline threw him an admiring glance. "You can draw?"

"Only maps." He smiled apologetically. "It's useful in the field."

As it turned out, a map wasn't necessary. After it was explained what was needed, a technician conjured up a perfect photo-realistic reproduction of the earth, complete to current cloud cover and terminator line. With the clouds eliminated, Ross Ed was easily able to locate the south Texas coast. So as not to attract undue attention, he pinpointed a location somewhat to the south of the city limits.

"Down there the metropolitan area peters out pretty fast. You should be able to slip your ship in without being seen."

Uroon yipped softly. "We could position it in the center of your capital city without being noticed, but this will be simpler. People will see you. They will not see us. We will appear to be nothing more than a localized climatological phenomenon."

"Like fog?" asked Caroline.

"Exactly. We will perform the transfer during the darkest part of the night. But before we can commence, there is one other matter that must be attended to first."

"Of course." Ross Ed didn't have a clue as to what the alien was talking about and was disappointed when Uroon didn't explain.

A number of hours passed, during which time Caroline in particular worried about the Culakhan undergoing a change of heart. When Ross's watch read four A.M. California time they were told to prepare. This entailed each of them taking several deep breaths when a technician directed them to the center of the depression.

"What happens now?" Ross couldn't keep from wondering how much air lay between the soles of his feet and the rocks of the surface.

"First we must resolve our encounter on a friendly basis, so that no feelings of enmity will remain between Culakhan and primitives. This is required by our Codes of Conduct."

Caroline leaned over and whispered to Ross Ed. "Might've guessed that one."

He shushed her. "Okey-doke. What did you have in mind?"

At a signal from Uroon a technician stepped forward and with great solemnity passed the Texan a large bright green ovoid some three feet in diameter. Performing a series of elegant bows, the deliverer then retreated.

The Frontrunner's tail stood straight up. "This is a representation of the Great Egg, from which life originally sprang. Take it as a symbol of our good feelings toward you and your kind."

"What does it do?" Ross Ed cradled the heavy lump dubiously.

"Do?" Uroon fiddled with his headband, as if he hadn't heard clearly. "It doesn't 'do' anything. It is a symbol."

"Like a cross," Caroline explained, "or a crescent moon, or six-pointed star."

"Oh. Oh, yeah." With an effort he forbore from asking the Frontrunner of the Culakhan if ham went with it. "Thanks!"

Uroon stepped clear of the circular depression. "Farewell, and take with you no ill thoughts of the Culakhan. You carry no onus from your association with the Shakaleeshva, for you knew not who or what he was. Resume your rudimentary lives as though nothing has happened."

"Easy for you to say." Ross gazed past the Frontrunner, to where Jed lay strapped to his bench.

A brief but intense light flared in the chamber and he stumbled. "What was that?"

Uroon barked at two technicians before replying. "The section of atmosphere through which we are currently passing is highly charged. Settings must be adjusted to compensate so that our camouflage remains intact. It can be difficult."

"I bet. The Gulf's only halfway through hurricane season."

Upon which observation the bottom dropped away beneath them. Caroline looked down, wished she hadn't, and moaned.

They were standing on nothingness approximately two hundred feet above dense, starlit forest. Ross Ed's last glimpse of the great ship's interior showed Uroon turning away to yelp at his associates. Having formally bade them farewell, the Frontrunner was no longer interested in the two humans. Or to put it another way, he had satisfied the relevant Code of Conduct.

Still cradling the ovoid, Ross Ed felt himself slowly falling. A gentle pressure exerted itself on every part of his body, firm yet comfortable. As soon as they made contact with the white sandy beach, the pressure evaporated. In front of them marching wavelets crooned to the coconut crabs while behind, inscrutable forest beckoned.

Above, a dark mass of cloud scudded with unnatural speed off to the east before vanishing at last over the horizon.

"Well, at least we're out of that, safe and sound." Caroline was pumped with a mixture of exhaustion and relief.

"Yeah. Safe and sound." Putting down the ovoid, the Texan continued to stare at the point on the horizon where the Culakhan ship had taken its leave.

She put a comforting hand on his arm. "There was nothing else you could do. Don't worry about Jed. He'll be fine; he's dead. Ross, we're alive and together." Spreading her arms, she whirled gleefully in small circles. "We're home!" Sand flew from beneath her feet.

"Back on Earth, yeah, not necessarily home. This doesn't look like Texas." He studied the forest's jagged silhouette. "It's not this lush near Corpus, or anywhere else in Texas that I know. I suppose it *could* be Padre Island. A forest reserve, or something."

At that moment an aural soufflé of screechings and chitterings filled the night air. Initially intimidated by the ominous mass of the Culakhan ship, the forest's inhabitants now resumed their nocturnal chorus.

"Doesn't sound like Texas, either."

Caroline joined him in pondering the raucous woods. "Of course we're in Texas. Where else would we be?"

As they considered the possibilities a couple of bats flew by overhead. Ross Ed knew that Texas was full of bats, but to the best of his knowledge none of them had four-foot wingspans.

"That settles it." He looked up and down the beach. "Let's get off the sand. We're too exposed out here." He started toward the coconut palms.

"Wait a minute. What about this?" She nudged the egg shape with a foot.

"What about it?"

"Maybe there's something useful inside."

"I thought you said it was just a symbol." He eyed the Culakhan's parting gift doubtfully. "I'm sure not hauling it all over creation."

"Then let's at least open it." She smiled encouragingly. "If nothing else, maybe we can make an omelette."

"Be my guest." He was more interested in the unidentifiable forest than the ovoid.

Kneeling, she examined the object gingerly. The surface was firm but giving, like Styrofoam. Drawing a fingernail experimentally along the curve, she was gratified to see a seam appear in its wake. The two halves of the ovoid fell apart.

The interior contained not a religious icon, not an oversized yolk, not a bundle of survival gear, but a familiar tripedal shape. Ross Ed jerked around sharply.

"Jed! How in blazes did . . . ?" Automatically he scanned the sky for signs of gigantic alien spacecraft or unnatural clouds.

The artificial larynx conveyed the deceased alien's sentiments admirably. He was still cocooned in pulsing Culakhan instrumentation.

"My defensive functions may have been disconnected, but my brain's still working just fine, thank you. During the interrogation I told the Culakhan that you and I had been together long enough to establish a Knes."

"Say what?" The Texan could only gawk at his motionless friend, whom he had never expected to see again.

"A Knes. It's a kind of unbreakable bond. I explained that it was vital to your primitive mental health that some way be found of maintaining this bond. When they're not making complete idiots of themselves, the Culakhan are a very spiritual species. They understood.

"The solution was to construct a kniessen, an artificial bonding reproduction of myself correct down to the smallest detail. It was part of the price of my cooperation. The Culakhan are excellent technicians and the mechaniflow replica they constructed turned out to be a damn good job. The idea was to present it to you upon your departure so that you'd have something to take home and worship."

"So you're a mechanism, a device, a reproduction. A dummy." He cleared his throat. "Well, I've had plenty of practice dealing with dummies these past weeks."

"You treated me like one often enough. Nothing like incorporating personal experience into a performance."

Ross Ed's brows creased. "For a mechanical reproduction you're mighty responsive."

Something like a subdued laugh emerged from the artificial larynx. "I'm no reproduction, Ross Ed. I'm the genuine article.

The real thing. The kniessen is on the Culakhan ship, programmed to respond like me, albeit with a much more limited vocabulary. At the last minute I pulled a switch."

"But how?" Ross Ed stared at the diminutive alien. "You're dead, mostly. You can't move, much less change places with a mannequin."

"That's not quite correct, my friend. I can't move my muscles, but that doesn't mean I can't move my body. Just because I cannot send instructions to bundles of meat fibers doesn't mean I can't send them anywhere else.

"I insisted that the kniessen portray me exactly as you had last seen me or otherwise your mental stability would suffer. This meant equipping the reproduction with a duplicate set of instrumentation. The Culakhan complied. During the rest period while you were asleep and after the kniessen had been placed nearby, I executed the switch. It was not as difficult as you might imagine.

"Working in teams of two, technicians made periodic checks on us. Though it looks no different from any other survival suit, the one I happen to be wearing represents the pinnacle of Shakaleeshva scientific achievement. Recharged and reenergized, it allowed me to contemplate possibilities of which the Culakhan were unaware. Remember our initial contact in the cave, Ross Ed, and your brief tour of the known universe?"

Ross started at the recollection. "Their minds. You influenced their thoughts!"

"Indeed I did. In the same way that I affected individual humans from maids to barflies to business travelers, I was able to alter the mental state of two of the Culakhan technicians. Since this particular function is part of my communications instrumentation, they neglected to disconnect it. Still, it was very much a touch-and-go operation. Or think-and-go, if you will.

"While I induced one to 'adjust' the on-site recording equipment, I had the other exchange me for the kniessen. I also had her, on my instruments, activate the context-sensitive intuitive response unit which had been included with the reproduction. Though designed to respond to and mollify your primitive emotions, with luck it will fool the Culakhan until they are spatially displaced and well away from your solar system.

"Delicious, is it not? They will be demanding replies and

revenge from their own automaton. I wish I could be there to perceive Uroon's expression when he realizes the deception."

Again Ross Ed looked heavenward. "What happens then?"

"We need to take certain steps. First, unstrap me from this stupid bench. Take care to leave the attached instrumentation intact so that we can continue to communicate."

Caroline helped Ross Ed free the alien. With the added gadgetry Jed fit a little more snugly in the battered backpack. A few modules and unrecognizable Culakhan accoutrements now dangled down Ross Ed's back.

"That's better," the Shakaleeshva declared. "We have places to go and beings to see. For a change, my friend, *you* will have to protect *me*."

"If we can find a phone I'll call my cousin in Corpus and he can come pick us up." Ross looked around uncertainly. "I thought I knew this area pretty well, but I have to admit I'm lost. We need to find a road sign or trail marker or something."

"So we shall, but it won't be one you'll recognize. As it happens, we are nowhere near the connurbation you selected."

The Texan sighed resignedly. "I had a feeling. Then where are we?"

"On the relevant coast, but a little farther south."

Caroline and Ross Ed exchanged a glance. "How much farther?" he asked finally.

"About a thousand of your miles. You call this region the Yucatán, I believe."

"Great! So we're in the middle of the jungle?"

"How do you know our geography?" Caroline asked curiously.

"As I have explained, it's all there in your heads, on the soft drive. Given the appropriate equipment, retrieval is not that difficult."

Ross frowned. "The Culakhan were supposed to set us down just south of Corpus Christi. How come we ended up here?"

"I altered your directions slightly. It was necessary. The Culakhan know nothing of your world's geography. To them this place lies in the same general vicinity as the spot you picked out.

"Now we must get moving. Time is of the essence. I wouldn't rely on the Frontrunner Uroon's Codes of Conduct to save you if he finds us again."

Caroline grimaced. "Whereas you, of course, will be perfectly safe. They want you."

"Of course," admitted the Shakaleeshva cheerfully. "Although being dead, I'm not sure how safe I can be made."

"Why here?" She eyed the surrounding jungle distastefully as they started inland. "Why'd you choose to have us set down in the Yucatán? Why not outside Paris?"

"It's cold in Paris," Ross Ed countered. "The Oklahoma border's always like that."

She gave him a gentle punch. "I meant Paris, France, you insensitive hulk."

"There's another one?"

Jed put an end to the byplay. "Several inhabitable worlds contain evidence of numerous but not vanished space-going species who predate the Culakhan, the Shakaleeshva, and all of our contemporaries. Many are ancient indeed. One is called the Veqq.

"Impressive archaeological sites which survive to this day on their home world show us that the Veqq were great engineers. Records indicate that eons ago they constructed not only ring structures around individual planets but energy-retaining spheres around suns. Their vessels exceeded in volume and velocity anything that can be built today. The galaxy is spotted with amazing relics which attest to their achievements."

Ross Ed stepped over a log after first checking to make sure no snakes were sleeping on the other side. He did so without thinking, the reaction instinctive in any Texan.

"Unfortunately," Jed continued, "as a technologically advanced species, the Veqq had one drawback. They were terrible drivers. They had an unfortunate habit of running their remarkable ships into large solid objects. Given the limited number of objects to mass existing in the stellar firmament, that's not easy to do. But apparently they exercised this foible on a regular basis.

"One of them ran into your planet."

"I don't remember reading about anything like that," Caroline remarked.

"That's because it happened about sixty-five million or so of your years ago. Right here. Left one *micrahc* of a crater, which has since more or less been filled in and covered up by the usual geologic and meteorologic forces. Your planet's a pretty active place.

"Naturally, all evidence of the ship was vaporized by the tremendous impact. Veqq construction techniques made extensive use of the platinum group of metals, particularly iridium. That's one way we know one of their ships struck here. Records indicate that the impact made things tough for the interesting life-forms which happened to be locally dominant at the time. Too bad. A lot of Veqq died, too.

"Thorough as ever, they sent out a team to check out the disaster site. In the unlikely event they missed any survivors, an archeon transmitter was set up so that Veqq who might have dispersed around the planet could someday get back in touch with civilization. Such transmitters were self-repairing and self-activating. When I first orbited your world I ran a routine check for the presence of advanced technology. The transmitter was all I found."

"It's still working?" Caroline couldn't believe it. "After all these millions of years?"

"Like I told you," the artificial voice replied, "The Veqq couldn't navigate worth shit, but they sure knew how to build."

"What's your point?" Ross pushed lianas aside, holding them until Caroline had passed.

"I know a bit about Veqq engineering. If we can get into the transmitter and make a few modifications, it might make someone curious enough to pop down for a look. Someone besides the Culakhan."

Caroline eyed the figure bobbing loosely in Ross Ed's backpack. "If you're not afraid of being picked up, then I guess you were telling us the truth. You're not a criminal."

"No, and I don't want to be picked up. That's why I planned to crash-destruct my ship and maroon myself here. But I don't want to end up in a Culakhan exhibit, either. Ah, there it is."

"There what is?" Ross glanced at the burden on his back. "You can't see anything."

"True, but I can perceive. You forget."

Pushing aside a branch, Caroline found herself face-to-face with a sleepy fourteen-foot-long boa. Reptile and refugee regarded one another evenly. Their respective responses were identical, except that Caroline stuck out her tongue first.

She didn't start to shake for another thirty seconds, until she was well past the snake tree. Ross Ed thought she was cold.

TWENTY-ONE

The temple complex was thickly overgrown. Rainforest trees as enormous as they were exotic soared above the tallest structure, while strangler figs embraced stone and stellae with equal ebullience. Vines and creepers snaked their way along walls or through windows. Monkeys chattered, birds screeched, and a toucan, its bill like a rush of spilled Halloween candy, perched clownishly atop the graven image of a noble.

Reclaimed by the jungle and hidden from the air, the city had been abandoned for centuries. In between football games, fishing shows, and the weather, Ross Ed had seen occasional glimpses of such places while idly flipping channels, but he'd never expected to actually stumble into one.

"Which way?" From where they were standing, all roads led to stone.

"Just a minute. The electrical activity of your brains provides a locus for my suit's instrumentation. Inanimate objects are much more difficult. I wish I could see!" The alien paused, then; "Turn to your left. There should be a particularly large structure."

"I see it." Caroline started forward.

"I think I see some kind of entrance." Ross bent over. "Part of it has caved in, and the ceiling is low."

"Doesn't matter. What we need to reach is the small temple on top."

Leaning back, the Texan could just make out the structure's overgrown crest. "That's just dandy," he muttered.

"It won't be so bad." Caroline started up. "There can't more than a thousand steps."

"You're not carrying mister interstellar hobo, Jed, here."

"Quit complaining. At least you're not dead."

"When I do die," Ross Ed shot back, "I hope I have the decency to keep quiet."

Vines and creepers made the last twenty feet difficult. That surmounted, they found themselves with a view of an endless sea of green, an undulating roll of jungle in all directions. To the east, a few specks of blue ocean were visible through gaps in the verdure.

"Your ancestors apparently moved the Veqq transmitter here, where they could worship it," Jed commented. "As an object of occasional veneration myself, I quite understand. I can perceive it."

"Just hang on to your perceiving for a minute." After first checking to ensure it was free of ants, Ross Ed slumped down on a creeper as big around as his thigh. "I'm bushed."

"Me, too." For a seat Caroline chose the exquisitely carved and stylized head of a jaguar, just missing the scorpion that scuttled quickly out of the path of her descending derriere.

Only after catching their breath and luxuriating in the spectacular panorama did they rise and enter the supreme temple. There was nothing inside but crumbling rock, rotting wood, the omnipresent vines and lianas, and a deteriorating tree stump.

"I don't see anything," Ross Ed announced.

"You're practically standing on it. Are you sure *you* can see?"

"Only rocks and jungle."

"Move to your left." The Texan complied, but the view didn't change.

It was Caroline who noted that the tree stump looked a little too unsoiled. It also was devoid of secondary growth, decomposing fungi, and insects.

"See if it moves," she suggested.

Ross nodded and set the backpack aside. Then he put his considerable shoulder to the wood. Unfortunately, the stump was firmly rooted to the floor. Its upper tenth, however, was not. As soon as he applied pressure, it whirred and slid aside.

Over the eons a few bits of plant matter had managed to squeeze inside. There were also the shells of unlucky insects. They lay atop what looked like a wastebasket full of crumpled gold foil. A mass of red filaments bound this together, as if a spider with the Midas touch had been at its nest.

Cautiously, Ross Ed peered inside. No sound emerged from the interior.

"Doesn't look like much." Caroline eyed the ancient mess dubiously.

"The Veqq were wonderful engineers," Jed reminded them. "It's probably powered by stray neutrinos. Don't ask me how. I'm no scientist."

Ross's hands hovered over the gold foil. "What do I do? It looks pretty fragile. I don't want to break anything."

"You won't." The little alien proceeded to furnish instructions.

Ross felt he was doing little more than moving filaments and crumpling foil, but after thirty minutes Jed pronounced himself satisfied. As far as the two humans could tell, nothing had changed. Although when Jed directed him to put an ear close to the opening, Ross thought he could hear something buried deep within hiccuping softly.

"Do I close it back up?"

"You bet. Just apply pressure to the lid."

Ross did so and was rewarded with the sight of the cover sliding silently back into place. Once again the transmitter looked exactly like an isolated tree stump.

"How come the Maya, or whoever hauled this up here, didn't accidentally open it and rip out the insides?" Caroline wanted to know.

"There is an activation sequence which must first be keyed in," the Shakaleeshva explained. "Otherwise the unit is impossible to open. My suit broadcast the necessary sequence. Your ancestors would have heard only an occasional humming. No doubt they believed some sort of spirit to be trapped inside.

"Now I suggest we depart."

"Wait a minute." Ross Ed frowned as he picked up the pack and swung it onto his back. "If your people are going to intercept the signal and come looking for you, shouldn't we be here waiting for them?"

"We need to remain in the general vicinity, certainly," Jed admitted, "but the Shakaleeshva may not arrive first. Others can pick up the modified signal as well. Not only the Culakhan, but the Tuniack, the Moespre, and half a dozen others may be drawn to it. I would rather not meet up with any of them. We need to remain in the region in order to monitor visitors, but far enough away so that we can be selective in who we greet."

"How do we manage that?" Caroline asked uncertainly.

"My suit will handle any necessary contacts. Meanwhile we should move away from here."

"Let's go back to the beach," Ross suggested. "Maybe we can find a fishing village or something."

"Sounds good to me." Caroline stretched tiredly.

"This is where I have to rely on your aboriginal expertise, Ross."

"I'd feel more at home in Austin," the Texan confessed as they started down the steep stairway, "but we'll do the best we can."

Breaking out of the rain forest and back onto the sand, he and Caroline debated whether to head north or south. Without knowing their position relative to the tourist towns of Cancún and Cozumel, they had little to go on. So when Caroline voted for the south, Ross had no reason to object. They walked for miles before he used a sharp rock to crack a couple of coconuts. The water within was deliciously refreshing, the meat cool and savory. Having no need of sustenance either liquid or solid, Jed perceived their actions with indifference. Sometimes being dead had its advantages.

Caroline sipped from her indigenous wooden chalice. "I always thought a real jungle would be very romantic." Her left hand brushed continuously back and forth in front of her face. "It's not. It's hot, sweaty, buggy, and dangerous."

"They usually are," Jed observed. "Aulaua Five is entirely covered in jungle and the 'bugs' there are so big and vicious that—"

She cut him off. "Never mind. What I'd really like to find is a shower."

"Wouldn't matter if we did," Ross Ed pointed out. "We don't have any money."

"Says you." From her omnipresent fanny pack she removed the credit card she'd alluded to back in Los Angeles, when they'd first discussed fleeing Tealeaf's hospitality for San Diego.

Her companion eyed it speculatively. "That's swell, provided anyone around here takes plastic."

"Where've you been, Ross Ed? *Everybody* takes plastic these days."

"In the jungle? I wouldn't count on it."

• • •

"Visa, MasterCard, Diner's Card, American Express, Sumitomo, Barclay's, and Banco Vera Cruz, señor. Any of those are acceptable. I was offered a Harrod's card once but could not figure out how to process it."

They'd met a couple of kids fishing from a point of rocks. The boys had shown them a trail which led through the rain forest, past newly cleared cornfields, to a dirt road, and thence to the village of Santa Luisa del Mar. There they had found the cantina, with its outdoor tables, Dos Equis umbrellas, and freshly painted stucco.

Santa Luisa was a boomtown, barely a few years old, which explained why its inhabitants had not yet found the temple complex hidden in the jungle to the north. Or perhaps they had, Ross Ed reflected, and were keeping its location a secret while they pillaged its passageways and tombs. In their covert search for gold and jade artifacts, acquisitive locals wouldn't pay much attention to a tree stump.

After inhaling a couple of cold Coronas apiece, the weary travelers consented to order food. High up on a wall a radio was blasting out a melange of Argentinian rock, Mexican pop, and American country-western. Ross Ed put his feet up on an empty chair and felt almost at home. With the backpack scooted beneath the heavy table, Jed remained comfortably out of sight.

The proprietor wore a bright, flowery shirt, jeans, and a white apron. His wide forehead, bulging cheeks, and enormous mustache framed a pleasant disposition.

"I'll bet you don't get many tourists here." Caroline swigged her Corona directly from the bottle.

"That is changing rapidly, señora. Ever since the start of something called eco-tourism, crazy people from all over the world are coming to the Yucatán. They bash their way through the jungle, frightening away the animals and birds, getting bitten by bugs and stung by scorpions and wasps, and then leave saying what a fine time it was they had. Some even bring their own drinks, which they sip all day long." His brown forehead creased. "What are lomotil and imodium, anyway? Some kind of milk drink?"

"But you still do business." Ross Ed saluted with his bottle.

The man smiled. "Enough, and it is getting better every month. They drink my beer and eat my food and some days my wife and daughters cannot make tortillas fast enough. Life is good, eh, señor?"

Ross glanced under the table. "It's interesting, anyway."

"Besides touristas we get archaeologists, oilmen, scientists, and surfers. You would be surprised, my friends, at the number of people who come this way."

"Your beer's very good," Ross Ed told him. "I hope your tamales, burritos, and frijoles are its equal."

The proprietor wagged a finger at him. "I know your accent, señor. You are from Texas, yes?" Ross nodded and the man smiled. "Then you are almost a Mexican."

"And you're almost a Texan."

"I will make sure the food is hot enough for you."

"I'd appreciate that. I like it hot . . . so long as there's enough cold beer."

While they waited for their food he and Caroline watched children brown as nuts roll hoops up and down the dusty street. Occasionally a donkey cart would trundle past, and less often, an old car or truck held together with bailing wire and prayers. The village was still sleepy, but like so much of southern Mexico, in the process of waking up.

There would be a telephone, he surmised. They'd make it safely back to Texas yet.

"Hey, haven't you kids got anything else to do? *Vamos!*" He sat up in his chair and waved at a couple of teenagers who were leaning on the railing and staring. When he started to rise, they fled. Had they noticed Jed? He couldn't be sure.

They were nearly through with their excellent meal when two of the three teens Ross had chased off returned. Three men accompanied them; lean, intense, no-nonsense-looking fellows. Two of them had weapons slung over their shoulders. M-16s, Ross noted even as he doubted they were used for hunting monkeys.

"Maybe they're just coming in for a drink."

"I don't like guns," Caroline announced.

"Then you wouldn't feel at home in Texas. Let's just ignore them."

This proved difficult to do when the new arrivals entered the patio via the swinging gate, turned sharply to their left, and marched straight up to the Americans' table. One of the teens immediately started jabbering away in a mixture of Spanish and a language Ross didn't recognize. As he rambled he pointed not at the Texan or his companion, but under their table.

"I don't like it," Ross whispered. "What do they want?"

"I'll get the owner." She started to rise.

Her effort was premature. Having taking note of the confrontation, the proprietor was already on is way over. Slinging the towel he'd been carrying over his shoulder, he engaged the newcomers in conversation. As they talked looks and fingers occasionally flew in the travelers' direction.

"Whatever happens, at least we got to eat." The big man drained the last of his iced Corona.

"They keep looking under the table." Caroline did her best to ignore the debate taking place behind her. "Maybe they want Jed for some reason."

"Well, the army couldn't have him, Hollywood couldn't have him, not even the Culakhan could have him." He sat up straighter in his chair, emphasizing his size. "And if I have anything to say about it, no bunch of farmers is gonna get him, either."

"Is there some trouble, Señor Santos?" Caroline asked the owner. She was relieved to see that the men showed no inclination to remove their rifles from their shoulders.

The proprietor looked apologetic. "It is the little creature you carry with you."

"What, Jed?" Ross tried to make himself look surprised and intimidating all at once.

"So that is its name." Santos nodded at the man. "They believe it is a reincarnation of the god Azalotl. They are Mayan, you see. Many of them here still believe in the old ways."

"Aza who?" Caroline made a face.

"One of the more powerful major deities responsible for prosperity," the cantina owner explained. "These men belong to a group that is in rebellion against the government. Myself, I happen to believe they have many legitimate complaints, but I do not support armed revolt." He lowered his voice. "Revolution is bad for the tourist business. However, we all have respect for one another. In a village in the middle of the jungle, that is necessary."

"Jed is not an ancient Mayan god," Ross Ed explained patiently. "He's an alien. A dead alien."

The proprietor looked resigned. "Nevertheless, that is what they believe. They feel that if they have Azalotl with them, they will have good luck in their fight against the government." His gaze narrowed slightly. "They want to buy him from you."

"Aza . . . I mean, Jed's not for sale."

"You are a big man, but you are not armed that I can see. I warn you to go carefully with these people. They have used these guns, and they will use them again for what they believe in."

Even though he knew he could longer rely on the diminutive alien to turn bullets as he once had or otherwise protect him, the Texan crossed his arms over his chest in a gesture he hoped was universally recognizable. "I'm not selling Jed, and that's final. You can tell 'em that."

Looking distinctly unhappy, the cantina owner proceeded to translate. As Ross and Caroline waited nervously the men caucused among themselves. Ross noted that the two young teens were included in the conversation.

As soon as they finished, several rifles were raised in the travelers' direction. These were held casually, but there was no mistaking the intent. The proprietor explained.

"They admire your determination and fully understand why you would not wish to be separated from so powerful a deity."

Ross Ed relaxed a little. "That's more like it."

"So if you will not sell the little creature, you will have to go with them."

"Go with . . . ?"

Caroline did her best to forestall his instinctive reaction. "Let's not push it, Ross Ed. I'd rather see the rain forest than get shot. Thanks to the Culakhan, Jed can't protect us anymore. It won't take them long to see that he's no god, that he's just a harmless corpse, and then they'll let us go. If they meant us harm they'd just shoot us now."

"Since Jed doesn't seem inclined to comment," Ross said as he peered under the table at their studiously silent companion, "I expect he doesn't perceive any direct threat. Maybe it doesn't matter so long as we remain in the general vicinity. Right, Jed?" While the proprietor gave him a strange look, Ross smiled blankly and waited for a reply. When none was forthcoming, he sighed and moved on.

"I'd rather stay here and drink Coronas, but it looks like we're going to take a tour of the jungle. I suppose it's a good idea to keep moving, so long as we don't get caught up in a local revolution."

She smiled ruefully. "Looks like it's too late for that." She turned to the anxious proprietor. "Okay, tell them we'll go with them, but ask if there's anyone among them who speaks English. I'm afraid our Spanish is kind of rusty and it would be nice to be able to talk to our 'hosts.'"

Nodding understandingly, the owner conveyed the query. When he turned back he was beaming. "They say there is one at their camp who speaks even better English than you who would be pleased to translate."

"Another Harvard-trained revolutionary," she speculated under her breath. Louder she said, "That'll do."

Ross Ed reached beneath the table and swung Jed back up onto his back. The guerrillas watched his every move intently. "Doesn't look like we have much choice."

Caroline was more confident. "I'll be all right, you'll see. It'll just take them a day or two to realize their mistake. If their leaders are more educated, they'll see it immediately and let us go. This is local politics and doesn't involve us. Besides, they aren't vicious. Look at their faces: don't they look kindly?"

"Look at their guns: don't they look lethal?"

An elderly, bearded man with a serape slung over his right shoulder came running toward the cantina. He was shouting and trying to steady the machete that bounced against his arm.

Breathlessly, he conversed in restive, low tones with the armed men. Then he looked up at the two Americans.

"There is no time. You must come with us now, please."

"We're pretty tired," Ross told him. "We've been walking for a long time and we've had a couple of pretty tough days."

"I am sorry. We will slow down as soon as we are safely beyond the town limits." He nodded back the way he'd come. "Government patrol."

Santos was all but wringing his hands. "Please, my friends, I have tried to help you. Do what you will, but do it somewhere away from my cantina."

Ross Ed and Caroline were escorted across the street and through a park overgrown with weeds and encroaching jungle vegetation. Half-naked children giggled as they played on a few sorry pieces of homemade playground equipment. Used tires had been employed inventively and were much in evidence.

Behind them, they could hear the cantina owner calling a

farewell. "When you are all tired of fighting, please come back! I am always open for good customers!"

The old man grumbled. "Santos takes money from both sides. He is neither a revolutionary nor an oppressor, but a businessman. He is not to be trusted." A grin appeared on the grizzled face. "But his *pollo molé* is wonderful."

The park was separated from true rain forest by a small stream, which they crossed as silently as possible. On the far side a narrow trail presented itself. This led uphill into dense jungle.

The teens had vanished into the verdure. In their absence the four men maintained a wary watch, their dark brown eyes flicking constantly over trees, bushes, and openings. They no longer held their weapons casually.

A little less than an hour into the hike a dull *boom* echoed behind them. It could have been caused by a falling tree, but Ross Ed thought otherwise. One sound a man quickly becomes familiar with out in the oil fields is that of explosives. He found himself hoping that the congenial cantina owner was all right.

It took the rest of the day for them to reach the rebel encampment, a carefully camouflaged collection of simple huts and lean-tos. There was no clearing for aerial spotters to locate. Fresh green leaves and branches concealed the dry thatch beneath.

The arrivals were greeted by a dozen comrades. Among their number were several women and children. All had the high cheekbones, dark brown skin, and prominent nasal ridges characteristic of the Maya.

As they stumbled into camp Ross Ed caught a glimpse of a small overhang. A couple of mortars lay hidden there, together with boxes of ammunition and one rocket launcher. As he took note of these heavy munitions someone sang out in clear, unaccented English.

"Well, you two don't look like the usual recruits!"

A lean, muscular man in his mid-thirties emerged from one of the huts. He had short, curly blond hair, light blue eyes, and pale skin. Above the tattered shorts, a very dirty photographer's vest bulged with an assortment of exotic equipment. His high-tech hiking boots, Ross Ed decided, probably cost more than the most successful of the rebels made in a year.

"Hi." He wiped his right hand on his vest before shoving it

forward. "I'm Michael McClure. Nice to meet you." He grinned at Caroline. "Especially you, miss."

She frowned. "Are you *with* these people?"

"In a manner of speaking. I'm sort of a guest. I'm a stringer for *The New York Times*. Who are you two?"

Ross Ed made the introductions, not neglecting Jed.

McClure eyed the Texan's burden with interest. "Dead alien, huh? I got to admit it's one of the better fakes I've seen. What are all the blinking lights for?"

"Christmas," Caroline explained dryly. "He goes on top of the tree instead of an angel."

"Need a helluva tree." The reporter nodded in the direction of the old man. "Reyman is saying they think your alien whatsit may be the reincarnation of one of their old gods."

"You're taking this pretty calmly," Caroline remarked.

McClure shrugged. "I've been here going on six months now, and I've seen and heard a lot of unusual stuff. I can't condemn these people for searching out a useful symbol. They need every edge they can get. The government's pressing them hard."

"So you're on their side?" Ross asked as they were directed to the shelter of a lean-to. A woman brought cold water in multicolored plastic tumblers.

"I'm just here to report on the rebellion. I don't take positions. These people have real grievances and the government insists it can't tolerate anarchy, so both sides can make a valid argument. I'm just a neutral observer and noncombatant." He smiled. "Of course, if I'm captured by government forces they may not take me at my word. That's always a danger in this kind of work.

"So far it's been mostly trivial skirmishes. Neither side really wants a pitched battle with lots of bodies."

"How do you get your reports out? Couriers?" As she spoke Caroline found herself envying the diminutive alien. The heat and humidity weren't bothering him. Dead people were pretty much immune to the vagaries of climate. "Surely you don't march down into Santa Luisa and put them in the mail?"

"Not hardly." McClure grinned. "I've got a Motorola Iridium phone."

"Iridium?" Ross Ed looked up. Hadn't Jed used that term?

Caroline saw which road his thoughts were taking and hastened to erect a roadblock. "It's just a coincidence, Ross Ed. In this instance Iridium's only a name for a low-orbit satellite communications system." She turned back to the reporter. "I've heard about it. I didn't think it was operational yet."

"Not all of it is, but the portion over the U.S. was activated just last year. Here, I'll show you."

Ducking back into his hut, he reemerged with a cellular phone larger than the models Ross Ed was accustomed to seeing in the oil fields or on U.S. Army belts. Of particular interest was the long, heavy antenna which McClure extended to its full length.

"I can ring anyplace on Earth that lies within the footprint of an Iridium satellite. If the full system was up I could call somebody in central Siberia from here and get clean reception. As it stands, it works fine for New York. That's how I file my reports. I've got a laptop with a built-in fax/modem. All I have to do is charge it and this with a car battery and phone my stories in to Manhattan. Goes through as cleanly as if I were reporting from Passaic." He walked around behind Ross Ed to get a better look at his burden.

"I can't get you out of here. These people have really fixated on your mannequin, or doll, or whatever it is. But if there's anybody you'd like to talk to, I can certainly let you make a call."

"Not interested." What Ross wanted was another drink.

Caroline was more agreeable. "I wouldn't mind chatting with my sister. She's in Omaha."

"My pleasure." McClure hefted the phone. "What's her number?"

Caroline told him and he punched it in. Much to their amazement, the call went through as smoothly as if they'd been using a pay phone in Dallas. While she supplied her sister with a carefully edited version of her recent travels, Ross Ed watched the movements of the Indian rebels. The silent Jed continued to act more dead than he was.

When she'd finished, Caroline handed the phone back to the reporter. "Thanks. It was nice to be able to tell her that I'm all right."

Ross glanced sideways from where he was sitting in the shade. "Think she believed the part about vacationing in Mexico?"

"Hey, my family isn't surprised at anything I do. They wouldn't bat an eye if I called from Madagascar."

He squinted at the surrounding rain forest. "One country I've never heard of at a time, if you don't mind."

TWENTY-TWO

In their excitement and surprise at being able to call Caroline's sister, neither of them had paused to consider the possibility that satellite telephone calls might be monitored and intercepted by assorted intelligence agencies. Especially calls that originated from obscure locales such as the Yucatán rain forest and happened to trigger a particularly sensitive hypertext reference on a number of government computers.

So it was that two days later a lookout came running into the camp, gesticulating frantically and yelling to his comrades.

Ross Ed raised up from the sleeping pad in the lean-to which had been assigned to him and Caroline. "What is it?" he called out McClure. "Army patrol?"

"No, something more." The reporter was listening closely to the excited conversation. "He says there are people in the U.S. Army uniform advancing with Mexican marines. They're puzzled why Americans have suddenly chosen to get involved in their internal conflict."

The Texan swung his long legs out of the lean-to and drew them up to his knees. "I think I can answer that."

McClure looked surprised. "You?"

"Yep. They're after Caroline and me. The army's been tracking us for weeks."

The reporter was genuinely dumbfounded. "But why?"

"They want me to turn Jed over to them."

McClure's eyes widened as he studied the backpack and its burden, which Ross Ed had propped up against the rear of the lean-to. "You don't mean that's a *real* alien? I thought you'd stolen a movie prop or something."

"Nope. He's real enough. Dead, though. We've been telling you all along. You just haven't been listening."

"I've been trying to cover a rebellion. It tends to occupy all your thoughts." Now the reporter couldn't take his eyes off the motionless body. "And the army wants it?"

"Army intelligence." Ross smiled thinly. "I bet if I had a good pair of binoculars, I could give you the names of some of the soldiers in the lead. Last time we saw them was in Malibu."

"Where else?" commented McClure sardonically. "I don't know if I believe you, but something's sure got the Mexican army in an uproar. This is the first time they've made a push this high into these mountains." Men and women were rushing too and fro around him, collapsing gear and loading packs. "We're going to have to move."

"Maybe," Caroline murmured as the reporter turned to load his own gear, "this will convince our Indian hosts that Jed doesn't bring good luck."

"Just so long as they don't decide to shoot the bearers of bad tidings," he replied.

Within an amazingly short span of time every useful item had been crammed into duffels, shoulder bags, or two-man slings and the entire encampment had started up the almost invisible trail. Rain forest closed in suffocatingly around them.

Ross Ed shoved a thorny branch out of his way. "How do they know where they're going in this?"

McClure looked back at him. "Are you kidding? These people know every tree, every stream, every mountain in this range, and half the monkeys by name."

And every Mayan ruin? Ross Ed found himself wondering.

"The government either has to settle eventually with these people," the reporter was saying, "or exterminate them. They're part of the forest and they're not going to go away."

Caroline was looking back the way they'd come. "What about the camp? Won't the army destroy it?"

"Sure, but it's no great loss. These people can raise a village out of virgin jungle in less than a day. You'll be interested to know that right now they're debating whether or not to get rid of you and your idol. Seems they feel they may have been mistaken about Aza."

"What do they plan to do about it?" Ross Ed asked guardedly.

"They're not planning to shoot you or anything. Relax. Maybe they'll leave you for the U.S. soldiers to find."

That would be about right, Ross thought disgustedly. When they hadn't wanted to go into the jungle, the rebels had taken them by force. Now that they might want to remain with the Indians to avoid the attentions of the army, their hosts were considering dumping them. He wondered how his friends, the captains three, were enjoying the bugs and humidity. The thought made him feel a little better.

"Is there much more of this climbing?" Caroline was starting to labor and her fair skin was suffering from the intermittent exposure to raw tropical sun. Like Ross Ed, she was perspiring profusely.

McClure could offer no solace. "This part of the Yucatán is all up and down. One near impassable ridge after another. That's why the rain forest here is still largely intact. Good for the environment, good for guerrilla fighters, not so good for hiking."

To the visitors' relief, the trail soon started down into the next lush, overgrown valley. Rain began to pelt them, the drops heavy and warm. Amid the gathering downpour, one cloud moved with significant independence.

The Culakhan Frontrunner stood before a vitreous wall in which assorted images were floating. Readouts drifted into the image, responding to retinal contact by sliding out again once they had been read.

"They are almost directly beneath us," reported one of the monitoring technicians. She sat sideways to her instrumentation, manipulating it mostly with voice commands and only occasionally with her prehensile tail.

"I can see that." Uroon stoically examined the screens.

"Do you wish us to descend to within lifting range and pick them up?"

"Not yet. There are too many natives in the immediate vicinity. This time we would be observed by a multitude. You know that portion of the Codes which restricts contact with primitive civilizations." He turned away from the wall of information. "Now that we have relocated the Shakaleeshva, there is no need to rush the matter." Reaching up and back with a foreleg, he scratched his belly. "Such transfers are best accomplished under cover of darkness. We will wait and see what opportunities the night brings."

"We could simply obliterate the immediate countryside and all observers located therein," suggested another technician. "Do you not, Frontrunner, sometimes feel the urge to overlook portions of the Codes?"

"I would sooner overlook mating." Uroon's expression was stern. "The Codes are the Culakhan. Without them we would be no better than the Shakaleeshva. I commend to you the chapter on patience." Suitably abashed, the tech who had ventured the recommendation hung her head down to her chest.

"We will repossess the vile Shakaleeshva and its attendant humans soon enough. This time there will be no mental tricks." Red eyes gleamed in the subdued light of the command chamber. "I do not enjoy playing the fool."

Later that afternoon the line of rebels halted beside the river that ran through the narrow valley. There was no sign of imminent pursuit and those in charge felt it was safe to stop.

No one was more pleased than Caroline, who was near the end of her proverbial rope. She was neither built nor dressed for cross-country walking. Plunging her face into the clear, cool river water helped greatly to revive her spirits if not her strength.

They were startled when sounds materialized in the forest up ahead instead of behind them. Ross Ed tensed and moved closer to the visitor from New York.

"What is it? Army?"

McClure was staring into the trees. "Don't know. I didn't give them that much credit. Flanking maneuvers aren't their style."

An Indian came bursting out of the trees to wade the shallow tributary. When this scout sat down and began chattering calmly to his seated comrades, the reporter relaxed.

"Whatever it is, it's apparently nothing to get excited about. For a minute I thought the army might have helicoptered some elite troops in ahead of us. That would mean real trouble. But the government prefers to hold its best soldiers back for parading, and for guarding government buildings. I really think they want to negotiate the end to his uprising. For one thing, it'd look better to the IMF." He drank noisily from his canteen.

"Then what's going on?" Having dunked her head completely underwater, a refreshed Caroline was now patiently braiding the sodden strands.

"Beats me. I expect we'll find out soon enough."

They did. Three heavily armed strangers appeared on the far side of the river and hailed the rebels. Granted safe passage, they proceeded to wade across. Two carried automatic weapons. The third wore a pistol on either hip, expensive (and now very wet) dress boots fashioned from some exotic leather, a clean cotton shirt, and an immaculate wide-brimmed Panama hat. Impressively, his holster leather matched that of his boots.

After glancing briefly at Ross Ed and lingeringly at Caroline, he took a moment to study Jed. Whispering something to one of his men, he turned and crouched to converse with the leaders of the rebel band.

"What's this all about?" Caroline edged closer to McClure. "Who are these guys?"

"Quiet. Let me listen." The reporter strained to overhear.

When he finally turned back to them, he wore an expression unlike any they'd seen before. "Well, you don't have to worry about anyone shooting you. It's been decided that you are to be turned over to these newcomers, alien and all."

"But who are they?" a suddenly tense Caroline demanded to know.

"I'm not sure. Haven't seen them before. Haven't been in this part of the jungle before. As near as I can make out, you've been sold."

Her eyes widened slightly. "I beg your pardon?"

"Hey, I'm not positive. My Spanish isn't perfect. But that's the way it sounds. You can't blame the rebels. They need money for supplies and weapons and this gives them a conscientious way to get rid of you and your bad-luck god. They're going to take the money and run."

"They can't sell us," Ross Ed objected. "We're not even for rent. And besides, we don't happen to belong to them."

"I couldn't agree with you more, but nothing can be done about it. Seems to be a done deal."

"Can't you help us?" Caroline pleaded.

"What, and compromise my reportorial neutrality? Sorry, miss. Best I can do is get on the phone and let the embassy know what happened to you. Of course, if you are trying to avoid the attention of U.S. government agencies . . ."

"Surely this man in the hat doesn't think he owns us?"

"He'd better not." Even as he spoke Ross Ed was acutely

aware there was little they could do to affect the proceedings, unless Jed could nudge the man mentally. And if such effects were only temporary or limited in scope, that might not be such a good idea. They'd still be stuck in the middle of raw jungle. Around them macaws squawked and monkeys chittered in the treetops.

At last the negotiations were concluded. The man in the hat rose and shook hands with the rebel leaders. Then he and his sinister escorts advanced on Ross Ed and Caroline. McClure thoughtfully moved to one side.

Quite unexpectedly, the hatted one broke out in a wide grin and stuck out his hand. Not knowing what else to do, Ross shook it. The grip was firm and straightforward. Even more unexpectedly, he then turned to Caroline, raised her right hand, and bent to kiss it, perspiration notwithstanding.

Confused and wary, she responded with a warning look. "That was nice, but don't go getting any ideas just because you think you've paid for us."

The man made anxious placating gestures. "I am Armando de la Vega. *Por favor,* wait until *los indios* have gone on their way and we will talk. I promise that no harm will come to either of you." His English was heavily accented but readily understandable.

An hour later Ross Ed and Caroline bid farewell to McClure, who wished them well. When the line of rebels was finally out of sight over the next ridge, their new host gestured for them to follow.

"Just a minute." Ross didn't move. "Why should we?"

De la Vega turned and walked back to them. "Well, for one thing, because I gave money to free you from the rebels. More to the point, if the army finds you here, you may very well be shot as collaborators, or at least arrested. Besides, you don't want your U.S. Army Intelligence people to pick you up, not after all the running you have been doing. Do you?" He winked.

The two startled Americans exchanged a look. "How'd you know about that?" Ross Ed asked him.

Again the expansive smile fell upon them. "I have my own technicians, who know their way around fax/modems and satellite telephones as well as radios and TVs. I have been reading with interest your Mr. McClure's reports back to New York. It is an excellent way for me to keep abreast of the rebellion. Encoded army communications are a little more difficult to decipher, but these days you can do anything with the right chip, *es verdad*?" He turned and beckoned.

"Now come with me. Or do you still prefer the jungle to cold drinks, cooked food, and a bath?"

"A *bath*?" Caroline all but swooned. "Take me, I'm yours."

"Caroline!" Ross Ed blurted.

She shrugged and grinned. "Well, figuratively, anyway."

They fell in alongside him, the two escorts spreading out to flank them on either side, guns at the ready.

"You live out here?" Caroline studied the slightly tannin-stained water with interest as they slogged toward the opposite bank. Meanwhile Ross slipped on smooth river rock and fought to right himself.

De la Vega nodded absently. His attention was focused on the Texan's burden. "Is that really an ancient Mayan god? The American officers speak frequently of a valuable 'parcel' you are supposed to be carrying."

"It's a dead alien," Ross Ed explained tiredly. "His name's Jed."

"Really? You don't say. I have seen such things in films, but never expected to encounter a real one."

Surmounting the opposite bank, they started up another slope. Not as severe as the one they had ascended in the company of the rebels, it soon leveled off. At this, Caroline was visibly relieved and Ross Ed silently grateful. It was the climate here that sapped one's energy, not the climbing. Occasionally they had to duck beneath fallen trees, but otherwise they made good progress.

"U.S. Army Intelligence must want something very badly to involve uniformed soldiers in a domestic Mexican rebellion. Since neither of you strike me as especially remarkable, I must assume they are interested in your alien."

"What's any of this to you?" Ross Ed tried not to sound too belligerent. "Why should you get involved?" He was afraid he knew the answer. De la Vega's reply went a long way toward confirming it.

"I am a businessman, and where there is opportunity for profit, I am always interested." He flicked an inch-long ant off his leg. "Also, I have no love for the armies of either country, and it pleases me to confound them. I do much business with the rebels, but I also am a confidant of the local police."

"So you're another amoral local," Caroline surmised, "like Santos."

"Ah, Santos!" De la Vega kissed bunched fingers. "Such food the man serves! It is not Vera Cruz, but for the hinterland he does wonders. What he can do with *camarones* is sinful."

"So you want Jed, too." Ross Ed was hardly surprised.

"A dead alien. A real dead alien." The man wagged a finger at them. "These are possibilities that are new to me, and require careful consideration."

"Just so you should know where we all stand," the Texan told him, "I wouldn't give him up to the U.S. Army, I didn't give him up to the rebels, and I won't give him up to you."

"Please, please." De la Vega assumed a hurt expression. "So much hostile." He looked at Caroline. "Is he always like this?"

"He's just being protective. Based on what he's told me about the things that have happened to him and on what I've seen for myself, he has reason to be."

"So. Now then, you are from Texas," he told Ross, "and you"—he studied Caroline intently—"I'm not so sure. Ohio?"

She shook her head. "Sorry. Nebraska."

"I have never been to Nebraska, but I have a feeling I would not do much business there."

They crossed a small bridge fashioned of logs bound together with strips of vine. Caroline picked her way carefully while Ross Ed, accustomed to working atop oil rigs, sauntered across effortlessly.

"What is your business?" Caroline inquired. "Oil exploration, gold mining, logging, cattle ranching?"

"None of those things. We are too far south for oil, there is no gold in this part of the Yucatán, and this is a protected region as far as logging and ranching are concerned." He straightened proudly. "I am a dedicated environmentalist, as you will see.

"I am a simple, small farmer who believes in preserving the rain forest."

"And what is it that you farm?" Ross asked him.

"Only native produce. Hemp, mostly. For rope, of course." He smiled sadly. "Is it my fault that instead of using it to make nets and things, misguided people choose to burn it and inhale the smoke? Except for your president, of course."

Wonderful, Ross reflected. They'd gone from being chased by the armies of two countries to being held by Indian rebels to being bought by a local drug lord. It was almost enough to make one wish for the cool assurance of the Culakhan. At least they operated according to a Code.

"You're a dope dealer."

De la Vega raised a hand. "Tut, *mi compadre*. A businessman, if you please. I sell only what my customers want. If *norteamericanos* want to smoke my produce instead of braid it, who am I to argue with them? I do admit that the laws I choose to pledge allegiance to are those of supply and demand."

Following in their host's agile footsteps, Ross Ed hopped lithely across a foot-wide stream of army ants. "So where does that leave us?"

"Please, not here. It is too hot. We will talk more when we reach my hacienda. It is just ahead, just there." He raised an arm.

Ross stared. "Ahead where? I don't see anything but more jungle."

De la Vega was pleased. "I subscribe to the aesthetic of natural landscaping. You will see."

The armed guard who emerged from the fake tree didn't salute but simply nodded at his boss, who waved graciously in passing. A gate fashioned of logs decorated with moss, fungi, and epiphytes opened to admit them to a luxuriously landscaped courtyard, all of which would have appeared perfectly natural to any airborne observer.

The moss-encrusted stone wall gave way to a complex of interconnected pavilions, each roofed with its own camouflage netting. Several of the structures had rainforest trees growing through their roofs. Dirt and gravel surrendered to exquisite marquetry and tile work.

"No carpeting here, I'm afraid," de la Vega explained. "The insects would have it for breakfast. Ah, here we are."

After passing through a spacious open den cooled by concealed air-conditioning units, they reached a glass doorway which admitted them to the pool area. Shaded by its own camouflaged canopy, it appeared to have been tiled in mother-of-pearl. At the far end a landscaped artificial waterfall mimicked those in the surrounding jungle. A second green-swathed wall of river rock defined the enclosure.

Their host directed them to several high-backed planter's chairs fashioned from imported rattan. A white-suited servant appeared briefly, vanished, and returned moments later with a tray of iced drinks. Despite his misgivings, Ross Ed gulped the contents of two glasses before finally taking it slower with a third. Caroline matched him drink for drink.

The unwalled side of the enclosure opened on an elaborate aviary alive with rainforest denizens, from sloths to quetzls. An expensive stereo system pumped Vivaldi through a network of hidden speakers. It was all very civilized and homespun, provided one ignored the guards and their automatic weapons.

Caroline could no longer contain her feelings. "This place is amazing!" She toyed with the little paper parasol which shaded her drink. "You have everything here."

"Well, not quite everything," confessed de la Vega modestly, "but I do have access to many modern conveniences."

Ross Ed's reaction was understated. "You must be one hell of a farmer."

Their host pursed his lips. "My interests are extensive. Everyone wants what I have, you see. My contacts with the rebels, the police, and the local government ensure my safety, even from Colombians. I do well enough and my wants are simple." He gestured with his glass.

"Well, I don't know about your other visitors, but *I'm* impressed," Caroline admitted. So was Ross Ed, if less effusively.

De la Vega leaned forward slightly. "And I am impressed by the attention you have attracted. Tell me truly now what it is that I have bought. What is a dead alien worth?"

"To tell you truly, I haven't the faintest idea." Ross had removed his backpack and set it down next to his chair. "Anyway, it doesn't matter, because he isn't for sale. I don't know what you think you 'bought' from those rebels, but it wasn't me, or Caroline, or Jed."

"I see. I do not wish to appear the inconsiderate host, but I did spend a considerable sum to rescue you from your situation."

"We weren't in any danger," Ross Ed shot back.

"You think not? Do you think the army's long-range weapons can distinguish between a rebel *indio* and a visiting Texan? You cannot debate politics with an incoming rocket, and artillery shells are terribly egalitarian.

"But I wish for us to be friends. After you have bathed and rested we will talk more. I am sure we can resolve our differences and come to an understanding."

Further conversation was cut off by a yelp from the far side of the pool, this apparently being the preagreed upon signal for All Hell to Break Loose.

The two guards instantly sprang into action, the staccato chatter of their automatic weapons threatening to drown out everything else. Alarms were going off all over the compound.

"The army!" Caroline had dropped her glass, which shattered on the tile floor.

"No." De la Vega had moved instinctively to take her arm and was pulling her back toward the den. "Inside, quickly!"

Neither of them needed any further urging. As soon as the glass doors slammed shut behind them, a trio of impact cracks appeared in their wake.

"Bulletproof," their host disclosed, "but not bomb-proof. I do not understand. I have never been attacked here."

The invaders who swarmed over the back wall were clad entirely in black bodysuits camouflaged with swatches of light and dark green, save for narrow openings that revealed their eyes. In addition to guns they wielded swords, knives, and a wide assortment of rococo shuruken.

One of the guards went down with several protruding from his torso while the other began a slow retreat. Shouts and screams resounded throughout the compound. More of de la Vega's men were starting to arrive. Despite the increased firepower being brought to bear on the attackers, two of them got within twenty feet of the den before being shot down.

An instant before, a sigh had emerged from the artificial larynx attached to Jed's now gently glowing suit. "A fine world I chose! Am I never to have proper time for contemplation? I perceive the presence of numerous additional hostile individuals. In the absence of my ability to effectively influence the trajectory of assorted explosive projectiles, I believe we should seek more effective cover."

"Good idea." Ross Ed dragged the backpack and its suddenly loquacious contents behind the polished purpleheart bar. Moments later something blew in both glass doors, sending a shower of sharp fragments flying through space only recently occupied.

"This is all very confusing," the alien remarked. "Don't you people *ever* cooperate with one another?"

"Not when there's big money involved." Ross kept his head

down as an astonishing hodgepodge of shouts in English, Spanish, and Japanese echoed across the compound.

Elegant and composed, de la Vega scrunched back against the wall and managed to open the compact refrigerator beneath the bar without exposing himself to hostile fire. "We may as well make ourselves comfortable until my people have driven these *pendejos* away. What is your pleasure? Rum, Scotch, gin, RC?"

"I'll have an RC." Caroline was unaccountably cheerful. "I'm still thirsty."

Though backed up in a corner, de la Vega somehow managed a bow. "My pleasure, señorita." He poured himself a rum and clinked glasses with her.

"You are not thirsty, my friend?"

"Sorry. I can't drink when I'm worried about dying." Ross kept sneaking glimpses over the bar, trying to divine which way the battle was going. The den had taken several hits but thus far only the decor had suffered. Most of the fighting remained centered around the pool. A coffee table had been brutally mutilated. Occasionally the sweet, sick sound of a slug smacking into wall or furniture rose above the general cacophony.

"Where do you suppose these people came from?"

"I cannot imagine." De la Vega eyed him speculatively. "Could it be that others besides the army were following you, hoping to relieve you of your alien friend? If the Japanese are aware, perhaps we may expect representatives of other countries and organizations to make similar attempts. I can see now that my investment may not have been a wise one." He winced as shells shattered the big mirror behind the bar.

"We can't stay here." Slipping on the backpack, Ross poised on hands and knees. "We're gonna have to make a run for it. Get ready, Caroline."

"Uh, I don't think so, Ross Ed."

Their eyes met. "You don't think so? What d'you mean, you don't think so?"

Her expression fell. "You're a nice guy, Ross Ed Hager, and I'm glad for the time we had together, and I'm glad I was able to help you out, but I don't see much of a future with you. You're running from too many people, and some of them aren't even people. Eventually they'll catch up with you, and I'm not sure anymore that I want to be part of the package." She coughed delicately.

"While you were seeing to Jed, Armando here asked me to stay with him. He says I can have anything I want. Trips to Paris and Rome, clothes, jewelry, anything. He's been very decent about it. Gallant, even. I mean, nothing against you, Ross, but you're still quite the country boy, if you know what I mean. I always did see myself with someone a little more sophisticated." Reaching out, she took their host's hand and squeezed it gently.

"Now don't be bitter. You can't help it if you can't give me the things I've always wanted." Edging forward and carefully keeping her head below the level of flying slugs, she kissed him fondly. "I'll always treasure our time together."

All Ross Ed could do was stare. "You haven't known this guy for a whole day yet and already you're prepared to stay in the jungle with him?"

"I'm kind of the impulsive type, Ross Ed." There was a twinkle in her eyes. "You of all people should know that. Besides, you have to confess that your immediate prospects are less than inviting."

Both statements were true, he had to admit. Hell, he liked de la Vega himself. He suppressed a grin. Somewhere down the line, in Venice or Istanbul or Hong Kong, she might just as readily dump the pot farmer for someone else. Her impulsiveness, her flighty nature, was something he'd been aware of from the beginning. He knew he really shouldn't be surprised, and it was hardly the first time he'd been dumped. But that didn't make it feel better.

"Have it your way. I'll move faster without you anyhow."

She looked hurt. "Please, Ross Ed. It's been a lot of fun, but all the variables are starting to catch up with me. First the army, then aliens, then rebel Indians, and now ninjas. Not to mention," she added with a shudder of remembrance, "Hollywood types. You have to admit it doesn't portend a very stable future for a simple girl from Nebraska. I'm ready to stop running, Ross Ed."

That much he could understand. He was ready to stop running himself. Unfortunately, it didn't seem to be an available option in his immediate future.

"All right, Caroline. If you change your mind—"

"If I change my mind I'll look for you around Austin. Or on the evening news." She kissed him again.

De la Vega looked on benignly. "I am sorry, my friend, but I have never seen one so beautiful as this wondrous Caroline. Or so big."

"Forget it. I owe her a van. Buy her one."

"A van? But she can have a Ferrari, or a Rolls."

Caroline was smiling again. "Take my advice and make it a van," Ross advised him. "You can give her that. All I have to offer her is a dead alien."

Their host crawled forward and pointed. "If you go that way you will reach the kitchen. Go through to the back door. There is a gate in the perimeter wall for service deliveries. The fighting seems to be concentrated here. You should have no difficulty reaching the jungle. If you make it out, head downriver and eventually you will strike the ocean. Oh, and help yourself to anything in the cupboards."

"Thanks. You think you'll be all right?"

The other man nodded. "I have confidence in my people. I have never understood these Japanese pajama-men who think they can beat machine guns with swords and sharpened Christmas ornaments. It is all very balletic, but I think maybe they watch too many of their own movies. Give me a good Russian rocket launcher any day. If you would like something to take with you . . . ?"

"That's okay. If I don't have a gun I'm not a threat, and maybe nobody'll shoot at me. Also, while it seems I'm generally considered expendable, nobody wants to risk damaging Jed."

"So valuable." For a moment the grower gazed longingly at the Texan's immobile three-armed passenger. "Good luck to you, my friend."

"Right. So long, Caroline."

She saluted with her cola. "Fare thee well, Ross Ed Hager."

"Whatever."

Charging out from behind the bar, he made the sharp left turn that de la Vega had suggested. Sure enough, he soon found himself in the deserted kitchen. While the thick walls muted the sounds of battle, he madly shoved dried fruits, nuts, packaged foods, and anything else small and portable into his pockets. Many of the labels were unfamiliar and indecipherable, but he doubted any of it would prove inedible. Not in the jungle and on the run.

Then it was out the back door after a quick look around revealed no sign of combatants. The continuing conflict did seem to be confined to the opposite side of the compound. Locating the small service gate, he slipped through and found himself once more in unpopulated rain forest.

Reaching the river without incident, he headed downstream and ran for another hour before he felt it was safe to stop and rest. A river-washed granite boulder provided a smooth seat relatively devoid of voracious insects.

Propping Jed carefully against the rock, he dipped his face into the river and took long, deep drafts of the cool water. When he'd slaked his thirst he took a seat and began sorting through his hurriedly acquired supplies. A small box instantly caught his eye.

Sugar Frosted Flakes. The label was in Spanish, but there was no mistaking either the grinning tiger or the front of the tooth-numbing sweetness of the contents. Munching the dry shards, he could feel the sugar rush starting.

"Well, after all this it looks like it's just you and me again, Jed." Around him the rain forest seethed and cried with extravagant life, but there was no sign of soldiers, rebels, drug dealers, or ninjas.

"I'm sorry, Ross Ed. I guess I've complicated your life. Maybe you ought to just stick me back in another cave somewhere. I don't think anyone will find me here. But then, I didn't think anyone would find me where I was before, either, and you did."

"Hey, I couldn't do that. You may be dead, but you're conscious again."

"That's easily fixed," the little alien replied. "I'll tell you which Culakhan contacts to disconnect and then I'll be a hundred percent deceased again."

"Is that what you really want?" Ross had lowered his voice. "Final death?"

"What I really wanted was peace and quiet. Death was only one option, which circumstances forced me to accept."

"I think you ought to give it some thought." Leaning back and putting his hands behind his head, the Texan gazed up into the sunstruck canopy. "Might as well. I'm beat and I need to rest a bit."

As the regular evening rainstorm gathered strength, the sky began to cloud over. He relaxed against the granite and closed his eyes. In seconds he was fast asleep.

He dreamed of hard work in the hot Texas sun, of putting his modest savings into a wildcat operation and bringing in a gusher big enough to make the old-timers forget even Spindletop. His silent musings turned to thoughts of good food and happier times, when he wasn't running from belligerents from all over the world, not to mention from off it. For the first time in days he rested easy.

Too easy. Opening his eyes, he noted with interest that he was floating twenty feet above the top of the tallest tree and rising through a pale yellow efflorescence.

Jed was nowhere to be seen.

TWENTY-THREE

Struggling violently, he found he was able to twist and tumble but could do nothing to slow his ascent. Which was just as well, considering that he was now a couple of hundred feet above the forest floor and accelerating. One spin allowed him to catch sight of Jed. The motionless alien was forty feet overhead and rising at a comparable speed. Moments later he disappeared into a white hole in the underside of a storm cloud. Rain fell all around, but not a drop penetrated the cylinder of yellow light.

His calmness surprised him. Obviously the Culakhan had discovered Jed's ruse and returned. Somehow they had tracked the little alien down a second time.

There wasn't much he could do, except be thankful that whatever happened now, Caroline was safely out of it. He hoped she and de la Vega would be happy. As he rose he vacillated between hoping the lift beam would be turned off and praying that it would not. If he fell, there was a chance that the dense forest cover would break his fall, although at his present altitude it would be more likely to break all of him.

Codes of Conduct or not, the Culakhan couldn't be happy with the ruse that had been played on them. This time they might not prove so hospitable. He stopped thrashing around and tried to enjoy the view. If it was to be his last glimpse of Earth, he wanted to remember it clearly.

Rain forest and rain clouds vanished as he rose into the interior of a silver glove. The mirrored surface reflected back several distorted versions of himself. This chamber was different from the one they had arrived via before. More secure, perhaps. The aliens would be taking no chances.

The lift beam vanished and he found himself standing on a solid surface. Lights embedded in the walls bathed him in bright, near-carnival radiance. Taking a step forward, he stumbled and heard voices urging him on. The translator headband was in his pocket. Pulling it out, he strapped it to his head. He wondered what de la Vega would make of Caroline's. Probably think she bought it at Wal-Mart, he decided with a rueful grin.

The mirror sphere opened onto a much larger chamber whose walls were solid instead of glassy, multihued instead of green, and rife with sharp angles instead of flowing curves. There wasn't a Culakhan in sight. Instead, waiting hands reached out to assist him. Real hands and not prehensile lips or modified tail-hairs. Of course, they weren't human, either.

Their owners barely came up to his waist. Each had three eyes, arms, and legs, a sharp keel running down the center of its face, and no tail. Allowing for mundane individual variations, they were virtual clones of Jed. Ross straightened.

So these were the Shakaleeshva. Cute little fellers.

He wondered if the translator band would work on their ship. Certainly they were as technologically advanced as the Culakhan, and had the ability to compensate for settings he couldn't begin to adjust himself. There was one way to find out. He tapped the strap.

"Does this gadget work for you guys?"

This prompted hurried consultations among several of the attending tripeds. Three-fingered hands manipulated delicate instrumentation. Their actual speaking voices, he noted, were so soft as to border on the inaudible, but the headband brought their meanings through sharp and clear.

"Yes, we can understand you." The Shakaleeshva who had spoken edged out from beneath the burden of Ross Ed's left arm. "Or rather, you should now be able to understand us." Triple arms stretched and quivered. "Can you now stand by yourself? You constitute a substantial organic mass."

"Hey, that's me," he replied cheerfully. He was still recovering from the realization that instead of having been recaptured by the brooding, vengeful Culakhan, they had been rescued by Jed's people. "Just your average Texas organic mass."

"We know. The Enlightenment has told us."

"The who?"

For an answer the Shakaleeshva turned and pointed with two arms toward the far side of the welcoming chamber, where a host of colleagues were swarming the limp, unmoving form of Ross Ed's deceased companion.

"Jed? He's the 'Enlightenment'?"

"Assuredly. What did you think he was?"

"Dead, mostly." Maybe the translator band wasn't accurate all the time, he decided. It was all very confusing. But then, pretty much everything that had happened since he'd dragged Jed out of that cave in New Mexico had been confusing, so why should this be any different?

He allowed himself to be led deeper into the ship, following a handful of Shakaleeshva who bore their deceased kindred shoulder-high. Several times he had to duck, and once he was forced to crawl the length of an especially low corridor, but eventually everyone gathered in a peculiar rectangular chamber which boasted enough head room to allow him to stand.

A gentle vibration jolted the floor and the room shifted, though he was unable to tell in which direction. When his surroundings eventually stopped trembling, one wall disappeared and admitted them to a truly enormous chamber. It was a good three stories high and reminded him immediately of the atrium in the Houston Neiman Marcus.

Multiple levels swarmed with busy Shakaleeshva. Images and motion scenarios drifted back and forth through the air like flocks of translucent birds. Several of the aliens rode tiny scooters that were nothing more than control poles protruding from flat disks. Racing through the cavernous room at high speed, they somehow managed to avoid running into each other or anyone else. The chamber was bursting with activity and energy.

Off to his right was an image he at first took to be another, larger screen but soon saw was an actual port. Two stories high and nearly as wide, it offered a view of interplanetary space bounded on one side by the curve of the earth. The spectacular blues, whites, and browns of a distant Central America assailed his eyes. More than the little room had moved, he realized.

Geometric designs were integrated into the matrix of the floor. Whether they were purely decorative or performed unknown functions he had no way of knowing. Leastwise, nothing happened when he stepped on them. Two Shakaleeshva seated atop a levitating mushroom brushed past him, arguing vociferously. As they approached, the Jed-bearers both rose slightly to execute a gesture of obvious deference.

All these genuflections suggested that his dead friend had been an individual of some importance among his kind. Furthermore, "the Enlightenment" was a term unlikely to be applied to a wanted criminal. He still couldn't be certain of anything, however. The Culakhan had had other, less flattering names for the deceased.

His attention was drawn to the port. A pair of enormous elongated structures that could only be spaceships hove into view. Lights glistened on their flanks, which except for several whitened sections which resembled the inner surface of a brand-new bathtub appeared to be fashioned entirely of brushed stainless steel. Without any basis for comparison he could only guess at their size, but they struck him as being truly massive. They were utterly different from both the Culakhan cloud-craft and the cube-ship of the saucer visitants. He wondered if the vessel he was aboard was equally impressive in appearance.

The procession halted before a console of mirrored metal from which three comparatively large Shakaleeshva emerged. One particularly impressive individual stood nearly four feet tall, towering above his companions. Or perhaps it was a her, he mused. He was just starting to become aware of subtle physical differences among the species.

Crowding around Jed, they addressed him in low, respectful tones while he replied via the Culakhan's artificial larynx. Ross Ed's headband allowed him to follow portions of the conversation.

"So we have found you at last, Enlightenment." The tallest one appeared to be drunk, but Ross soon realized there was a deliberate pattern to its oscillations. As others spoke they, too, swayed or twitched respectfully. Coordinated movement of the upper body with the three arms was graceful to behold.

"You have made things very difficult for us," avowed another. "We feared that the Culakhan would find you before us."

"They did," Ross heard Jed reply. "Surely you didn't think the electronics attached to my person were engineered by the primitive inhabitants of the world below. Nothing personal, Ross Ed."

The Texan shrugged. "Hey, I'm getting used to it."

One of the supplicants bent to more closely examine the relevant instrumentation. "Is it so. These appurtenances are surely of Culakhan manufacture."

"How did you manage to escape them? Your condition is not conducive to flight." It was impossible for Ross Ed to tell if the speaker was being facetious.

"By dint of a little inventiveness, and with the aid of my large aboriginal friend here." Jed couldn't point, but he didn't have to.

The tall one trained two eyes on the human while keeping the other focused on Jed. "A clumsy, overgrown species. Only bipedal as well, indicative of unsophisticated neuromuscular development. Evolved from primates, I should say. Remarkable that it can stand upright without falling over."

"All true," Jed agreed, "but given those constraints, still not to be underestimated. More importantly, they have aesthetic potential, although they have far to go before their moral development evolves equivalently."

"If you will permit me," appealed another, "why? Why have you done what you've done?" It moved a little closer to the body by advancing first its middle leg and then the other two.

"Because it was something I felt was required. I suppose a more detailed explanation is in order."

"To say the least," agreed the tall one. "However, it will have to wait. The Culakhan have become aware of our presence. We barely had enough time to make a quick dive into the atmosphere with a landing craft and extract you. They are even now assembling a portion of their Third Grand Fleet for an all-out attack on our expeditionary force."

"Uh, 'scuse me here a minute." Turning as one, all eyes focused on the tall human. "Grand Fleet? Expeditionary force?"

Turning as one for a second time, all eyes proceeded to ignore him. Jed was speaking anew. "We must move away from the planet as rapidly as possible. It is not feasible to conduct a battle so near to an inhabited world. For all their fury and frustration, the Culakhan will be of like mind. They will not attack until the safety of the ignorant primitives and the inviolability of their planet is assured. In this, our respective Codes are alike."

"We are already engaging the necessary system," announced a technician from nearby.

Glancing up at the port, Ross Ed watched the moon whiz by.

At that speed it didn't look like much. He would have preferred a more leisurely encounter.

One of the attending Shakaleeshva pressed a finger to the side of its head. "The Culakhan Third Fleet has turned to pursue. Formal engagement will occur shortly."

"If you don't mind my asking," Ross Ed interrupted, "could someone please tell me what's going on?"

"Come closer, Ross Ed." Jed could only beckon aurally. Ross moved nearer to his dead friend.

"What's the point? You can't see me any better."

"No, but you can see me better, and I know how important visual contact is to you humans. Stand easy," he instructed his suddenly edgy attendants. "He won't fall on you.

"There's going to be a fight, Ross Ed. Quite a big fight."

"Over you?"

"Over me."

"The Culakhan said you were a criminal."

Muted murmurs of outrage came from the circle of officials and officers who had gathered close.

"Silence!" Jed roared (as much as the artificial larynx would let him roar). "The primitive knows only what the Culakhan have told him. As I've said before, Ross Ed, I'm not a criminal. It's worse than that. I'm a writer."

"A writer?"

"That's the closest I can come to describing to you what it is I do, or rather, did. I craft aesthetic perceptions. Because of the specificity of its nature it's nearer writing than your painting or sculpture, but still quite different. The best I can do by way of an explanation you are capable of comprehending is to say that I am a writer.

"I have designed and conceived . . . I have written . . . a great deal. Some of it dealt with the Culakhan. Myself found it diverting, but they were less than amused. Outraged, in fact. Your equivalent of a price was put on my head. It all has to do with their rather rigid Codes of Conduct, to which you have already been exposed. It was requested that I be turned over to them for punishment. Naturally, my people refused. I am, or was, somewhat revered among them. Advanced technology can supplement but not replace artistic invention. You can lead a machine to water, but you can't make it paint."

"Who did you think your companion was?" wondered one of the attendants. "He was among the Twelve Systems and Twenty Worlds of the Shakaleeshva accounted the greatest of all artisans, oft proclaimed a living treasure."

"Shoot, and all along I thought he was just a dead . . ." It abruptly occurred to Ross that this might be an auspicious time to shut up.

Another alien picked up the tale. "Then one day long ago he simply vanished. We have been hunting for him ever since, as have the vindictive Culakhan. So have the T-trimot and the Jaarawamba."

"T'trimot and Jarra-whowa?"

Jed was quick to explain. "Two additional species with no sense of the self-absurd."

Ross Ed scratched the back of his head. "You seem to have insulted a lot of folks."

"It is in the nature of the creative to be controversial." The deceased did not sound in the least contrite. "A tremendous responsibility, which began to weigh heavily upon me."

The tallest of the onlookers bent low over the motionless corpse. "You have given us a worrisome time. All these many years of searching and then, out of nowhere, the modified Veqq signal. It is regrettable that the Culakhan also detected it. In addition to which, you are dead.." The official straightened. "Nevertheless, there will be rejoicing at your return. If you can still create."

"That is so. Unfortunately. To be perfectly honest, I was much happier ambling about the world we have just left in the company of my primitive friend. You see, I was tired of creating, exhausted by the burden, worn out by the responsibility. That's why I fled, seeking a place where I could recharge my enthusiasm and regain my interest. In their mental nakedness and lack of sophistication, backward worlds can often be inspiring. I found one such place. Unfortunately, while I can easily manage great epics, I am less comfortable with technology. I made a mess of my approach, and the planet in turn made a hash of me. I'd still be nothing but dead meat if the human hadn't found me.

"And incidentally, before I forget, please convey my compliments to the manufacturer of this survival suit."

"It will be done, Enlightenment. Much remains to be discussed, but as I said, first we have a battle to win." He touched a finger to his head. "The Culakhan are attempting an englobement. Steps must be taken to prevent it."

"Look here," Ross inquired, "should I put on a seat belt or something?"

They blinked at him, a reaction that was disconcerting when performed in concert. "You may remain here with the Enlightenment. All necessary steps are being taken."

Three mushroom-shaped chairs emerged from the floor, each beneath a different Shakaleeshva. One zoomed off with the tallest, hurdled the console from which he and his companions had emerged, and promptly climbed the nearest wall. The others split in opposite directions. Once again Ross Ed was alone with his friend.

Brilliant bursts of light began to dominate the scene beyond the port. One time the huge chamber shuddered, causing several mushroom chairs and their riders to spill to the floor. Shipmates hurried to attend to the fallen. One Shakaleeshva lay unmoving where he had struck.

Again the room trembled. Feeling very helpless and left out, Ross took a seat next to his deceased companion, sitting cross-legged on the floor.

"That's a big window, and I still can't see who we're fighting."

"The distances are vast. It's rare for vessels engaged in combat to ever come within eyesight of each other," Jed explained.

Far off in the blackness of space something blazed mightily before burning out. "Seems like an awful lot of fuss over a dead writer."

"I couldn't agree with you more, but there are other standards besides human ones. You cannot imagine what it is like to be a permanent prisoner of one's own abilities. Your creations never leave you, and you can never live a normal life. Neither your public, your critics, nor your own brain will allow it."

"I wonder how many ships are involved?"

"According to what I was told earlier, ten of the Shakaleeshva and eight Culakhan."

Ross Ed whistled, startling those aliens within hearing range. "Eight against ten. They must want you real bad."

"I'm afraid they do. I was a very good, or if you are Culakhan, very bad, writer. It pains me that lives may be lost on my account. I, who wished only to be left alone to ruminate in peace."

"What happens if we lose?"

"Then you will doubtless have the opportunity to experience the same condition as I currently exist in myself, albeit with a likely lack of comparable volubility."

"Say again?"

"You'll be dead, too, only you won't be able to tell anyone about it."

"Oh." Ross looked around the vast, frenetic room. "I don't guess there's anything I can do to help."

"I'm afraid that as a specimen of lesser life your efforts would only hold you up to ridicule."

"Wouldn't be the first time. I remember once in the eleventh grade . . . " He went quiet for a moment. "I wish I had a gun or something."

"Spoken like a true Texan, from what social lore I have been able to acquire. Have courage, my friend. The Shakaleeshva will prevail and I will see to it that you are returned to your home."

"Being designated an Enlightenment must be a pretty big deal among your people, huh?"

"It's Supreme and Exalted Enlightenment, actually."

"Yeah, well, whatever. You ought to be proud."

"It's too big a thing, Ross Ed. Too much accountability for any one individual."

"A dirty job, but somebody's got to do it, is that it?"

"Not so much dirty as relentless."

Left alone and with nothing else to do, they proceeded to debate the difficulties of Jed's previous profession while the battle raged furiously around them.

Not so very long thereafter one of the original three attendants rejoined them, his mushroom seat screeching to a halt. Inclining his head, Ross looked for wheels or treads beneath the seat. Whatever was holding it off the floor was not visible.

"The *Chenisisult* has been damaged, the *Kalavak* less so."

"And the Culakhan?" inquired Jed.

"Three ships so badly crippled they have been forced to withdraw. Two more battered. I regret to say that the Culakhan vessel *Utchu* has blown up."

"I'm surprised they're still maintaining contact," Jed commented.

"As are we, but the Culakhan are nothing if not tenacious. Their—"

"Codes of Conduct, I know."

"The tide of battle has turned and continues to turn in our favor. It was thought you would wish to know." Ignoring the tall human seated on the floor, the messenger sped away on his mushroom.

Fifteen minutes later a vast sigh whooshed through the chamber. It was a concerted exclamation on the part of the Shakaleeshva, who had at last received the information they had been waiting for. The battle had been won.

Further confirmation took the form of the Shakaleeshva commander, who arrived with two new associates in tow. "The Culakhan flee. We regret the mutual devastation, especially the destruction of the *Utchu*. All could have been avoided if our opponents were less rigid in adherence to their Codes. With only three undamaged vessels remaining to them, it became clear they could not win. They have conceded control of this system and withdrawn to deep space, leaving only regrets and imprecations in their wake." She, for Ross Ed had asked a few questions and was now better able to distinguish gender among Jed's kind, bowed to the deceased.

"They vow retribution at an unspecified future date. The Shakaleeshva will expect them."

"I'm dead," the artificial larynx gargled. "You'd think that would be enough."

"They seek another kind of redress. They wish you to reform certain of your compositions which pertain to them and which they perceive as insulting."

"Screw 'em, aesthetically speaking. My work is immutable."

This time all three officers bowed. "The Shakaleeshva would not have it any other way."

"So we're safe now?" Uncrossing his legs, Ross rose and stretched. One of the Shakaleeshva officers instinctively drew back.

"Yes. Unless the Culakhan choose to assemble even more craft and pursue the matter by attacking the home world of this expeditionary force. I don't think even my work has managed to insult them quite that much."

Through the impressive port Ross Ed could see Shakaleeshva starships gathering. A lambent sphere glowed in the distance. He thought it might be Jupiter. "What happens now?"

One of the officers explained. "Repairs must be carried out on those of our own vessels which suffered serious damage. When this has been accomplished we will commence the long journey homeward."

"You mean your home, not mine."

This time it was the commander who responded. "If the Culakhan translator is functioning properly, I detect despair in your voice. Please be of good cheer. As protector and savior of the Enlightenment, you will be feted with honors. Anything the Shakaleeshva can provide shall be yours. It would take you a hundred of your lifetimes to enjoy all the wonderments that the Twenty Worlds have to offer."

Ross was quiet for a long moment before replying carefully. "That's real generous of you, and I admit I'm curious, but I'm afraid what it boils down to is that the Twenty Worlds just ain't Texas. Bet you can't get a decent chicken-fry on any of 'em."

"The concept does not translate," declared one of the officers. His superior gestured eloquently.

"I am afraid that it does." To show that she indeed understood, her peculiar mouth twitched. "We certainly do not have that of which you speak."

"How about chili? Mesquite-grilled steaks? Longnecks? Biscuits and gravy?"

"Alas, no." This time the commander gesticulated simultaneously with all three hands. "Perhaps some of which you speak might be synthesized. Our nutritional chemists are renowned for their inventiveness."

"What about football? Deer hunting? Bass fishing?" These invocations produced the same sorrowful negative. "See? That's why in spite of all the great things I couldn't see in a hundred lifetimes, I don't think I'd have a very good time if I went back with you. Not even with twenty worlds in twelve systems to choose from."

"I see." The commander deliberated. "The Twelve Systems count among their orbiting bodies several small inhabitable moons. Considering the service you have rendered, it might be possible to make you master of your own world."

"I don't think so," Ross Ed replied immediately (well, perhaps not immediately, but after a moment's thought). "I've been around long enough to know that I'm not the executive type. Also, the few masters I know about don't seem to have many friends."

The commander was obviously disappointed. "Very well. You may meditate on these proposals while we conduct repairs. When they have been completed we will do whatever you desire, though should you chose to return to your world, I will miss the opportunity of introducing you to the Twelve Systems. This I would personally regret."

"Hey, you can give the rest of the Shakaleeshva my best wishes."

"As is common, I have under my command the usual scientific complement. They will want to carry out cursory studies of your world before we depart. This is nothing for you to concern yourself with. Rest assured their exploratory vessel is equipped with the latest camouflage equipment."

Ross Ed smiled. "Glad to hear it. Tell 'em to keep a close lookout for weather balloons."

"We shall, whatever those may be."

He and Jed were escorted to a private room, the equivalent of an officer's suite. It was more than comfortable, provided he was careful not to bump his head on the ceiling. Jed was able to help explain the operation of unrecognizable devices, most of which Ross had no use for anyway. One he did enjoy was the control that expelled bubbles of ice water in midair. Sipping through a magnetic field was a new experience.

Now if they could only do it with beer, he mused.

The food that was provided was pasty and soft, not surprising when one realized that the Shakaleeshva had no teeth. After being reassured by a biochemist that his body would find it nutritious, he forced himself to swallow a few patties. Relatively tasteless, it cried out for pepper or Tabasco, neither of which he expected could be found among the ship's stores.

Having learned the trick of inhaling water globes without getting any up his nose, he sucked down several in the wake of the paste.

"So you decided you were burned out and came to the conclusion that the best way to recharge your creative juices was to maroon yourself on some primitive planet like Earth."

"Yeah, only I didn't make a very good job of it," the deceased one muttered. "'Earth.' What an egocentric appellation. Believe me, Ross Ed, it's tough being the Enlightenment. You have a lot more privacy and much more of a real life if you're just a little flash that blinks on and off once in a while. I *had* to get away. I was desperate." From the artificial larynx came something that sounded almost like an oath.

"Now I'm dead, and thanks to the Culakhan recharging this suit, I have to decide if I want to stick out this specious existence for another fifty or so of your years."

"There are those," the Texan replied quietly, "who would be glad of the opportunity."

"What do you expect me to do? Be grateful? I'm a writer, dammit! They'll take me home and venerate me. I'll become an honored exhibit. Supplicants will badger me in hopes of obtaining original creations. I'll have no peace, least of all in my own mind. Once the spigot is turned on, there's no shutting it off. Some of our philosophers believe the creative energy lingers even after extermination. There is a formula for it."

"You think you've got problems?" Ross Ed toyed with a bowlful of blue paste. "When I go home I've got to find a way to get the army off my back. Talk about being badgered and bothered! Then there's that Hollywood woman and her friends. I'm sure they're looking for me, too. And there'll be others."

It was quiet in the room for a long time. At last Jed asked, "Is there nowhere you could be comfortable and free of harassment, noplace else on your world that you would like to experience? Someplace similar, perhaps, to your beloved Texas?"

"There is one place that might work. Just one. I've heard a lot about it."

"Then tell me, and I will see that it is arranged."

"That's mighty fine of you, Jed. A change of scenery might do me a world of good. I just don't want to change to a whole new world. Who knows? It might even help me to forget about Caroline."

"Take it from me, my friend. She wasn't right for you anyway."

Ross snorted. "As if a dead alien knew what kind of woman was right for me."

"Don't underestimate me just because I'm a dead member of another species. I'm very perceptive, as you know. Now, if you will provide me with your chosen coordinates I shall see to it that the commander is properly informed."

Ross Ed rolled his eyes. "Coordinates again! How's about I just use another one of those slick map globes. If the Culakhan had 'em I'm sure your people do, too."

"Complete with full relief, moving cloud patterns, and circulating ocean currents," Jed assured him. "Look at the wall behind you. There is a series of small depressions. . . ."

When Ross had finished isolating and describing his chosen locale, the deceased Enlightenment pondered the result thoughtfully.

"I perceive that this locale is even bigger than your Texas."

"Yeah," Ross Ed conceded grudgingly. "Not many places are."

"You're certain you will be comfortable there?"

"Hey, nothing's certain. One time I thought I'd be comfortable in Snyder, until a tornado ripped through town and scattered everything I owned between Abilene and Austin." He fingered the slowly rotating globe, his hand wholly encompassing the region he'd isolated.

"I heard the folks hereabouts are a lot like Texans, and the country itself is damn interesting. One thing's for sure: I don't think U.S. Army Intelligence is going to look for me there. Not for a while, anyways."

"I'll take care of it," the deceased Enlightenment assured him.

TWENTY-FOUR

It was with considerable fanfare that Ross Ed found himself placed early the next morning in a small, automatically piloted vehicle that had been programmed to deliver him safely to the site he had chosen. Directions had been installed in the craft by the Enlightenment himself, operating in tandem with the flagship's systemology and utilizing the remarkable capabilities of his survival suit. The tiny craft could be dropped from the camouflaged scientific survey ship during its first orbit of Earth.

As he lay prone in the harness which was designed to support three Shakaleeshva but which had been modified to accommodate his single, far larger human frame, Ross contemplated what had been a most remarkable relationship. He was going to miss Jed. Certainly the Enlightenment was the most interesting dead person he'd ever known, even if he wasn't human.

It was a good thing he wasn't claustrophobic, because the drop craft was only a little bigger than a single-engined plane. His shoulders barely fit the confines of the life-support compartment.

Something clicked softly and he was suddenly falling, the tiny vessel being much too small to support any kind of artificial gravity. For several minutes he was afraid he was going to spew partially digested blue paste all over the interior, but as the craft entered the earth's atmosphere and gravity returned, so did control of his stomach.

Considering the size of his vehicle and the velocity at which it was descending, it was just as well that there were no ports or windows. He had to rely entirely on the Shakaleeshva, though even if he could see where he was going he couldn't affect the outcome. If he slammed into an ocean there wasn't much he'd be able to do.

The feeling of falling at great speed lessened. There was a bump, then another, and then all sense of motion ceased. Hidden servos whined and the top of the little vessel slid back. Moist, thick air filled his nostrils, then his lungs. It stank of green growing things.

A single touch released the restraining harness, allowing him to sit up. The ship rested on damp soil, surrounded by tall trees and stately palms. Strange bird sounds fluted the air. An iridescent blue butterfly the size of his palm investigated his face before moving on. It was rain forest, but very unlike the Yucatán. The trees and palms were too widely spaced, the undergrowth utterly different. No monkeys gibbered in the canopy, and while plentiful, the local insect life seemed less aggressive.

Climbing out, he was careful to step over a line of green ants traveling single file. As he bent to inspect an indifferent pair of bright green golden-eyed tree frogs squatting on a nearby log, a panel popped open in the drop ship's side.

Gliding out under its own power was a singular figure. The survival suit was of different design; a little sleeker, a touch more elaborately instrumented. No doubt it was some of the latter which granted the unit mobility. As it inclined to the vertical he got his first look at the contents.

Three eyes shut tight, arms and legs hanging limply, Jed the dead could not stare back at him. But he could perceive, and he could talk. Somehow the artificially reproduced voice succeeded in conveying amused delight.

"Hello, Ross Ed."

"Jed!" Ross would have enveloped the alien in a true Texas bear hug, except he feared damaging the suit's external instrumentation. "What the hell are you doing here?"

"I was not designated the Enlightenment because of a paucity of imagination. Even deceased, I like to think I'm a little smarter and a little cleverer than the majority of the living."

"That sounds like a writer, all right." Shaking his head and grinning, Ross Ed chose an antless log and sat down. "How'd you pull it off?"

"While everyone else was busy attending to your needs, I was attending to mine. I had been offered a new survival suit immediately after our arrival on board the flagship. I accepted, but put off making the transfer until last night. Once broadcast neuromuscular facility had been regained, it was a relatively simple matter for me to program not one, but two of these marvelous little craft. My old survival suit, together with my personal signature, was on my instruction loaded aboard the duplicate vessel. None of the scientists aboard the survey ship which dropped us here paid it any mind, assuming it to be part of someone else's experiment.

"Similarly, I was able to maneuver myself when no one was looking into the modest cargo bay of your craft long before you were loaded. My only fear was that I would be discovered during the ceremony of departure. But only the life-support bay was checked, to ensure your comfort. I, of course, was perfectly content in the cargo compartment, since I carry my own survival system with me.

"When this craft was released, so was its mate. Instrumentation on board the survey vessel will record the event as a single drop signature. Adjustments I performed to camouflage instructions will have hidden our craft not only from your kind's primitive detection devices but also from my own."

"They'll still come looking for you," Ross Ed warned.

"And they'll find me, by tracing the drop signature. Or at least, they'll find my old survival suit. Then they really will be confused. They won't know whether I've gone to ground on this world or simply shot myself out into space, where, if nothing else, there can be found eternal peace. No trace of my manipulations remains aboard either the survey vessel or the flagship. I made certain of that before I put my little enterprise into effect.

"Your world is large, crowded, and off-limits to general exploration. This time I won't be found."

"No? What if they come looking for me, to ask me questions?"

"My dear aborigine, did you think I ever gave them the coordinates you selected for me? If they come looking for you at all they will have to find a way to search a large metropolitan complex halfway around the world. The Culakhan, should they return, will have an even more difficult time. I don't think anyone will try it. Besides, it doesn't matter. You and I are here, not there."

Half expecting to see an isolated storm cloud drifting speculatively through the sky overhead, Ross Ed rose from the log.

Sweat was pouring down his face. He wasn't properly dressed for the climate, but that could be fixed soon enough.

"Sure this is what you want?"

A hissing sound issued from the larynx. "I am nobody's monument! I intend to enjoy my death, thank you."

"What about this little ship, and the other one?"

"The other's self-destruct sequence was preengaged. I will now activate this one."

In less than five minutes nothing remained of the Shakaleeshva drop craft except a few wisps of smoke, its molecular structure having been completely broken down. A prospector passing through might have been struck by the remnants of certain exotic metals and other substances underfoot, had he bothered to examine the ground in the immediate vicinity, but such an encounter in this place was highly unlikely.

"Much better," the Enlightenment observed with satisfaction. "What now? You chose this location, Ross Ed. Not I."

"I guess we walk. Or rather, I do. I'd better carry you in case we're seen. If we landed in the right place we ought to find people or a road pretty soon."

"I can finesse my new suit's levitation function to ease your burden. We need to acquire another backpack." The corpse rose and drifted forward to settle gently into the Texan's waiting arms.

Sure enough, it took less than an hour's walk to hit a narrow, paved road. Hitching a ride into the nearest town, Ross Ed chatted amiably with the trucker who'd picked them up. The man glanced at Jed but asked no questions. As Ross was soon to learn, he'd chosen an area where folks didn't pry into other people's business.

With the little money remaining in his pocket he bought Jed a nice new backpack. There was plenty of work to be had in surrounding towns, and with the alien's assistance and advice, money was soon no longer a problem. Given enough cash, a man could buy anything in the Top End, including new identification and a valid passport.

He was going to like it here, he decided. True, it wasn't Texas, and to the locals iced tea seemed an alien concept, but other than that he was content. There were even a couple of decent Mexican restaurants in Cairns, just down the highway apiece, and all the hotels showed American football on their closed-circuit cable systems. Furthermore, even he had to admit that where beer was concerned, there was simply no comparison.

He made new friends, who politely forbore from questioning him about his history. Occasionally he would pull out his alien dummy and treat them to the damnedest ventriloquist act any of them had ever seen. It was suggested that he turn professional, but he demurred, insisting he performed only for his own amusement and that of a close chosen few.

Eventually he met a girl who was even taller and more beautiful than Caroline. When Jed approved, they were married. At first wary of the alien shape, his new wife came to accept her husband's explanation that it was an old movie prop lovingly brought over from the States, and thereafter she became as big a fan of his ventriloquist act as any of their friends.

As for Jed (whose real name was far too long and difficult for a simple country boy like Ross Ed Hager to manage), the Enlightenment of the Shakaleeshva, venerated artist of the Twelve Systems and the Twenty Worlds, creator of aesthetic marvels and stylish insulter of the Culakhan, he was more than content to sit propped erect on the porch of their rainforest home and perceive the daily passing of strange creatures and even stranger humans.

On rare occasions, when Ross Ed and his wife were out of the house and the irresistible muse could no longer be denied, he even composed. Fortunately, the nearest neighbors were too far away to complain.